# THE CITY OF VEILS

### S. Usher Evans

Sun's Golden Ray
Publishing
Pensacola, FL

Cover Design by Jo Painter
Line Editing by Danielle Fine, By Definition Editing

Sun's Golden Ray Publishing
Pensacola, FL
www.sgr-pub.com

For ordering information, please visit
www.sgr-pub.com/orders

# DEDICATION

To the girls who can take care of business

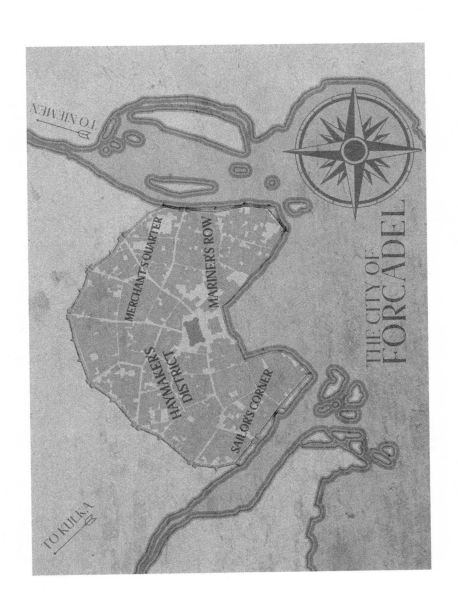

THE CITY OF
FORCADEL

# Chapter One

"I'll have your money tomorrow, I promise."

"See, that's a problem, because you promised Lord Beswick you'd have it tonight."

The man struggled against the giant, pig-faced guards who kept an iron-clad grip on his arm. "P-please, give me more time. I need more time."

Ignacio, a tall, thin man with a pencil mustache, sighed dramatically. I didn't know the specifics of what the shopkeeper owed, but it didn't matter. If I knew Ignacio, one of Lord Beswick's most ruthless lieutenants, there would be no pleasing him.

Leaning over the ledge of the roof, I counted the guards again. Two held the shopkeeper, another had his young son, and the fourth stood behind his boss. On a good day, I could take two—maybe three, if they were particularly slow. But four? That would require a little help.

Reaching into the cloth sack beside my black boots, I dug around for something I could use. Knockout powder could work, but I didn't have enough for the entire crew. Still, if I could incapacitate two or three of the guards, it would give me enough time to take down the rest.

Another wail pierced the night, and I returned to the ledge to scope out the scene. Ignacio had procured a knife, presumably to chop off one of the man's fingers.

No—his son's. The boy was barely ten, and the source of the wailing as one of the guards held out his hand.

Four guards and two victims made this more complicated, but I couldn't let them maim an innocent child. My fingers closed around a hard ball at the bottom of the bag. I hesitated only a second then lobbed it to the street on the other side of the building.

A loud explosion followed, with a plume of black smoke billowing up into the night sky.

"What was that?" Ignacio asked. He nodded to the two guards furthest away. "Go check it out."

Two of the guards peeled off, and I followed them on the rooftop, attaching the bag of knockout powder to my small crossbow. I knelt on the edge and aimed for a spot just above their heads. The arrow sailed through the dark air, sticking into the brick side of the building. The bag ripped and a small stream of powder poured out. Like fools, both men walked over to investigate, and shortly thereafter, fell forward onto each other, sound asleep. They were large, so I didn't know how long the powder would last.

Another wail echoed from the victims, and I hurried back to Ignacio and the shopkeeper. Everyone's appendages were intact, but not for long. I wrapped the bag of tricks around my shoulders then adjusted my cloak. Curling my fingers around the hem, I leapt over the ledge. Air gathered in the sewn-in pockets, and I gracefully floated to the ground, landing in a crouch between Ignacio and his victims.

Slowly, I rose, letting Ignacio take in the full effect.

"You again?" he scoffed. "Didn't you learn your lesson after the last time?"

"I considered that a tie," I replied, lowering my voice to a whisper. "Three of your men needed help walking away from it."

"How is that a tie?" Ignacio said.

I smirked and untied the cloak and bag from around my neck, letting them fall to the ground. "Because you walked away at all."

"We don't have time for this," he said to his goons. "Make her bleed."

They rushed to me, but I was faster, yanking a length of metal twine from my belt and swinging it over my head. The two weighted balls on the end gave it momentum, and as I released it, the ends tangled around a guard's legs, tripping him. I used his falling body as leverage to boost me into a flying kick toward guard number two.

Before I could land my blow, he grabbed me by the neck, pushing me upward as black spots danced in my vision. With a cry, I slammed both my elbows into the inside of his forearm, and he released me. I dropped to a crouch, flinging my leg out and chopping him down like a tree. He fell onto his back, and with a swift kick of my foot, he was out.

I spun, pulling my knives out of my belt, ready to take on Ignacio himself. But the bastard had run, leaving the shopkeeper and his trembling son in the corner of the alley along with his two goons, who were out cold. I released a soft curse as I unwrapped the weighted twine from around guard number one's legs (kicking him once more in the face to make sure he stayed out). It would be hard to find Ignacio again.

"T-the Veil!" the shopkeep cried. "I can't even begin to thank you for what you've done. I thought you were a myth, but this, tonight—"

"What does Beswick have on you?" I asked quietly.

"He's my landlord," he replied, stroking his son's hair. "But with the long winter, we haven't had the produce we normally get from the Kulkans. And I'm..." He shivered. "I'm ten gold pieces short this month."

That was usually the case. I walked to one of the goons and found his coin purse on his belt.

"From the weight of it, you'll probably have enough for a few months of rent until you get back on your feet," I said, tossing the purse to the man. "In the meantime, you should probably find a new place to live. And perhaps leave this area until the goons wake up."

He nodded, holding the bag close to him. "Thank you, Veil. I'll tell everyone what you have done. The city is safer thanks to you."

I reached down to grab my cloak, tying it around my neck and replacing the hood over my head. I gave the man and his son one flash of a smile before dashing toward a stack of crates, and ascending to the rooftops once more.

A bright, full moon loomed overhead, providing the only light I needed to travel across the rooftops soundlessly. The tile was still warm from the sun, which had set hours ago. Sweat gathered under the cloth mask around my eyes, both from the air and from the fight. Summer hadn't yet arrived, but the nights were growing thicker with humidity. Soon it would be downright miserable, with no escape except to dive into Forcadel Bay itself.

I continued my hunt for Ignacio, although I knew it would probably be fruitless. Most likely, he'd slithered back to his boss's hideout, licking his wounds, and out of my reach. Lord Beswick was neither high-born nor high-class. He was nothing but a common criminal, a man who'd built himself an empire on the backs of the most vulnerable. Beswick had been mostly immune to prosecution. No matter how many of his henchmen I placed at the feet of the captain of the king's guards, he continued to deal shadily with merchants and threaten innocents—cashing in on King Maurice-Pollox Archer Lonsdale's lack of control over his domain.

I swallowed, a bit of unease creeping through my brain. The king had died three weeks ago, and his funeral would be next week. Even though he wasn't my favorite person, it seemed wrong to disparage the dead, especially when they hadn't yet been buried.

Beswick, on the other hand, I would readily disparage at any given moment. He was ruthless, extracting exorbitant rents from everyone, like the man I'd just saved. And then, when the tenants could no longer put food on the table, Beswick would loan them money and make them work it off as part of his criminal underground. It was a vicious cycle of poverty that was difficult to break.

I did what I could to help the citizens fend him off—whether it was a few gold pieces to help with the rent or just beating back the goons who terrorized them—but it was like trying to defeat the tide. The only way to end the cycle would be to remove Beswick himself.

Unfortunately, he had a lot of high-powered friends. Taking him down required more than beating him up in a back alley and dropping his crooked ass on the doorstep of Captain Mark, who ran the king's guard in the city of Forcadel.

It had become clear to me these past few months that the only way to permanently get rid of Beswick and his kind would be to gather enough evidence to charge him with a crime—and not petty crimes like theft and violence. I'd have to find something big. Like treason.

There were rumors that he'd been illegally importing goods from the neighboring countries, selling them to Forcadel merchants at a high markup, and pocketing the difference. Screwing our own citizens was bad enough, but it was prohibited for any businessman to sign international treaties without the express permission of the king.

The only thing I needed was proof.

Tonight, I'd been following Ignacio and hoping he'd lead me to Beswick's bookkeeper, Eric Poole. I had a feeling the money man would have what I needed. But now, the sun was peeking over the rooftops, a sign that my nightly patrolling was done. Tomorrow, I would don the hood and try again, as I'd been doing every night for the past three years.

As quietly as I could, I ascended the perfectly-placed crates on the side of the butchery I called home during the day, climbing into an open window. My dark room held very little—a wardrobe with a few tunics for the day, a tub for washing myself and my weapons, and a mattress. There was already a form sleeping there—Tasha, the butcher's son. We had a nice arrangement—he never asked where I disappeared to (nor anything else about me), and on occasion, he gave me a few minutes of stilted lovemaking. To him, I was simply Larissa, the mysterious girl who swept the floors in exchange for a room.

I undid my cloak and unwrapped the mostly empty pouch of tools from my hips, hiding both under a loose floorboard, along with a spare mask and my beautiful sword. I nudged the snoring Tasha out of the way and took my spot on the mattress next to him.

Just as I drifted off to sleep, voices outside the still-open window grabbed my attention. It was too early for his parents to be up and about. Careful not to wake Tasha, I crept from the bed and retrieved my sword and mask. I swept out of the room, landing with a soft *thump* on the crates outside my window. There was a crowd of royal guards in the alley—all I needed to see before I took off along the rooftops.

A chorus of cries followed my leap onto the next building. Before I could take two steps, disembodied hands grabbed my wrists, legs, ankles—and no matter how much I struggled, I couldn't break free. My sword dropped from my hand as a bag fell over my head. A tremor of fear rumbled through me.

Had Beswick sent for me? Was this the end? I'd barely spent eighteen years on this world. No, I wouldn't go out that easily. Even captured, I still had my wits.

I let them carry me, deciding to save my energy for the right moment. I wouldn't get very far shackled with what sounded like a horde of guards, but I could certainly try.

Finally, they placed me on a seat and removed the bag. I blinked in the dim light. My mask was still on, but I didn't know how long that would last. The handcuffs were removed, and I gingerly rubbed my wrists, calculating my next move as I furtively glanced at my captor.

Captain Mark's young second-in-command, Felix Llobrega, walked to the other side of the table, the handcuffs swinging in his hands. A man in his mid-twenties with short-cropped black hair, he wore a satisfied smirk on his thin lips as he settled in the seat across from me, his dark brown eyes sparkling with something like victory.

"Good morning," he said. "Would you like a cup of coffee?"

I rolled my eyes. "With a side of poison, I assume?"

He smiled, giving him something of a wolfish look. "Now why would I poison the princess of Forcadel?"

# Chapter Two

I clenched my jaw shut, inhaling then exhaling deeply. Then, painfully, I reached behind my head to untie the mask. It fell to my lap, and I felt naked. But there was no hiding my identity anymore. Not in this room, anyway.

"How long have you known?" I asked, after a moment.

"We've never not known, Your Highness." My title sounded more mocking than respectful. "After all, a mask doesn't hide much. And you haven't changed since running out on your wedding five years ago."

I begged to differ. Back then, I'd been a scared thirteen year old and I'd accumulated a few more scars since. But I was more surprised he'd bothered to remember my face. In my youth, he and my brother had been best friends, and considered me more a thorn in their side.

"I suppose August sent you?" I said casually, making a big show of placing both my boots on the table. "He wants to continue what my father started? Marrying me off to the most politically advantageous lord."

"Your brother is dead."

My feet dropped to the floor with a loud thud. "What? When? *How*?"

My brother and I weren't particularly close, as there were nearly five years between us. But, more importantly, with my father gone, *he* was to be king. And with August dead as well...

"No," I said, standing up. "I'm not—"

"Please, sit down," Felix said. "I know this must be a shock to you."

Shock didn't even come close. Here I thought I was being arrested—potentially having to claw my way out of the dungeons. And now they wanted me to sit on the throne. My stomach threatened to come to the surface, but I swallowed it. There was no need to panic yet. Perhaps they just needed my signature to move onto the next warm body.

I glanced at Felix, who actually looked sympathetic. Not a look I'd seen on him before. I needed more time to plot my escape, so I asked, "Why haven't I heard about August's death?"

"Because it happened two nights ago," Felix said. "The Council knows, but we haven't announced it to the kingdom yet. Not until we had you."

"You don't have me yet," I said, continuing to pace. My brother dead, my father dead, my kingdom without a Lonsdale to rule it for the first time in three hundred years. Because I sure as hell wasn't up to the task. "How did he die?"

"In his sleep," Felix said. "Same as your father."

My footfalls stopped. "And has it killed anyone else? Servants? Maids?"

He shook his head.

"Poison, then," I said, running my hand over my face. "Do you know who's responsible?"

"We have theories," he said. "We can discuss that later. The point remains that whoever did it assumed there would be a power vacuum. But we have you, so—"

"And one slip of a flask into my morning porridge and I'm dead as well," I said with a grimace. If I was going to die, it was going to be on the end of a sword, fighting for my city or someone who needed saving. Not the victim of some regicidal maniac.

"We are taking precautions," Felix said. "I promise we won't let anything happen to you."

"I'm sure you said the same thing to August."

He stopped, his mouth falling open. "I'm sorry?"

"Your track record speaks for itself, *Lieutenant*," I seethed. "Two kings dead under your boss's watch."

The corner of his mouth turned upward, but there was no humor in it. "That's *Captain* Llobrega now. Mark has been fired." My gaze dropped to the shiny badge on his breast, signaling his new position overseeing the elite soldiers that guarded the castle and the royal family. "And as to surviving, our heir apparent seems perfectly capable of keeping herself from ingesting poison."

"You don't have an heir of anything," I muttered. "I can decline your request. I don't have a lot of love for the throne."

Felix's gaze never left me as I paced the room. "And yet, you've been here all this time, protecting Forcadel."

"My mistake. Had I known you knew I was here, I never would've come back." This lunacy needed to end, and quickly. I could easily fight off Felix in this room, but how many guards waited outside?

"Brynna," Felix said, coming to his feet. "Your kingdom needs you. Why not protect it as queen, instead of behind a mask?"

I hated how much that tactic worked on me. I needed to stall until an escape plan came to me. "So what now? I just walk into the Council's meeting room and become queen? And what are you planning to tell my father's court about where I've been? I'm sure *they* don't know about The Veil."

"We leave for the castle now, and I'll formally introduce you tomorrow afternoon," he said, walking to the door and resting his hand on the knob. "You'll need your rest before you face the Council. And to prepare."

More time—I needed more time. "May I have a moment to collect my things?"

"And give you a chance to run?" The son of a bitch actually smiled. "Do you really think me that dumb?"

With no other options, I followed Felix out of the small room and regained my bearings. They'd dragged me into a fabric shop across the street from the butchery. No less than twenty guards surrounded a dark carriage, all of them armed to the teeth. If I was going to run, now was my chance.

Felix pressed a firm hand on my shoulder. "Don't even think about it."

"Think about what?"

He tightened his grip in what I assumed was a comforting gesture. "I promise, it won't be as bad as you think. We'll help get you acclimated to your role."

"How very generous of you."

The commotion had awoken the neighbors, some of whom were openly gaping out of windows above. My name was on their lips, but the name I'd given them. Larissa the blood sweeper. Perhaps they thought I was being arrested for sweeping too much blood.

Felix and I spoke no more as I sat in the carriage, the weight of panic pressing on my chest like a stone as we lurched forward. I was still looking for options to escape, knowing they'd all be futile, but needing to keep my mind busy. I pulled the fabric back from the window, the vast, white-stone castle looming in the distance. It reminded me of a prison, with tall spires that stretched into the night sky. My musty mattress at Tasha's side had always seemed more welcoming.

"I also shouldn't have to say this, but your nightly activities as the Veil will have to end," Felix said.

"I can take care of myself, and being queen is mostly a figurehead position," I replied, giving him a look. "None of that precludes me from continuing to protect the city."

"You mean, besides the fact that vigilantism is illegal?" He snorted. "It's dangerous. We need our queen alive. And we can't do that if you've broken your neck falling off a roof or been bloodied up by one of Beswick's goons."

"Well, aren't you just *so* fortunate that I haven't fallen off a roof yet?" I said, ignoring the fall off a roof that had broken my arm last year. That was beside the point. I crossed my arms over my chest. "I suppose you'll be arresting Beswick today?"

"On what charges?" he asked. "Being a general creep?"

"Running illegal trade deals, bullying, preying on the poorest in our city. Or don't you care about any of that?"

"I care if my queen and Council tell me to care," he said with something of a meaningful look. "And while the former seems invested, I think you'll find the latter to be something of a hurdle."

I sighed. "All the more reason you should let me take him down under the mask. I promise you, I'm very close."

"Sure you are."

"Did I or did I not deliver Chiara Raker and Zita Oriola last year?" I replied, lifting my chin. Two very big illegal importers, and two nice feathers in my cap. "All that lovely evidence deposited at your boss's doorstep. Clean conviction, too."

He cast me a look. "Thank you, Brynna, for the assistance. But Beswick isn't some low-level slumlord. He's a dangerous man, and you'd do well to keep away from him."

"Then get around to arresting him. You're captain now, you can do that."

"I'll get right on that," he drawled, casting me a tired look.

"Just as soon as I have enough evidence."

The carriage came to a halt and the door opened, revealing Felix's guards. He stepped out first and extended his hand to me, but I ignored it. I could get out of a carriage without needing help; I wasn't that delicate yet.

We entered the dark castle through the servants' quarters, I assumed to keep the whispers of my arrival quiet until the morning. Felix and two female guards escorted me up the stairs to one of the tall towers. He opened the door, leading the three of us into an expansive room with a front sitting area, complete with table, and another door that probably went to the bedroom.

"This is your suite," Felix said. "You'll have your meals here and will remain in this room when not escorted by myself or a member of my guard."

"My prison cell, you mean," I said, walking to the window and gazing down the stone tower. Far below, the guards moved like ants in the early morning light. Even worse, the stone was smooth around the window. I could find footholds, but not many—not enough to get me safely to the ground.

"We will have a tailor this morning," Felix said behind me. "You'll be fitted for a wardrobe appropriate for your position. After that, we'll introduce you to the Council."

"Great. They'll know my face so they can kill me." The room was getting hotter as my chest tightened, so I pressed my forehead against the cool glass.

"I told you. I won't let that happen," Felix said, reaching over my head and pushing against the glass until the pane opened. A cool wind touched my cheeks, and some of the tightness left my chest.

"Can I sleep on the roof, at least?" I asked, turning my head upward as I sat on the sill and leaned out.

Felix grabbed me by the shoulder and pulled me back inside. "Please don't. Remember what I said about breaking your neck?"

I bit my tongue instead of firing off another retort. It was late, and I wasn't in the mood for another argument. Besides, with the other window open, I had a nice view of the sunrise.

"Get some rest," he said, walking to the door. "You'll need it."

And suddenly there was silence.

I turned back to the room. None of it looked familiar, and yet it did. This had been my life for thirteen years. Corsets and dresses and sitting quietly while those with more power decided my fate. I'd been born second, and therefore, I was the one who would be married off for alliances.

My husband-to-be, I'd been told, was a young man. They'd said my marriage contract was merely insurance for his father, that I wouldn't be required to consummate the marriage until I was eighteen. Even still, I hadn't been able to stomach being sent away like that, having to trust complete strangers to not do what they wanted with me. I'd run, far away from Forcadel, and made a life of service and independence, far away from all things royalty.

And yet, after all I'd been through, there I was, back in the same prison.

I shook my head, anger clearing away the panic. No one—not even Felix Llobrega—would decide my fate. I would make it for myself. Walking to the door, I pulled two hair pins from my braid. They'd taken my swords, but I still had a few things up my sleeves.

I knelt and picked at the lock, listening for the tumblers turning over. I quietly opened the door...

Only to come face to face with a sword point.

"Back to bed." Felix stood on the other end of the sword, his face a mask of indifference.

I glanced behind him to see no less than five guards sitting in chairs down the hall. "A little much, don't you think?"

"Go to bed," he repeated, tapping the broad side of his sword against my cheek.

With a scowl, I closed the door behind me and leaned against it, closing my eyes. Exhaustion tugged at them, overtaking the panic that had set in since I'd been captured. So I let myself fall asleep against the door, praying I'd wake from this nightmare soon.

# Chapter Three

Someone was in my room.

I reached for my sword just as wakefulness reminded me it had been taken from me and the rest of the previous night's excitement came rushing forward. I cracked open an eye; there was a maid dusting the mantle above the fire, adjusting the hanging wall art as she swept her feather brush along the edges. She hummed a soft song, and when she turned, I got a better look at her. She was maybe twenty or a little older, with delicate features and dark brown hair she wore in a bun at the nape of her neck.

"Beata, you're being watched."

I jumped, sitting upright at the sound of Felix's voice. He was perched in one of the two chairs by the fireplace, next to a table with what looked (and smelled) like a delicious breakfast.

The maid swiveled around, a blush appearing on her cheeks. "P-pardon, Your Highness. I didn't mean to wake you."

"You didn't," I said, yawning and rubbing my face. "Apologies for scaring you. I'm not used to people in my *space*." The last biting remark I aimed at Felix.

"Well, you've slept long enough," he said. "Come have breakfast. We have a lot to discuss."

Only the promise of a strong cup of coffee could've roused me from the bed. I still wore the same clothes as the day before, a dark tunic and pants, although my hair had half-fallen out of the long braid. Leaning into my disheveled appearance, I plopped down on the second seat and helped myself to coffee.

"Beata, is it?" I asked, after taking three sips.

"Yes, ma'am?" She hurried to stand in front of me, hiding her hands under her apron and wearing a helpful smile on her face. "What can I do for you?"

"Nothing," I said with a smile. "Thank you for breakfast."

She beamed at me, sharing a warm look with Felix. "It's my pleasure."

"Normally, you would have a staff to help with your day-to-day needs," Felix said, turning back to me. "But considering the risks to your life, Beata will be handling all of it."

"That seems grossly unfair," I said with a frown to Felix. "And besides that, I don't need a servant. I can handle myself."

"It's no trouble. I'm glad to do it," she said with almost overly-enthusiastic optimism that faded slightly. "I was... I attended to your brother for the past few years. It was my honor to serve him, and it's my honor to serve you."

I nodded slowly, taking another sip of coffee. "If it becomes too much, let me know and I'll make Felix find you some help."

She glanced at Felix for a moment, and they shared an unspoken conversation. I downed the rest of my coffee then poured myself another.

"Beata, if you could give us a minute," he said. "And let Kat know that she's awake."

Beata nodded, bowed to me, then hurried from the room, closing the door behind her.

"So we're sure she didn't kill August, right?" I said, after a moment.

"Absolutely sure," Felix said. "She was his attendant and loved him dearly."

"So what? She was sleeping with him?" I settled back into my chair. "Everyone is a suspect until they aren't. Maybe she got mad at him for something."

"I know for a fact that she was not in the castle the night he died," Felix said. "But as I told you, August's death, and your father's, isn't your concern. We'll need to get you presentable, and educate you about the Council—"

"I know who's on the Council," I said, placing my feet on the ground.

He paused, seeming to collect himself before he snapped. "When you disappeared before your wedding, your father informed the court that you'd gone to study abroad, so we'll have to stick to that story."

I snorted. "And they bought that?"

"To be frank, Your Highness, they barely even remember you're alive, not with your father's ailing health and your brother's tenuous grip on the council." His brown eyes held all the annoyance he was keeping from his tone. But they softened as he looked away. "Their deaths are...untimely in more ways than one."

"Yes, murder usually is."

"Before you will be crowned, we will need to work on..." He tilted his head to the side, making a motion with his hand. "All of this. You are not fit for the throne as you are."

I shoved a scone in my mouth. "Are-th thou insinuating that I have-eth forgotten-eth my manners?"

"I'm saying that the Council will eat you alive the moment you set foot in there," Felix replied with a grimace. "At the very least, you need some new clothes. Kat—"

"Yes, who is this lovely Kat I keep hearing about?"

There was a soft knock at the door, and a Niemenian woman

poked her head in. Most of Forcadel shared the same bronzed skin, dark hair, and dark eyes, but our mountain-dwelling northern neighbors were fair-skinned with light hair and eyes. She wore a lilac dress that accentuated her white-blond hair, which had been pulled into a bun almost as tight as Beata's. She held herself confidently, with squared shoulders and a high chin as she stared at me.

"Brynna, this is Lady Katarine Meradeth Hasklowna, fifth princess of the kingdom of Niemen." He paused. "And your sister-in-law."

"Oh right," I said with a nod. I'd forgotten that August had been married a few years before in an arrangement similar to the one I'd run out on. Now that her husband had been killed, Katarine was a foreign woman in search of purpose. Or, perhaps, a murderer herself.

"Kat has agreed to help tutor you," Felix continued, giving me a warning look. "She's spent the last six years studying Forcadel politics and trade, and is uniquely positioned to help you understand where you need to act."

"Mm." I broke apart another scone, this one with little blueberries stuck in the middle.

"I must admit, Brynna, it's wonderful to meet you," Katarine said, a bright smile on her pink lips. "August spoke of you often."

"And I'm sure he was glad to be rid of me," I replied. "So tell me, do you know who killed my brother?"

Katarine licked her lips and shook her head. "I cannot say for certain—"

"You shared his bed, you should know who wanted him dead."

"Brynna," Felix warned.

I glanced over my shoulder at him, "Captain, *you* will address me—"

"When you act like a queen, I'll treat you as one," he said with a fierceness I hadn't expected. "Katarine is an ally, and you have few of those at the moment."

"It's quite all right, Felix," Katarine replied, folding her hands across her skirt. "I understand why Her Highness would be so wary of me." She swallowed. "If it's all the same to you, Brynna, I'd prefer not to speak of it for a few days. After all, it just happened two..." Her eyes shifted and she cleared her throat. "Three nights ago. It's all been so quick, I still believe he'll be waiting for me in our room."

There was something Katarine wasn't telling me—and it wasn't due to grief. Even the most stoic of women showed more emotion than this when their husbands died. Especially husbands they'd been betrothed to for their entire lives. From what I could tell, she and my brother weren't unhappy, even if they'd had no say in their marriage. But the scathing look I was getting from Felix told me to let that topic go for now.

"And why should I count you as my ally, Lady Katarine?" I asked before taking a bite of the scone. "Other than that you're a widow in a foreign land. Why not just run back to Niemen? Too cold up there?"

"Forcadel is my home," she said softly. "My sister has no use for me, other than, perhaps, to marry me off again. I would much rather stay and help you. We are sisters, too."

"By marriage," I scoffed. "Well then. Speak. Tell me what you know."

Katarine's eyes flashed and her face shifted. "In the first place, I know that if you walk into the Council room with that chip on your shoulder, they will toss you right out. You are a princess who hasn't been seen in years, so you'll need allies—and fast. It's much easier to do that if they think you're docile."

"So I'm learning," I said. Perhaps Blondie wasn't as much of a pushover as I'd thought. "What else do I need to know?"

"As queen, you'll have to have an understanding of our economic policies, our main trading partners, our allies, our enemies, and more. Most of what goes on in this castle is finely tuned, like a clock. One wrong move, and all the gears stop working."

I doubted that. A lot went wrong in the kingdom on a daily basis, and things kept moving forward. "For the Council today, what should I know?"

"Today is the first meeting since the Council was informed of my husband's death," she said, as if the event had occurred a year ago, instead of three nights. "It's important that you observe today and try not to make any waves."

"Ma'am, Captain." Beata was back. "The tailor is here."

"Excellent," Felix said with a grin. "Send him in."

The tailor, an older man named Norris with bottle glasses, seemed to be overly excited to be handling my wardrobe. Felix told him that my trunk of clothes had fallen overboard in a bad storm on the way back, which was why I had nothing but my tunic.

"I am honored to be dressmaking for you," he said. "I designed your mother's wedding and coronation dresses. Would you like a similar garb to hers to honor her? Perhaps a signature flower or her favorite color?"

"Sure," I said then added when Katarine gave me a sharp look. "I mean, that would be very special to me. Thank you."

Norris nodded and disappeared to his supplies, muttering about pins and scissors and fabric colors. Felix stood next to me in the mirror and shook his head.

"I know you carry no love for your parents, but the kingdom loved them very much," he whispered. "Try to be a little more cognizant of that."

Norris returned with rolls of fabric in every color but black, holding the swatches up to my skin and making notes on how it contrasted. Then, with his measuring tape, he inspected every inch of my body, right down to my feet. But when he came to my chest, he stopped, poking at the thick binds I wore.

"What is this?" he asked.

"I prefer to keep everything secure," I replied.

"Oh, no, no. This won't do." He pointed toward my lavatory. "Undo these things and come back so we can get an accurate measurement."

"I don't—"

"Brynna," Katarine interjected with a pleading look, seconded by Felix, who'd retired to the other side of the room to stay out of the way.

I groaned and stomped toward the small room with an ivory tub and face washing bin. With the door closed, I pulled off my tunic and stared at my binds in the mirror. I'd been wearing them for years, if only to keep my breasts from flopping around when I ran around the city. After carefully unwinding the cloth, I exhaled and stood for a moment, letting the cool air hit my skin before I pulled the tunic back on.

"Brynna?" Katarine called then when I walked out, her eyes grew wider. "Oh, my."

The dressmaker hurried forward and measured quickly. "Your bust is much larger than it looks. You are very lucky."

"It's not luck. They're a pain in the ass," I remarked. I'd used them when I needed to, but for the most part, I would've rather had Katarine's flat chest.

"I had no idea you were so...womanly," Katarine said, tilting her head, her gaze still on my breasts. "Why do you bind your breasts so tight?"

"It's not all that easy to swordfight when your tits are hitting you in the face," I replied.

"Mother above," Felix swore, looking at the ceiling. "Brynna, you can't talk like that."

"Like what?"

"Referencing your previous life," he said, casting a warning look at the tailor.

"Fine." I huffed.

"Do you have anything available for her to wear now?" Katarine asked. "She has a Council meeting and I'd hate for her to go in her tunic."

"Pardon," Beata said, walking in with a sky-blue dress. "Lady Katarine, I took the liberty of finding a dress of yours that might fit the princess, if it were adjusted a little."

I gazed at Katarine's waifish figure—almost a foot taller and about thirty pounds lighter—then back at Beata. "You think?"

"Ah, this will do," the tailor said, going to his kit. "Just give me a moment to adjust the seams."

———⇒————

Even with the tailor's adjustments, the dress was tight and uncomfortable, and showed way too much of my cleavage. Felix arrived just as I was being sewn up, and he, like Katarine, stared openly at my chest before remembering himself.

"How quickly can you have more dresses made?" Katarine asked.

"I will send another by the end of the day," he said, packing up his sewing kit. "And I will have a closet made by the end of the week."

"Excellent," Katarine said.

"And tunics?" I asked hopefully. "I can't be expected to wear dresses every day, can I?"

Katarine made a noise, but Felix nodded. "If you have scraps, you can make the princess a few tunics. But in bright colors only."

I scowled, turning back to the mirror as the tailor left. "It's not as if I can escape anyway."

"Well, better to limit your clothing options," he said, picking up my discarded black tunic and leggings. "Though it might be a sight to see you running around the rooftops naked."

"I can't move in this," I said, swishing the petticoats around.

"And I can't wear a sword. Where is my sword, by the way?"

"In safekeeping," Felix said. "I'm your sword now."

"I feel so safe," I said, with a sugary sweet smile which melted under his glare. "Give me back my weapon or I will find it myself. Obviously, there are still dangers in the castle. I would feel better if I had more than my fists to protect myself."

"If you behave yourself in the Council meeting, I will consider it."

I exhaled as much as I could against the tight seams. "Who cares about poison? I might just suffocate in this thing."

"Oh, nonsense," Katarine said, returning with Beata in tow. "You look lovely—and regal. We just need to do something with that hair."

"Don't you dare chop it off," I said, grabbing my braid.

"Of course not," Beata said, gently taking it from me. "We'll just need to brush it out."

I sat in the uncomfortable dress while Beata worked on my hair and Katarine gently took a golden circlet out of a velvet box.

"What's that?" I asked, wincing as Beata found another knot in my hair.

"Until you're crowned as queen, you'll wear this," Katarine said, running a cloth around it lovingly. "Your brother had one just like it."

"Was that his?" I asked.

"No," she said, looking off into the distance. "His remains on his head."

Finally, the woman showed some sadness for the death of her husband. But I still wasn't convinced. "What else can you tell me about the Council?"

"For today, you'll just need to know names: Garwood, Vernice, Octavius, Godfryd, and Zuriel."

I blinked. "Zuriel, as in the mayor of Forcadel?"

"Yes. Your father thought it appropriate to have the mayor on the Council to keep a finger to the pulse of the city," she said. "You'll be able to decide who stays and who goes when you're queen."

I nodded, mesmerized by the swift way Beata re-braided my hair then twisted it into an intricate bun on the back of my head. She set it with pins and smoothed the top of my hair with a little water. Then she took the circlet from Katarine and set it on my head.

"There now," Beata said with a smile. "We can officially call you Princess Brynna-Larissa."

I took in my reflection, the tight blue dress, the delicate diamond earrings on my lobes, the gold circlet resting in my hair. Perhaps I was now Princess Brynna, because I sure didn't recognize myself.

# Chapter Four

My large skirts extended on either side of me, so Felix and Katarine had to walk in front of and behind me, respectively. Perhaps Felix assumed I was too sewn in to run, but in fact, I was just biding my time and building a map of the castle in my mind. It had been dark when I'd arrived, but now, sunlight streamed through the windows. The castle was four floors, and my tower was on the southwest corner. I counted sixty steps to the first landing, the fourth floor of the main castle, then another ten to the third floor, which was where we exited the well.

We walked down a long hall which, based on the view out the window, was on the outer rim of the castle, as the open front gate was visible, and the city square beyond. Sweet freedom—a day that should've been spent snoozing after cleaning blood from the floor of the butchery.

"The Council room," Felix said, as we came to a pair of carved, closed double doors. "They're probably already in there."

"Are you ready?" Katarine asked, smoothing my skirts.

"Do I have a choice?" I asked, glancing out the window to the city beyond.

"You're going to do fine," Felix said with an affirming smile. "Just don't say anything and get through this first meeting."

I wished I had pockets, or enough room in my dress to cross my arms across my chest. I settled for gripping the folds of my skirt as Felix opened the doors.

A gasp and consternated sounds arose from the five people sitting at the table. I'd seen many of these men and women before but Zuriel was the only one I immediately recognized. One of the three men rose, the look on his face similar to someone who'd just farted in his own bed. "What is the meaning of this, Captain? I know you haven't been in your position long, but we are not to be interrupted."

"My apologies for the interruption, Lord Garwood," Felix said, bowing low at the waist. I caught the smirk on his lips that said he wasn't sorry at all. "But this couldn't wait. May I present Princess Brynna-Larissa Rhodes Lonsdale of the Kingdom of Forcadel."

Zuriel let out a cry of surprise, and the drunk-looking man to his left covered his mouth. The older, grizzled-looking woman just nodded while the purple-clad lady licked her pastel lips with a curious, surveying look.

The man who was still standing straightened. "Are you...uh... sure this is the right girl?"

"With absolute certainty," Felix replied.

The distrust on his face was clear as day, but he sat. I decided I'd call him Distrust until I learned his real name.

"Well, let's not all stand around gawking at the girl," said the man I considered drunk. From the capillaries on his cheeks, this state wasn't an uncommon occurrence. I dubbed him Drunkie. "Welcome home, Your Highness. You've certainly grown from the small girl we—"

"Tried to marry off as a child?" I finished.

Felix made a sound, and I felt his angry glare on the back of my dress.

"Don't be silly," Distrust replied, with a laugh that said all it needed to about his involvement. "You were betrothed to a boy a few years older. King Neshua would have been an excellent guardian until you came of age."

"I met the king. I felt differently. That's why I—"

"Decided to study abroad," Katarine interjected. "Aren't we so lucky that she did?"

"Lady Katarine, how very convenient that you're here with the princess," the woman who'd been surveying me said. Her lips were a vibrant shade of purple, so I'd call her Purple.

"And why wouldn't I be, Lady Vernice?" she replied. "Princess Brynna is my sister-in-law. We've obviously kept in touch these past few years while she's been abroad. She was already on her way home after word reached her that her father had died, and now, with August..."

My, my. How easily Katarine lied. I would have to keep that in mind.

"And where has our fair princess been?" Distrust asked, reclaiming his seat.

"Off studying the arts in Palivka across the sea," Felix replied. "But now, of course, she is willing to take up the mantle. We must keep a Lonsdale on the throne to maintain continuity and confidence in our kingdom."

"Must we?" Purple drawled. "I would much rather place a regent until we can be sure of this girl's abilities to rule. I doubt this girl is old enough—"

"I'm plenty old enough," I snapped.

"It's clear she's the right age," Distrust said, leaving the unspoken "but is she the right girl" dangling in the air. He sat down again and scooted his chair into the table. "Very well, I suppose we should continue, now that we have a *representative* here." He glanced at Felix with overt loathing in his gaze. "That will be all, Captain, Lady Katarine."

Katarine curtseyed and hurried from the room. Felix bowed, offered me one warning look then left, closing the door behind him. And then it was just the six of us—five older Councilors who barely trusted I was who I said I was, and one princess who was ready to jump out the window.

"I don't want to be here all day, Garwood," Purple said, taking her seat.

"Fine," Distrust—Garwood—replied, pulling a chair out for himself. The others followed suit, leaving only the gaudy chair in the front. After a moment's hesitation, I quickly took it.

"First and foremost," Garwood said, "my condolences on the loss of your brother. Hearing the news yesterday was...very unsettling."

My gaze swept around the room, searching for any sign of guilt. They were all innocent—or good actors.

"Thank you," I replied. "I was very unhappy about it as well."

"And yet, here you are," Purple replied. "If you were across the sea, how did you arrive so quickly?"

"I was coming for my father's funeral, as the good Lady Katharine said," I replied. It was a convenient alibi, and would help us get on with things. "But I believe we have Council business to attend to? My history isn't the focus of the meeting."

Zuriel, seated across the table, smirked. "Too right, you are, Your Highness. Vernice, let's let our princess off the hook for a bit and focus on what we need to do today. We're already weeks behind on decisions thanks to all the turmoil."

She huffed, but didn't argue.

"First order of business," Garwood said, looking down the bridge of his nose at the sheet. "There's been a petition to replace the cobblestones in Haymaker's District."

I knew it well. The northwest part of the city backed into the large stone wall, and was at least thirty blocks from the water and commerce. It was very poor and in need of help. A new road might not fix all the problems, but it would certainly improve transportation.

"How much?" Purple asked.

"Twenty thousand gold coins, it says," Garwood said, looking at his paper again. "There's additional work to the street foundation."

Drunkie scoffed. "Twenty thousand coins? For Haymaker's District? We might as well just throw the money into the bay. It'll do about as much good."

I gripped the folds of my skirt, wisely remaining quiet until this conversation played out. It should've come as no surprise to me that the leadership in Forcadel thought so little of the people.

"We have a similar petition for Mariner's Row," Purple said. "Twenty thousand. And it requires much less work."

On the southeast corner of the city, Mariner's row was the complete opposite in all ways. It boasted the nicest homes, the ritziest merchants, and the finest goods. They certainly weren't suffering from a lack of access.

"This is the fifth year Haymaker's has petitioned," Zuriel said. "What say you, Princess?"

"It seems to me that Mariner's Row has fine streets," I replied after a moment. "I say we help those who need it first."

Purple rolled her eyes. "You don't even know what you're talking about, girl."

"That would be *Your Highness*," I said with a steely-eyed gaze. Purple's face grew blotchy and she looked away.

"I have to agree with Lady Vernice," Garwood said. "Although I appreciate the sentiment, there are businesses on Mariner's Row who provide jobs and tax revenues to the city. Investing there makes more sense than repaving a perfectly usable road in Haymaker's District."

"Agreed," came the chorus from everyone except Zuriel. Lady

Vernice—Purple—elbowed the drunk man who'd fallen asleep and he let out a half-hearted 'Aye' before falling back asleep.

"That's settled then," Garwood said, making a note of it. "Next order of business, General Godfryd has a report from the front lines."

The grizzled woman stood, revealing more of her dark blue military uniform. Her face lacked any levity or emotion other than stoic reverence, and the awards and ribbons on her left breast were impressive. Her face looked like it had seen its share of battles, and when she spoke, her voice crackled with age.

"We've dealt with the pirate issue on the Vanhoja River, and we believe they've moved out of Forcadel and into the Kulkan territory. And on the northern front, we've maintained a solid presence throughout the winter to keep the Niemenians away from the city of Skorsa. I do strongly urge the Council to reconsider the position of the navy, however. Forcadel's location in the bay leaves us vulnerable to attack."

"What's our current position?" I asked. As far as I knew, our bay was impenetrable from the ocean, thanks to our cannons on the coast.

"Our fortresses on the inlet are very well stocked," she said. "And we believe our efforts on both the Vanhoja and Ash Rivers are working. But we've had to send our strongest ships up the river to deal with the pirate problem, and I'm concerned we might need to move some of our ships back. There's always an uptick in merchant activity in the summer."

"Agreed," Garwood said, followed by a resounding, "Agreed," from Zuriel, and, when prompted, Drunkie. Garwood marked it as approved and moved on—without any input from me. "Now, onto the next bit of business. We've gotten another request from Finkle out on the eastern front to send more ships to help."

"No way," Vernice said, looking at Godfryd. "Nata, we can't possibly spare any ships, can we?"

She shook her head, making a face like she had indigestion. "Not for the eastern front."

"Then it's settled," Garwood said, putting that page down.

I held up my hands. "No comment from me?"

"If your general recommends not moving forces," Garwood said, "then we don't. You should've learned that in your tutelage wherever you were."

I didn't miss the subtext in his voice. "So am I merely supposed to sit here and nod, or am I actually going to be allowed to do something? Because if you're all going to ignore my presence then I have much better things to do."

"In my opinion, Princess, you do not yet have the ability to make decisions," Garwood said, stacking up the papers next to him. "And, in fact, until we determine your true lineage, it would be advisable if you didn't attend our Council meetings."

I paused, glancing around the room and looking for friends. The only one who wasn't staring defiantly at me was Zuriel, but his gaze was on the ground, as if he were too afraid to speak up at the risk of angering the rest of them.

"Fine," I said, rising. "By all means, continue this meeting without me. That's the smartest thing anyone has said all day."

# Chapter
# Five

I pushed open the door, praying there would be no one waiting for me, but my two new shadows were there. And by the look of surprise on their faces, they hadn't expected to see me walking out so soon.

"That was a disaster," I said, passing them.

They quickly fell into step beside me. "I'm sure it wasn't," Felix replied.

"They all think I'm an idiot—or worse, an imposter," I said, running a hand through my hair and finding it confining. Everything was confining—from this damned dress to the shoes on my feet. Breathing became difficult, and I had to stop and lean against the window. It was bad enough that I was completely out of my element, but now I had to convince others I was who I said I was when I didn't even want to *be* her?

"They'll accept you eventually," Katarine said.

"I'd like it if they didn't," I replied.

"And I'd like your brother back to lead this kingdom," Felix shot back. "But as it stands, we have you. And that will just have to do for both of us. You have a duty. You will fulfill it. That is the end of it."

"Is it?" I said, pushing myself off the sill and marching back the way we'd come. "I'm not a queen, Felix. I don't even know where I'd begin."

"Then let us help you," Katarine said. "We can teach you everything you need to know."

"Everything *you* need me to know," I said under my breath.

"And what is that supposed to mean?" Felix said.

"It seems to me, Felix, that there are two very interested parties who want me to be queen. And I can't help but sniff out an ulterior motive. You fabricate this intricate lie about me studying abroad? Katarine sending me letters?" I nodded toward Katarine. "And it's clear Vernice wants *her* gone. I don't appreciate being used as a political puppet."

Katarine's face was a mask of indifference—years of training had groomed her for such a face. "If you want me gone, I will leave, Your Highness."

"We don't want you gone," Felix said, exasperated. "Brynna, she's on our side—"

"See, I don't exactly trust that either of you are here for the right reasons," I said, the anger in my veins the only thing that seemed real at the moment. "My brother's been dead less than a week. You're his best friend, you're his *wife*. And yet, your eyes are dry. Have either of you even shed a tear for him, or are you too busy scheming how to take over the kingdom?"

Her hand connected with my face before I could stop it. "Don't you *dare*," she seethed, more fire in her blotchy face than I'd seen yet. "I loved your brother. I mourn in my own way, and that is that." She straightened. "We don't all have the benefit of wearing our emotions on our sleeve, Brynna."

I rubbed my cheek, waiting for the sting to wear off.

"I know you don't trust me, and I understand why. But I have

44

lived in this castle since I was eighteen years old. Betrothed to your brother before I was even born. My safety was predicated on our marriage contract. And now..." She swallowed. "Now he's gone, and I don't quite know my place. So forgive me for trying my best to make myself useful to my new queen. That, Brynna, is my ulterior motive."

She gathered her skirts and stormed away.

Felix worked his jaw, watching for a moment before turning to me.

"Let's take a walk," he said, offering his arm. "You look like you could use some fresh air."

"Can I change first?" I asked, tugging at the sleeve of the dress.

"C'mon."

Felix escorted me down to the bottom floor and out a side door into the lush green gardens on the western side of the castle. I felt better outside, but the dress was still constricting my breath.

"What happened in the Council meeting?" Felix asked.

"The usual. The well-off in Forcadel are shafting the rest of us," I said. "And the Council proceeded to make decisions without my approval."

"Yes, that's what they do," he said with a smile. "Typically, if you want something done, you have to meet with them one-on-one, sway them to your side, and then when they arrive to vote, it's a done deal." He glanced at me. "Which Kat would've explained to you, had you not just accused her of murder."

"You have to admit, it's a little fishy," I said. "Why were you the one to retrieve me?"

"Because I was the only one who knew where you were."

"Well...true," I said. "But if I'm not *your* puppet, whose am I?"

"Brynna-Larissa Archer Rhodes Lonsdale, do you *honestly* believe *anyone* could make you a puppet?" he said with a quirked brow. "I'm honored you think so highly of my manipulation skills."

"Then what is your end goal?" I asked. "What do you gain out of all this?"

"Keeping the city out of civil war," Felix said, as if discussing the weather. "Preventing one faction from destroying the city. Maintaining a neutral party on the throne who's beholden to the city and not herself." He cast me a sly look. "If I had to pick a queen, I'd like someone who's been sacrificing herself for her people. Even if it has been as a masked vigilante."

My cheeks warmed slightly. Perhaps he was telling the truth, but I still couldn't trust him.

"What did you think of the Council?" he asked.

"What do you mean?"

"You kept gazing at their faces. Trying to read them. Probably trying to figure which one killed your brother. I'm curious what you found."

"No suspects jumped out at me, probably because they were too surprised to see me," I said, gazing up at the blue sky. "Lord Distrust, maybe."

"Distrust... Garwood?"

I shrugged. "The one who kept looking at me like I was a fraud. More than the others."

"That would be Garwood. He could be an ally, once you get on his good side."

"Drunkie's familiar. I've seen him around town too much."

"Octavius Liswith," Felix said with a chuckle. "He is the only direct descendant of the original six families of Forcadel. Besides yours, of course. What else?"

I stopped to admire a beautiful pink rose. "What does it matter?"

"It matters because I think you're better at this than you think you are." His brown eyes were sharp. "What else did you notice?"

"There's a power vacuum, obviously," I said, slowly. "They didn't expect me to show up to fill it. So it stands to reason that whoever killed my brother will also try to kill me. Do we have any leads on who might be committing regicide lately?"

"Several, all of which I'm currently working through."

"Then perhaps you should inform your queen about them."

"You aren't queen yet," he said. "And to be honest, I don't trust you with this information."

I looked over my shoulder. "And why is that? I get results."

"Your results are short-term wins, which end up screwing up the long-term, larger goals I've been working toward," Felix said, walking by me with a smile I wanted to wipe off his face. "You aren't going to be able to find the parties responsible for killing your family. Leave that to me."

I pursed my lips. "Humor me, Felix. If you aren't going to let me be a vigilante, at least let me help you unravel this mystery. Tell me who your prime suspects are."

"Chatter in the kitchen points to the food staff, but..." He shook his head. "I don't think so. If you're murdering the king, you aren't that sloppy."

"Obviously, since it's worked twice."

He turned to me, shock in his eyes, but it disappeared quickly. "It wasn't until August died that we considered the possibility. Your father wasn't the healthiest man. He succumbed to a stomach illness, and then just didn't wake up."

"What about August?"

"Katarine found him dead," Felix said, staring out into the lush, green garden. "And speaking of, you should apologize to her."

"She could be a suspect. As could Beata."

Felix barked laughter. "If you knew Kat, you'd know that's absolutely ridiculous."

"Why? Was she so in love with my brother? I don't buy it—"

"Whether she was or wasn't in love with him isn't the

question," Felix said. "She has no motive to kill him. They were trying for a child to seal the treaty, and now, barring some miracle, that treaty won't be ratified. She would've had more power had August lived." He glanced at me. "Now, she's at your mercy."

"So I wasn't too far off that she was trying to use me," I said with a smirk.

"She's also your sister-in-law," he added, quietly. "Perhaps the only family you have left. And, I might add, a very good woman."

I didn't miss the tone of his voice. "It's plausible that you and Katarine conspired to kill them both."

His brows knitted together. "To what end?"

"I don't know, so you two could run off together?"

He burst out laughing, catching me by surprise. "Oh, Brynn. You are so very far off there. And if you think I would jeopardize the stability of this kingdom, potentially causing civil war, death, and destruction simply because I was in love with Katarine..." He wiped a tear from his eye. "You aren't as smart as I thought you were."

"Fine," I said, flushing. "You aren't madly in love. But there's still something going on between you two."

"It is entirely possible for a man and a woman to be dear friends," Felix said. "And for those two dear friends to help their best friend's little sister gain her footing in a kingdom. Is that so hard to believe?"

It was the simplest solution, but there was something more afoot. But for the sake of keeping Felix satisfied, I shrugged. "I suppose not."

"I know you're angry that I've taken you from the life you knew," he said. "But I honestly believe it's the best place for you. I meant what I said—if I had my choice of queens, I'd pick the one who's been protecting the city from behind a mask any day."

I looked down at my hands, filled with callouses from swordfighting. "And you won't let me—"

"No, Brynna," Felix said. "Your home is here now. You need to focus on how you'll be saving the city from your throne, not by the point of your sword."

I was escorted back to my room by just two of Felix's guards this time—the same two women as before. One was at least a head taller than me, and the other, while more my height, was stocky and muscular. They kept their distance from me, perhaps believing me to be too tired from the emotional toll of the day to try anything.

"What are your names?" I asked, raising my voice so it echoed in the stone hallway.

"My princess?" asked the taller one.

"I asked for your names," I replied. "I like to know who I'm dealing with."

"Joella," she said, with a bow. "And this is Riya."

"How long have you been with the King's Guard?" I asked, continuing to walk.

"The guard recruits at six," Joella said. "I've just passed twenty-four."

"And I'm twenty-nine," Riya replied.

"Do you like it?"

From their silence, I could tell they were trying to figure out my game. Perhaps Felix had told them I wasn't to be trusted. Or maybe they just weren't used to being asked questions by those they were guarding.

"I...suppose," Joella said. "Captain Felix is fair and an excellent leader and we're very fortunate to have him with us."

"He came the same year I did," Riya replied. "I'm not surprised he became the captain so young. He's quite brilliant."

With their backs turned, I let my eyes roll. "And I'm sure that being best friends with the crown prince didn't help his cause."

"Oh no," Riya said, throwing me a look over her shoulder. "He earned it fair and square. He was unanimously recommended by the guard to be second-in-command."

I chewed my tongue, wanting to pry more into why they seemed to love him so much, but not wanting to rouse their suspicions. "Then you must be thrilled that he took over for Mark."

"Mark was..." Joella began then decided against it. "We're just honored Felix has kept us in his inner circle. Not everyone in the guard has been entrusted with protecting you. Or knowing your secret."

"Ah, well," I said. "So you were part of the contingent who came to get me, then?"

"The captain was concerned you'd be unwilling to come."

"The captain was correct."

"But..." She glanced over her shoulder. "You are...the princess, aren't you?"

"*Joella*," Riya scolded. "Of course she is. Look at her."

"F-forgive me," Joella said. "I never met the princess before she left."

"You mean before I was bartered off like livestock?" I drawled. "Yes, it's me. If Felix was going to find a fake, I would assume he would find a more willing individual."

"I suppose that's true," Joella said. "There are just whispers. You should be aware of them, Princess."

"I got a council full of them, thank you." I chewed my lip. "Who do you think killed my brother and father?"

"Uh..." Joella looked at Riya, who shook her head. "We aren't at liberty to say. Much like your secret, Captain Llobrega has kept this investigation close to the vest."

Interesting. Felix had concerns about his own guards, which certainly seemed odd considering what I'd just learned about how tight-knit they were. But every person has their price.

We arrived at my tower and Joella unlocked the door with a ring of keys. "Sleep well, Your Highness. We'll be outside."

I closed the door and leaned against it. Perhaps Felix thought a vigilante would make a good queen. But wanting to do good for the kingdom and having the freedom to do good for the kingdom were two different things. Between a council who didn't trust me and a potential poisoner out to get me, I didn't think the best place for me was at the castle.

It was time to make my escape.

# Chapter Six

I shimmied out of my dress and searched my room for something I could actually work in. Felix had left me with a tunic for tomorrow—a bright blue velvet number that would be visible from anywhere, but that would have to do. It was only temporary, anyway.

A plan had been forming in my mind since the Council meeting. I would leave Forcadel for a few months, until another monarch was put in place. Then, when everyone had forgotten my name, I would return and don The Veil once more, cleaning out my city in peace.

I went to the window and opened the glass, letting the cool night air brush against my face. I didn't like the idea of being gone for so long. How much more damage would Beswick cause? What might happen if the Council picked someone who didn't have the city's best interests at heart?

But what alternative did I have? It was lunacy to even consider becoming queen. I'd been taught to be a wife then a thief, a swordsman, a vigilante. But I'd never been taught how to lead.

Especially a country that most assuredly did not want me as its leader.

My mind made up, I slid my hands along the smooth edge of the tower. It was designed to keep assassins out, presumably not to keep princesses in. Some fifty feet below, the roof was slanted, so if I jumped, I might slide off if I hit it wrong.

I turned back to my room, looking for anything I could use to rappel with. There were curtains, bedsheets, that damned dress. With little ceremony, I pulled them off, placing them in long strands around the room. I laced the curtains together then added the bedsheets. I threw the sheets out the window and surveyed the distance. It was still a far jump, but not as far. I could manage it.

Pulling the sheets back into the room, I searched for something to tie them to, as the window wasn't going to work. The four-poster bed was an attractive option, but getting it over to the window might be loud. There was a chair next to the fireplace; that could work.

As quietly as I could, I pulled it toward the window, stopping every few minutes to listen for the lock on the door turning over. When nothing happened, I tied the end of the bedsheets to the bottom of the chair and tested my weight. The chair moved, so I pushed it right up against the window, hoping it would be strong enough.

I climbed over the chair and tested the weight just out the window on the ledge. Then, with a quick exhale, I stepped out of the window, leaning back. The chair rocked but didn't tip. So I climbed out further, the slippers on my feet poor for this effort with their lack of grip. But I carefully slid against the stone, moving surely and slowly.

Finally, I came to the edge of my rope—there were perhaps ten feet separating me from the roof, so I let go, landing with a bit of a slide on the steep slope. I remained still until I found my balance and listened for guards or anyone else who might've heard me.

Confident I was still unheard, I moved slowly. It was difficult, but with every step, I found more of myself. I was no longer Princess Brynna-Larissa. Once more, I was a creature of the night. The only thing missing was my sword, and while I was *very* upset to be leaving her behind, I would procure another. Perhaps sometime in the future, I'd ask Felix for it back. When someone new was on the throne.

Now, the important part was to disappear.

My tower was located in an interior square, the roof of which I was scurrying along. It connected to nothing else, so in order to escape, I'd have to find a window to climb down into. I stopped at the corner between two walls, climbing to the edge and hanging down by my fingertips. There were windows every few feet, most of which were locked. I didn't have the strength to break into any of them.

And yet…did my eyes detect an open window halfway down the roof?

I pulled myself up and counted the steps to the center then hung down again. The window was wide open. Perhaps a maid had left it when she'd been cleaning.

Dangling, I swung my legs back and forth to get momentum then released just as I had the distance. My feet landed on the carpet, and the rest of me landed in a heap.

Success.

I crept to the door and opened it, peering out into the hall. Empty to the left, empty to the right. Slipping out, I hoped my face wasn't so well-known that I couldn't blend in as the help until I escaped. After all, nothing about my clothes screamed queen-to-be, even if they were bright.

I found the spiral staircase at the corner, and took the steps two-by-two, expecting a guard or a barrage of arrows at every turn. But I arrived at the bottom floor without meeting either. There were more servants walking through down here, but none of them gave me a second glance.

After some starts and dead ends, I finally made it to the kitchen, which led me out onto the dark green between the main castle and the external walls. From there, I kept to the wall, running my hand along the brick and praying I could make it to the front gates before—

I saw it before I felt it, the flash in the torchlight then the sharpness against my throat. I stood still, knowing who had thwarted my escape.

"Back to your room, Princess," Felix breathed softly.

I stepped away from his sword, and my back hit the wall. "Felix, this is madness. Why can't you find someone else?"

"Do you know who succeeds you? Your great uncle, who is near to death himself and who lives two days' ride away," Felix snapped, his face shrouded in shadow but his eyes wild with anger. "His son is a drunken fool who would sooner fill his own glass than make sure his people have food."

I frowned. "Who's after him?"

"Do you think he'll step aside when offered the crown?" he asked, taking a step closer to me.

"I think I'll force him to," I replied, running my fingers along the brick at my back and avoiding his gaze. "Does he have any children who would make suitable kings?"

"After him is your father's other brother's son, who is a monk near the sea," Felix said, closing the space between us even more. "Are you going to force him to take the crown?"

"If I must."

He growled and pressed his hand against the wall next to my head. "As an option, *Princess*, perhaps you might consider just taking the crown yourself, especially if you are so concerned for its owner."

I glanced at the dark sky above, allowing my shoulders to sag. "I just..." Seeing he had dropped his guard, I slipped under his arm and ran as fast as my feet could carry me. I didn't care to look back nor did I worry whether he was in pursuit. I had one chance to run and this was it—

His weight crashed on top of me. We wrestled on the ground as he turned me to face him, even as I wriggled and thrashed against him. He took my wrists in his hands and slammed them into the ground above my head. Try as I might, I couldn't shake him off—as if he predicted every movement.

"*Let me go!*" I screamed.

"I will when you agree to return to the castle." His calmness was infuriating. "You have a duty—"

"I don't want it," I said, laying my head on the ground and closing my eyes in shame. Let him think me weak, maybe he'd see just how stupid this idea was.

"Brynna," he said, releasing my hands and sitting up. "It's not like you to run away."

I remained on the ground, defeated. "What do you know about me, Felix?"

He was silent for a few moments, and I cracked open an eye to look at him. He was staring at the stars, resting on his heels.

"I know it's a scary prospect," he said, turning to me once again. "But you've spent your life staring down the worst criminals this city has to offer. You can't tell me a couple of old lords and ladies terrify you that much."

"It's not just that." I could no longer hide my emotions as tears spilled down my cheeks. "This is all just...too much. I was happy in my life before. It wasn't the best life, but it was mine. And now I'm being forced into dresses that don't fit and being told what to say and..." I wiped my cheeks and sniffed loudly.

He sighed.

"And more than that..." I shook my head. "I was *so* close to getting Beswick on treason charges."

"Are you?" Felix asked with a quirked brow. "How?"

"I think he's running deals with the Kulkans," I said, brushing my hair out of my face as I sat up. "So far, it's just conjecture, but I was closing in on his bookkeeper. Now, all those leads are going to go cold..."

He actually laughed. "They won't if you give them to me and let me take care of it. I want him gone as much as you do, so if you have a lead..."

"Felix, you can't operate the way I do." I limply raised my hand into the air. "People are much more eager to speak with me than with the captain of the king's guard."

"You mean you threaten them."

"Well?" I shrugged. "It gets results, doesn't it? And I can get more, just...let me continue what I started. Let me *finish* it, at least." I closed my eyes as more tears fell. "Before you take away all the best parts of myself. Please, just let me have this one thing."

Felix was quiet for a long time, sitting there on the dirty ground outside the castle.

"I suppose..." He sighed loudly. "If you *promise* to be careful, and you remain injury-free, I would consider letting you continue your investigation."

My eyes opened, torn between indignation that he was allowing me to do anything and relief that he was. "I'm listening."

"You will continue to make all your appearances during the day," he said, sounding as if he already regretted what he was saying. "And if your nightly activities interfere in any way, I will handcuff you to your bed."

"Is that a promise?" I said with a grin.

His dark eyes met mine, and there was nothing but annoyance in them. "And when you are officially crowned in three months, you will hang up your hood for good and that will be the end of it."

I licked my lips. "Counter offer. I will find and dispose of Beswick. Then I will become queen."

"Your coronation is in three months," he said, standing and holding out his hand to help me up. "I suggest you work quickly."

I could do three months, so I let him pull me upright. "Give me my mask and sword back."

"Tomorrow," he said, releasing my hand. "Please, just sleep tonight. I have a feeling we'll both need it. You have a very busy day tomorrow."

"Oh, yeah? Doing what?"

He smiled. "You've got a lesson with Katarine. Bright and early."

"Really?" I said with a quirked brow. "She still wants to be in the same room as me?"

"We all want to see you succeed, Brynn. Even when you're a pain in the ass."

# Chapter
## Seven

When I woke up the next morning, I was well-rested and feeling less like the walls were closing in on me. I had three months to find enough evidence to convict Beswick with treason. It had taken me weeks to suss out the name of his bookkeeper, but now—now I had a fire at my back. And, presumably, an unlimited budget.

Beata arrived bright and early with my breakfast, and I spent a few moments getting to know her further. She'd been there for a number of years, knew just about everyone who worked for the royal family, and would probably prove to be an invaluable asset.

"Oh, no," she demurred, shaking her head and glancing down at the floor. "I'm just a simple maid. Nobody important."

"Very important," I said, inhaling the scent of coffee. "Nobody ever notices you, and you hear everything. I'll have to make sure to keep you happy. You've worked in the castle a long time, right?"

She ducked her head. "Yes, ma'am."

"Did you serve my father? Or just August?"

"I was your brother's attendant," she said. "His and Lady

Katarine's for the past few years."

"And what was the relationship like?" I asked, nibbling on a piece of fruit. "Katarine and August's?"

Beata's eyes softened a little. "Your brother was a wonderful man. We both miss him terribly."

"You didn't answer my question," I said with a knowing smile.

"That's because, and please forgive me, it's not my answer to give," she said, gazing at the ground in deference even as she deflected my question. "The relationship between Lady Katarine and Prince August remained between the two of them. If she opts to share it with you, that's her decision, not mine."

So Beata was loyal to Katarine. Good to know.

The woman in question walked in the door, bearing a stack of books and papers. Beata left so quickly, I thought she might be on fire. Katarine barely gave her a second look, as she came to the center of the room with a stony look on her face.

"Good morning, Your Highness," she said, bowing. "Felix asked me to help you learn about Forcadel's history, and some additional things you might want to know before you meet with the Council again."

I sat back and surveyed her. She showed no sign of the woman who'd slapped me the day before and seemed determined to forget the momentary lapse in judgment. I could practically smell the desperation.

So, mindful of Felix and wanting to keep our agreements intact, I cleared my throat. "I'm sorry for what I said yesterday."

She straightened, her pale cheeks growing rosy. "What?"

"Yesterday, about my brother and you. It was out of line," I shrugged. "I'm sorry I doubted your intentions."

"You don't have to explain yourself," she said, although she looked rather relieved. "I know how it looks. But know that I'm only here to be helpful."

"I know," I said, sucking down more of the coffee. "So you said something about history?"

⇀————

Katarine took me to the room where I'd learned to read and write as a girl. Now, she was using it to impart all her geopolitical wisdom. Maps and drawings hung on the walls, flag colors of our allies and enemies, and my indefatigable tutor seemed to know everything. She'd obviously been preparing to become queen for many years, as her knowledge of not only Forcadel, but also Kulka and Niemen, was impressive and thorough. And to her credit, she never once mentioned her almost-position.

But that didn't mean any of what she was telling me made sense to me.

"So, okay," I said, looking down at the map of Forcadel and surrounding countries. "Forcadel is basically centered around the capital city here in the bay, and our borders extend across the southern half of the continent, with these two rivers connecting us directly to Niemen and Kulka, right?"

"Right. And we receive a lot of money from these other nations to ship their goods on the rivers in Forcadel," Katarine said. "And those tariffs pay for...well, all this."

I looked around the room and scoffed. "Well, we've got all this already. Why can't we just give them free access?"

"Then they would no longer need us," Katarine said. "Forcadel doesn't have mines or farmland or even glass. What's to say Kulka wouldn't add a three hundred percent tariff to their food? We'd have no recourse, and our people would starve."

I furrowed my brow. "But they wouldn't do that, would they?"

"It's best to keep things as they are so we don't find out." She smiled brightly, but there was the hint of impatience in her voice. "Forcadel's position on the coast makes us a hub for many of our land-locked neighbors."

"You mean, we bullied and conquered our way to the best

position," I said with a loud yawn. "Please, don't skip over our bloody, conquest-heavy history."

"Oh, don't worry, we'll be going over all of it," Katarine said, rising to walk to the map hanging on the wall. "Niemen and Forcadel have only recently become amicable trading partners through a carefully negotiated treaty. Obviously, my being here was part of that." She stared at the paper for a moment. "I would hope that even if a Niemenian queen doesn't sit on the throne, we can continue to have peace."

"I don't see why not," I said, watching as a bird flew by the window. Oh, to be outside today. Or sleeping and resting up for my big night out.

"*Because*," Katarine said, gaining my attention back, "the treaty was highly controversial, including and especially the marriage. It's one thing to make a treaty, quite another to mix bloodlines. Do you understand?"

"But you...didn't mix any bloodlines?" I said. "Unless there's something you want to tell me."

"No," she said, her eyes a little sad. Then she shook it off and went back to the map. "Obviously, I'm here as your link to the Niemenians, but there is someone on your Council who links you to Kulka. Do you know who it is?"

I blinked. "Uuuh..."

"Lady Vernice."

"Which one was she?" I asked, straining my memory. "Purple?"

"She was wearing purple, yes," Katarine said with a smile. "She was also the one who was very unfriendly to me."

"Oh yeah." I nodded. "Why?"

Katarine laughed, although there was no humor in it. "Because if it were up to the Kulkans, the treaty between Niemen and Forcadel would be nullified, my head would be on a pike, and war would probably break out between Forcadel and Niemen."

"But how would that benefit...oh..." I nodded. "Kulkans

would be our only source of metal. Metal that we would use in a war against Niemen."

"See? You're getting the hang of it," Katarine said with a smile.

"But if she's a Kulkan, why is she on the Council?" I asked.

"Forcadel was formed when six warring dukedoms came together under a single flag. The idea was that they would rule the land together, so each family would still have a seat at the table." She pointed to the flag of Forcadel, which contained a shield with six smaller crests. "Of course, the Lonsdales had the biggest army and the most gold, so they crowned themselves kings after a few decades."

"As one does."

"Your present Council bears little resemblance to those original families," Katarine explained, walking to the chalkboard where she'd listed the names of each of the participants. "Your father stocked the council with political allies like Garwood—"

"Garwood? An ally?" I snorted. "Yeah, right."

"He and your father were aligned on many issues," Katarine said. "He appointed Vernice because of her hold on the northwestern section, which has a heavy Kulkan population. Conscious of my betrothal, he appointed Vernice to appease both the country and the citizenry up there." She drew her pointer down one name. "Councilman Zuriel is the mayor of the city."

"Well acquainted," I said. "I like him."

"General Godfryd commands your naval forces. She's a force to be reckoned with. Hard, and oblivious to political headwinds. If you can count her as an ally, you're doing well. And of course, Octavius, who does whatever the others tell him to."

"So I could clean house, couldn't I?" I said. "Get rid of Vernice and the rest of them?"

"You could, after your coronation." She looked at the map again. "But with all the turmoil these past few weeks, the country needs a steady hand. And despite their personality differences, your

Council isn't as bad as it seems."

I placed my finger on the country to the west of Niemen. *Severia.* "And what about that country?"

She shook her head. "Desert country. We get glass from them, and that's about it. They're very poor, so we do what we can."

"I see." I looked back at the other two nations. "And how do our allies feel, knowing that the last two kings were poisoned?"

"It happened so quickly," Katarine whispered, another veil of sadness dropping over her eyes and disappearing before I got a good look at it. "But that's why Felix was so eager to get you back on the throne. If we can keep a Lonsdale on the throne, we can weather this storm without breaking any of our treaties and causing more damage."

"Assuming I don't make an egregious mistake."

She chuckled. "That's why we're here studying. There's a lot to keep up with, and until you have a set of trusted advisors to help guide your opinions, you're on your own making decisions."

"Right, decisions." I pushed the map away, tired of seeing it for the moment. "Let's talk about these kingdoms some more. Any of them suspects in murdering August and my father? Maybe the Kulkans are trying to undo the deal, like you said?"

"It would be brazen," she said. "It's much more likely that it was an internal attack."

"They could be working together, the Kulkans and Vernice," I said with a small shrug. "That happened two years ago—there were two crime families fighting against each other. The younger son got in with the enemy family and wiped out his father and older brother. Then he got himself a deputy position..." I cleared my throat. "Until his old cartel got wind of his betrayal. Think they drowned him—"

"*Brynna.*" Katarine's face had grown quite pale. "Crime families and retribution murders are not your concern anymore."

So Felix hadn't told her about our agreement. "I mean, they're still my subjects. So yes—"

"That is the concern of Felix and his men. Delegation is a key skill you need to learn. And quickly." I opened my mouth to argue, but she held up her hand to silence me. "As queen, you should be focused on the larger issues of the kingdom. Foreign dignitaries and the kingdom's coffers. Making sure your lords and ladies are able to manage their holdings effectively."

"You mean help them make deals to keep themselves rich while taking from—"

"Brynna..." Katarine sighed. "I'm trying. Please try, too."

"Fine," I said with a frown. "Continue, please."

The sun was low in the sky when Katarine finally released me from our session. Felix's guards Coyle and Zathan escorted me from the classroom back to my tower, where Beata had a succulent dinner waiting. I wasn't hungry, though, not when excitement pounded through my veins.

I changed into a simple tunic and pants that were now hanging in my wardrobe. When I came to the door again, Zathan rose so fast, I thought he might attack me.

"My lady?" he said. "Is there something wrong?"

"Take me to Felix," I said.

Zathan cast a glance at his partner, who nodded. "He said to take her down to the barracks."

I followed them down the stairs, bouncing with every step. I was honestly prepared for a fight, not yet trusting Felix to be a man of his word. Especially where me leaving the castle was concerned. But perhaps this first night would convince him that I wasn't a delicate flower to be guarded at all times.

Coyle and Zathan led me into a green patch inside the castle exterior walls. Two squads of twenty soldiers each jogged in perfect formation around the track, while another group, perhaps aged fifteen or sixteen, squared off against each other. A still younger group sat cross-legged while they rigorously cleaned weapons. In the center, watching everything, was Felix.

"Wait," Coyle said as I started for him. "He's in the middle of training."

"And the sun is setting, so I don't have time to wait," I said, shoving off her hand and walking up to Felix.

"Afternoon," he said, not tearing his gaze away from the jogging teenagers. "Is there something I can help you with?"

"I want my sword and hood," I said. "You promised."

He rubbed his chin, his late-in-the-day stubble scratching under his thumb. "Promised?"

"I can't very well investigate Beswick without them," I said. "And yes, you did promise."

"I'd prefer it if you went with just your cloak," he said.

I spun on him. "Don't make me hurt you, Felix. You said I could continue my nightly activities. I can't do that without my weapon."

Just as I was about to lay him out in front of his soldiers, the corner of his mouth turned upward. "Yes, Brynn. Once drill is over, we'll retrieve your things."

"Is it customary for the captain to oversee this training?" I huffed.

"No, but I've been a bit preoccupied and haven't set a second yet," he said, eyeing me. "I promise. Ten minutes."

Drill took longer than ten minutes, as the sun was gone and the moon overhead when Felix finally released his soldiers to their barracks. Even then, they still marched toward the barracks with steely expressions, no one daring to look even remotely like they were enjoying themselves.

"Tough crowd," I said, falling into step beside Felix.

"Is that sarcasm?"

"Yes." I nodded toward a pair of kids who jumped to attention as we passed. "It's like they've been brainwashed to worship you."

"I believe they're saluting you, Princess." Again, he wore that smirk. "It's a great honor to be chosen to participate in the King's Guard."

"Unless you're August." My brother had been forced into service by my father to try to beat some of his more rebellious tendencies out of him. It appeared to have worked.

His stoic face fell a little. "Yes, unless you're the prince."

We continued into the barracks, filled with the stench of body odor and the sound of young boys and girls cutting up drowning out all my thoughts. Each dark brown door was adorned with a single number; Felix stopped in front of number twelve.

"Doesn't the captain get nicer quarters?" I asked as he opened the door. There was a small bed in the corner, the humble wool blanket tucked under the mattress, and a desk with a small oil lamp with a neat stack of papers. It fit the tidy, military view I'd come to expect from the man.

"Supposedly, I get a room in the castle," he said, walking to his closet. "But as I said, I've been a little busy." He opened the simple wooden closet and I got a whiff of musk and old wood. His tunics hung neatly, along with a few extra sets of pants. He carefully pushed aside them both and reached into his closet, retrieving a familiar bundle.

"Your hood," he said, placing the black material in my hands before returning to the closet and finding my scabbard. "And your sword." He kept his hand on the pommel, preventing me from tugging it away. "Remember that our agreement is null and void if you get injured in *any* way."

I yanked the sword from his grip. "Luckily for you, I'm good at hiding bruises."

"Brynna—"

"This isn't my first trip out into the night, Captain," I said, already feeling better with my mask under my fingertips.

"Promise me you won't run."

I looked up at him, my lips parting in surprise. Not at his words, but at the soft way he'd spoken them. It wasn't a demand; it was a plea.

"I won't run," I replied. "I still don't think I'm the best for this, but...a deal is a deal."

That seemed to placate him, and he nodded. "I'll take you to the stables to get changed. From there, I'm sure you can make it out through the front gates without being seen."

"Naturally."

He pursed his lips, the ghost of indecision on his face. But thankfully, he said nothing else and led me to freedom.

# Chapter Eight

It had been two nights since I'd donned my hood, but it felt like a lifetime. The warm air, the cloth against my cheeks, my sword a comforting weight against my hips, it was easy to believe the past two days had been a bad dream.

But they hadn't been.

A small voice begged me to continue running—beyond the bay and out into the great unknown. But if I left now, Forcadel would descend into chaos. And perhaps, if I were being totally honest, Felix might have made some sense about those in line behind me. I did care about who sat on the throne, because I cared about the people here. That damned captain seemed to know more about me than I cared to admit.

My first stop of the night was back at the butchery. My room was empty; Tasha and his parents were still cleaning the slaughter room. I wondered how long it would take them to find a new girl. Would Tasha bed her, too? Marry her? She'd be a lucky woman, to live a life so free of responsibilities.

I knelt and removed the loose floorboard, digging among the

paper and other trash I'd stored to throw off any looters. My fingers made purchase on something hard, a necklace. A simple blue stone on a silver chain that had belonged to my mother. It had been a gift on my wedding day, and the only thing I'd kept as a memory. I slipped it around my neck and hid the stone between my breasts for safekeeping.

Then I was gone.

I spent a few minutes reacquainting myself with the city's rooftops, thinking about my next move. I could frequent one of Beswick's many bars, locating a lieutenant and following him until he led me to Poole. But with my pressing deadline, I needed to be more proactive. And luckily for me, I'd snatched a fair bit of gold from Felix's closet while he'd left me to change.

Which might explain why he was very noisily following me on the rooftop.

"You're clodding around like a cow," I said, stopping short and spinning around to face him.

"I apologize," Felix said, wearing a black tunic and pants. "But I'm unaccustomed to walking on rooftops. Maybe we could try the street?"

"And yet I ask myself why you're here at all?" I placed my hands on my hips. "We had an agreement."

"Which said nothing about me following you to keep you safe," he said, before his foot slipped on the slanted roof. He windmilled his arms for a moment before regaining his balance. It would've been funny had I not been on the brink of throwing him off myself.

"Still want to follow me?" I said pointedly.

"Considering it's my sworn duty to keep you alive, yes."

I closed my eyes, counting to ten. Perhaps if I took him around for one night, and made a point to steer clear of trouble, he would realize his presence was a hindrance and go back to the castle. I could barely stand him during the day, there was no way I'd survive his overbearing supervision at night, too.

Without a word, I climbed down from the roof and landed on the ground in a crouch. I waited, grateful my mask hid the look of annoyance on my face as Felix took his sweet time joining me there.

"I'm looking for a man named Eric Poole," I said as Felix's heavy footfalls caught up with me. "I believe he's Beswick's bookkeeper, and when I find him, I'll find the evidence I need to charge Beswick with treason."

"And how are you planning to do that?" Felix asked. "Just walk up to the man and ask him to hand it over?"

I quirked a brow. "The usual ways."

"You can't go threatening people, Brynna."

"If you can't adhere to our agreement then I'll be happy to go alone," I said, pressing a hand to my hip.

"And I told you that's not happening."

I released a frustrated noise. "Regardless, I have to find the man first. And for that, I think I'm going to have to pay someone to give me information."

"You didn't try that before?"

"I didn't have this lovely gold before." I flashed him the coin purse I'd nicked off him earlier in the day. I hadn't stolen money in eons, but I figured Felix could spare a few gold coins.

He clicked his tongue. "Just give me the purse back when you're done. It's a keepsake."

"But of course," I said, pocketing it. "My informant knows a lot about everything. She'll recognize your face, so you'll need to stay in the shadows."

"Will she recognize yours?"

I cast him a look, pointing to the mask. "Hasn't yet."

My informant was at the usual spot, waiting tables at Harm's Cafe. It was still early in the evening, and couples out for a romantic night shared coffee over small iron tables. A woman with red hair caught my eye, and she gave me an imperceptible nod. I turned and made my way to the backdoor, waiting in the darkness for her to appear.

After a few moments, the door opened. "My dearest Veil, how are you?"

"Ruby, always a pleasure." I grinned, taking her hand and shaking it. "I need some information about Beswick's men. Got a moment?"

"I have a moment if you have money to pay for it."

At that, I laughed. Ruby had an extensive network of people to inform her, and therefore, her information didn't come cheap. I placed five gold coins on her outstretched hand, and her eyes lit up.

"A downpayment," I said, shaking the bag to make the rest of the coins clink. "What do you know about Eric Poole?"

"Hm..." She stroked her chin. "I know where you can find him tonight. Titta O'Sullivans. He's usually there on Thursdays."

I groaned, but handed her another five gold coins, making sure to tuck the bag back in my belt for Felix. "Titta's, huh?"

"Yes, ma'am. Time to break out your dancing clothes."

⇒━━━━━

"You are not going to Titta's," Felix grumbled behind me. "I cannot allow the princess of this kingdom to—"

"You're not. The Veil is going," I said.

"Somebody will recognize you."

"Nobody will be paying attention to my face, so don't worry about it."

"Have you..." He sputtered incoherently, his face growing redder. I gleefully wondered if the good captain had ever seen anyone in any state of undress, and from the red-faced sputtering, I guessed not.

"Yes, I have," I replied, getting a delicious vengeance from his discomfort as we closed in on the three-story building, flooded with purple lights. "And I'm quite a good dancer, in case you didn't know."

"I don't think you should go in at all, Brynna," Felix said, his face etched into a permanent frown. "You're to be queen—"

"And if you think my brother never came here, you're dumber than I thought," I said before dashing down the street. Two large men stood in front of the door, allowing me passage and denying it to Felix.

I wandered into the dressing room, with lighted mirrors lining the walls and men and women scurrying about half-dressed. The eponymous woman was sitting at a desk in the middle of a hall of dancers, her small legs crossed as they dangled from the tall stool. She was smoking a long cigarette and barking orders to the dancers who came for their final inspection.

"You! More eyeliner. You! Hike up your skirt, we're giving them a show, not taking them to church. You! Rouge on the stomach muscles. I want them more defined." She tapped her cigarette. "And you! Take off that ridiculous cape. No capes!"

The dancers nodded and scurried, and another group quickly took their place. But now, Titta had noticed me, and she hopped off her stool and waddled over.

"Ah, my lovely Veil," she said, meeting me with a chaste kiss on either cheek. "Are you here for pleasure or business?"

"The latter," I said, handing her the rest of my gold that I had in my pocket. "Looking for a man named Poole, if you've seen him."

She tapped her finger against her small chin. "Mm. Not familiar. What do you want from him?"

"Just to know where he lives, so I can question him in a few days' time." Titta traded in secrets and lies, so if I wanted access to them, I paradoxically had to tell her the absolute truth.

"A few days?" she said, rubbing her chin. "Make it three. I can't have men thinking they're being pumped for information here."

"Three will work," I said with a nod. And if I did it one hour sooner, she'd know it and bar me from coming back. "Thank you."

She waddled back to her stool, picking up her cigarette again. I turned to the dressing room, finding my usual stall to change out of my hood. There was a loose board behind the mirror that was perfect for stashing my hood and tunic. Walking the room required the proper attire—and shaking my ass in front of everyone else until I found him.

The outfits were flat-out ridiculous, with a strip of fabric to cover the breasts, and a long, flowing skirt that was mostly see-through, over a pair of tight underwear that cupped my butt cheeks. The male dancers wore the same, sans the top. It was a deliciously deviant evening for anyone who could afford the entry fee. I stifled a giggle as I thought of Felix paying a few gold coins to enter.

In the small dressing room, I unbound my breasts and replaced my tight cloth wrap with the much looser one of the dancer's uniform. Once I was dressed, I hung a transparent veil over my face. It wasn't the same as my mask, but it would do for now.

I queued up with another set of dancers. The closest one gave me the once over.

"You're new," she said.

"Yep," I said, lowering my voice. "First night. Any tips?"

"Don't take it personally."

Titta barked for the next group, and we stood in front of her. She dismissed me without another look and I hurried away, as the girl I'd spoken to was sent back for redder lips. I pushed my way through the velvet flaps that served as doors and into the smoky room.

There were dancers everywhere, and even more patrons. It was mostly a free-for-all, find a single person and dance until they gave up their money. A woman nearby grabbed my ass, but I kept walking.

Poole would've been a well-dressed, clean-cut man, perhaps middle-aged or older. There were ten men in the room who fit the bill, so I sashayed up to my first target. The sheen of sweat on his forehead and the lascivious look in his eye told me he wasn't a man who got women easily. So pumping him for information would be a breeze.

I rested my hands on the man's shoulders and wiggled my hips to show off the goods. "What's your name, sweetie?" I purred.

As predicted, the man's gaze was on my chest. "M...Merrick —"

"Never mind," I said, straightening and walking to the next.

But before I got there, someone grabbed my wrist and yanked me to him. Luckily, I recognized Felix before I broke his arm. "What are you doing?"

"What are *you* doing?" he whispered through clenched teeth. "You look... You look..."

"Like a dancer," I said, faking a smile and grabbing his hips. "You're drawing attention to me. Go sit in the corner until I find who I'm looking for."

"I can't let you continue this," he said, his hips moving stiffly under my guidance as he tried to look everywhere but my exposed cleavage. "This is indecent. You're the princess—"

"Right now, I'm a dancer," I cooed, glancing over his shoulder to the portly man who'd just walked in. "And I think I found my guy." I stood on my tip-toes and kissed his cheek, leaving a blood-red stain. "Stay here and stay quiet."

Felix sputtered and hissed, but did as he was told, leaving me free to finish my mission.

I circled the room a few more times until I found the man who'd piqued my interest. He had a look that said he was a man accustomed to making a lot of money doing shady things. So I danced my way over to him slowly.

"Hey there," I said, leaning over to land on his knees. "What's your name?"

"Eric," he replied, his gaze landing right where I wanted it to.
"Eric what?"

"Poole," he said, his fingers dancing along my collarbone.

"That's a fantastic name," I said, rising and turning to sit down.
"Why don't you tell me about yourself?"

And he blabbed, without much prodding or guidance from me, just as they always did. It was a wonder the girls didn't go mad from boredom. From Mr. Poole, I learned everything about him in the span of five minutes, including his mother's name and his favorite flavor of candy. Most importantly, I found out where he lived.

"Thank you, sugar," I said, dropping my voice into a sultry whisper. "You have a good night. See you around." I left a lipstick stain on his cheek and walked away slowly to make sure he got a good look.

⇒━━━━━→

"Well?" Felix asked, waiting for me out back.

"Well what?" I asked, wiping the remnants of lipstick off before sliding my mask back into place. "I learned what I needed to. In three nights, I interrogate him."

"Why not tonight?"

"My agreement with Titta was three days. And besides that, if a masked vigilante shows up at his front door an hour after he was chatting up a girl at Titta's, he might remember that girl's face a little better. If I go tomorrow, he might make the connection, too." I adjusted my gloves over my hands. "I've been doing this a long time, Felix."

"You say no one was looking at your face," Felix said. "But Titta did. Can you trust her not to spill your secret?"

"She's kept a lot of secrets," I said. "I've seen every one of the Council in there on more than one occasion. Octavius is a weekly patron."

Felix tripped over his feet. "Have you ever..."

"Ever what?"

"How many men have you taken to bed in there?" he asked in a low voice.

I glanced at him as I slid my mask back in place. "That, sir, is none of your business. Now, if you'd like to continue our evening, I need to find some lowlifes to beat up."

"You should go back to the castle. It's already midnight."

I sighed. "This is going to be a long three months."

# Chapter
# Nine

Morning came too quickly, as did Beata with my breakfast. I wasn't sure if she was part of the inner circle Felix had allowed to know my secret, so I mumbled some excuse about insomnia when she asked why I was so tired.

"Would you like me to send up some calming tea at night?" she asked, genuine concern in her eyes. "You need your rest for the funerals tomorrow."

"No, no," I said, shaking my head and trying to clear the smoke from my eyes. "But thank you."

She tutted, reminding me of a mother hen, and I was fairly sure there would be tea tonight whether I wanted it or not.

Katarine arrived shortly after that, nodding once to Beata as she made her exit. "Well? Were you successful last night?"

I allowed my mouth to drop in a large yawn. "So Felix told you?"

"He did, this morning over breakfast when I asked him why he was late to our morning run," she said with a disapproving scowl. "I really think you should reconsider. It's hard enough for you to manage all your responsibilities when you get a good night's sleep. I don't know how bad you'll be when you're distracted."

"I'll manage, I suppose" I said, rolling over onto my side. "I'm not in the mood for whatever nonsense you're here to tell me. So please, just give me the short version."

She made a noise. "The short version is it's time for our lesson."

"Lesson? Again?"

"Yes." She ripped the covers off me. "We have a lot of ground to cover."

Perhaps there might've been some wisdom in not staying out all night, especially as my eyes drooped most of the morning. Katarine seemed to have grown more confident that I wasn't going to kick her out, because she'd become more militant in her lectures. And to make things worse, she'd stuffed me into what she termed a "posture modification sleeve." In fact, it was worse than a corset, keeping my shoulders upright and my back arched perfectly. There was a wooden crown on my head, larger than the gold piece I'd been wearing, and my neck ached as I remained still and alert.

And still, my mind was elsewhere, scheming how I might go about getting Mr. Poole to talk, and what I was going to do for my three nights of free time.

A loud smack on the papers woke me up. Katarine stood in front of me, holding a riding crop between her hands. "*Please* pay attention. It would be terrible if you made a gaffe in front of the Council. They're already still complaining about how you walked out of the meeting the other day."

As my hands were already bright red, I smiled and nodded like the good little queen. Perhaps I could borrow the riding crop to beat Felix with later for making me sit through this.

"Sit up," Katarine said, poking me in the back.

"I am sitting up," I said, adjusting myself as much as I could without letting the wooden crown fall. "I couldn't slouch in this thing if I wanted to."

"Your shoulders. Level them out. Chin up. Don't roll your eyes at me."

"Then quit barking orders," I said, crankily. "I am quite capable of sitting like a queen. I just don't see the point. If I'm queen, who cares?"

"Your title is only yours as long as your kingdom bestows it on you," Katarine said. "The Council already has misgivings, and the rest of the kingdom is wary of you. In order to gain their trust, you have to look like you actually care. And *yes*, that means sitting up and not acting like you'd rather be anywhere but here."

"It appears I'm out of practice lying," I said, adjusting myself.

"You lie all the time as The Veil," Katarine said. "You played a role during the day, didn't you?"

"It didn't require me to smile and wave like a prized doll."

"From what I hear, it required a lot of dancing," she said, shuffling the papers on the table.

"You and Felix have a lovely conversation about me?" I asked, trying to get more comfortable. "Has he been intimate with another person before? Seemed awfully put out by the human form. Maybe I'll hire one of the dancers to give him a thrill."

"You'd do well not to piss him off," Katarine replied. "He's only looking out for your best interests."

I bit my tongue instead of answering the way I wanted to. My head was aching and arguing with Katarine would just make it worse.

"Now, back to our discussion," Katarine said, turning to the map. "Where were we?"

"Kulka's rich farmlands," I said with a yawn.

"Right. Kulka delivers over half of the food the kingdom consumes, including most of the fruits and vegetables. Therefore, they're a very important partner. They do share a border with Niemen, and have begun mining more, as we talked about. There's an outstanding treaty that I'm sure the Kulkan envoy will want to discuss when he arrives for your coronation."

"Oh yeah?" I said. "What treaty is that?"

"The one that wasn't completed when you ran away from your wedding," she said with a knowing smile. "The good news is that Kulka's King Neshua is in his forties, having taken over from his father fifteen years ago. He's fairly even-tempered, although he's been more aggressively guarding the border and the mining. He also has a variety of siblings at your disposal to marry, if you are so inclined. I'm sad to say the man you were supposed to marry, Prince Ammon, is married to another."

"He looked like a frog," I said. "No loss there."

"Be that as it may, you should be mindful when dealing with the Kulkans that they're still sulking about you walking out on them." She turned to the map again. "Our other allies are the Niemenians, my home country."

"Who are also out a treaty, since you and my brother didn't screw enough." She turned to me, flushing bright red, and I remembered my brother hadn't even been dead a week. "Sorry, that was out of line."

"A-anyway," she said, turning back to the maps, presumably to hide her emotions. "Niemen has Queen Ariadna, my eldest sister. I'm the youngest of six, and the only Niemen royal to be living abroad. There was talk that one of my brothers and one of Neshua's sisters would marry, but it hasn't happened yet. And if they keep squabbling over the border, it might never happen. I'm not sure who my sister is sending as an envoy to your coronation, but I assume it will be one of my siblings."

"And our relationship with them is fairly positive?"

"Yes, I would assume so," she said. "I recently wrote to my favorite brother Luard and told him of August's passing, but I haven't received his response yet. I would..." She sighed and looked out the window. "I'd assume Ariadna would ask you to find me another husband. And while not the same as marrying into the direct royal family, it would still meet the terms of the contract."

"You could always marry me," I said, fluttering my eyes at her.

"Sadly, Brynn, you are not my cup of tea," she said with a laugh.

"What about Severia?" I asked, pointing to the map. "Who's in charge up there?"

"Ilara," she said. "I know very little about her. She's young, I believe. Sickly. Doesn't travel. But as I said yesterday, you'll mostly be dealing with the Kulkans and the Niemans, in terms of international affairs."

"And what about internal affairs?" I asked.

"Oh, that, my love, is a lesson for another day," she said. "I don't want to overwhelm you."

"I would pay attention better if I didn't have to wear this stupid..." I adjusted myself again and wished I could exhale. "Thing."

"Come here," Katarine said, beckoning me to her. I pushed myself to stand and waddled over to her. She spun me around and fussed with the cords. "Oh, darling, these aren't tight—"

"Don't you *dare* tighten it," I growled.

Blessedly, I received a small reprieve as she undid the ties.

"Can I outlaw these when I'm queen?" I asked. "I prefer my bindings. At least then I can move."

"When you can demonstrate a queenly posture, I will stop the training device." She patted my cheek. "Now, back to Kulka. Last year, we received no less than fifty ships a week down the river from Kulka..."

The torture didn't end until lunch, when Beata arrived at our small training room with another fantastic meal. Katarine released me from the posture device and I caught twenty minutes of a nap before someone was shaking me awake. I opened my eyes to Felix's brown ones and groaned.

"What now?" I asked.

"We have paperwork to complete. Let's go."

"Hooray," I whispered, coming to my feet. The late night and early morning were catching up with me, as was the very heavy lunch of fish and pasta. I followed sluggishly behind Felix, scowling at the look of amusement on his face. "What?"

"You look tired. Maybe you should take a night in."

"I have," I yawned, "three months to deal with Beswick. That's not a lot of time."

"You also have three days before you can question Mr. Poole," he said, nodding to the guard Coyle as he walked by. "So perhaps you should take one of those nights to recover?"

"I'll be fine," I said. "Any chance Beata could bring me some coffee?"

He led me into the east side of the castle, where my father had conducted most of his business, and into a circular room with large windows overlooking the bay. A smattering of wooden ships sat in the water, their sails billowing in the wind and looking like small toys from this distance.

In front of the vista was a grandiose desk, carved from the finest dark wood with gold-plated drawer knobs and a glass covering. There was a tower of papers in a wooden box to my right, and an empty box to my left.

I plopped down in the leather chair I assumed was mine and picked up the first sheet of paper. "What is this?"

"Documents that require the sovereign's signature," Felix said, pulling up a chair beside me. "So sign them."

"Without reading them?" I asked, although I wasn't quite sure I understood the small print I was reading.

"They've already gotten your Council's approval, or else they wouldn't come to you," he said, leaning back.

"What if I'm signing away my kingdom?" I said, picking up

another paper to see if there was something more intelligible there. "Can we trust the Council?"

"Yes, Brynn," he said. "As much as you can trust anyone in politics."

"So no," I said, fighting off a dull headache between my eyes. "Is it an absolute requirement for you to be here, looking over my shoulder?"

"I'm standing guard."

"You're sitting guard."

He quirked a brow. "Why are you so eager to get rid of me? Want an early start on your vigilante work? Or..." He smiled. "Just want to take a nap?"

I didn't want to give him the satisfaction of knowing I was exhausted. "Just wondering why my captain is in here when I'm doing paperwork. It should probably be my Councilman or at least my attendant. Don't I have one of those?"

"You've yet to appoint one."

"Then Katarine will work. She's smart enough to know what's going on around here."

"You two are getting along now?"

"As long as she didn't murder my brother, we'll get along fine," I said, finally seeing something I recognized. "Why is it my job to sign for a side of beef?"

"Because the sovereign is responsible for paying for your daily meals, including, it seems, a side of beef."

I quickly scrawled my signature on the paper and put it in the done pile. There were still so many to go. Perhaps it wouldn't be so bad to just...sign them. After all, they might've been reviewed before my brother had died—one was dated before my father had died. Perhaps I could trust them, just this once.

No. Until I knew who was responsible for the killing, I couldn't trust anyone. Not even the Council.

I rested my hand on my chin and forced myself to comprehend

the boring document in front of me. It was a request to repaint a south wall of the castle that had fallen into disrepair. The next was a notice that a Forcadel bank was increasing the interest rate on my account from one percent to two percent. And on and on...

After I'd signed ten in a row, I looked at the pile remaining and whined audibly.

"How about this?" Felix spoke up. "Why don't you finish half of them, and then I'll take you back to your room so you can rest up for tonight."

"R...really?" I stood up so fast I knocked over the chair.

"Yeah. Since you're obviously too stubborn to take care of yourself, I suppose I'll have to make some adjustments. I'll have Beata bring the rest to your room at breakfast tomorrow before the funerals."

I blinked. "Funerals are...tomorrow?"

"Obviously, we had only been planning one," Felix said, casting a long look out the window. "But I suppose Maurice won't mind sharing the dais with his son."

I chewed on my lip. "Am I going?"

He sighed. "You're the sovereign."

"So? Doesn't mean I have to go."

"Yes, Brynna, you have to go. And you have to look sad and lead the nation in healing. As much as you don't care for your father and brother, they were very well-liked."

"Maybe in your areas of the kingdom," I muttered. My brother was tolerated, but I heard more gripes than praises for Maurice.

"Which is why I *strongly* recommend that you stay in tonight if you're this tired," he said.

"I strongly recommend you keep your recommendations to yourself."

# Chapter Ten

Four hours of sleep later, I was wide awake and ready to take on the night. This time, Felix brought my mask and sword to my room, and beckoned me to follow him silently.

"We can't continue letting you leave through the barracks like you did last night," he said. "There are people who might see you, and it's too much of a risk."

I slowed my gait, ready for him to lower the boom. "So…?"

"So I'm going to let you in on one of my most closely guarded secrets." He stopped, spun, and pointed at my chest. "You cannot breathe a word of this to anyone, understand?"

"Felix," I said with a grin, pushing his finger away. "Are you about to show me a secret exit to the castle?"

"There are several that have been built in over the years," he said, turning back around and continuing down the stairs. "I will show you the closest. That is the only one you'll get."

"Fine, fine," I said. "You're certainly full of surprises."

The closest was inside my father's office where I'd been not a few hours before. Felix walked toward a statue in the corner and pushed it out of the way with ease—it was probably on casters of some kind. Then he tapped the solid wall, and a thin crack appeared. He pushed it open, revealing a dark passageway.

"*Full* of surprises," I said, walking past him into the passage.

"You can thank your brother for this," he said quietly. "He was always looking for escape routes."

"And, let me guess, you followed along to protect him," I said, lowering my voice to mimic his.

"No, I followed along because it was fun." He held out a hand, blocking my path. "Brynna, I'm giving you this option for tonight, but rest assured I will post a guard at the exit if you try to leave on your own."

"Where's the trust?" I said with a sad shake of my head.

The passage ended in a door covered with ivy and foliage, which Felix pushed open. We now stood in gardens on the western side of the castle. When Felix closed the door, I couldn't even see it amongst the greenery.

"Fascinating," I said. "But we're still inside the castle walls."

"Come with me."

He led me through the green garden, ignoring the buzzing of the summer bugs around our heads. We reached the castle wall, where he pushed aside another ivy-coated door to reveal another hallway, although it smelled more like a drainpipe. We ducked our heads and walked through the wet muck, reaching another grate that Felix easily removed. And then, finally, we were out of the castle.

"Where are we?" I asked, trying to orient myself in the city.

"Northwestern wall," he said, replacing the iron grate. "Facing Haymaker's District."

"Right," I said, stretching my arms. "Do all the secret passages lead out that garden door?"

"Ah-hah, I'm not telling you about any more of them," he said with a smile.

"So no," I said. "Good to know there are more, though."

"Brynna—"

"Felix, relax. If I wanted to lose you, I could," I replied. "I would've thought last night was enough to prove that to you."

"It proved to me that you're reckless and don't care if the whole kingdom finds out you're the Veil," he said.

I rolled my eyes. "Fine. Come with me."

"Where are we going?"

"To show you that I can be trusted."

We didn't go far, walking the length of the castle walls to the market square, a large open area south of the castle. Directly across was the large, white tower church. The black front doors were wide open, beckoning worshippers to come inside and light a candle of prayer. But for today, I motioned for Felix to follow me to the side of the building, where a pair of loose boards came away from behind a stack of crates, revealing a staircase.

"After you," I said, offering him entry.

"This isn't a trap, is it?" he asked with a scowl.

"Fine, I'll go first," I said, walking through into the dark room. Once Felix joined me, I replaced the wood and grabbed him by the tunic. "So you don't trip."

I led him toward the staircase, where I found the lamp and lit it with the matches underneath. It illuminated the room a little.

"So what is this?" Felix asked as I started climbing.

"It's my lair," I said, leaning over the wooden railing. "Come on."

"Not much to look at." He tilted his head back, taking in the room. The bells hung above our heads, giant metal ghosts that made too much noise when they were used. But for now, they just echoed our conversation.

"Well, all right, it's more like a safe storage place," I said with a laugh. "A central location where I can keep all my gadgets and spare potions. Easy to get to. Nobody comes up here. And plenty of places to hide stuff."

"Your butcher's apartment didn't suffice?"

"No," I said, walking to one of the floorboards and pulling it up. I'd thought I'd had a few extra pouches of knockout powder, but I found nothing except a spider's web. "That place was always temporary."

He made a noise as he kicked one of the boards. "So why didn't you just live here?"

"Because vigilante work didn't pay," I said, finding my stash of masks and throwing a spare one at Felix. "Here, if you're going to be following me around, wear this. You're too recognizable."

He lifted it up, staring into the eyeholes. "Where do you get all this stuff?"

"Different places," I said, sitting back on my heels. "These knives I got from a pirate passing through. They use them to quickly tack boxes to the hull of the ship in bad weather, I use them to stick bad guys to walls when I'm in a bind." I picked up a small pouch. "Knockout powder. Can fell a two-hundred-pound man for thirty minutes." I held up my crossbow. "The tension on this is strong enough to pierce through ceiling. I use the rope to climb up."

"That's...pretty impressive," Felix said. "That you've accumulated all these things."

"This may come as a surprise to you, but as good as I am at hand-to-hand, I can't exactly fight off a group of people," I said, digging around for another bag of knockout powder and coming up empty. "So I employ little cheats. Use the element of surprise. Anything I can do to keep myself one step ahead of them and still save the day."

He wrapped the mask around his head. "It's nice to hear you admit you're human, at least."

"I don't understand why you think I'm some reckless kid who intentionally goes after the biggest, baddest bully and who needs constant supervision so she doesn't break her neck."

"Says the woman on the prowl for Lord Beswick." He smiled, and the mask gave him a bit of a roguish look.

"*Prowl*, not recklessly attacking," I said after a moment of staring at him. "I've been after him for months and I haven't moved yet. I know how to wait for the right moment." I straightened. "And lucky for you, tonight, we may get to avoid rough and tumble altogether."

"Yeah?" He quirked a brow. "Back to the castle?"

"Nope." I jangled his coin purse, which I'd replenished before we'd left. "We're going shopping."

Out of courtesy for Felix's lack of balance, I took to the streets instead of the rooftops. The city was slowly transforming, with black flags replacing the colors of Forcadel.

"So this funeral tomorrow," I said. "What do I have to do? Speak?"

"No, Mother Fishen will be taking care of that," he said.

I cast a glance behind me at the church. I'd been in the bell tower almost every night, but I hadn't made it inside the church in years. But that was tomorrow—tonight, I had other things on my mind. So we went on in silence, as we'd come into a more nocturnal part of the city, and I didn't want anyone to recognize Felix's voice.

My destination was Slack's Bar, a dive of a place that sat one gusty wind away from toppling into the ocean. The old sign was barely hanging onto the side of the building and music and conversation were audible from the street. It was popular with sailors and criminals alike, as the sailors sometimes got too drunk and spilled their secrets to the barkeeps (or anyone who'd listen). The owner, John, had made so many enemies over the years that they were now all his friends.

"I'm well aware of this place," he said. "The better question is, why are we here?"

"Because it's the best place to find things I can't buy at a store," I said, pulling my hood over my face to hide my mask. "I know you want to come with me, so here's the ground rules: don't speak, don't look at anyone, and definitely don't touch anyone. There are people in here who'd sooner punch your lights out than shake your hand." I paused. "I'm *not* going to leave you, but it would be best if you came in after me and looked from afar."

He grabbed my arm. "Please try to stay out of trouble."

"I *always* stay out of trouble." I flashed him a grin as I left him to walk inside.

It wasn't crowded, which was a good thing. On days when I couldn't even get a seat, I usually couldn't get any information either. With my hood and dark clothes, I blended in with the rest of the patrons, and I sidled up to the bar and took an empty seat.

"What do you want?" Frank the bartender asked, walking over.

"Whiskey," I said. I placed two gold coins on the table. "And John."

He nodded and took both coins, pocketing them and pouring me a small shot of dark liquid. He slid it over before disappearing into the back room. I put the drink to my lips but didn't imbibe.

A few minutes later, a man took the seat next to me. In his youth, John had been a sea captain, and his skin was dark and leathery from the sun. Now, he sported a bushy beard, but his sharp blue eyes were as aware as ever, especially as he took me in.

"Haven't seen you in here lately."

"Been busy," I said, putting down the glass and playing with it. "I need some stuff. Who's in town?"

"Pretty light at the moment. King's guard's been checking our shipments lately."

I snorted. Damn Felix. "I'll take light. What do you have?"

"Kieran's down at the docks, but he's leaving tonight. I hear he's got some of that sleepy powder you're such a fan of. Maybe some arrows. Couple knives. Few surprises, too."

"Then I suppose I'll head down." I placed five gold coins on the bar. "Thanks for the tip."

"I'm hearing rumors that Beswick's bringing in some Severian artisans for the summer festival," he said as I rose to leave. "Those Severians have some funky weapons." He raised his gaze to me. "That one's a freebie."

I smirked and walked away, my cape trailing behind me as I walked outside.

Felix was waiting for me, leaning against the door. "Well?"

"Surprised you didn't go in," I replied. "Trust me that much?"

"Not at all. It's just that everyone in that bar wants me dead," he said, falling into step beside me. "I don't think a mask would hide me very well."

"You're right about that," I said, although it did make him a touch more handsome in my opinion. "And on that note, quit disrupting my weapons suppliers."

"Perhaps the royal armory could provide you with what you need."

I smirked. "I sincerely doubt that, Felix. What I need is more than just a sharpened sword."

We continued down to the labyrinth of ships and crates, Felix's questions ending in favor of keeping a low profile. My target was a pirate of sorts, although his lawful to unlawful shipments ran about fifty/fifty, the lawful half allowing him access to the official docks.

"Ah, that guy," Felix said, when we came to the dock that held his ship, a large schooner with tall masts and a flag that currently bore the Forcadel crest.

"Another friend of yours?"

"You could say that." He shook his head. "I may have to stay out of this one, too."

"Just stand guard," I said, as we arrived at the wooden ramp.

"Kieran likes me sometimes. But I also disrupted a very profitable shipment about six months ago. He's still a little salty about that."

Felix turned to me, and I could almost see his eyebrows go up under his mask. "Oh?"

"It's okay, I gave him a wild night, so we're even."

My partner stumbled over his feet. "Wait, do you mean you—"

"Bye, Felix." I laughed as I continued up the ramp.

There were a pair of fierce-looking Kulkans standing guard, but they said nothing as I passed them, walking toward the back office. A light shone through the window, meaning Kieran was open for business. I just hoped he had something for me.

The man himself was seated at his desk reading a leather-bound book. He was a Kulkan, with sandy hair bleached from the sun and dark brown skin. His white leather boots rested on top of his desk, presenting a very relaxed image. But I wasn't fooled.

"You have a lot of nerve showing up here," he said, turning a page. "I thought I was very clear that I was no longer doing business with you."

"Don't do business with men I'm trying to take out, and there won't be any problems," I said, walking into the office.

"Beggars can't be choosers, Veil. Between you scaring off all the thieves and that infernal captain scaring off all my smugglers, it's getting harder and harder to make my money." He finally looked up at me. "And don't you dare lecture me on going straight."

"Wouldn't dream of it," I said. "Because if you did, I wouldn't be able to get what I need."

"Always trying to play both sides, aren't you?" He shook his head. "Whatever you need will cost you double."

"Then it's a good thing I brought triple." I tossed the bag of gold onto the table.

He quirked a brow as he pulled his legs off the table, opening the bag. Then his sneer disappeared in favor of a grin. "Well, all right then."

He led me down into the belly of the ship, where boxes and crates were stacked against the hull and attached by thick leather straps.

"I'm so glad we're not fighting," Kieran said, walking toward the back. "Because I have some wonderful new things to give you. I met with a very creative Nestori witch."

"Don't call them witches," I said with a shake of my head. The Nestori were one of the last remaining groups that practiced the old ways, religious and mystical arts from before the four kingdoms had been formed. Most thought it nothing but smoke and mirrors, but I'd seen enough to know that at least some of what they did was real. And even if it wasn't, they knew more about plants than anyone else I'd ever met.

"Fine, a creative Nestori medicinal," he said with a roll of his eye. "Either way, she gave me some doozies. Your favorite knockout powder, of course. And your flash-bangs. And look at this." He handed me a small button-like mushroom and a pair of spectacles with a green tint. "Put on the glasses."

I slid them over my nose. The mushrooms now glowed iridescently, and every few seconds, sprouted little puffs of green spores. When I took the glasses off, the spores were invisible, and the mushroom a dull gray color.

"What is this?" I said, putting the glasses back on. "And how would I use it?"

"You could smoke it—craziest night of my life, I'll tell you that," he said with a wave of his hand. "But the Nestori told me that these mushrooms like to attach to stuff. And these spores last for up to five minutes, which means that if you attached the mushroom to someone's cloak..."

"You could follow them," I said slowly. "Those Nestori just come up with the best ideas, don't they? I'll take ten."

"Ah, these are expensive," he said. "You may have one."

I grumbled and put the mushroom into my satchel. "What else

do you have?"

There was a reason Kieran was worth the trouble. He provided me with a cornucopia of options—powders, arrows, a new set of knives that I could more easily hide under my dress, and a slingshot with pellets that could glue a man to a brick wall for an hour.

"You always have the best stuff," I said as I added all my new trinkets into my slingbag.

"So you've said." He rested his hands on my hips, and I forced myself not to stiffen. "Any chance you want to see more of my *stuff* before I leave?"

I smirked and leaned into him. "You just want me to take my mask off this time."

"What can I say? I want to know what your forehead looks like." He pressed feather-light kisses to my neck. "I already know about the rest of you."

I spun in his arms, offering him a coy smile. "If you come back with more mushrooms, I might be obliged."

"Oh, you drive a hard bargain, Veil," he said, running his finger across my bare cheek. "Can I get a taste of the merchandise?"

I leaned in close, so close we were almost touching, and whispered, "Next time, pirate."

Then I left him.

# Chapter Eleven

After replenishing my supplies, I wisely took Felix's advice and returned to the castle. A light drizzle had started, which usually put a damper on street-level criminal activity. And more importantly, I was to be front and center at a pair of funerals, on display not just for the Council but the entire kingdom. I needed to be at my best.

When I awoke, the drizzle had turned into an all-out deluge, with dark gray skies and the occasional flash of lightning. Beata lacked her usual spark, her eyes downcast as she set my breakfast down. She dressed me in a long-sleeved black dress with gray petticoats and white lace at the wrists and collarbones. She brushed and braided my hair, winding it around the back of my head. Then she rested the delicate gold band atop my dark hair, pinning it with several hair pins.

"I hope it's not out of place, but...I am sorry for your loss," she said, her cheeks turning pink once she stood back to look at me. "It's never easy to bury a loved one. And your brother was very loved."

I took her hand gently and squeezed it. "You are absolutely not out of place. Thank you."

Rain pounded on the carriage for the short ride from the castle across the market square to the church. Felix was silent on the ride, his dark eyes faraway and glassy. Instead of his usual blue and white uniform, today he wore a black velvet tunic with the Forcadel colors on his breast. It made him look more severe than usual, and I missed his mask and stubble.

The carriage ride was short, and Felix held an umbrella over my head as I stepped out. A roar of cheers erupted from onlookers. I barely got a chance to see the crowd before Felix was hurrying me inside the church.

"How do I look?" I asked, sweeping my hands along my hair to smooth down any flyaways.

"You look beautiful," came a withered old voice from my left.

Mother Fishen beamed down at me with watery brown eyes and a kind smile that accentuated her wrinkles. She'd been the spiritual leader since my grandfather had been king, and had baptized me in the church we stood in as a babe. My heart fluttered at the sight of her, my words silenced by reverence and nerves.

"My sweet child," she said, taking my hands in hers. "I'm so sorry about your losses, but it is wonderful to have you back with us."

"Thank you," I whispered.

Felix had resumed his spot in my shadow. "We've got to get you seated. You'll have a moment with…with them, if you like."

I nodded as the doors to the main church opened wide. A soft murmuring followed me as I walked through the pews, head held high. I focused my gaze on the ornate carvings at the front of the chapel. My black skirt swished against my legs but was soon drowned out by the whispers. I didn't dare look at them, not wanting to give them the satisfaction of knowing I'd heard them. Instead, I lowered my gaze to the two open coffins at the front of the room, bathed in an ethereal light that seemed impossible based on the cloudy, rainy day outside.

I kept my gait steady until I reached the bottom of the steps to the dais. Then, I pulled my skirt and ascended the stairs. Up close, the coffins were ornate and beautiful, surprising considering the short notice of the funerals. I stood between both caskets, clasping my hands behind me.

There they were, my father and brother. Faces I hadn't seen in five years, faces I'd done my best to forget. And yet, looking at them now, I was struck with an overwhelming nostalgia.

I felt Felix's presence behind me and turned my head. "Can you give me a moment?"

He nodded and walked to the front pew, standing at attention with the rest of his guard. I gazed past him at the rest of the cavernous church, filling with citizens of Forcadel. My people.

I turned back around, exhaling slowly to calm my racing heart. My father's coffin lay to my right. His beard was grayer than I'd remembered, his skin pale. At his chest, his hands clasped his sword hilt, the length of it ending around his knees. And the crown atop his head was the same he'd worn when I was a little girl, bejeweled with red and green stones. Did he ever consider that he'd be buried in the crown when he wore it?

The simple gold band around my head felt heavy.

I turned to my brother's coffin, taking another step toward it to clear my head. His face seemed out of alignment, his skin too pale. His fingers were clasped gently over his chest. I didn't dare touch him, knowing that there would be no life there. If I concentrated, I could still hear his booming voice as he chased me down the hallway when I was a girl. A phantom chill skated up my spine as I recalled how he'd throw me over his shoulder and carry me through the garden like I was a sack of potatoes. His scent, a mixture of cologne and musk, wafted past my nose, replacing the overbearing smell of flowers.

I rested my hands on the casket and allowed a tear to fall. I had been furious at him for so many years, but now, looking at him, I felt a mixture of grief and something else. Regret, perhaps?

"Brynn?" Felix's soft voice asked. "Are you ready?"

I nodded, wiping my cheek quickly and leaving the coffins and my heavy thoughts behind. We continued toward the front of the church, past the pulpit where the priest would give the eulogy, to the carved seats against the wall. Felix unlatched the gate around them and I passed through, moving to take the seat to the right.

"Ah, Brynn," he said. "Yours is the main seat."

I stared at it for a moment, memories of long holiday services and fidgeting next to my brother and father pulling me back into a lull. But I forced myself to sit in the chair, ignoring the uproar of voices in my mind telling me it wasn't right, it wasn't my seat. But it was. Now.

I loosed another long breath and lifted my gaze out onto the church. Rows upon rows lay before me, spreading farther and wider than I'd even though possible in this place. And not just one floor; three tiers of audience tilted down before me.

And every single seat was filled.

Movement toward the front of the room caught my gaze. Katarine walked to the two caskets, a vision in black. She reached into the casket and held my brother's hand, flinching as her skin touched his. Her lip trembled, but she didn't let much more emotion show than that. Having been around her a few days now, even that small show was enough. What might happen behind closed doors, when she finally let that stony wall fall away?

My words about her not mourning came back to me in full force. Hers was a look of a woman trying hard to keep it all together—and terrified for what tomorrow might bring. Guilt bubbled up from the back of my mind. I had her fate in my hands, and I'd been careless about it. Looking at her now, I saw her for what she was.

She caught my gaze, and I gave all I could, a half smile. She nodded in my direction, turned and walked back to the pews.

Fishen ascended the stairs to her pulpit, pausing only for a moment to wink at me before finishing the climb. The chattering in the chapel quieted. The architecture carried her soft voice to the upper echelons of the church.

"Good morning."

*"Good morning."* The swell of voices rejoined.

I scanned the room for others I recognized, and my gaze landed on the Council. They looked every bit the somber, desolate group, with Vernice dabbing her eyes and Octavius blowing his nose. I wished the culprit would jump out at me.

"Today is a very sad day," Fishen continued. "We are grieving the loss of our great king, a king who was, to many, a father figure. A man who led us into prosperity. And his loss, so suddenly, has left us all adrift. But to lose Prince August so soon after..."

Katarine ducked her head into her hand then straightened.

"For me, the loss of both King Maurice and Prince August is personal," she said. "Maurice was a young prince when I ascended the ranks, and I was the lucky priest who brought August into our church when he was born. I cried like I've never cried before when I heard the news."

To my right, Felix shifted, quickly wiping his cheek before resuming his attentive stance.

"But there is cause for celebration," she said. "For our princess Brynna-Larissa has returned to us from her studies across the great sea."

At once, I felt every eye in the room swivel toward me, and I wanted to dissolve into a puddle. Even as my palms began to sweat, I kept them resting comfortably on the chair that wasn't mine. This was the kingdom's first look at me, and I wasn't about to disappoint them.

"I have seen in her heart. She loves this city, has bled for its people. She will make a fair and just ruler, and carry on our many beautiful traditions. If you will join me in a prayer so that we might send our good wishes to her to find courage during this troubling time."

The congregation bowed their heads, and my chest constricted.

"Dear Mother, please look down upon Princess Brynna as she takes the mantle of queen. Please guide her to make wise decisions. Help her see the greater good as she makes proclamations. Give her the strength to lead us further into divinity and prosperity. Keep Your hand upon her, oh Mother, and keep her safe. Amen."

"*Amen.*"

The ceremony continued with the more religious aspects—a reading from the scriptures, a song of prayer, a long, emotional tribute from Garwood, more reading, and finally, a song that lasted ten stanzas longer than it should have. Then, finally, the service was over, and people shuffled from their seats.

"Can we go now?" I asked Felix, working my numb butt on the seat.

"Receiving line," Felix said, nodding to the line of people queueing up.

"Am I to receive everyone?" I said with a whine. There were probably thousands there.

"No," he said with a little chuckle. "Although it would be funny to watch you squirm. You'll receive the Council and a few others."

The Council came first, pausing at the caskets first. One by one, they bowed their heads and dabbed their kerchiefs against their eyes. Then they continued their procession toward me.

Vernice was first, the tip of her nose red as she reached her hand to me. Felix nodded imperceptibly, and I took it, squeezing it awkwardly from behind my gate.

"I forgot just how young the prince was," she said. "'Tis a pity Katarine was not with child."

"Yes," I said. That would've solved everything. "Pity."

She left me, and Octavius took her place. He was already three sheets to the wind, the pungent odor of whisky flowing from his breath.

Felix must've noticed him because he nodded to Coyle and Octavius was shuffled away. Garwood and his husband took his place, both wearing stiff collars that accentuated their cheekbones.

"Your Highness," Garwood said, disdain dripping in his tone. "You look most uncomfortable on that throne."

"Perhaps because I never envisioned I'd be sitting on it," I replied icily.

Felix shot me a look of warning.

"We'll see how much longer you'll be on it," he said, adjusting his coat and walking away with his husband casting me a scathing look.

I caught Felix's eye, sure a lecture would be coming about how it was important not to piss Garwood off. Luckily, I was saved by Zuriel who took great pains to tell me how sad he was about my father and how happy to have me back. General Godfryd offered her condolences but nothing else, before assuming her spot in the front row.

Once alone, Felix turned, his shoulders still straight and his face alert. "Just a few more then we'll leave."

"Was there a lottery or something?" I muttered.

"There was, actually."

"Oh, boy."

"Your Highness," the woman said. Her dress was a patchwork of black fabric, perhaps hastily sewn together, and although her hair was washed and combed and pinned, the pins were rusted. She'd given all she had to be here and make herself presentable for me.

"What's your name?" I asked softly.

"Henriette," she said, amazed, perhaps, that I was speaking to her. "My brother and I own a small shop that deals in ship needs.

Ropes and sails and that sort of thing. We don't make a lot, but it's an honest living." She clamped her mouth together then laughed nervously. "Apologies for babbling, Your Majesty."

I reached forward to take her hands, ignoring the look of annoyance on Felix's face. "I'll come visit your shop soon, all right? I'd love to know what you do. Where is it?"

"Down by the docks. Green's Supplies." She was now bright red. Felix gave me a look to send her along.

"Thank you for coming," I said as Joella appeared to escort her away.

"Please be careful who you touch," Felix muttered. "Someone might try to poison you through skin contact."

"She's so precious, though. Wouldn't hurt a fly." I imprinted her shop's name in my mind. Perhaps The Veil would...

I lifted my gaze to the next well-wisher and my heart stopped in my chest.

"Your Highness," Lord Beswick himself bowed low before me. "It is most wonderful to see you back in your rightful place."

# Chapter Twelve

I blinked several times, sure that I was dreaming. The man I'd spent months searching for, unable to get within striking distance, was now less than two feet away. So close, I could count the pores on his nose. Smell the sickly sweet cologne that always wafted from him.

Felix cleared his throat beside me, and I cast him a look. "Princess, this is Johann Beswick. He's one of the most prominent businessmen in the town. Perhaps you've heard of him?"

I looked at him, having found my tongue but not sure I trusted it. "Pleasure to finally meet the man behind the reputation," I said after considering my words carefully.

"Brynn," Felix whispered harshly, warning in his eyes.

"It's quite all right, Captain," Beswick said, giving me a once-over. "It's been quite a day for her, I'm sure. I can only imagine how difficult her position must be."

"You have absolutely no idea," I said, calculating what moves I could make to subdue him. Would Felix back me up if I ordered him arrested?

"Perhaps it's time for the princess to leave," Felix said. "All this excitement has made her faint."

I glared at him, but was flanked by his two lackeys and escorted away from Beswick before I could say another word. I watched over my shoulder as he met with Vernice *and* Garwood, even giving Octavius a warm hug. That son of a bitch had the entire Council in his pocket.

The doors shut behind me, and I was finally released.

"Brynna, calm down," Felix said.

"Calm down?" I spat. "*Calm down*? There's a wanted criminal in our midst."

"Yes, but nobody knows you're a vigilante," he said with a smirk.

I opened my mouth to argue, but then realized what he was saying. "That's not funny, Felix. *Beswick* is a wanted criminal. He's a thug. And he's out there shaking hands with the Council? Talking to me like he's some kind of titan of the kingdom?"

"As far as you and the kingdom are concerned, he's just a businessman."

"The kingdom knows what he is," I said. "And I can't believe you haven't taken care of him yet. He ruins people's lives."

"You have no proof of that. Nothing I could take to a magistrate that would hold up in court." He sighed. "Believe me, if I could, I would do something about it. But my hands are tied."

"Yours are," I said, adjusting my black sleeves. "Mine aren't."

"As princess—"

"No, as The Veil."

He exhaled loudly. "Later. The only thing you need to do is wipe that murderous look off your face and go back out there to greet your people," he said. "Or you're going back to the castle. Your choice."

⇾————→

In the end, I opted to return to the castle, feigning distress at the thought of being in that room any longer. In reality, with Felix tied up at the service for a few more hours, I could sneak out early and enjoy some well-deserved alone time.

My stomach rumbled, reminding me that I'd skipped dinner. So with my head bowed and cloak still tucked under my arm, I ventured into the dwindling market. In the day, the place was packed with shoppers. Now, it was limited to a few people here and there, which meant I needed to be quick. A gold coin rested in my hand.

I spotted a small child tending her family's stand, an assortment of meats and fruits on display. Keeping my head down, I crossed the square and began pointing at goods I wanted her to package up for me. If I was lucky, she'd think me mute and not engage. She gave me a kind smile and took the coin. When her shirtsleeve slipped, I spotted a tattoo and my heart fell.

"You're one of hers, aren't you?" I whispered.

The girl's eyes widened, and she quickly replaced her shirtsleeve. "Not anymore. My family bought my freedom back."

I wished I had more than one gold piece to give her, but that was all I had in my cloak. Instead, I thanked her and moved along, unable to shake the fear in her eyes and the way the ink looked on her young skin. I could've probably guessed the rest of her story—perhaps her parents had died, or perhaps she'd been kidnapped. Celia said children came to her, but I never believed it. Once there, the child would've been inked as a member of the gang and pressed into service. This girl was lucky her family had the coin to pay for her freedom. She was lucky she had a family at all.

I climbed onto the roof with my purchase, sitting down against the ledge and allowing the remaining light from the dying sun to warm my face. I pulled down the cloth on my left arm, pressing my fingers to the unmarked skin. Celia never ordered me marked, perhaps knowing one day I might return to the throne. It was one thing to kidnap peasant children; quite another to hold the princess of the kingdom captive. My father might've put a little more effort into disrupting her operations had he known.

Maybe.

"It's not dark yet."

I cursed my bad luck and covered my arm again. "What do you want, Felix?"

"You aren't allowed to leave until the sun sets," he said, standing next to me in that infernal black tunic and pants. "And there the sun is, still up."

"Close enough," I said, sitting back and unwrapping my sandwich.

"People might see you."

"Oh, no."

Another sigh was brewing, but he stifled it. "I thought you said you were going to wait to talk to Poole?"

Smiling, I dusted the crumbs off my hands. "Three days, per my agreement with Titta. Tonight, I'm going to do my rounds."

"Rounds?"

"Rounds," I said, pulling my hood over my head. "You can't fight crime if you don't find it, Felix."

If I'd been by myself, I might've taken the extra hour or two of sunlight to catnap on a roof somewhere. But since Felix was determined to babysit, I gave him a good show. Sitting on rooftops, watching high-crime spots. I hoped he was bored out of his mind and would end this ridiculous obsession with watching my every move.

"So this is what you do," he said. "You sit here and wait for crime to happen."

"Sometimes," I said. "Sometimes I sniff it out and prevent it from happening. You have to mix it up, or things get boring."

"If I were you, I wouldn't be wasting a night watching for crime to happen. Surely, you have more leads than just Poole."

"You aren't me," I said, glaring at him. "And no, I don't. I didn't expect that I would have to finish this thing in ninety days, so I'm not quite prepared for it."

He opened his mouth to respond but I lifted my finger to silence him. There was movement below, two figures moving in the darkness. I crept to the edge of the rooftop to get a better look then relaxed when I saw it was just two old women rushing home before things got dark.

"So terrifying, Brynn," Felix whispered in my ear.

"They know The Veil is out there," I said. "Crime's down in the city."

"Says who?"

"Ssh."

A voice had carried over the wind, but I couldn't make out who was speaking or what they were saying. I closed my eyes and listened. Another muddled cry, coming from my right.

"Let's go," I said, pulling my hood over my head. After creeping toward the edge of the roof, I shimmied down and listened again.

"What is it?" Felix asked.

"Could be nothing, could be something," I said. "Until I find it, I can't tell you. So shut up and let me find it."

A scream echoed in the night, and we both took off running toward the sound. Three streets over, there they were. Two large figures and one smaller one stood in front of a young girl—the same girl who'd sold me a sandwich earlier that afternoon.

"P-please, I already paid my debts," she said.

"Ah, see, my records here say you still owe a thousand gold pieces."

I turned back around the corner and shook my head. It wasn't Beswick's man, but it was just as bad. Jax was one of Celia's

The City of Veils

henchmen, carrying out her directives with as much ruthlessness as Beswick. But unlike Beswick, Celia didn't condone bullying. Which was why she wouldn't mind if I roughed up her favorite man.

"That's not true, Celia said—"

"Then how about we all take a trip out to the forest and ask her about it," Jax replied sweetly.

"N-no," the girl whimpered. "If you take me there, you'll charge me two thousand gold pieces to let me out. I know how it works."

"Then we'll just take the gold out of your hide."

"How about I take it from yours?" I said, appearing in the alley with my hand on my sword.

"Ah, Larissa," he said with a chuckle, turning to face me. "Still masquerading around in that hood, are we?"

Out the corner of my eye, I saw Felix getting into position. I just hoped he wouldn't show himself; the last thing I needed was for Celia to find out I had the captain of the King's Guard following me around. Although she'd probably heard I was back on the throne.

"It works," I replied with a shrug. "Now we both know I can dispose of all of you, so how about you let this nice girl go and we can talk it out amongst ourselves?"

"Celia sent me on a mission to retrieve her," Jax said. "Can't have the locals thinking they can get away with stiffing the Pirate Lord."

I folded my arms across my chest. "The girl says her debt is paid. And I doubt Celia would've let her out of her sight if there was anything outstanding." I chuckled. "As you well know, no one leaves until their debts are repaid."

My insinuation landed as I wanted it to, and his face darkened as he pulled out his sword. "Almost no one."

I pulled mine and tested the weight as I surveyed him. "Must we really come to blows, Jax? You know how it's going to end."

"You forget, I have backup—" No sooner were the words out of his mouth than I pulled my small knives from the belt and flung them at the two bodyguards, pinning their shirts to the brick wall. A figure moved behind me—whether one of Jax's or Felix, I didn't know until I shot my foot out to kick them backward and heard his familiar *oof.* I just hoped Jax hadn't noticed the new figure in the alley, or, worse, recognized him.

Luckily, his attention seemed to be all on me.

"Why don't you take off that mask and we can talk about it?" he snarled. "It's not as if I don't know your face."

Yes, but it had been several years since he'd seen it, and I didn't want to chance him noticing that the new princess bore a striking resemblance. Still, his distraction was enough to give me an opportunity. In one fluid movement, I found his outstretched hand, pulled it to my body, and forced it downward until I heard a crack, followed by a howl of pain.

"You *bitch*," Jax growled, grabbing his arm. "You broke my arm!"

The two bodyguards wrestled free and hurtled toward us. I fell to my knees as they barreled over me and into Jax, sending him backward. Before they could recover, I grabbed the girl by the arm and we dashed out of the alley, finding a hiding spot behind a large pile of garbage, and waiting. She clung to me, pressing her sweaty face into my shirt and panting with fear and exhaustion. I patted her head, holding her close and listening for Jax and his boogeymen to run by. But I doubted they would—not with Jax injured. They'd go crawling back to the forest and Celia could add to the number of goons I'd sent back to her in tatters. Served him right.

"You're fine," I said to the girl. "Now tell me the truth. Do you owe Celia or was Jax just being a shit?"

"W-why does it matter?" she asked.

"Because I need to know if Celia will be sending others."

She shook her head. "No, I know for a fact that I paid my dues. Why would he come and tell me I still owed?"

I sighed as I stood upright, brushing the wrinkles out of my tunic. "Because Jax is a liar. He'd pump you for that money then keep it himself. He won't be back to bother you, as he now has to explain to Celia why he has a broken arm. And he surely won't tell the truth."

"You said...you said that no one leaves," she said. "Does Jax still have a debt to Celia?"

"Until he dies," I said. "You're lucky you were able to get out with money. Now make sure you keep yourself out of trouble, understand? Go home and stay there."

She nodded, gathered her skirts, and raced out of the alley as fast as her little feet could carry her. I made a note to come back and check on her this week.

"You *kicked* me," Felix grunted behind me.

"Well? Stay out of my way," I said, adjusting the hood over my head. "I told you I didn't need your help. And you damned near gave me away. When I say stay hidden, I mean it."

"You *kicked* me," he said again, rubbing his stomach. "I'm probably going to have a bruise."

I rolled my eyes and turned to him. "Are you really so delicate? Do you need a tincture or something to get you through the night?"

"No," he said, dropping his hand from his stomach. "But I'd appreciate it if you'd not attack me when I'm trying to keep someone from murdering you."

"And I'd appreciate it if you'd just go back to the castle and let me do my job."

"Your job is being queen. This is just nonsense."

"It's not nonsense to the girl I just saved. Jax would've extorted her poor family for the next six months. Now he's nursing a broken arm and Celia won't have her favorite henchman to send out for a few weeks."

"How do you know so much about her?"

I stared up at the sky, debating if I should share and then deciding it was pointless to hide it.

"Because Celia is the one who trained me."

Felix spun me around, his wide eyes a hair's breadth from mine. "Are you...*Celia* trained you?" He turned my wrist over, pulling the cloth back, no doubt looking for the brand. "Celia, the forest pirate who steals children and holds them for ransom."

"She knew who I was. She wasn't going to brand me," I said softly, taking my arm out of his hand. "But I'm sure she'll appear soon enough, wanting a favor in exchange for the food and shelter she gave me as a child. Surprised she hasn't come to the castle yet."

But Felix wore a look of pure horror, as if he were envisioning some terrible childhood. "Brynna, I had...no idea."

"You said you never lost track of me," I said, hoping we could get off this subject quickly.

"I lied," he said. "I'd heard rumors about a vigilante two years ago. I saw you fighting some thieves and followed you home to arrest you."

"Gee, thanks."

"I didn't arrest you, knowing who you were," he said. "But I thought you'd been in Forcadel this whole time. I had no idea... Celia. Why didn't you come to me for help?"

"It wasn't so bad," I said, climbing a nearby drainpipe. It was too hot in the alley, and hard to breathe. I stood on top of the roof and inhaled the warm night air, allowing the memories to disappear on the wind.

"I can still save the rest of the children there," Felix said, coming to stand next to me on the roof. "Tell me where her fortress is. I'll send the best I have. They'll—"

"Despite what you think, most of the children are there

because they have no other choice," I said, interrupting him before he got rolling. "Celia may be depraved, but there's food and shelter for every child. Most of those kids would rather die than change their loyalties."

"You did."

"My loyalty was never with her," I said, walking to the edge of the roof and crouching down to watch the street. "I got what I wanted from her and got out."

"She taught you how to use a sword?"

I looked down at the streets below. "She taught me how to survive."

"And why did she let you go?" he asked, after a moment.

"She didn't," I said, my pulse quickening as we drew closer to a secret I wasn't ready to share with Felix. "I left."

"And she let you?"

"I'm sure she knew, eventually, I'd be back on or near the throne," I replied, letting my feet dangle on the ledge as I sat down. "And when she needs a favor, she'll come knocking. Then we'll have some decisions to make."

He stared at me as if he were just seeing me for the first time. "Did you really break his arm?"

"Easiest way to take someone out of the fight," I said, trying to shake off the way he looked at me and the memory of a dead man's eyes. "Now if you aren't dying from a kick to the stomach, let's continue on our night."

# Chapter Thirteen

I'd barely laid my head down on my pillow before Beata was opening the blinds and walking around my room with a feather duster. And before I could get a good snooze in, Katarine arrived and yanked the covers off of me.

"Get up," she said. "Can't have you lying about all day."

"No," I said, grabbing the covers and pulling them back over my head. "Come back later. I don't want to hear about economics."

"Luckily for you, we won't be talking economics today," Katarine said. "It's time for your weekly meetings with the citizenry."

"What?" I poked my head up, and that was all the opportunity she needed to yank the sheets away from me.

"It's a tradition started by your father," she said, throwing my blankets to the ground. "Maurice would meet with citizens for three hours, once a week, and let them petition him for whatever they wanted."

"Great, so I'll just approve everyone," I said, grasping my

pillow and covering my head.

"No," Katarine replied, tugging the pillow away from me with a force that seemed superhuman. "You don't have the money in your royal account to do that sort of thing. And agreeing to one thing might set off a chain reaction to a whole set of outcomes you don't want. Hence why we will discuss them."

"Listen to Kat," Beata said, picking up the sheets Katarine had discarded. "She's quite smart."

"Thank you, Beata, that will be all," Katarine snapped.

Beata nodded and scurried from the room with the blankets in hand, her face growing red as she shut the door behind her.

"Don't be mean to her," I said with a scowl.

"What?"

"Beata," I replied, helping myself to the strawberries and cream Beata had left on my small sitting room table. "You bark orders at her and she won't spend more than three seconds in the same room with you."

Katarine's face flushed, surprising me. "I'm not gruff with her. She's just efficient. Servants should be seen and not heard."

"She's human, Katarine," I replied. "You can treat her with a little decency. Besides that, she just complimented you."

"I treat her fine," Katarine said.

I waited for more, but I wasn't going to get it, so I changed the subject. "Who decides who gets to come see me?"

"The Council approves them," she said, going to sit at the small table where my breakfast was waiting.

"Of course they do," I said with a shake of my head. "Surprised they're letting me see anyone at all. Thought they just made decisions without me."

Katarine sighed. "The Council is responsible for internal affairs, the treasury, and the military. You are responsible for the city of Forcadel and the castle, international affairs, and treaties. This business today is about the city. You are, of course, advised to speak with them for input. But for today, you and I will discuss the requests that are coming to you, and how you're going to handle them. It's probably best if you just not agree to anything."

"What?" I bit into another strawberry. "But what if I want to do it?"

"Just give them a noncommittal answer then bring their grievances back to us. We'll discuss and make a decision together."

I narrowed my eyes. "You don't trust that I can listen to a problem and come up with a solution myself?"

She pursed her lips and considered her words carefully. "I don't believe you have a firm grasp of what you can and can't do as queen, or if you do, you don't care. I just want to make sure you don't make a mistake."

I stuffed a scone into my mouth and chewed instead of responding.

At the end of our morning lesson, I still couldn't understand why a two percent tariff on fruit was better than a three percent tariff on vegetables, but Katarine left me to have my lunch in peace. Instead, I fell face-first into my bed and caught as much of a nap as I could, until I was roughly shaken awake by Riya.

"Time for your citizen parade," she said.

"Where's Felix?" I grumbled, looking around. I hadn't seen the man all day, which seemed weird for my shadow.

"He's taking a personal day," she replied. "Apparently, he's dealing with some stomach issues this morning. But he sends his sincerest regards."

I snorted. "Then perhaps he should stay out of the way."

She glared at me, as if she wanted to retort something, but kept her mouth shut.

Beata arrived with another dress, a yellow frock with elbow-length sleeves and white lace at the bottom, then set to getting me presentable. All the while, I watched Riya's expression—a mixture of loathing and impatience.

"So, Riya," I said, as Beata painted my eyelids a dark brown color. "How's things?"

"We've lost two kings in a month, my captain has been distracted by a vigilante princess, and now he's injured," she said with deadly calm. "How do you think things are?"

"I'm not the one who told him to go with me," I said, opening my mouth as Beata painted my lips a rose color.

"Be nice to Riya," Beata whispered. "She's one of Felix's closest confidantes."

If that was supposed to mean something to me, I didn't get it. "Amazed that he delegated my protection duties to someone else. I could have sworn he was glued to my side."

"The captain takes his job very seriously," she replied. "We'd all like to avoid a repeat of what happened to the previous two occupants of your throne. As it's your life at stake, I'd hope you felt similarly."

"I feel very similarly." I opened my eyes and checked my appearance in the mirror. "But unlike the other two, I know how to stay alive. I'd just appreciate a little credit from the captain."

Riya had no response to that, or none that she wanted to share with me, even as we ventured down to the first floor of the castle. I followed her down a long walkway, flanked on either side by wooden doors. The kitchen was nearby, based on smell and noise, and I only supposed the formal dining room was nearby. At the end of the hall, Riya fumbled with a set of keys then pushed open the door, revealing the larger throne room.

"Thanks," I said to her wordless sneer.

I craned my neck backward, gazing upward at the murals painted on the ceiling, the chandelier that hung so beautifully above my head. Large oil paintings of sea battles hung on the walls, depicting Forcadel's conquests of kings past. In the center of the room sat a golden chair with spires that reached toward the ceiling. I could picture my father sitting here, his crown settled upon his gray head, stroking his chin as he spoke to those who'd come to meet with him. Twice, I'd had a tutor haul me in front of him to get my behavior to change. Perhaps that was why he'd wanted me married and sent to Kulka.

"P-princess?" a small voice asked behind me.

I spun to see a younger man, his hair short like the rest of the guards, but his tunic a light blue, versus the darker ink-colored guard uniforms. A page, perhaps?

He was waiting for me to confirm who I was, so I pointed to the crown on my head. "Yes, that's me."

"O-oh, right!" He laughed nervously then straightened. "My name is Cherry, Galton Cherry. I'm your royal attendant today."

"How's this going to go?" I asked, before adding, "It's my first time doing this."

"Right. Well..." He pointed to the golden chair in the middle of the room. "You'll sit there. I'll bring in the guests and announce them to you. You'll listen, and then...well, make your decision. I'll record it and make it happen."

"Sounds easy enough." I approached the chair, which had red velvet-covered cushions and arm rests, both showing a heavy amount of wear. I doubted it would be comfortable, an assumption confirmed when I sat squarely on top of the cushion. There was barely anything between my butt and the gold.

"Are you ready?" the page asked from the front of the room.

"As I'll ever be," I said, resting my chin on my hand then remembering I needed to look queenly. "Send them in." When he gave me a look, I cleared my throat and called out, "Send them in."

My words echoed across the room, and the boy turned and rushed from his perch. A few moments later, he reappeared with a woman. She carried her shoulders straight, her chin high. Her clothes were well-made, her shoes sporting metal buckles instead of pure leather.

"May I present Carla Oliver," the attendant said. He nodded to her and walked to the edge of the room, waiting at the doorway for the meeting to end.

Carla bowed at the waist, giving me a bird's eye view of her graying hair. When she came upright, she wore a look of desperation, albeit a forced one.

"It's a pleasure," I said, nodding to her. I had no idea what else to say. "What can I help you with?"

"I own the Oliver shipping company. We operate mostly between the Severian border and Forcadel. Lately, our shipments have been...well, not arriving on time. Or at all. I think it's bandits."

I looked around. "And what do you want me to do about it?"

"Stop it, of course," she said with a little laugh. "Send a missive to the queen of Severia and ask her to up the security on the border. Assign a contingent of your armed forces to help guard us."

I chewed my lip, "no" on the tip of my tongue. Katarine had been very clear that I should refrain from agreeing to anything, but at the same time, this didn't seem like a huge ask. I had tons of ships and guards at my disposal, and parting with one or two to help my own people at the Severian border was a good thing.

"You know what?" I shrugged. "Let's see if we can't help you out. Attendant!"

The attendant jumped and rushed forward. "Ma'am?"

"Take a note. We're sending some ships to help our merchants on the eastern front."

His eyes widened. "Are you...um...Captain—"

"And make a note to draft a letter to the queen of Severia," I said, interrupting him. "Will that suffice, Carla?"

"Yes, thank you." She took a step forward, like she was going to hug me, but the attendant yanked her from the room, grumbling under his breath. A moment later, he was back with another person, an older man this time. Like Carla, he was well-dressed and carried himself with an air of confidence.

"My princess," he said, bowing. "I come on bended knee, asking for your help."

"Shoot," I said, sitting back on the chair. It was damned near impossible to get comfortable, but I would sure try. "What can I help you with?"

"I'm a vendor of fine goods, furniture," he said. "I'm asking for the sovereign's help in reducing the tariffs on wood imported from Kulka. You see, the Forcadel oak is of lesser quality than those deep in the forests. The Kulkan wood is better and cheaper, except that the tariffs make it twice as expensive."

"Um... Sure, why not," I said. "I'll see what I can do."

He grinned and rushed from the room, barely even needing the page to follow him.

"Well, this is fairly easy," I said, drumming my hands on the throne. I assumed their requests had been vetted, especially if they'd already gone through the Council.

Over the course of the next hour, I approved lots of requests, from small ones like border disputes between business owners to approving the construction of a new dock down by the water, so Forcadel could accept bigger ships.

"Your last one of the day," the page said with a smile. "Mayor Zuriel."

I frowned, sitting up. Why was Zuriel coming to me here instead of seeking an audience in person? He was a Councilor, wasn't he?

"My princess," he said, bowing. "Thank you for letting me meet with you."

"Of course, but...aren't you on the Council? Couldn't we talk about whatever you want there?"

"I'm coming to you in my capacity as Forcadel's mayor," he said with another bow. "As you know, we put on the summer festival every year at the end of the season."

I nodded. "I've been a few times."

"This year, the festival coincides with the week of your coronation," he said. "I had spoken briefly about it with your brother, but alas, he passed before the official decree was signed. As well, I wanted to know—"

"You want to do them together?"

He nodded.

"Why not?" I said with a shrug. "The kingdom will be celebrating, right? Give them something to celebrate."

He bowed. "Excellent. Thank you."

As he walked out the door, my page came back in, this time bearing an envelope.

"More?" I asked, taking it from him.

"This just arrived," he said. "I'm not sure—"

I opened the envelope, pulling out a small card with loopy handwriting and a letterhead bearing Garwood's name. It was an invitation to dine with him that night in his private residence. Was it an olive branch? Or something more nefarious? Smart money said the latter. As much as I didn't want to take time away from The Veil, it would be an opportunity to meet with Garwood privately. Even if he had ill intentions, I could always use it to my benefit.

"Tell him I accept," I said, folding the invitation.

"Accept...what?"

"His invite to dine," I said. "Get my carriage or whatever I use to travel around the kingdom."

"Pardon, but..." The attendant became red in the face. "Captain Llobrega said I wasn't to let you leave the throne room until he came for you himself."

I made a noise, folded the invite, and stuck it back in the envelope. "What was your name again?"

"I'm sorry?"

"Your name, attendant."

"It's...um..." He swallowed, a look of sheer panic on his face. "It's Galton, m'lady."

"Galton," I said softly. "Tell me something, is Captain Llobrega the king?"

"N-no..."

"And who is sitting on the golden throne of her ancestors?"

"Y-You, m'lady."

I smiled and handed the envelope back to him. "Very good, Galton. You're a smart boy. Now, why don't you run along and tell Lord Garwood that I would be delighted to dine with him tonight. And be sure to bypass informing the good captain, hm?"

# Chapter
# Fourteen

Knowing my window of opportunity was very slim, I immediately called for a carriage and set out. Felix would throw a fit, but I didn't care. I was tired of being handcuffed to rules I didn't understand. And after all, he wanted me to find allies on the Council. Garwood would be quite a win.

I stepped out of the carriage, thanking the footman with a soft smile. Garwood's house was a three-story, white-brick beauty with iron railings and pristine glass windows in Merchant's Quarter, on the northeastern side of town. An assortment of multicolored flowers grew in beds under windows, giving it something of a homey look. There were other, similar houses down the block, but this one had an extra air of refinement. Fitting for a man who controlled part of the kingdom.

"Ah, Princess. So kind of you to meet me at my home."

Garwood stood in his doorway, his arms crossed over his velvet tunic. His gray beard was extra pointy today, as if he were proving something with it. I was sure this was the beginning of his power play, and for once, I decided to play the beta.

"Thank you for the invitation," I said, walking to the bottom of the stairs. "May I come in?"

He offered me the door and I walked up the steps, giving him a gracious smile as I followed him inside. The house was as immaculate as the exterior. A wide hallway with a narrow staircase greeted us, with gas lamps flickering on the wall. The air smelled of old wood and dust, and I caught a glimpse of a library before we found the back sitting room. It was encased in glass, all bearing the seal of Severia in the bottom corner. Two sitting chairs were in the center, along with a table bearing a silver kettle and two white cups.

"Please, have a seat," Garwood said.

I took the seat to the left, keeping my posture as straight as if I were wearing that infernal device of Katarine's. "Thank you for the invitation. It's nice to get out of the castle."

"I've heard you aren't adjusting well to your new confines," Garwood said. "There's been much discussion in the kitchen about your arguments with Captain Llobrega."

"Has there been?" I'd have to tell Felix that there were some loose lips on his staff.

"Mm-hm." He poured the tea into the two cups. "Sugar?"

"None for me, please."

"That's so interesting," Garwood said, catching my eye. "Because when she was a girl, Princess Brynna liked three sugars in her tea."

I quirked a brow. "Sure, when I was eight. That was a decade ago. I hate to inform you that tastes change." Especially when three of those years had been at the hands of Celia, who'd probably never seen a sugar cube, let alone let us have any.

"I suppose they do," Garwood said. "You look much different than the girl I remember."

"In what way?"

"When you were a girl, you favored my sister," he said. "Now, it's impossible to tell who you favor."

I furrowed my brow. "Wait, you're my uncle?"

He chuckled. "Yes, Brynna. Or did Captain Llobrega fail to mention that to you when he was teaching you about yourself?"

"If there's anyone to blame, it's my nursemaids," I said, trying to recover. "As my mother died in childbirth."

"She was always so fragile," Garwood said. "She lost five children between August and Brynna. But she was so happy to finally bring one to term. I was there, you know, when she died. Held the baby girl in my arms moments after she was born." He took a sip of his tea. "I don't believe you're that girl."

"Why? Because I lack my mother's fragility?" I snorted. "Clearly you don't remember me very well then. I was climbing trees and raising hell long before I ran away."

He gave me a look. "And where did you run away to? The girl who left was wild and untamable. The woman who sits before me now is scheming, wise, and manipulative. I'm curious who was responsible for such a transformation."

Oh, how much I could tell him about that. "I am responsible for the way I am. I didn't want the life my father had planned for me, so I chose a different one."

"Where did you go?"

"Away. Next question."

"Are you really Princess Brynna-Larissa?"

"Am I the daughter of Maurice? Yes," I replied. "Whether or not I want to be her is another question."

"Why is that?" he asked, tilting his head.

"Because this wasn't a place I ever wanted to return to," I replied. "And I'm not yet convinced I'm the right person for the job."

"Finally, something we agree on," he said, sitting back with something of a smile on his old face. "Which brings me to my next question: If you don't believe you're the right person for the job, why are you still here?"

"Because I haven't found a suitable replacement yet," I replied smoothly. "And I think it's important to find out who's been committing regicide." My gaze was averted, but I watched his reaction out of the corner of my eye. His eyes flashed at the word regicide, but showed nothing more. Knowing he was my uncle—and August's—made it less likely that he would be responsible for his death. I doubted he was in line for the throne; Felix hadn't mentioned it at all. And if he was my mother's brother, that took him out of contention completely.

"We seem to be working toward the same goals, then," he said after a moment. "We both want a good, strong leader for Forcadel and we both want to see the murderers of King Maurice and Prince August brought to justice."

"Same goals, perhaps. But our methods will probably differ wildly." I let a coy smile play on my lips. "I do hope if you find an answer to either, you'll share with me."

"But of course," he said. "Do you have any theories?"

"Some," I said quietly. "Llobrega is on it."

"He's a young fool," Garwood said with a grimace. "He still believes he can fix everything by controlling it. And in doing so, he misses all the shades of gray. I doubt very much that he'll find the one who killed our kings, as he's convinced of everyone's goodness."

"And are you good, Garwood?" I asked. "Do you swear fealty to Forcadel and the Lonsdale throne?"

"You may not remember, but your father and I were very good friends," he said, looking down at his hands. Sadness entered his features, and his hard gaze softened. "Since boyhood really. Much like Llobrega and August. It was the greatest honor of my life to serve your father."

"It probably won't surprise you to know that my memories of my father aren't the most positive," I replied with a scowl. "To him, I was just a means to an end. I firmly believe I was born to be traded to Kulka for peace."

"Of course you were," he said. "The second child of a king has no other use. Unless, of course, there's a vacancy." He tilted his head in my direction. "There are some who'd say you were eager for the throne."

"Then those people are *blind*," I said, not bothering to hide my disgust. "I was happy living my life, and Llobrega comes along and drags me back here. If there were *any* other option, I would find it."

There was a soft knock at the door and a very worried footman appeared.

"Excuse me, Lord Garwood. Captain Llobrega is h-here. And he says it's urgent that he speak with the princess."

"Ah, my babysitter has arrived," I said, putting the saucer down.

"Was he unaware that you'd accepted my invitation?" Garwood asked, sipping his tea.

"I don't believe, as princess, that I answer to Captain Llobrega." I shrugged as I walked to the door. "Thank you for a very enlightening tea. I'll see you at the next Council meeting."

"It was a pleasure, Brynna."

I stopped, glancing back at him with a knowing smile, before continuing out the door.

"What in the *Mother's name* were you thinking?" Felix snapped as soon as we were inside the carriage. "Do you not understand what's going on here? Garwood could very well have been the one responsible for all this!"

I shrugged. "He's not."

"And how do you know?"

"Gut feeling," I replied with a smile. "And I'll thank you to quit sending pages in your stead."

"Obviously, I can't leave you alone."

"Obviously, you're wrong," I said, looking out the window. "Garwood is my uncle. Thanks for telling me."

"I...thought you knew that," Felix said. "How did you not know that?"

"Nobody told me anything as a child," I said. "He's not in line for the throne, is he?"

"No. Your mother's family was a landed, wealthy group, but not royal." Felix cleared his throat. "But that's beside the point. Why the *hell* did you go to his house? Alone?"

"He and I had a good chat. I believe he's on my side now. Or, at least, he now believes that I am who I say I am."

"You're wrong about that." He shook his head. "In the first place, the *princess* doesn't meet with the Council outside of the castle. If you wanted to talk to him, he should've come to you. You're royalty. He's not."

"Sometimes, Felix, it's best to make your opponent think they have the upper hand," I said, looking out the window. "You thought I would be compliant if you sent Riya. I obviously wasn't."

He worked his jaw. "Still. You weren't ready to talk to him."

"I think I did just fine."

"I'm sure you *think* that—"

I released a loud sigh. "I swear, Felix. I will break *your* arm if you don't back off. I'm not a child, and more importantly, I'm not an idiot. You don't need to control my every move."

"Is this how it was with Celia?" he said. "I can't imagine she let you talk back this much. Or was it merely because you're the princess?"

My anger spiked, but I held my tongue.

"I've just been informed about all the things you agreed to at today's grievance hearing," Felix said. "Even though Kat specifically told you *not* to agree to anything."

"And why shouldn't I? I'm the princess—"

"Because you have *no* idea what your decisions mean, or how they affect other people."

I threw my hands in the air. "Give me one example."

"You told a shipper on the eastern front that you'd send a few ships from your navy to help secure her shipments to Forcadel."

"Yes, I did. She said her shipments are getting hijacked on the Severian border." I opened the curtain to the carriage window and peered out. "I'm going to write a letter to the queen and send some soldiers to help guard her stuff."

"You... Brynna, you can't just agree to things like that," Felix said, rubbing his face. "If you offer royal help to her, you'll have a thousand shippers at your door, asking for military support."

"Well, if they all need help—"

"And from which forces were you going to send? Your navy is spread pretty thin at the moment, and Forcadel's ground forces are primarily concentrated here in the city."

"I'll send your guard," I said with a smirk. "You can lead them. Take a nice six-week vacation to the western front."

He growled. "This isn't a game, Brynna."

"So why do I feel like a pawn?" I said heatedly. "You come in, ordering me around, following me at night. All these rules and regulations. I have some idea of what I'm doing, and you yelling at me every time I do something *you* don't approve of is bullshit."

"It's not about approving," he countered. "It's about doing what's best for the kingdom—the *whole* kingdom—"

"Then why does it feel like we're only helping the well off and leaving the rest of them to fend for themselves?" I asked, throwing my hands in the air. "You told me I could help the people as queen, but you aren't letting me do anything!"

"Because nothing you're doing is helping anyone but yourself!" He barked, his words echoing in the carriage. "You're just an egocentric little asshole hell-bent on doing exactly the opposite of what anyone tells you. And maybe, just maybe, if you pulled that chip off your shoulder and *listened* to the people who just want to help you, you could do some good instead of ruining *everything.*"

My jaw fell and the door to the carriage opened, revealing Coyle's shocked face. Leveling a death glare at Felix, I pushed past him and marched out toward the castle.

# Chapter Fifteen

*"Egocentric little asshole"*
*"Ruining everything."*

Felix's jabs echoed in my mind as the sun disappeared over the horizon and the moon rose over the bay. My door was locked as soon as I walked into the room; more proof that my guards thought I wasn't to be trusted. I half-expected to remain in there all night, but eventually, the lock turned over and Felix appeared wearing his dark tunic.

"I want to apologize for losing my temper earlier today," he said, as if that would fix everything. "Are you ready to go?"

I snorted, having decided I wasn't speaking to him, and brushed past him. Partly, I just couldn't stand to look at him. And partly, I hoped if I ignored him long enough, he might just leave me alone.

"So, are you just going to ignore me all night?" Felix asked, coming to walk beside me. "I'm letting you out to do vigilante stuff. That should count for something, right?"

With a brisk pace, I marched through the city, listening for the sound of trouble and finding none of it. Of course, the one night I wanted to get into it with someone, the criminals all decide to stay home. I even stopped by the house of the young girl I'd rescued the night before, hoping I might've been wrong and Celia had sent more thugs. But no, the girl was seated around the dinner table with her family, sharing what looked like a delicious meal of fish and vegetables.

"Suppose she was telling the truth about Jax extorting her, huh?"

I bit my lip so hard I was sure I'd made myself to bleed. I spun and kept walking, his presence making me angrier by the minute. In a fit of stupidity, I made a break for it, bolting into the darkness. But no matter how fast I ran, he was right behind me.

"You can try all you want, but you aren't going to shake me," he said, on the fifth time I tried. "So I suggest you just accept it and start talking to me again."

I closed my eyes, ready to snap finally, when I caught sight of the lit steeple of the church. *There* was a place I could lose him. At least temporarily.

I walked into the church, now empty of parishioners as it was closing in on midnight. The dais where my father and brother had lain was gone. Now there was the pulpit and a wall of lit candles, flickering lights that represented a prayer wish of someone in the kingdom. There were more than usual; a sign, perhaps, that people were worried about the future.

"What are we doing here?" Felix asked.

With a smirk on my face, I marched toward the side of the church where a small wooden room was set aside. The confession box, and only one confessor in at a time.

"Oh, Brynn—"

I pulled open the door and slammed it behind me, settling into the hard, wooden seat and sighing in relief.

"So what, you're just going to hide in there all night?" Felix asked. When I didn't respond, he sighed. "Look, fine. I'll be outside when you decide to grow up."

His footfalls disappeared and some of the tension released from my shoulders. I pulled my mask off my sweaty face as it felt wrong to hide myself in here. This was a ploy to get him away, sure, but it was also a sacred space.

As if on cue, I heard the rustle of cloth in the booth next to me. "Is there someone in there?"

I smiled. "It's me, Mother."

"Me. There are many mes. Which me am I speaking to?"

"Brynna," I whispered, allowing the stress of the day to wash away. There was something reassuring about being myself in this box. Not the princess, not The Veil. Just me.

"It's been many years since you've come to see me in here." Her brown eyes sparkled through the mesh screen. "You seemed to have some more weights on your chest since the last time we spoke."

"At the funeral?"

She chuckled. "No, the night you saved that woman. The night you first donned the mask."

My eyes shot open, the memories of that fateful night coming back in a rush. I'd just run away from Celia's camp, seeking atonement for the horrible thing I'd done. But along the way, I'd stopped a young woman from being raped by some thugs. Fishen had witnessed it and suggested instead of throwing myself in jail, I keep the mask on and find atonement through service. And thus, the Veil had been born.

I chuckled. "So you knew it was me, hm?"

"The Mother works in mysterious ways," she said. "So tell me, what's troubling you tonight?"

I traced my finger along the carving. "I'm frustrated."

"With?"

I closed my eyes, the fight I'd had with Felix in the carriage coming back to me. "It seems every decision I make is the wrong one. And it feels like I'm being forced to do things that I don't agree with."

"Your captain, the one standing guard. He can help you."

"Who do you think keeps telling me I'm wrong?" I said with a laugh. "He wants me to be queen, but a queen that makes decisions he likes. But what if those are the wrong ones?"

"Do you think his decisions are wrong?"

"I think he doesn't see the bigger picture," I said. "It seems like all he cares about is maintaining order at the expense of people he's sworn to protect. We have to make the rich richer, because otherwise... I don't know." I looked at my hands, allowing myself to be vulnerable. "Tonight he said I was selfish. How can I be selfish when all I've done for the past three years is dedicate my life to helping others?"

"Hm..." She was quiet for a while. "Perhaps instead of focusing on how you feel, you could consider the world from his perspective. He's been thrust into a new role after the deaths of two monarchs, one of whom was his best friend. I don't think it's a reflection on you, but perhaps his own insecurities and fears." She paused. "But he's allowing you to continue as The Veil, isn't he? Doesn't that count for something?"

"You mean second-guessing every decision I make?" I said with a snort. But she had a point. Felix would be well within his rights to lock me in the castle, *especially* after all the events of the past few weeks. Yet, he'd been allowing me to continue, even if it was for a short time.

"Felix is a good man," she replied. "He only wants to keep you safe. Perhaps if you approach it from a place of understanding, you might be able to communicate better."

I nodded and pulled the mask back over my face. "Thank you,

Mother."

"Any time, my child."

I walked out of the box and Felix was nowhere to be found, but I knew he wouldn't be far behind. So I crossed the chapel to the wall of candles. I pulled a small matchstick from the jar at the top, striking it and finding a half-used candle in the center and pressing the tip of the flame to it. As a tiny flame emerged, I whispered a small prayer for myself. To give myself strength and wisdom as I tried to balance these two lives.

Felix came to stand next to me. He took his own stick from the set and lit it, pressing the new flame onto an unlit candle next to mine.

"What are you praying for?" I asked softly.

"You," he said. "I prayed that you'd start speaking to me again."

I rolled my eyes so hard it hurt the muscles. "I swear, Felix."

"Don't swear. We're in church."

I might've laughed had I not wanted to punch him in the face.

"I would like to apologize again for calling you an asshole," he said, turning toward the candles again. "That was out of line. Truthful, but out of line. I shouldn't have lost my cool like that, especially with you."

That he thought me selfish was still rubbing me the wrong way. "I fail to see how spending my evenings protecting the kingdom under a mask is egocentric."

"You're right, that's not. But disobeying a direct order just to spite me is an asshole move."

"Funny, I didn't think you could give me orders."

"Fine, you ignored a request," he said. "I thought we were friends, Brynn. I thought that you trusted that I was trying to help you."

I craned my neck to look at the sculptures above us. "I think you think you're trying to help."

"And I think you think you know everything," Felix said. "This may come as a surprise to you, but your way isn't always the best way. You have this habit of running in, fists bared, fighting your way to resolution. But when it comes to politics, to getting people to do what you want them to, you've got to have more finesse."

"I have plenty of finesse," I said. "Garwood trusts me now. All it took was some one-on-one time, a little honesty, and I know he's on my side."

"What about all those other decisions you made? Combining the summer festival with your coronation?" He snorted. "You're going to get me killed by the rest of the guards when I tell them."

"Why?"

He waved his hand. "Because it's our busiest weekend regardless—three guards on every street, jails filled with drunks and petty thieves. And you want your coronation the same weekend?" He shook his head. "It'll be madness."

"Then let's delay the coronation," I said, leaning back on my heels. "Winter would be a good time, I think."

His brown eyes caught mine again. "Nice try." He nudged me slightly. "Are we okay?"

I exhaled, leaning onto the bannister and staring at the candles. "Why do you care if we're okay? Think I'll fire you if you piss me off too badly?"

"Well, that would truly devastate me," he said with a wry grin. "As I've put a lot of time and effort into your guard over the past few years." The grin faded. "I want us to be okay because you're my friend, Brynna. I don't like it when my friends are mad at me."

I cast him a wary look. "Do you really think we're friends?"

"I hope we are." His smile was genuine, but his eyes grew sad. "You're a lot like August in so many ways. Just more hot-headed and a lot better in a fight. Kat and I feel like having you around is a little like having him back. Although he listened to us more than you do."

There was something honest about the way he stared into the candles, something that tugged at my heart and gave me the urge to pull him into my arms and comfort him. Instead, I settled for nudging him back.

"We're okay, Felix. And who knows? Maybe if I'm a good little princess, you'll let me out on my own one day."

"That is entirely possible," Felix said.

I almost toppled off the bench. "Seriously?"

"Perhaps." He smirked. "If you're a good little princess."

I smiled and turned back to the candles, lighting one more as relief swelled in my chest. "And while we're on the subject of concessions, you can't schedule me from morning until evening. I have to sleep sometime."

"Fine," he said, rising to his feet and offering his hand. "Where to next?"

Although I could patrol the city again, perhaps take down a few bad guys, my body was crying out for sleep. Knowing Felix would never let me live it down if I made a mistake, I admitted defeat.

"To the castle," I said. Then, to his raised eyebrows, I added, "Don't look so surprised."

"With you, Brynn, I am constantly surprised."

# Chapter
# Sixteen

Felix was a man of his word, and neither Katarine nor Beata came to my room until mid-morning. It was the longest I'd slept in days, and it certainly put me in a fine mood. Not only that, tonight was the night for my little chat with Eric Poole.

First, though, I had to get through my agenda. My lesson with Katarine was cut short due to yet another Council meeting. I could scarcely believe it had been a week since I'd been plucked off the street. But I was feeling a bit surer of myself, especially after my dinner with Garwood.

When Beata was finished dressing me (I was finally able to convince her that a tunic was just as formal as a dress), Joella escorted me down the stairs to the Council room. Vernice and Garwood stood just outside the door, discussing something in hushed tones.

"Good morning," I said, by way of announcing my presence. "Lovely day, isn't it?"

"Princess," Garwood said with a nod toward me. "Thank you, again, for an enlightening evening last night."

Vernice shot us both a look, and I could practically see the wheels turning in her head. Whether she thought us plotting against her or sleeping together was debatable.

"I was glad to do it," I replied. "Lady Vernice. Always a pleasure."

"Hm," she said, nodding her deference as an afterthought. "Much to discuss today, Garwood."

"Indeed. Shall we get to it?"

I followed them into the Council room, which somehow felt more familiar and more stressful at the same time. I sat in my chair, taking the time to feel the velvet under my fingertips and move around on the cushion until I found a comfortable spot.

General Godfryd was the next to arrive, shaking hands with everyone in the room before coming to sit in her customary spot. Zuriel came after, looking harried and ruffled as he smoothed his hair.

"I apologize for being late." He glanced at the last empty chair. "Though at least I made it before Octavius."

"Are we sure he's coming at all?" I said.

"Well," Zuriel replied, leaning in close to me, "we usually have a pool for how late he's going to be. Five silvers per guess."

"Oh, well, put me down for not coming at all," I replied with a smile.

"Fifteen minutes," Garwood said, glancing at the clock behind him. "Vernice? Godfryd? Care to wager?"

"We could always begin without him," Vernice replied.

"I've left my coin purse at home," Godfryd said, although she probably found the whole thing as distasteful as Vernice.

In the end, he was ten minutes late on the nose, and Zuriel collected the silvers from the group with a grin. Even from across the table, the stench of booze was palpable. It was amazing he even got himself dressed.

"We have several items to discuss today," Vernice announced, clearly eager to get moving. "The first is, of course, this treaty with the Niemenians."

The one that had been ratified on the day of my brother's wedding to Katarine. "What about it?"

"Well, I believe the Niemenian queen is wondering if it's still valid, considering her sister is now a widow."

"I don't see why it wouldn't still be valid," I replied. "Unless you're asking me to revisit what's been a settled agreement? If Ariadna wants us to marry her sister to someone else, I can find her a suitable replacement from somewhere in Forcadel."

Vernice sniffed, obviously expecting me not to know much about the subject. "That particular agreement may have been settled, but there was another one that has yet to be fulfilled. Your marriage to the prince of Kulka."

I groaned. "Not this again."

"King Neshua has been excessively patient with us. But I fear he won't be patient forever. The eldest son is obviously not an option anymore, but perhaps one of the younger siblings."

"I've been in this seat less than two weeks," I replied with an even tone. "How about we wait a few months before you start lining up suitors, hm?"

"It would be a wise move," she said. "To ally yourself with Kulka and prove you are a queen of your word. They have such a low opinion of you…"

"Why? Because I didn't want to be whored off at thirteen?" I snapped.

"It's not a game," Vernice said.

"No, it's not," I said. "It's my life. And if I don't get to choose where I go or what I do or even who I dine with, I damned well get to choose who I'm going to sleep with for the rest of my life. If the Kulkans want their treaty ratified, I'm sure I can find them a suitable breed cow. It just won't be me."

"Perhaps it's wise to wait," Garwood said, holding up his hand.

"Princess Brynna is right—we've already had several leadership changes this month alone. She's obviously very capable of leading us on her own, and we can deal with the Kulkans in some other way."

My brows shot up in surprise and he winked at me. Around the table, no one made any further objections, and Vernice just bristled.

"What's next on the agenda?" I asked Garwood, feeling very affectionate toward my uncle.

"The queen of Severia has asked for an official invitation to your coronation," Zuriel said, after a moment.

Based on the expressions in the room, I only supposed that wasn't normal, and it was confirmed when Garwood said, "That's awfully presumptuous of her to invite herself to a Forcadel coronation."

"Queen Ilara is a presumptuous woman. I believe she wants to renegotiate some trade agreements while she's here," Zuriel said. "Your father, Princess, wouldn't meet with her. But perhaps you might?"

I narrowed my eyes. The Severians were supposedly one of the two countries Beswick was working with, along with the Kulkans. Inviting the queen here might be a good way to flush Beswick out.

"I'll consider it," I replied, Felix's voice ringing in my ear. "I have a few months to decide, don't I?"

"We'll need an answer sooner," Zuriel said. "It takes months to get messages across the desert plains of Severia to the castle. And if she doesn't leave soon, she'll be stuck there while the sandstorms rage."

"Then perhaps Queen Ilara should move her home a little closer to civilization," Vernice said with a snort. "Princess, I must object to giving the desert people an audience. They offer pottery and glass for trade, the bare minimum compared to Kulka or even Niemen. What kind of message would we be sending to our other trading partners if you let such a lesser country come to your coronation?"

"Have they asked?" I asked casually.

Her mouth hung open like a fish. "Pardon?"

"Have they asked to come to my coronation?" I asked, buying myself a little time to think.

"Well, n-no, but it's not usual for the *royals* of a foreign country to witness. Envoys are one thing, but..."

"I said I'll consider it." I shrugged and turned to the mayor, offering a smile. "I'll have an answer for you next week, Zuriel." By then, I'd know more from Poole and I'd be better able to decide if inviting the queen was worth the complaining.

"Our next item of business happens to be your coronation itself," Garwood said, adjusting his glasses on his nose. "Am I to understand that you will have your coronation the same week as the summer festival?"

I nodded. "Might as well have a celebration. I've discussed it with Captain Llobrega and he has no objections. I would much rather pare down the coronation celebration to the bare minimum and allow the people their celebration."

"The Forcadel coronation is one steeped in tradition," Vernice said. "We can't just throw out tradition—"

"And we aren't," I said, glancing around. "We can do both. It won't strain our resources too badly. And I would much rather the focus be on the people than on me."

She huffed but said nothing else. Perhaps Vernice was used to getting her way on the Council, as she spoke over the other four in the room. I would have to think about how I could win her over. As much as I didn't want to, she would be less inclined to cause trouble if she thought me in her pocket.

"Llobrega mentioned it to me," Godfryd said, clearing her throat. "I don't think it will be an issue."

"Well, if Llobrega thinks it's a good idea, then we should take our time in considering it," Garwood scoffed. And to my surprise, the look was shared by Vernice and Godfryd—even Octavius looked doubtful.

I sat back, schooling my expression. "And has the Council lost faith in the good captain's abilities?"

"Of course not," Vernice said with a heavy wave of her hand. "But his abilities are stretched thin at the moment. Between a coronation and the summer festival, finding a murderer seems to have dropped off his list."

I nodded slowly. "Then it's a good thing I've ordered my own internal investigation."

Every eye on the table—even Octavius's bloodshot ones—swept to me.

"You...have?" Garwood asked.

"Indeed. I have my own sources looking into it." I smirked. "She's very good."

Vernice bristled. "And who, pray tell, is she?"

"Unfortunately, I've said too much already," I replied, sitting back. "Because you see, I have my theories that the killing was done by someone internal to Forcadel. Perhaps even to this Council."

"You can't be serious," Godfryd said.

"I'm not saying any of you are under investigation," I replied, my voice naturally dipping into a lower octave as I channeled The Veil. "But of course, if you're innocent, there's nothing to fear, am I right?"

# Chapter
# Seventeen

The meeting ended shortly after that, with Vernice and Octavius rushing out deep in discussion. I steepled my fingers together as they disappeared through the door, casting a look at Garwood. "Curious behavior, don't you think?"

"Oh, leave them alone," Zuriel replied with a laugh as he rose. "I'd wager they're more worried about the other skeletons you might uncover."

I tilted my head toward him. "And you don't have any skeletons, Mayor? General?"

"None worth mentioning," Zuriel replied.

"You can count the skeletons on my medals of honor," Godfryd said, gruffly. "May I have a word with you privately, Princess?"

I nodded and followed her out of the room, leaving Garwood and Zuriel at the table. I would ask Garwood what he thought about the whole exchange later.

"No need to follow us, Lieutenant," Godfryd said to Joella, who'd fallen into step behind us. "If I'm unable to protect the princess from attackers then I might as well give up my position."

She hesitated, only for a moment, and I gave her an affirming nod. "I promise I won't disappear into thin air. Or disappear at all. General Godfryd will take me down to the captain."

"Very well." She bowed and walked away.

"Those guards keep a tight watch on you, don't they?" she said as we walked the length of the hall outside the Council room.

"More than you know," I muttered. "So what did you want to talk about?"

She grumbled for a moment, rubbing her wrinkled chin. "I'm concerned that you're being too flippant with your naval forces."

"In what way?"

"You've sent two of our best ships to help a merchant on the eastern coast instead of positioning them here, in the bay, where they need to be." She turned to me, a frown on her old, weathered face. "We can't simply send ships to every merchant marine who cries for help. We have priorities, resources to allocate. First and foremost, we need to maintain the protections around the bay."

"What ships remain in harbor to defend us?" I asked.

"Just two, and both are older and have less firepower than the ones you sent." She cleared her throat. "But more importantly, you didn't seek my counsel before making this decision."

"I'm sorry," I said softly. "I thought I could help someone. But it appears I just made things worse."

"I would like to help you help others," she said. "But first you need to come to me. Your father and I had weekly talks over tea. You've yet to even speak to me outside of a Council meeting."

*Ah, so she just wants face time.* "It's been a whirlwind these past few weeks. I'm just coming to terms with all the meetings I'm supposed to be having. It's a miracle Felix lets me out of the tower at all."

"Yes, your captain." She pressed her lips together in a thin line. "He came highly recommended, of course. But there is clearly someone out to destroy the kingdom, and there's yet to be any progress on the investigation. It's not right for the princess herself to have to hire her own staff."

"That's purely for my own benefit," I said. "I have full faith and confidence in Felix as a captain."

"That makes one of us," she said. "It was clear after Prince August was assassinated that a leadership change was required. Felix was the obvious choice. He was smart, he was dedicated, and he had a personal investment in finding the assassin." She shook his head. "But it seems he's become distracted as of late. I wonder if it's time to find someone else to replace him."

Last night, I would've jumped at the chance to replace Felix with someone much less clingy, but as we walked out onto the garrison where he was holding drills with his young cadets, I didn't have it in me. We'd come to an uneasy truce the night before, and I preferred the devil I knew.

"Thank you for your insight," I said. "If you'll make an appointment with whoever is responsible for managing my schedule, I would love to take tea with you weekly."

She beamed and nodded once, leaving me to cross the green grass alone.

"Was that the general?" Felix asked when I came up beside him. Today, the youngest were running around the track while the older ones had paired off to spar with wooden weapons. It reminded me a little too much of Celia's camp, although we'd trained with real weapons.

"Yep. Wanted to know why I haven't been paying her any attention."

"I'm sure." He turned his gaze back to the sparring teens. "The Council meeting went well, then?"

"Mostly," I said, wincing as the girl landed a particularly painful blow to the boy's head. "Garwood was especially helpful."

"Oh?"

"Told you it was smart to visit him." The boy yielded, and the girl returned to her friends, sharing a short celebration before sitting on the bench. Head hanging, the boy walked to another bench and poured water over his head.

"How was the rest of the meeting?" Felix asked, taking my attention away from them.

"Vernice continues to be a pain in the ass. I don't like how everyone's already trying to line up suitors. It's like everyone's trying to kill or marry me."

"Unfortunately, that's how it goes when you're the queen." The ghost of a smile played on his lips. "What else?"

"The Severian queen wants to come to my coronation."

"Queen Ilara wants to come to your coronation?" Felix turned to me, brows knitted. "Why?"

"I think she might be coming to renegotiate with Beswick," I said.

"Uh-huh." He shifted back to his cadets. "And what does that have to do with the Council?"

"Oh, nothing. Just wondering if it's a good idea to bring her here," I said. "It's treason for Beswick to enter into agreements with countries I haven't sanctioned. Perhaps if we brought her here —"

He stopped me with a hand on my arm. "Brynna, I know it's tempting to want to use your position as queen to get to Beswick, but you have to be careful about it. There's a very fragile alliance between our four countries, and that alliance is the only way we retain our borders. If you invite Ilara and neglect the other two nations, they could revolt. We could lose our carefully crafted agreements, and our industry. Without our industry, your people starve—"

"So I invite them, too."

"It's not that simple. Kulka considers themselves to be Forcadel's number one trading partner, even though it's been

Niemen for the past few years," he continued. "They'd consider it an insult if you invited them as an afterthought. There are other ways to find out what he's up to without potentially endangering the entire kingdom."

"I got it, I got it," I said, waving him off. "Fine. I won't invite her. But I still think it would've been a good idea."

"What else did they talk about?" he said, turning back to his soldiers. Most of them had shrugged off their losses, except for that one boy. He hung his head, staring at the grass as his fellow soldiers compared notes.

"I don't think they have confidence in your abilities," I said.

His eyes widened, and I knew what I'd said had hit somewhere deep, even if he didn't want me to know. "Oh."

"So I suggest, Captain, that you find us a murderer. And soon." I chewed my lip. "Any...news on that?"

"Unfortunately, no. We've questioned everyone with access to August's food and bed. We don't even know what poison was used."

"Katarine see anything?"

Felix shook his head. "No. Just...found him dead one morning."

"Wasn't she sleeping next to him? Why didn't they kill her, too?" I stared at the moon out the window. "Did you check the bedsheets?"

"Yes, Brynn. We've checked everything. And unfortunately, until they...try again, we won't have anything more to go on."

"Well, you'd better hope I can sniff out a poison before I drink it," I said. "Luckily for you, I can."

"Luckily, indeed," Felix said. "Stay here, I'll be right back."

He dismissed the rest of the group, but halted the boy, taking a seat beside him. It was clear this kid hadn't been performing; none of the other kids seemed as affected by their loss. And based on Felix's gestures, and the lost look on the boy's face, Felix's help wasn't useful.

"Maybe I can help," I said, picking up a wooden sword and walking over there.

"I don't think Page Jeremy wants a lesson from the princess," Felix said, his eyes warning me against it.

"Oh, come now," I said, tossing the sword from one hand to the other. "I'm already in my tunic." I thrust the dull tip into Felix's chest. "And now you're dead, so you can't stop me."

"Enough, Brynna," Felix said, tapping my sword away. "Go wash up for dinner, Jeremy. You'll try again tomorrow."

The boy jogged away, and I shrugged. "I could've helped him."

"Oh yeah? How?"

"Easy." I stuck the sword into the ground. "We'll train with some real weapons. It's amazing how clear the mind gets when you're fighting for your limbs."

Felix sighed. "No, Brynna. That's not the way to deal with him. He just needs a bit of confidence, that's all."

"Confidence." I snorted. "What he needs is a win. I could show him how to win."

"You'd show him how to fight dirty."

I stepped back, picking up the wooden sword again. "Oh? You think I fight dirty, do you?"

"I think you have a certain way in the ring, yes," he said, knocking away the wooden sword when I poked him again. "I don't teach my soldiers to break arms and ribs."

"Whose ribs did I break?" I said, tapping the back of his thighs.

"Mine, almost," he said, grabbing another sword that had been left lying around and smacking away my thrust. "I don't think you want to go toe-to-toe with me."

"Oh," I cooed, as our wooden swords met again. "I think it's you who doesn't want to go toe-to-toe with *me*. Are you afraid of The Veil?"

"Don't say that too loudly," Felix replied, trying to hit me in the shoulder, but I was quicker. "These soldiers don't yet have my trust."

I jumped away from a well-timed swing and came back with one of my own, tapping him on the shoulder. "And why do Joella and Riya have your trust? And Coyle?"

"Because they've proven themselves," Felix said as our swords met in the middle. I pushed against him, my arms shaking with the effort. His smirk said he felt my struggle, but no matter how deep I dug, I couldn't find the strength to push him back. When his blade drew precariously close to my face, I finally relented.

"And that, Brynn," he said, his breath warm on my cheek, "is why the queen remains in the castle."

"Because I'm too weak to defend my kingdom?" I said, annoyed that I'd let him win.

"Because *someone* needs to," he replied, casting his weapon away. "You're more than just a person. You're a symbol—it doesn't matter who you are. Someone has to be a beacon of hope. Someone has to make the tough calls. Someone has to be looking farther than the next blade to see the entire army."

I paused, kicked the sword into my hands, and yanked Felix down to the ground, pressing the wooden blade into his neck.

"What was that?" I said, breathing in his ear. "Perhaps I'll just lead the army myself."

"It'll be awfully hard to decapitate everyone you see," Felix said. "Remember, you have just one sword. That's not very useful against an army."

I released him and stood upright, tossing the sword between my hands with ease. "But sometimes, sticking your blade in the right person makes all the difference."

He got to his feet, shaking his head. "Go get changed. I'll meet you down by the garden door."

# Chapter
# Eighteen

An hour later, I was dressed in my mask and hood, hopping on one foot while I waited for Felix. Tonight, finally, I could move forward. Perhaps even find the contracts themselves. But I didn't want to get too ahead of myself.

Felix was late, and more than once I considered leaving without him. But the trust we had in each other was starting to grow, and it seemed foolish to overturn the apple cart after we'd just righted it. I heard his footsteps before I saw him, bathed in shadow and wearing his mask with a bit of stubble around his jawline.

"Off to see Mr. Poole?" I said with a cheery grin.

"Indeed." He pulled the iron gate away from the drain and we crawled through. "Sorry I was late. I was dealing with Jeremy."

"Hope you took it easy on him," I said.

"We just talked," he said softly. "Perhaps there's some merit to what you said about him needing a win."

"Of course there's merit to it," I said as we came to the other side. "I'm not saying you send the boy out into battle, but maybe I could meet him on a dark street and rough him up—"

"I think that might cause more harm than good," he said with a shake of his head. "He's never won a single match in the two years he's been in my care. I'm sure that's contributing to his issues."

"Maybe he's not a soldier then. Can we find another place for him?"

"I don't know if that would devastate him more," Felix said. "He's actually my cousin, my father's youngest brother's son. I have several family members in the guard now. It's in our family's blood to protect the crown."

"Maybe it's not in his blood," I said. "Or maybe he can protect us some other way. It's not all about waving a sword around, you know."

"In our family, it most certainly is," Felix said with a grim expression. "I would hate to be the one who sent him home." He glanced at me. "Metaphorically speaking. The Llobregas live in Mariner's Row."

"Of course they do," I said. "Maybe we can stop by on our way to Poole's. You can stay there, even. Catch up."

He made a noise and didn't respond, so we set off.

My first stop of the night was the bell tower to replenish my supplies. I lit all the lamps, pulling the loose floorboards and wall pieces and laying out my pouches, weapons, and whatever else I had on hand. I wasn't sure what to expect from Poole, so I hung my small knives on my belt, leaving my sword behind. In my sling-pouch, I added my last bag of knockout powder (Kieran needed to come back already), my weight-ended ropes, and a rolled-up strand of binding twine. I even packed those little mushrooms and eyeglasses Kieran had given me, though I hoped not to use them.

"I don't think you have enough stuff," Felix said, leaning against a wooden pole. "Maybe you need to add more knives."

"You should be impressed," I said, tying my hood around my neck. "I'm preparing adequately for the unknown. Look at all the risk I'm not taking."

"You're still breaking into a man's house. A man connected to the worst criminal in the city."

"And if I'm lucky, maybe he's over for tea, and we can resolve this whole thing tonight," I said, breezing by Felix with a wink.

We left the bell tower, and not even the thick, summer air could dampen my spirits. A light sheen of sweat coated my brow under my mask, and the back of my shirt was wet beneath my slingbag, yet I kept up my pace as we passed Mariner's Row on our way to the northeastern quadrant of the city, Merchant's Quarter. It was upper middle class, not as expensive or gaudy as Garwood's mansion, but still nice enough to be proud of. Most of those who lived here were business owners or well-to-do lawyers and bankers.

Poole's house sat in the middle of a row of townhouses painted white with black shutters. Two lights were on, one in the bedroom and one in the living room. My guess was he was downstairs, and he lived alone, so the light upstairs was just burning unattended.

"So what exactly is your plan?" Felix asked, looking over my shoulder.

"I generally don't have one," I said, turning away from the house and sorting through my bag. "I'll creep in through a window, assess the situation, then decide what to do from there."

"I don't like that," he said. "You need to have a plan *before* you get in there. What if he has a knife?"

I sighed. "Then it's a good thing I have two."

"What if he ambushes you? What if he has friends there? What if—"

"What if you leave me alone to do my job, Felix?" I snapped. "I can handle the interrogation of a rich accountant."

"A rich accountant on the payroll of one of the most dangerous —"

I covered his mouth with my hand and pulled him down to hide as the back door opened. Poole stood, bathed in light in nothing but his boxers and a stained white shirt. He scratched his belly and turned around, closing the door behind him.

"If you want to come with me," I whispered, "you *will* keep your voice down. Now I have to change my plan."

"Why? I thought you said you didn't have one?"

"My plan is usually creep in through the window, surprise, bind then interrogate. Now you've ruined the surprise part, so I have to think of something else."

I crawled up to the house and crouched next to the window, testing it to see if it was unlocked. Unfortunately, no such luck tonight, but I was able to see inside. Poole was sitting in a large leather-bound chair with an oil lamp overhead. He seemed at ease, which was good for me.

"You aren't going in there alone."

I growled as I pulled out my knife and slid it through the glue connecting the pane to the wood. "Fine. You can come. But stay in the kitchen and out of sight."

The glass popped out easily, and I unlocked the window, sliding it up softly and crawling into the kitchen and where I hid behind a table. In the other room, the chair creaked as Poole stood to investigate, but he wasn't two steps inside the kitchen before he froze.

Poole sucked in a loud breath. "Who's there?"

I smirked and stood so he could see my outline in the moonlight.

"Who are you?" he said, his voice trembling.

"You know who I am," I growled, lowering my voice.

Felix snorted behind me and I tried not to let it bother me.

"W-what do you want?"

"I need information about your boss," I said, pulling one of my knifes and letting it catch the moonlight. "I want to know where he keeps his contracts—especially those with Kulka."

The man swallowed, wearing a look of indecision. Would he

save his own neck or his boss's, that was the question. I'd never met a person yet who'd chosen the latter.

"Beswick keeps his most...er...interesting contracts on his person at all times."

I straightened. "On his person. As in...in his suit pocket?"

He nodded. "The ones you want are probably there. He doesn't trust them with anyone else."

"What can you tell me about them?"

He shook his head roughly. "N-nothing, I can tell you nothing about them."

I paused, just for a moment, then rushed him. In three moves, he was on his knees with my knife pressed against his neck.

"Still want to be quiet?" I whispered. "I will *kill* you."

"This death would be quick. Beswick would..." He swallowed. "I've heard tales. It would last for days. And he wouldn't just kill me, he'd kill everyone I'd ever come into contact with."

"You seem like a man who's pretty selfish," I said, pressing the blade harder into his skin. "Fine books. Fine things. I can give you protection."

"Not from him, you can't. No one can." He whimpered against my blade. "P-please. I've told you all I can."

"You've told me *nothing*," I growled, releasing him. "I'll be back in three nights. If you don't have anything of value then, I'll torture you worse than Beswick ever would. Perhaps I'll start with your fingers..."

With him trembling in a ball on the floor, I stormed to the window, jumping through and rolling to a stop in the bushes. I dashed away down the alley, hoping Felix was smart enough to follow without me telling him so. A few streets down, I finally slowed, cursing my luck that I'd wasted so much time on such a useless endeavor. Poole probably wouldn't tell me more tomorrow than he did today. The only way I was going to get those contracts off Beswick was to pickpocket them myself.

"Brynna."

I stopped, but only for a moment. "What?"

"That was too much," Felix said as he fell into step with me. "You can't...you can't kill people."

"The Veil has never killed anyone," I drawled.

"You broke a man's arm the other day."

"Well, he deserved it."

"Still, though," Felix said as he joined me on the roof. "I know you're frustrated, but chopping off accountants' fingers isn't the way to get information. That's what Beswick does, and you're better than that."

"Threatening, Felix. Only threats." I cast him a coy look. "I promise I'm not as much of a monster as I tell people I am."

He joined me on the ledge, agitation clear in his body. "You've already been out all night. What more could you have to accomplish?"

"Find Beswick. Get close to his person. Steal the contracts from his pocket."

Felix turned fully to me. "No."

"Why not?"

"Because, save yourself, Beswick is one of the most closely-guarded people in the city," Felix said. "There is no way you'll get close enough to spit on him, let alone pickpocket him."

"You doubt my abilities?" I asked.

"I doubt your sanity right now."

I pursed my lips. "Then how about we just go watch him for a bit?"

"I don't want you anywhere *near* Beswick," Felix said. "Find your proof some other way."

"Felix, I don't have time for another way," I replied, sidestepping him.

But he blocked my path. "We'll figure one out together. Something that doesn't require you putting yourself in unnecessary danger."

"Then I'm at a dead end," I said, throwing my arms in the air. "I have no idea what to do next."

"What do you normally do when you hit a dead end?" Felix asked.

I crossed my arms over my chest and frowned. "I get more information. I keep digging until there's a break and then I take action. But now I have information, and someone won't let me take action on it."

"Then perhaps you need more information," Felix said. "Beswick's contracts may be permanently out of your reach for the moment. Instead of stewing over what you can't have, figure out a different way to get what you want."

I could've argued with him all night, but he had that particular look in his eye that told me it would be completely useless.

# Chapter

# Nineteen

After thinking about it all day, I still saw no easier path to my end goal than to spy on Beswick or try to pickpocket him. But Felix was stubborn, and although it was *incredibly* tempting to leave him behind, it would only cause more headaches. There was also the option that one day, if he trusted me enough, he'd let me out without him. So when he joined me, I at least wanted to show that I was trying.

"I'm going to ask all my regular informants," I said. "Maybe one of his lieutenants is in the know."

"See? That's a much safer option."

Safer, sure. But it felt a bit like going backward.

Ruby was nowhere to be found, perhaps taking the night off, so I ventured down to the docks to hit up Stank's to see what John knew. As usual, Felix waited outside, although his stern looks and annoyed snorts told me he didn't quite trust me not to make a break for it. But I gave him a sweet smile and told him I'd be out in half an hour, which seemed to placate him somewhat.

I pushed open the door and the odor of beer and sweat washed over me. The place was more packed than usual, and it made moving around difficult, but eventually, I found an empty stool at the bar. It took Frank the bartender a few minutes to make his way over to me, and he poured a shot of whiskey before I even asked for it.

"John's out," he said.

"Really?" I said, looking around. "Everyone else is in."

"Which is why he's out. Made too many enemies with his loose lips," he said. "Especially with the folks bringing in this big shipment tonight."

"Shipment?" I lifted my gaze. "What kind of shipment?"

"Been all the conversations down here," he said, picking up a glass and wiping it down with a rag. "All these guys are waiting for them to arrive."

"Waiting for whom?"

He shrugged. "Nobody knows. The captain's guard doesn't even know about it."

"What the captain doesn't know could fill the bay," I replied, putting five gold pieces on the bar. "But what you do know could be worth twice this."

"Keep your coins, all I've heard is rumors. Nobody knows what's coming except the people on the ship."

I pushed the coins toward him again. "Is Beswick behind it?"

He shrugged. "Rumors, Veil. That's all I've heard. But if you want to talk about Beswick, the gentleman in the corner is the one you need to speak with." He nodded behind me to where Ignacio was talking in low voices to individuals with hoods like mine.

"And you can't give me anything else?" I asked, rising.

He shrugged then set to cleaning the bar, so I turned to face Ignacio, formulating a plan. I still had Kieran's mushrooms in my slingbag, now might be a good time to use them. I disappeared into the crowd, pulling my bag around to the front and finding the small mushrooms. They were fairly insignificant, smaller than my thumb, but I hoped they wouldn't be noticed. I slid the stalks between my middle and ring fingers, holding them tight as I moved my bag around to my back again.

Ready for battle, I made my way across the bar as casually as I could with all the people packed inside. Squeezing between two beefy women, I adjusted my hood and continued toward the table in the back.

"Evening, gentlemen," I announced.

Ignacio's face grew dark immediately as he scowled. "There aren't any sniveling idiots here for you to save. Get lost."

"Really?" I said, gently pressing one of the mushrooms to the man closest to me's shoulder. "Are you not counting yourself among that number?"

"Don't make me throw you out of this bar, little girl," he replied.

"I'd love to see you try," I replied, pressing a second mushroom to the other man's shoulder. "But don't embarrass yourself again. A little fire scared you so much."

He glowered in my direction. "What do you want, flea?"

"I want to know if you know anything about this shipment coming in tonight," I replied, as I did need an excuse for bothering them.

"I know nothing, and if I did, I wouldn't tell you, little flea. Now *get lost.*"

I bowed with a flourish, turning before either of them could see the smirk on my face as I exited the bar. Wordlessly, I beckoned for Felix to follow me as we ascended to the roof of the bar and waited.

"So, what'd you find out?" he asked.

"Nothing yet," I replied, pulling the spectacles out of my pocket and slipping them on. "We'll just see how well Kieran's Nestori friend can use her mushrooms."

"You look ridiculous," Felix said, the ghost of a smile on his lips.

"Ssh." The door below me opened and the two men who'd been talking to Ignacio walked out, both bearing a visible lime green circle on their backs. And even better, every few feet, the mushrooms spat out little spores, leaving a trail behind them.

"What is it?" Felix asked.

I pulled off the glasses for a moment, seeing nothing then put them back on. "I owe Kieran a drink, that's what. Let's go."

We followed the men at a safe distance. The spores lost their luster a few moments after hitting the ground, but it was enough to track them.

"What are you planning to do to them?" Felix asked.

"Ask what they're doing for Beswick." I held up my hand as the men walked into a small inn. That would be helpful—I could use the element of surprise. And perhaps, if they were in separate rooms, get the truth from them both.

"Stay up here and let me do what I do, okay?" I picked the lock on the back door of the inn then stepped over washtubs and around hanging laundry toward the front. Cracking open the door to the front room, I spotted an innkeeper at the desk, counting coins and putting them into a bag. Without any other options, I kicked over a washtub, causing a loud *bang* then pressed myself against the wall next to the door.

The keeper came running into the back room, rushing past me in the dark, and I was able to slip out behind him. With my glasses, the spores were still barely visible, but I trailed them up toward two rooms down the hall. I pressed my ear to the closest, listening for the sounds of movement. Instead, all I got were soft snores.

Working with my lock-picker again, I slowly pushed the door open, praying it wouldn't creak, then crawled inside. I rested on my hands and knees for a minute, waiting for the man in question to wake, but he snored on. They'd had a few pitchers of beer between them, so it might not be that tough to make him speak.

I yanked the covers off him, but he didn't wake. So I kicked him a few times until he roused, blinking in the darkness.

"What the—"

I yanked him upward by his shirt collar and snarled in his face. "*What are you doing for Beswick?*"

"I-what?" He shook his head. "Who are you?"

I pulled a knife from my belt and pressed it against his throat. "Your worst nightmare. Now tell me what you're doing for him?"

"I'm... I'm... I'm..." His face, pale in the dim light, grew wet as he trembled in my hands.

"And I'm losing my patience," I seethed. "Speak now, or I'll permanently remove your ability to do so."

"I'm bringing in artisans from Severia!" he cried, closing his eyes and dissolving into tears.

I lowered him slightly. "What?"

"Please don't hurt me!" he said, tears streaming down his face. "The Forcadel planning committee limited the number of foreign vendors who can show, but Beswick cut a deal with Mayor Zuriel to let more Severians come than were allowed and—"

I made a disgusted sound and tossed him back down toward the bed. "Are you serious? Artisans?"

"Y-yes, what did you think?"

With a growl of frustration, I threw open the window and climbed out without another word.

⊃———→

"Quit laughing at me."

"I just can't help it," Felix said as we sat on the edge of the docks with our feet hanging over the side. "You bullied some poor man who's just trying to get Severian artists some extra cash."

"Through Beswick," I said, but there was no heat in my tone. "And it's still illegal."

"But not...devastating to our local economy," he said, nudging me gently. "And definitely not treasonous."

I blew air out between my lips. "Maybe. Maybe not. Could it be a front for something? Beswick doesn't do anything nice for anyone unless he's getting something out of it."

"I think you're obsessed," Felix said. "I'll have my squad ask around tomorrow, and we'll find out what we can. If it's that important to you that some poor desert-dwellers don't make their coin..."

"This isn't funny," I snapped, sitting up. "This is how Beswick operates. He finds desperate people, gives them a hand with strings attached, and then they're stuck in his cycle forever. These Severians may make some coin, but they'll be in debt for much more."

"I know, I know," Felix said, casting me an amused look. "Perhaps the princess could intervene and grant a special waiver to the artisans."

I opened my mouth, ready to continue arguing then closed it. "I suppose she could."

"See? This is what I'm talking about," he said, leaning back on his hands. "You don't always have to save people by wearing a mask. There's a lot of good you could do as queen."

"Sure it won't mess everything up?" I asked, picking at the edge of the dock. "Take good paying jobs away from Forcadel citizens? Disrupt a treaty?"

"We always welcome foreign artists to the summer festival, but it's usually Kulkans and Niemenians because they're the only ones who can afford to travel here." He cocked his head to the side. "Why are you arguing with me about this?"

"Because I want Beswick to be guilty," I said, slumping my shoulders. "It's not just about the timeline. Every night he remains on the street, another person gets sucked into his web. Surprised the entire kingdom isn't indebted to him for something."

He covered my hand with his, sending a warm zing from my fingers to my toes. "You'll get him, Brynn. You just have to be patient."

I nodded, turning to the inky black waters of the bay as he held my hand. I willed the fog to dissipate so I could see more than creaking shadows, but nothing happened. "What do you think this big shipment is?"

"Could be those artisans. Could be something else entirely. The summer festival isn't for another two months." He turned to me with a smile. "Could be exactly what you need to take down Beswick, delivered on a silver platter."

"Now you're just being mean," I said, ripping my hand away from his. Not just because of what he'd said, but the reminder that time was passing quickly, and I was no closer to Beswick than when I'd started.

# Chapter
# Twenty

The next morning, three strange-looking ships sat in the bay with white hulls and billowing orange sails. Our own naval forces had surrounded them at daybreak, preventing them from getting any closer to the main city.

The only thing we knew about them were that they were Severians. And, if what they said was true, the queen was here, too.

"This is new," I said to Katarine as we stood in front of the window. "Right? This is new."

"Exceptionally." She chewed her lip. "It's unheard of for a queen to arrive unannounced."

"How'd they manage to get all the way into the bay?" I asked, squinting and wishing I had a telescope. "The fog was heavy last night, but we have some kind of defenses, right?"

She cleared her throat. "Presumably. But someone sent our two fastest ships to the east, and they haven't returned yet."

"Ah, well..." I shifted against the window. "What do you know about the queen?"

"Not much, unfortunately. She's young, maybe twenty?

Twenty-one? Her father was quite old, but most of the children he'd sired died in childbirth. She was his last, and the only one who survived."

"Tragic."

"It's a hard life in Severia, even for the royals." Katarine tapped her fingers on the windowsill. "It's very rare for the royal family to leave the kingdom, let alone the queen. The weather in Severia is unpredictable. Sandstorms, that kind of thing."

"So maybe she's on vacation?" I asked.

"Queens don't take vacations," Katarine replied with a small laugh. "It's more likely she's here to petition you directly to allow them access to the ocean. Severia has a coast, but it takes months to get from the castle to the coast on the western side of the country. It's closer for the Severians to travel into Forcadel and pick up the river at Skorsa, but of course, they're subject to tariffs."

"It sounds like she could use some help," I said, chewing my lip. "Do we have to charge them tariffs?"

"The problem is if we give the Severians an inch, the Kulkans will want one as well, and Niemen," she said. "As much as I know you'd like to help them, the other two nations are much more strategically important to Forcadel's future. It's best to leave things the way they are."

"And yet, here's the queen," I said, squinting out at the ships again. "It's gonna be bad to tell her no, huh?"

"It will be enough to receive her," Katarine said. "And perhaps you'll be able to figure some way to help without causing too much distress. Just be sure to use your resources."

"Ma'am," Beata said from behind us. "Felix has asked me to get you ready for the Council meeting."

"Council?" I shared a confused look with Katarine. "I don't have a Council meeting today."

"Emergency one, I'd guess," Katarine said, walking to the door. "I'll see what I can find out while you get ready."

Beata grinned and held up a bright blue dress. "I thought you could wear the Forcadel colors today. And perhaps your diamond tiara."

"Fine, fine." I sat down at the vanity and stared at my reflection in the mirror as Beata undid my plait. "Is it weird that I'm nervous?"

"I don't see why you wouldn't be," Beata said, her gaze focused on her hands in my hair. "It's certainly a new situation. I daresay nobody really knows what to expect."

"I can handle the Council, I can handle crime lords, but I'm not really sure I can receive a queen."

"Sure you can," Beata said, catching my eye in the mirror. "It's no different than meeting with anyone else. Be kind, smile, and don't agree to anything she asks."

"Oh?" I glanced behind me. "Have you been talking with Felix and Kat?"

"I hear things," she said, tying off the plait with a flourish. "You're very lucky to have so many people looking out for you."

No sooner had Beata helped me into my dress than the door opened, and now Felix strode in with a grim look on his face as he rested his hand on his pommel. "Riya got eyes on the queen, confirming she's here. Do you want to receive her?"

"Um..." I glanced at Beata, and she nodded. "What do you think?"

"I think it's weird she came unannounced," he said, walking to the window and staring out it as Katarine and I had done earlier. "But there were no signs of arms, and I can't imagine the queen would put herself in danger if she planned to do anything nefarious."

"So why's she here?"

"Her handlers wouldn't say. They're very protective of her, and when Riya tried to speak to her, she wouldn't answer." He cleared his throat. "The handlers said she'd only speak with the Crown

Prince."

"Ah, well." I laughed. "That's going to be a one-sided conversation."

"Brynn."

"Sorry, sorry," I said, catching Beata's eye as she fluffed my skirt. "What do you think I should do?"

"Receive her," he said. "See what she wants. *Talk to your advisors* before you agree to anything. It's clear she thought there was a leadership change, so my guess is she wants to renegotiate some borders, tariffs, or something else."

Katarine poked her head in. "Brynna, the Council is down in the receiving room, if you're ready."

"I guess." I turned, smiling at all of them. "Let's meet a queen."

My receiving room was already filled with people when Felix and Katarine escorted me inside. The members were huddled off to the side, and the royal guard had lined the room at the posts, all wearing leather armor and carrying swords. Coyle, Joella, and Riya stood closest to my throne, their gazes centered on the double doors where, presumably, the queen of Severia would enter.

I bypassed my throne and went to the Council, gauging their reactions from extremely concerned (Vernice and Godfryd) to curious (Garwood and Zuriel) to absolutely bored (Octavius). Garwood nodded in my direction when I approached, but the conversation continued without me.

"I don't like it," Vernice said. "Send them back to the dustbowl from whence they came."

"There has to be a reason," Godfryd said, her gaze on the doors like her soldiers. "Captain Llobrega reports they had limited arms on board, just enough for royal protection."

"Perhaps it's because they consider us weak, since we have a young princess on the throne," Vernice said.

"That's interesting, because they came here to meet with August," I said, tossing a hard glare at Vernice. "Would you say the same thing about him?"

"Which makes it more probable they're here to invade," Vernice said.

"Invade?" Zuriel laughed. "Come now, Ana. Don't be ridiculous."

"What's ridiculous is entertaining her at all," Vernice said. "We should send her back to the desert."

"I don't think there's any harm in receiving her," Garwood said with a look to me. "May I have a word before we begin?"

I nodded and allowed him to walk me to the throne. "I've already had three lectures about not agreeing to anything from these so-called 'pathetic desert-dwellers,' I don't need a fourth."

"Three?"

"Beata reiterated the point."

He chuckled as he released me and I sat down. "Then I will be brief. You haven't much experience dealing with international dignitaries, especially royals. They're usually interested in one of two things—doing the best they can for their kingdom or growing it. View everything she says through that prism, and you'll be well-equipped to make good decisions."

I nodded. "Thank you."

The front doors groaned as they swung open, silencing the chatter in the room. Zathan walked in, shoulders back and hand on his pommel, coming to stand at the center of the room and bowing low at the hip.

"Your Majesty," he said, coming upright. "The queen of Severia has requested an audience."

"Well, send her in," I said, with a flick of my wrist. "Or else we all assembled here for nothing."

He smirked briefly then turned and walked through the open doors. An anxious energy permeated the room as the moments ticked on, and I tapped my fingers on the armrest of the throne, trying to keep all that everyone had said to me in the back of my mind. I wasn't sure what I was ready for, but as loud footsteps echoed in the hall outside, I released a long exhalation.

The soldiers came in first, carrying orange flags that almost scraped the top of the large doorframe. Their leather armor was more cracked and worn than my guards'. They wore severe looks on their tanned faces, perhaps a few shades darker than my own, moving as a unit in two columns and stopping in the center of my throne room.

An older gentleman walked through the break between them, wearing dark red robes that dragged along the floor behind him. He came closer to my throne, and out the corner of my eye, I saw Felix grip his sword tighter. But the man simply bowed.

"Your Highness, may I present my queen, Ilara Hipolita Särkkä of the great kingdom of Severia."

Behind him, the queen herself appeared. Unlike the rest of her countrymen, she was wide-eyed, with long black hair that hung to her hips. She wore a light brown dress that seemed a lot cooler than the velvet one Beata had stuffed me into, and no less form-fitting. Her painted toes poked out of leather sandals as she walked, her hands clasped in front of her. On her head, she wore a simple gold chain with diamonds and other gems resting against her forehead.

She caught my eye and averted her gaze immediately.

"Your Highness." She tilted her head as she curtseyed, but still didn't look at me. "I am Queen Ilara Hipolita Särkkä of the kingdom of Severia. It is an absolute honor to be in Forcadel."

"Raise your head," the old man whispered sharply. "You are a queen, Ilara."

Ilara's head shot upward, locking eyes with me. In her gaze, I read fear and embarrassment, and about as much anxiety as had settled in my stomach.

I glanced at Felix and he nodded. "I'm glad to welcome you," I said after a moment. "But a little surprised. Isn't there normally protocol for royal visits?"

Her eyes widened. "Did you...not receive my letter?"

"I received a note that asked for an invitation to my coronation," I said. "And I believe we declined it."

Her jaw dropped, and pure horror dawned on her face. "W-what?"

I shifted on my seat, glancing at her handler whose face had turned red. An awkward silence descended in the throne room as Ilara wrung her hands, searching the room for what to do.

"I apologize," she stammered. "I never would have come unannounced had I known. They didn't tell me that... They just said that—"

"Stop stammering," her handler snapped.

Ilara's lips clamped shut and her eyes filled with tears as she stood in the center of the room, which was quickly filling with awkward tension. I glanced at Felix, then Garwood, then made a decision.

"You know what?" I rose from my seat. "Let's take a walk. You could probably use a walk."

"Your Highness—" Felix began.

"Captain," I said, cutting him off. "Please accompany us." I glanced at her handler and narrowed my eyes. "What's your name?"

"Jozef, ma'am—"

"You should probably head back to the ship," I said, walking down the throne to meet Ilara in the center of the room. "I don't think the queen needs your help from here on out. Seems like she's fully capable of talking with me without you."

His eyes bulged, but Ilara didn't contradict me.

"Shall we?" I said, offering my arm.

And without another word to anyone else, I led the queen of Severia out of the throne room and toward our gardens.

# Chapter
# Twenty-One

"I am mortified," Ilara whispered as soon as we were out of the receiving room. "I wish I could disappear on the spot."

"That Jozef guy needs to learn his place," I said, glancing behind me to make sure the little snake hadn't followed us. "I'm not even queen yet, and I wouldn't let anyone talk to me like that."

"He's...my tutor. I value his guidance." She, too, glanced behind us. "But yes, he's become a little too overbearing of late."

"I could tell." My own overbearing handler was no less than three steps behind us. "Captain, I don't think the queen is going to stab me, and if she tried, I'm pretty sure I can fend her off. So give us some more space, hm?"

Felix glared at me, but kept his distance.

"So what's really going on?" I asked. "Whether or not you meant to barge in, why travel here at all?"

"We heard rumor that King Maurice had died," she said softly. "He refused to meet with us—ever. But we'd heard Prince August was a lot more amenable. So we set sail. We'd hoped to get here closer to the coronation, but we arrived much sooner than anticipated." She cast me a look. "And to a much different ruler than we'd expected."

"You and me both," I muttered. "What was your goal? Just to give your congratulations?"

"No." She sighed. "We need help. My country is dying from famine, exacerbated by our trading partners' harsh policies."

I swallowed. "Such as?"

"The closest trading route is the Ash River, and to get there, we must enter Forcadel at the border city of Skorsa," she said. "We must pay five gold pieces per shipment to cross the border. Then another five gold pieces at every checkpoint. To enter the city, ten gold pieces. And we stand to make maybe twenty-two pieces per box, assuming our shipment hasn't been damaged."

"That sounds grossly unfair," I said.

"It is standard for shipments from all countries," Felix said from behind me. I practically felt his gaze burning a hole in the back of my neck.

"I suppose it is," I said with a smile.

We walked out to the front of the castle, where the glittering blue bay spanned out before us, filled with ships and activity. Ilara's boats were still surrounded, but it appeared the guard around them had lessened somewhat.

She inhaled deeply. "The salt water smell is exhilarating. And the wind is so refreshing. Not at all like in Severia. Here, the air is moist. There, your lips bleed from the dryness."

"It sounds terrible," I said.

"But it's not all bad," she said quickly. "At night, you can see every star in the sky. The sand glows, practically, shifting and moving in the night winds. It's absolutely magical." She turned back to me, looking up at the castle that rose above us. "This place, though. It's more incredible than I could have dreamed."

I followed her gaze, squinting as the bright sun reflected off the golden accents. "Tad ostentatious for my tastes, but I suppose it has its charms."

"A castle must be opulent, for it represents the best of its people," she recited. "Or that's what my tutors used to say. Have you been able to explore every inch of it?"

"Not really," I said. "Felix keeps a close guard on me at all times."

"Mm," she said, turning to me thoughtfully. "You know, my siblings and I used to explore our castle when we were young. Look for secret entrances and tunnels. Old castles, you know, they always have them." She turned to me. "Do you know of any?"

I shook my head, if only to keep from smiling. "Not particularly."

"You should look for some," she said with a devilish look. "Maybe one day you and I can give our handlers the slip and go out to explore your wonderful kingdom on our own."

"I doubt that," Felix said from behind us.

"Felix," I said. "Space, please."

Felix glared at me, but turned and walked to the castle entrance.

"He seems as overbearing as Jozef," she said with a giggle.

"He thinks he is," I replied, turning back to the ocean view. "But I know how to handle him."

"Jozef believes my health to be very delicate. You can't even imagine the tinctures they force me to drink every night."

At that, I had to smile. "I understand the sentiment. But you look fine to me." Sure, she was a little on the thin side, but I chalked that up to a hard life in the desert.

"I feel like we're kindred spirits," she said. "You're what? Eighteen?"

I nodded. "You?"

"Twenty. Jozef and the rest of my ruling tribunal think I'm too young to make any decisions on my own. They coddle me as if I don't see everything around me, as if I'm not observing what they say and how they say it."

"You're telling me," I said with a half-laugh. I was already warming up to her. Barging in unannounced, talking crap about her handlers. We might as well be sisters. "I wish I could help you."

"I appreciate that," she said, patting my arm. "But I have a feeling all parties would be much better served if we did our negotiations in full view. For now, I suppose I need help finding the best inn in the city to stay in."

"You can stay in the castle," I replied with a wave of my hand. "There are a thousand rooms and most of them are empty."

Felix cleared his throat loudly behind me, but I ignored him. I failed to see how letting her stay in the castle would cause an international incident.

"I don't wish to put you out," she said.

"You absolutely aren't," I replied. "And if my so-called 'handlers' get mad at me for inviting someone to stay in my own castle, they can just deal with it."

We returned to the receiving hall, where just two of Ilara's soldiers remained, along with Jozef, who cast me the meanest look he could get away with. The Council had already dissipated, but Garwood and Godfryd remained in the room.

"Lord Garwood, General Godfryd," I said, guiding Ilara over. "Queen Ilara. Ilara, two members of my Council."

They bowed their heads slightly and Ilara curtseyed. "My humblest apologies for barging into your kingdom."

"Indeed," Garwood said, glancing at me with a promise that we would discuss this later. "Princess Brynna, I believe it's time for the queen to return to her ships to rest."

"Yes, about that," I replied. "I think it would be best if she remained in the castle." Garwood's eyebrows shot up, so I added hastily, "If only temporarily, until our nations can conduct discussions formally."

"Ah, well..." He scratched his nose and glanced at Godfryd, whose face was unreadable. "It's unorthodox, but I don't suppose there's any harm."

"Felix," I said, glancing behind me at my red-faced captain, who was most assuredly going to lay into me once we were alone. "We have a few hundred rooms here, right?"

"Seventy-five."

"Can we spare, I don't know, three or four?"

He exhaled. "I'm sure we can make arrangements."

"See? Perfect." I beamed at Ilara, who was staring at the floor. "Ilara, I will leave you in the capable hands of my captain while I speak with my Councilman. And if you'll do me the honor of joining me for an early dinner with Lord Garwood, we can discuss the tariff situation further."

Before anyone could argue, I grabbed Garwood by the arm and led him away.

"Very interesting," he said. "What did she say?"

"She came hoping to talk to August," I said. "She wants us to give her a break on tariffs."

"We can't adjust our tariffs," he said with a shake of his head. "Unless we lower them for everyone. And I don't see a reason to do that. The Severians should just charge more for their goods."

"But then they won't be competitive with Forcadel glassmakers," I replied. "I just think we should consider it at the next meeting. Perhaps there's something we could do to help them."

"I understand your concern," Garwood said, patting my arm. "But your focus needs to be your own people. Let Ilara do what she must to help hers." He paused as I gave him a pleading look. "I'm not saying it's a no, but it's a no right now."

"So what do I need to do to make that no a yes?" I asked.

"I'd say," Garwood rubbed his gray beard, "you should work on Vernice. She sways Godfryd and Octavius."

I scowled. "She hates me."

"Then change her mind," he said, putting his hat on his head. "If it's that important to help the people of Severia, I have no doubt you'll figure out way to do it."

Crossing my arms over my chest, I pouted at his retreating back. I already had enough on my plate between The Veil and preparing to be queen. Getting on Vernice's good side seemed like one too many tasks. But Ilara's complaints hung in the back of my mind. Perhaps if I dealt with Beswick quickly, I could free up some time to help her out, too.

Dinner was less about tariffs and more about Ilara's harrowing journey to Forcadel. Garwood, clearly glad I'd invited him to dine with the queen, was a vociferous dinner guest. When we parted, it was already dark out, and I was itching to put this odd day behind me and get back to the business of treason hunting.

Felix was already waiting for me at the secret exit to the garden with his mask and frown in place. "How was your dinner with your best friend?"

I slowed, resting my hands on my hips. "Jealous?"

"Cautious," he replied. "Don't trust everyone you meet. Especially a queen from a foreign nation."

"Felix, I saw a girl about to be crucified, and I thought I might save her from that humiliation," I replied. "It's clear she didn't mean to just drop in."

"Uh-huh. You really believe that?" Felix asked.

"Everyone's been telling me what a horrible kingdom Severia is, how nobody can live there, everything's difficult. It does not surprise me that she would've gotten news a few weeks late."

"And perhaps, *perhaps*, she's telling you a sob story so you'll give her special treatment," he said. "I can't believe you offered her a whole wing of the castle. We're trying to get ready for your coronation, we can't be dealing with this many guests."

"Felix, come on." I rolled my eyes. "The coronation is in—"

"Two months," he replied. "Eight weeks."

I shuddered. "It's fine. I didn't tell her she could stay until the coronation. We'll just see what we can do for her then send her on her way."

"And I don't like it one bit," Felix said, glaring at the ground with all the animosity he probably felt toward me. "There's something fishy going on."

"You just don't like any of my friends," I said with a mock look.

"Oh, so you're friends now?"

I turned to him, batting my eyes at him and pouting. "Felix, you will always be my number one sidekick."

"Funny," he said with a sneer.

I grinned and nudged him. "At least we know what that big shipment was here for."

"Yes, although I'm not convinced that it was just Ilara," Felix said. "There've been an awful lot of Severians arriving on our shores of late."

"Probably because it's summer, we're having a festival, and they could use some money," I replied. "Isn't that what you said the other day?"

"That was before the queen herself showed up unannounced."

"She's a kitten, Felix," I said as we walked through the grate. "Poor thing is half-starved and desperate."

He gave me a long, piercing look that warmed my cheeks then shook his head. "I think we shouldn't take what she says at face value. Maybe we should go back to Stank's and find out the real reason she's here."

"I'd much rather focus on Beswick," I said. "Considering he's the threat to the kingdom at the moment, and not Ilara."

"You don't know that," he said, stopping in the middle of the road. "I understand that you've got a one-track mind about things —"

"I do *not*."

He crossed his arms and quirked his brow—a feat considering half his face was obstructed by the mask.

"Look, Princess Brynna is monitoring the situation," I said, uncrossing my arms and sticking my hands on my waist. "The Veil is focused on Beswick and his treason."

"So now you're two people?" he asked with a teasing smile as we headed out into the dark streets.

"Well, if you're so concerned, why don't *you* go to Stank's and ask around? Let me focus on Beswick." I shrugged. "After all, *we* are two people."

"What? And let you walk right up to Beswick and get yourself killed?"

"First of all," I said, elbowing him in the stomach, "I don't make moves that will get me killed. And second, as I've been telling you, all I want to do is *listen* to him."

"And as I've been telling *you*, it's impossible to listen to him without being in the room with him, and that's too dangerous."

"Oh, is it now?" I twirled on my heel to face him with a smirk as an idea came to me. "How about this, Captain? If I show you that I can get close to Beswick without him being the wiser, I'll *lend* you the gadget so you can listen in on Ilara. That way we both get what we want."

Now both his eyebrows went up. "Go on."

# Chapter
# Twenty–Two

We returned to the bell tower, and I made a beeline for a trunk in the back of the room. It was where I kept my lesser-used toys, specialty gadgets I'd picked up over the years.

"So how are you planning to listen to him without him knowing?" Felix asked, standing over me.

"Here," I said, pulling a round metal cup attached to a string from the bottom of the trunk. The string was made of a special material, and on the other end was a small metal tube.

"What's this?" Felix asked, as I handed it to him.

"You put that tube inside the room and you can hear what's going on," I said, running my hand along the bottom of the trunk as I searched for the other half of the contraption. "I think it's Niemenian ore, or some kind of ore from the mountains. Kieran got it for me."

"Hmph," Felix said, pressing the cup to his ear. "And how are you going to get this little tube into the room without them knowing?"

"Ah!" I pulled a small hand drill from the bottom corner of the trunk. "Here. You use this to make a hole in the window pane, then slip the tube through. And then you can sit on the ledge and listen all you want."

"Hm," Felix said, reaching into the trunk and grabbing a pair of gloves. "What are these for?"

"Climbing walls," I said, snatching them out of his hand and tossing them back in the trunk then closing it. "C'mon, we've got to find him before we can eavesdrop on him."

Beswick owned many clubs in the city, and while it wasn't a guarantee that he would make an appearance at any of them, he'd never be caught dead in an establishment he didn't own, and he was very careful not to mingle with the crowd. His managers were also paid a lot of money to make sure to know every face—thus infiltration was always difficult. And now I couldn't play the part of faceless patron as Beswick would recognize me.

"But I'm getting ahead of myself," I said, glancing at Felix. I was yammering on like an excited child, but I didn't care. "We need to find out where he'll be first. And for that, we're going to visit Ruby again."

The town square was still bustling, although the later-night crowd was mostly drunks wobbling home from the tavern and some beggars and thieves trying their luck against them. There, as usual, I found Ruby standing in front of her coffee shop, grousing and talking with clients as she flirted her way to higher tips.

I took a seat at the farthest table and waited for her to come find me.

"Ruby, how are you this evening?" I said.

"Fair to middling," she said, leaning over the chair. "It's been a while since you've come to see me. Been busy saving the kingdom?"

"You could say that," I replied. "What's the good word?"

"Celia has a bone to pick with you, as you picked a bone with her favorite lieutenant."

I snorted. "Then maybe her lieutenants shouldn't be threatening innocent girls in my city."

"My dear, you don't want to pick a fight with Celia unless you're ready to take her on."

"Celia isn't my focus tonight," I said. "Curious where Beswick is spending his nights."

"Aren't we all." She rolled her shoulders. "Beswick keeps his movements fairly tight. But I know things. Hear things. For a price."

I dug into my pocket and handed her five of the gold coins in my pocket. "Will that suffice?"

"Oh, my sweet love, it's very expensive information I have. It's not every day you come asking about my employer."

"You work for Beswick?" I said, struggling to keep the surprise out of my voice.

"Everyone works for him down here," she said, gesturing to the surrounding buildings. "But my loyalty is worth a price. As long as you don't speak my name."

"I won't." I pulled another ten coins from my pocket then thought better of it and added what else I had. "Enough?"

"Oh, yes, I believe so," she said, gathering the coins in her hand. "Beswick isn't really well known for staying in the same spots. He likes to inspect his clubs himself, usually by surprise. But there's always someone who knows, and you'll always see a flurry of cleaning at the club he's visiting." She smiled. "Tonight, the Bird's Nest, over near the docks, was getting a good scrub down."

I nodded. "Thank you for this."

"Don't come back to me if my information is incorrect. Sometimes they clean for no reason."

"I have no reason to doubt you," I replied.

I filled Felix in as we made our way down to the Bird's Nest, another seaside bar popular with sailors. Tonight, though, the place was mostly empty, and none of the inn's windows spilled light. That boded well for Ruby's information, and for me.

Felix and I swept around to the back of the place, keeping out of the moonlight to peer into the windows. The taproom was empty, save a few regulars at the bar and a bartender. So we continued around to the back, spotting a lone light coming from the top window.

"I'm going to get up to the second floor," I said to Felix. "The room next to him may be empty, and I can listen in from there."

"Are you sure about this?" he asked.

"Felix, trust me," I said with a grin. "And give me a leg up."

I found some foot holes in the brick and shimmied up the side of the building with my knife between my teeth. Instead of going to the lighted window, I moved to the darker one, one room over. With one hand on the window ledge, I stuck my knife through the joint where the pane met wood and carefully cut through the glue. With a small suction device, I pulled the pane out and stuck my hand through, unlocking the window. Once inside, I pressed the pane back into its spot, reattaching it with a little glue in my pocket.

As I'd suspected, this top room was merely a storage place, filled with boxes of glassware from Severia, the royal seal imprinted on the boxes. Taking extra care not to lean too hard on any of the floorboards, I crossed to the other side of the room and knelt down to the floor. From my pouch, I pulled the small drill and pressed it against the wall, slowly rotating the handle to turn the bit. Once I'd reached the other side, I carefully pulled the instrument out and threaded the metal tube to the other side. Then I pressed the cup to my ear and listened.

"...my good man. Excellent nosh tonight."

I smiled to myself. Beswick was speaking, none the wiser that he was being listened to.

"I was just at the Night Horse, and it's a total shitbox. They've really let it go. May have to fire everyone on the staff. But you, Terrence, you've run a tight ship, even with, well..." He chuckled. "All the shipmen here."

"They're a rough bunch, but good people." Ignacio was in the room with him.

"I'm in the market for another ship again," Beswick said. "Things are moving out in the Vanhoja River, and I'm still trying to recover from that ship I lost last summer."

I smiled to myself. *You're welcome.*

"The Kulkans think that with this new princess in charge of Forcadel, they've got an opportunity to go around me. Well, they have another thing coming. I've got that princess wrapped around my finger. Just where I want her."

*Oh, do you?*

"She's a simpleton. I still don't believe she is who she says she is. And if she is, she's certainly in no position to be queen."

"Do you know where she's been all this time?"

"Art school or something ridiculous. It doesn't matter. I doubt she'll do much to disrupt our business here. Vernice has done a good job of keeping her in check. I think the good lady is hoping I'll lower the rates on Kulkan produce." He chuckled darkly. "She'll keep believing that until she dies, I'm sure."

"Sir, we did receive a note from the Severian delegation that arrived. A request to meet with you."

"Oh, right. The desert-dwellers came in today. Mucking up my ports and causing all kinds of havoc. Bad enough I have them flowing in from the festivals." He paused, and I heard a wrinkling of paper. "Of course, they want to discuss our agreement."

My heart thudded in my ribcage.

*Come on, Beswick. Give me something to work with.*

"I'm not in the habit of meeting with Severians, and I'm not about to start now," he said. "Tell them our agreements remain as they are, and if they want to renegotiate them, I'd be happy to cancel them altogether. Let them try their luck against the bandits along the Niemen river."

"You mean your bandits?"

Beswick chuckled. "The trick, Ignacio, is to lull people into thinking they're your friend. Then they won't see you taking them coming and going."

Beswick continued to wax poetic for some time after that, but his poetry become less lucid the more he drank. But it was clear after I got a cramp on my left thigh that this was a dead end. Not totally, though, as now I knew what to look for to predict his movements.

I let myself out of the room, padding silently down the street as I considered my next move. I needed to be in a room alone with Beswick, and there was very little chance of that happening unless I got very, *very* lucky.

"Well?" Felix asked, when I joined him on the street. "What'd you find out?"

"Beswick has some kind of a protection deal with the Severians," I said, hurrying to leave the bar behind before Beswick's people came out. "I don't know the details, but he said he'd sooner cancel it than renegotiate the treaty. Ilara or someone in her entourage sent him a note to discuss it." I chewed my lip. "Is that treason?"

"Even if it were, all I have is your word," Felix said. "We need concrete proof before I can take action that will stick."

I ran my hand across my sweaty face. "He's not going to meet with the Severians, he said so himself. And most of the activity he's doing is up on the Vanhoja, where their glass comes in. I wonder how much of the two gold pieces per shipment they're giving him."

"Not your concern," Felix said with a warning look. "We need to get back to the castle and see what the others found out."

I nodded. "I mean, short of inviting Beswick to dinner with Ilara, I don't see how I could get anything more out of him."

"So why don't you do that?"

I stopped. "What?"

"Invite him to dine with you," Felix said. "He's a businessman. It's not unheard of for you to entertain leaders and merchants at a private dinner. If Ilara is looking for an audience with him, why don't we give it to her?"

I fumbled for my words, finally spitting out, "Are you serious?"

"Well, if you insist on having Ilara here, might as well use her to flush out Beswick," he said. "But first, we'll need to prepare. And you'll need another round with Kat to relearn the finer points of being a proper dinner guest."

Of course. Always give and take with him. "I feel like you've got an ulterior motive here. If we find out that Beswick is teaming up with Ilara, if we have proof, are you going to use that against her? To expel her from the country?"

He paused. "Not unless we find some reason to."

# Chapter
# Twenty-Three

I wasn't wholly convinced Felix wasn't using this dinner to get at the Severians, but I also couldn't argue that it was an elegant solution to our problem. Beswick may even be so bold as to bring the very proof I needed to the castle. One quick dive into his coat pocket and he would be finished.

"What are you scheming about?" Katarine asked when she arrived at my room the next morning.

"I'm planning a dinner party," I said, sitting up. "How do I go about doing that?"

"Felix told me as much." She sat down, opening a small folder filled with papers. "Normally, you would work with Beata to schedule and plan everything. But as there are some very specific things you wish to accomplish—"

"Pickpocketing a wanted criminal."

"—I've decided to take the planning on myself." She cast me a look under her lashes. "And also, well...you've never arranged a dinner party, so I thought you might want some help."

"As long as Beswick is seated next to me, I don't care what we do."

Katarine smiled. "Be that as it may, it would be a little strange to invite only him to your dinner table. Thus we'll have to think about a larger reason to invite him. I have several proposals here, most of which will perfectly fit the ruse."

"It's important that we invite Ilara as well," I said. "If we can catch the two of them in conversation with each other, even better."

We settled on hosting an introduction dinner, and I penned invitations to each of the most popular merchants. I had no idea who any of them were, but Katarine promised I would be intimately acquainted by the time the dinner started. It grated something in my chest to pen a note to Beswick, but I persevered.

"Excellent," Katarine said, gathering the invitations and handing them to Beata. She made a big show of checking off the first item on her list. "Now, we've still got a full day today. We'll be going to the tailor then paying a visit to the butchery, the vintner—"

"Hold on," I said, swallowing and pointing to my closet. "I have dresses and I thought I had servants to walk around the kingdom and get stuff for me."

"Well, on occasion, it's good for the sovereign to get out among her people," Katarine said then, with a smile, added, "Unmasked, of course. You haven't been seen since the funeral, and Felix is confident that you'll be safe in the city today."

"Uh-huh." That didn't sound like the Felix I knew. "Did you have something to do with this?"

She lifted a shoulder innocently. "Perhaps."

Beata brushed and braided my hair, placing the dainty gold ring on top of my head and securing it with pins. Then, dressed in my finest tunic, pants, and perfectly shined boots, I joined Katarine in a gold-plated carriage pulled by two giant white horses.

"A bit ostentatious, isn't it?" I said, resisting the urge to play with my plait.

"You're the heir apparent," Katarine replied, nodding to the footman as we sat inside on lush, red velvet seats. "There's something to be said about appearances."

"I'll say."

It was odd to watch my kingdom through a glass window instead of from the rooftops. We passed the square, already bustling with merchants and buyers. An older couple passing by stopped and bowed to the carriage, but a group of kids dashed down the street without giving me a second look.

"I received a letter from my brother Luard today," she said with a smile. "He sends his condolences, as does my sister, and they both wish you luck on your upcoming coronation. My sister will be sending an envoy."

"Did your brother say who it would be?"

"No, but I assume it'll be one of my siblings." She smiled warmly, a rarity for her. "It'll be nice to hear the latest from my homeland. Letters only do so much. And Luard isn't the most descriptive person, except when he's describing the girls he's bedded." She pursed her lips. "I'm sure I have more than a few nieces and nephews he hasn't told Ariadna about."

I tried to picture a male version of Katarine doing *anything* except scowling and scolding me, and I couldn't do it. "Which butchery are we going to?"

"Not the one you used to live in."

"Oh." It might've been nice to see Tasha again, and show off my fancy new crown.

"They are the regular butcher for the castle now," Katarine said, catching my eye. "And will remain so as long as they don't divulge that you used to live in their attic and bed their son."

"That might throw off my story about living abroad, wouldn't it," I said with something of a laugh. But I was honestly glad for it —not that they were being bribed into silence, but that Tasha's father was making a good living. He was a decent man, giving scraps and older meat to the beggars on the street instead of throwing it away. Perhaps now he could help more people.

The other butcher had a much smaller store than Tasha's father, but the scent of raw meat put a smile on my face. Behind the counter, a young girl was sweeping blood from a fresh kill, and I could barely take my eyes off her until Katarine nudged me silently, drawing my attention back to the butcher.

"It is our supreme honor to serve you at your first dinner," he said. "Might I suggest a succulent lamb? Or perhaps a seasoned pork roast?"

"I believe we've settled on pheasant," Katarine said with a smile to me. "There will be seven at the table, so perhaps we'll order ten in case of any mishaps."

"Ah, smart thinking, Lady Katarine," the butcher said. "As luck would have it, I have a fresh batch just arrived this morning."

"Then it was meant to be," Katarine said. "Is there anything else you might recommend for an aperitif?"

She and the butcher examined the case of sausage and cheese, discussing which might pair better with what wine. I hadn't seen much of Katarine outside the castle walls, and for the first time, I saw the queen she could have been. No matter how hard I tried, I would never reach her level of sophistication.

"Thank you," I said as we climbed into the carriage.

She smiled. "For what?"

"For sticking by my side," I said. "And doing all this, when I'm sure you probably wish you were the one being fussed over."

She wore a look of surprise, but only for a moment. "August would've wanted me to take care of you, Brynn. Besides that, it's nice to have something to keep me busy." She cleared her throat and checked her perfectly-written list of errands. "Ah, yes. Next we'll be visiting the tailor."

I groaned. "Don't I have enough dresses?"

"Indeed. But we'll be visiting him to do a fitting of your coronation dress," she said. "And picking out some new fabric for your dinner outfit. I was thinking something cream-colored, what do you think?"

"All the better for me to spill wine on..." I grumbled.

The tailor's shop was a tidy little place in Mariner's Row. Titta's bar was around the corner, too. Perhaps this fancy tailor also dressed the dancers on the side. The thought made me chuckle, especially when I saw the same tailor who'd dressed me weeks ago come through the curtains.

"Your Highness," he said with a bow. "How have you been liking your gowns?"

"Oh, um..." I shared a look with Katarine and decided to humor him. "Very lovely. Thank you."

"I'm so thrilled you've come for your first coronation gown fitting," he said, walking to a wooden wardrobe against the wall. He pulled the double doors open to reveal a large white dress with wrist-length sleeves and a neckline that scooped low, but not too low.

"It's gorgeous," Katarine said, joining him on the other side of the room to help him get it down. "Brynna, you're going to look so lovely."

I half-smiled as they brought the gown to me. Small diamonds sparkled from the fabric, casting an intricate pattern like stars in the sky. It was certainly a dress fit for a queen, but I really didn't want to see myself in it. I didn't have a choice, though, as Katarine helped me into the dress in the fitting room.

"Brynna," she kept repeating as the dress settled against my skin. She flitted with the sleeves and smoothed the fabric on my back, tugging at the skirt. "Brynna."

"You can speak, you know." I softened as her eyes filled with tears. "Kat, what is it?"

"You just..." She swallowed, and took my hand. "You look so beautiful."

"Kat." I held her hand closer to me. "What is it? Really."

"It's silly," she said, wiping away tears. "Goodness, I don't even know—"

"Yes, you do," I said, searching for something I could use to wipe her eyes with and settling on my dress sleeves. "Is it what I said in the carriage about August?"

She nodded. "I suppose this is the first time...I've really thought about what might've happened if..." She cleared her throat and struggled to come back to her stoicism. "Not as if I had any great designs on being queen, but..." The tears broke through again. "I really wanted to wear a pretty dress."

At that, we both began to laugh. I wiped Katarine's cheeks again and she helped me out of the dressing room.

"Sorry, Norris," Katarine said, her tears gone in favor of a happy smile. "We were just bonding."

"This dress took quite a while to put together," he said, inspecting the sleeve lengths and pull of the fabric. "It would be devastating if it were to be ruined before the princess's coronation."

I caught Katarine's eye and cleared my throat. "Is it possible to make Lady Katarine a dress?"

"Ma'am?" He looked at Katarine and frowned. "I suppose I could. But it would cost—"

"I don't care. I'll pay," I said, squeezing Katarine's hand. "I want my sister to look as beautiful as I do. Perhaps a lovely blue color, to match her eyes."

Katarine beamed, and not even Norris's under-the-breath comments could wipe the smile from my face.

⟫━━━━━━━➤

We wrapped up our day with a trip to the vintner, where I

smelled a concoction of different wines, but ultimately Katarine made the final decisions. So we piled back into my carriage and headed to the castle. My head hurt from all the action, and probably the wine, and I leaned on Katarine's shoulder.

"I think we've accomplished all we needed to," she said softly, putting away her list and resting her head on top of mine. "Are you going out tonight?"

I sighed. I sure didn't want to. "The city needs me."

"I suppose," she said. "I worry about Felix, though. He's not built like you, for staying out all night. Joella was telling me that he's become a little cranky."

"He's always cranky."

"Felix is actually a lot of fun, once you get to know him." Again, she smiled warmly, and it livened her whole face. "He's just under a lot of stress lately. And I know he hasn't yet mourned August's loss. He hasn't had a chance to."

I thought about what he'd said to me in the church, about how I was like my brother. I would've given anything to hand the crown and all its responsibilities over to him and Katarine, and they would've gladly accepted them. Katarine's loss wasn't just of a husband, but of all the plans and dreams she'd had of being queen. And yet, there she was, helping me take the spot she'd been preparing for her entire life with an understated and beautiful grace.

"What is it?" Katarine asked, smiling at me with that warm, inviting look in her eyes.

"Nothing," I said, settling my head against her shoulder. "Just glad you're on my side."

# Chapter
# Twenty—Four

"One more time," Felix said.

I sat in front of the mirror as Beata brushed my hair, looking at the captain in the mirror. He was already dressed in his finer uniform, the dark blue setting off his brown eyes and purple bags under them. Katarine and I had spent the last three days painstakingly going over every intimate detail of the dinner, but as usual, Felix wanted to hear for himself.

"Seven guests. Four merchants, Lady Vernice, and Beswick," I said. "And Ilara."

"Tell me about the merchants."

"The first, Rosita Finkel, has a good relationship with the Severians. She manages the pathways from the border to the water. She's a short woman with bright red hair. Unclear if she's allied with Beswick."

"Got it. Who else?"

"Aran Stolliday," I said, wincing as a pin dug into my scalp. "Youngest brother of the Stolliday clan. A few years ago, one of the other siblings, Marta, decided to go a little rogue. Use one of her brother's ships to smuggle in some diamonds from Niemen. So I pointed out to Corbit that if he didn't stop his sister from smuggling, I'd sink three of his ships. And to prove I could," I grinned, devilishly, "I sank the one carrying three thousand pounds worth of ore from Niemen."

Katarine gasped, and I was sure the pin digging into my scalp was intentional. "Do you know how much work it took to pull that from the mountains?"

"Relax," I said, moving her hand away. "I switched out the shipping lists with a boat full of produce from Kulka. The ore was fine, the produce not so much, and our fair Corbit got the point."

"Yes, well," Felix said, adjusting his shirt. "None of that is germane to the discussion tonight. Who else are you dining with?"

I thought it entirely germane, but let it go. "Deric Fitzsimmons and Rayne Obuch. Fitzsimmons is a shipbuilder, and Obuch is another merchant, although his domain is to the south with the Kulkans."

"And Vernice and Beswick make six," Felix said.

"What's your plan to get the contracts off Beswick?" I sat a little higher as Beata placed a more ornate crown on my head. I preferred my simple gold band to this, but tonight, I needed to be flashy.

"We'll see how dinner goes," he said. "I doubt we'll be able to pull it off his person during the coat check—he'll be looking for us to remove things. So we've cranked up the heat in the room, and hopefully he'll take off his dinner jacket at some point. Then, if you have an opening, take it."

"And where, pray tell, am I supposed to put it?"

I motioned to the white dress, which flowed out from my hips but was tight around my chest. Much to my chagrin, my breasts were on full display in this outfit. The tailor had taken wild liberties with the cut and stitching. I personally thought I looked like a dancer at Titta's, but both Katarine and Beata had gasped and

195

applauded when I twirled for them. Felix, however, hadn't mentioned it at all, though he kept his eyes averted.

"Ah, I have a solution for that," Katarine said, reaching for the folds of my dress. Where I'd thought there was a seam was actually a deep pocket. "I told Norris you needed a place to put your cheat sheets."

"You're brilliant," I said with a grin. "I think I could fit a few knives in there, too—"

"No, Brynn," Felix said. "No weapons. We can't have the sovereign slicing people up."

"Or worse, you'll slice up your dress," Katarine said, smoothing out the folds.

"Fine, fine," I said, looking at myself in the mirror. For the first time, I thought I actually looked like a princess, what with the crown and the cream-colored dress, and the attendants staring lovingly. And when no one was looking, I slipped one of my knives into my dress and felt a little like myself, too.

My private dining room had been transformed, with the usual garish place settings replaced by much more ostentatious ones. I hadn't thought it was possible to add more gold to the table, but there it was—gold-trimmed plates, goblets, napkin rings—even the silverware was gold. Forcadel flags hung around the room in place of the usual tapestries, and the Lonsdale crest hung right behind the biggest chair at the head of the table. I was loath to sit in it, so I remained standing.

"You'll greet your guests outside," Felix said. "A short service of appetizers and drinks will be served, then you'll make your way in here."

I noted the temperature of the room, which was warm, but not uncomfortable. "And when will you stoke the fires?"

"While you're out there entertaining your guests," he said,

handing me a list. "Some topics you could discuss."

"Thanks," I said, putting the list in my secret pocket next to my knife.

"You're going to do great," he said softly. "Just try to forget about Beswick and enjoy yourself for the first hour."

"Right," I said, glancing down at the dress. "Because walking around in a tent is my idea of an enjoyable time."

"You look beautiful," he said as the door opened. "Now, I think I see your first guests. Go be charming."

I forced a smile onto my face as I walked out into the receiving room. A redheaded woman and a man in a nice suit coat were there, whispering under their breaths. When they saw me, their faces changed immediately.

"Your Highness," Rosita said, curtseying. "It is an honor to be invited to your first dinner. May I introduce my business partner, George Pheros."

"Pleasure," I said, nodding as he bowed. "Let's see about getting some wine, shall we?"

Almost as soon as the words left my mouth, an attendant appeared with a tray of glasses. I plucked one off the tray and raised it.

"Cheers."

"To a long, happy reign," George said.

"To a prosperous reign," Rosita replied.

"Indeed." I took a sip, needing a little more liquid courage to get through the day. "So tell me, Rosita—may I call you Rosita?"

"You may call me whatever you like, Your Highness." The forced smile said otherwise, but I went with it.

"How are things on the western front?"

"Oh." She twirled her drink around. "Well, as well as usual. We can't all have the queen swooping in to help us when we ask."

I furrowed my brow then realization dawned. "You're talking about the ships I sent to assist? Surely the extra guards help you too?"

"No, m'lady," she said, and the truth behind her distaste of me was clear. "There are several trade routes and ports the Severians used. You sent extra ships to Milaard. We trade out of Brockle. There are about three hundred miles between them."

I sipped on my wine, giving myself some extra time. "And how might you resolve that problem? Of the pirates?"

She looked taken aback, sharing a look of surprise with George. "W-well, I might consider upping the reward for pirates on the eastern front. And perhaps increasing military presence on all ports, not just Milaard. Because the Forcadel navy is spread so thin, often there's only the local governor, as the navy moves between all the ports."

I nodded, taking another sip. "I'd like to talk more about this. Piracy concerns me, obviously. Ilara says they deal with it on their end as well."

"Who cares about them?" Rosita said with a snort.

"I do," I said with a cool look. "And if the Severians work with us to resolve the issue, you might benefit from it."

She opened her mouth to argue, but luckily, I was saved by the Stolliday boy. Although I was barely eighteen myself, and the man who walked in was perhaps twenty, he gave the impression that he was a baby. He bowed clumsily and shook Rosita and George's hands.

"My lady, my brother sends his appreciation that you invited our family to your first dinner," he said.

"Sent the child, I see," Rosita mumbled under her breath.

I cleared my throat. "Glad you could join us, Aran."

Fitzsimmons was a tall man with a pencil mustache who offered his congratulations on my impending coronation. Vernice was the next arrival, arm-in-arm with a handsome man with a charming smile, Obuch, I assumed. He seemed to be the only one in the room actually glad to be there.

"It is an honor to meet you," he said, taking a glass from the passing attendant. "I'm looking forward to discussing how we can continue to use our Forcadel navy to enhance our alliances with the Kulkans."

Rosita snorted; she was on her second glass. "You've taken plenty of the navy's time, Obuch. It's time the rest of us got some consideration."

"You are welcome to move your ships to a more prosperous port, Finkle, as am I," he said with a casual shrug.

As they got into it, calmly sniping at each other's businesses, my gaze drew to the door. One final invitee should've been on their way, and I was starting to get antsy.

"Your Highness," Stolliday said, coming to stand next to me. "Are you settling in into your role?"

"Somewhat," I said with a forced smile. Perhaps Felix was just taking his time in inspecting him, or maybe he'd run into trouble. Or maybe, I hoped, Felix had found the contracts, arrested the man, and was coming to tell me so.

"Are we going to dine or are we going to stand around all night?" Rosita asked, now on her third glass.

"One moment," I said, my hopes rising as Felix walked into the room. I hurried over to him, rubbing my sweaty hands on my dress as he pulled me into the corner. "What's going on?"

"He's not coming," he whispered, pulling a small piece of paper from his back pocket. "We just received this."

I snatched the scrawled paper out of his hand and read it three times before understanding what it said. Beswick sent his regrets, but he had a business emergency to attend to.

"An *emergency*?" I growled, crumpling up the paper. "What's more important than meeting *me*?"

"Take a breath," Felix said, glancing behind me at the partygoers, who were undoubtably watching. "We'll try again some other way. Ilara couldn't make it either. Apparently, she's taken ill."

"But now I have to make do with these idiots and there's no upside for me," I said. "Can I fake an illness, too? Maybe I'll throw up."

"Go entertain your guests," he said softly. "It's a good opportunity to try to get on Vernice's good side."

I glared at him, hoping that the string of vulgarities on the tip of my tongue was accurately conveyed, but all it seemed to do was make him laugh.

"Do you want me to join you?" he asked softly. "After all, it's no fun to dine without at least one friend."

I would've rather dined with Beswick, but in the end, I nodded.

It was hard to hide the fury back on my face as I stormed into the dining room. I had the good sense to be patient as an attendant pulled back my chair and I sat down. The rest of the guests took their seats, Felix in the one set aside for Ilara, and I glared angrily at the empty one set for Beswick.

"Is the queen not joining us?" Rosita asked.

"Ah, no," I said, grabbing my napkin from the plate. "She has taken ill."

"Perhaps she shouldn't have traveled so far from home," Vernice said, fanning herself. "It may be my age, but it's awfully toasty in here, isn't it?"

"Yes," I said, waving my hand. "Tell the attendants to put out the fires, we're warm enough."

"But—"

"I said," I smiled thinly, "we're warm enough."

The attendant nodded and set about the room, as the first course arrived, a green vegetable soup that Katarine had picked out a few days before.

"So we were just discussing your navy," Obuch said, his spoon delicately perched in his hand. "It seems you've sent a fleet to help out our neighbors to the north. Does this have anything to do with Queen Ilara's arrival?"

"No," I said, pushing the green, creamy liquid around in my bowl. Damn, it was hard not to pout.

An awkward silence followed as they waited for me to continue.

"I'm concerned," I began slowly, "with something Ilara did tell me though. Apparently, the Severians are paying for protection from some unknown parties."

"Why don't they just use their own people to protect their shipments?" Vernice asked.

I picked up my fresh goblet of wine and lifted it to my lips, wondering if getting drunk was an acceptable alternative to this nightmare dinner. But I stopped myself before I put it to my lips, smelling something...new. The wine I'd been drinking had been a pungent red, the bitterness contrasting nicely with the powerful flavors of the pheasant. But this glass smelled sweet.

Almost like poison.

"Are you all right?" Stolliday asked.

"I'm feeling a touch under the weather myself," I replied, putting the goblet down and wishing I could throw it across the room. I casually lifted my fingers to my nose, smelling for traces of poison there, but blessedly finding nothing. It must be confined to my goblet.

"Something amiss with your wine?" Vernice asked, hesitantly.

A smile curled onto my lips. "Why so interested in my food, Vernice? Something here that I absolutely *must* try?"

Felix caught my gaze and his brow furrowed.

"Because it seems to me that this wine has soured somewhat," I said, picking it up and smelling it again. There was no doubt now —it was poisoned. "But please, try it and tell me your opinion."

"I have my own," she said, but didn't reach for her glass.

"I would try it," Aran said, reaching across the table.

I pulled the glass out of his reach, shaking my head. "Unless you'd like it to be your last, I wouldn't. My drink has been poisoned."

Vernice laughed loudly, a noise that sounded guilty. "Poisoned? Your Highness, you must be getting paranoid."

"Must I be?" I replied. "Then I welcome you to drink it."

Her eyes narrowed. "I have had enough, thank you. But perhaps your captain could try it."

"Perhaps he could," I said, rising to my feet. "Believe me, it's crossed my mind more than once to poison the man, but as it stands, I need him to arrest you."

Felix cleared his throat as he rose from the table. "A word, Your Highness."

I followed him out of the dining room and into the main hall, still within sight of the guests, who were watching me with unabashed curiosity. I kept my gaze on Vernice, who was conferring with Obuch and one of her attendants.

"First of all, you have no proof it was Vernice," Felix said, gently turning my chin back to look at him. "So quit staring at her like you're going to murder her."

I blinked at him. "The cup is poisoned, I promise you. And based on her reaction—"

"You can't hang a woman on her reaction," Felix said. "And if you go around accusing your Council of poisoning you—"

"What?" I said. "Did you see the look on her face?"

"Lower your voice," Felix commanded, and I nearly saw red.

"Don't you *dare* say that to me again," I said, poking him in his velvet-clad chest. "And if you won't do the work to get rid of this murderer then maybe The Veil will. If I hadn't smelled that poison, I'd be the third royal dead. Not a great way to start your career as captain of the guard, Felix."

He brushed off my jab. "The Veil would do well not to go after a Councilwoman. Vernice is well-liked and, more importantly, well-connected. It smacks of paranoia to accuse her of attempted murder, especially on such flimsy evidence."

"Then I will *find* better evidence," I snarled, spinning and walking out of the room.

"And where are you going?" Felix asked. "What about your dinner party?"

*"Where do you think?"*

# Chapter
# Twenty—Five

I donned my mask and hood that night, filled with righteous indignation. I was to be queen and still had no power to vanquish my enemies. I knew—in my gut—Vernice was the one who'd ordered my poisoning.

Unfortunately, I was stopped before I even began.

"You can't murder a Councilwoman," Felix said, leaning against the garden wall as I passed by. He was still in his uniform, his sword at his side.

"I told you, The Veil doesn't kill," I said. "If she did, Beswick would be a dead man already."

"Fine, you can't maim her either," he said, following behind me. "I don't arrest you because the people like what you do, however illegal it may be. If you hurt Vernice, I will have no choice."

I straightened. "You would arrest your princess?"

"I'd have no choice but to unmask you." He put his hands on my shoulders. "I've already got my men questioning the kitchen staff. It was poison in your glass, by the way. And yes, Vernice is one of our suspects."

"No shit." I stepped away from him. "So why the lying in the dining room?"

"Because I can't very well tell the subject of my investigation that she's being investigated," he replied. "I had to make her think I wasn't going to do anything, so when I do, she doesn't have time to cover her tracks."

Shifting from foot to foot, I tried to find fault with him. "Well, you waited too long."

"Joella left the room the moment you mentioned poison," he said, coming to stand behind me. "I've been expecting this for some time, and they know what to do."

I was grateful for my mask, because it hid my red cheeks. Perhaps he wasn't as stupid as I'd thought. "I'm not going sit idly by while someone out there tries to kill me. You can't ask me to do that. Not when you know I can help."

He exhaled loudly and yanked a piece of paper from his trousers. "We're starting with the staff. Here's a list of them. I'm giving you this—" He pulled it out of my grasp as I reached for it. "Brynna, I'm *giving* you this with your promise that you won't threaten, maim, or hurt anyone on the list. And that you won't go after Beswick or do anything stupid."

"I could give two shits about Beswick tonight," I growled. Then, I realized what he was saying. "So...you're trusting me?"

"I trust that you're more fired up about the poisoner than Beswick." He took a step back. "But don't be surprised if we find him first. We're very good at what we do."

"I'm so sure."

⊃———————

My first stop of the night was Stank's. If the poisoner had spent any time in the slums, John would know. I arrived at the bar in record time, enjoying the return to freedom without Felix trailing me, but also kind of missing his constant breath on my shoulder. Pushing open the bar door, I searched for familiar faces and saw few. The room was filled with Severians, which I supposed made sense considering the numbers Ilara had brought. They paid me little attention, talking in low voices as they played a dice game I'd never seen before.

"Evening," Frank said. "John's in the back."

"Thanks," I said, throwing a couple coins on the bar.

"Ah, my dear Veil," John said, sitting against the window. "Sorry I missed you a few weeks ago, and for meeting back here. All these Severians hanging around." He shuddered. "I've made one too many bad deals with them and they aren't very fond of me."

"So they don't know you own this place?" I asked, walking closer.

He nodded, kicking out the chair for me to sit. "Nobody else is in port, either. Nothing but Severians as far as the eye can see. Kieran was supposed to be back this week, but I doubt he can even get into the bay."

"Are they all here for Ilara?" I asked.

"No, apparently they're all here for the summer festival," he said, shaking his head. "Beswick opened the floodgates and let as many of them in as could fit on a boat. Surprised they even know how to sail."

"Yes, well..." I cleared my throat. "There was an attempt on the princess's life tonight. A poisoning. Know anything about it?"

His brows shot up—not a good sign. "Poor girl. Somebody's trying really hard to make sure the Lonsdale line ends."

"Luckily for us, she can scent a poison," I said, thankful my anger at Beswick not showing up hadn't gotten the better of me. Had I not been paying attention, things could've turned out quite differently. "I take it you know nothing about it?"

"When the prince died, there was some talk around here, but it disappeared pretty quickly. Nothing concrete, of course, just rumors. You know how it goes. They say it was done by someone in the kitchens."

"The captain's searched the kitchens, hasn't found a trace of it. And they're pretty good about keeping track of who's touched the royals' food—for obvious reasons. And I saw...know that the princess's wine came from the same bottle as the rest of the room's, so—"

"Ah, yeah, but..." He picked up the goblet next to him. "Are you checking the glasses?"

My mouth fell open and I hopped to my feet. "John, you're worth your weight in gold."

And with that, I dumped the contents of Felix's coin purse on the table and ran from the room.

Of course, of *course*. It would've been the person who set the table. It was the perfect crime—Felix and his men would've been so focused on the food that they never would've suspected. As soon as I was out of the bar, I yanked the list from my pocket, scanning the names and their roles. I was beginning to worry that Felix had missed the place setters; after all, they hadn't been on his suspect list. But there they were at the bottom.

Most of them lived in the poorer neighborhood in the northeast, so I took off toward that side of town. Would they have left? Or would they be so confident in their cover-up that they remained at home? My heart pounded in my chest as I turned the corner to the first house...

Only to stop short—Felix's men were putting a man into a carriage in handcuffs.

"I told you."

I nearly jumped out of my skin at his voice behind me. "Don't scare me like that!"

"I thought you would've heard me," he said with a smirk, coming to stand next to me. "Bit distracted tonight."

"It was poison on the glass," I said then deflated. "And it appears you came to the same conclusion."

He nodded. "One of the maids mentioned she'd poured the wine from the same bottle. Therefore, it made sense not to look at the kitchen staff, as we had with your brother and father, but the one who set the table." His smirk grew. "And thus we found our poisoner."

"And?" I said, breathlessly. "Was it Vernice?"

"It was not," Felix said. "His name is Horace and he says he's working alone. Anarchist, wishes the entire royal family dead."

I narrowed my eyes. "That's bullshit."

"It's plausible," Felix said. "And until he says differently, that's where this investigation ends. He'll be tried for the deaths of your father and brother and hanged, probably."

I stared at the carriage. What could Vernice have over him that he would willingly give up his life for her?

Soft cries drew my attention. I craned my neck to see two small children in the window, tears falling down their faces. A woman appeared behind them, her face red and wet, and hurried them away from the opening, closing the glass behind her.

"He's being paid off," I said.

"He owes ten thousand gold pieces to Beswick," Felix said. "That debt is probably paid and then some. I assume his children will now be able to attend school."

I swore filthily under my breath. "So this was Beswick's doing?"

"No. I think that the debt was merely an incentive." He stared at the dark window. "Find the man with nothing to lose and everything to gain, that sort of thing." He sounded tired, but I wanted him to be angry. I wanted him to be looking until he uncovered the truth, not taking the word of a man who was offering his head so his children would live.

"What if I offered him twice what he was being bribed?" I put my hands on my hips. "He gets to live, his kids get their father, and I get Vernice."

He sighed. "If it *was* her, she could just say he's lying to save his skin. It's her word against a signed confession."

"*Damn* it, Felix," I growled. "Why aren't you on my side?"

"I am *always* on your side," he said, pointing to the crest at his left breast. "Which is why I'm trying to keep you from making a mistake. Whoever tried to poison you will make another move, of that I'm sure."

I looked up at the window, now dark. "And what about Horace, hm? Just throw an innocent man in jail?"

"We'll draw out the proceedings," Felix said. "He'll stay in the dungeon, but at least he'll be alive. Once we get to the bottom of things, he'll be a free man."

I swallowed.

"Patience, Brynn. Sometimes you have to let the small fish pass to be ready for the big one."

I was tired of his wise words, especially as I couldn't argue with them right now.

# Chapter
# Twenty–Six

I was wide awake when Katarine arrived. Felix hadn't yet filled her in on our eventful night, although she, too, doubted Vernice was responsible.

"What would she have to gain from killing you?" she asked. "Or your brother, for that matter? If she wanted the treaty disrupted, she would've been better off killing me."

"An innocent man is going to prison," I said, pacing in front of the window. "I'm so glad you can be blasé about the murderer of your husband."

"I'm not blasé about anything, Brynn," she replied with a small sigh. "We have no proof that she's guilty, other than your very keen gut. And even if she was, you don't know if she killed your father and brother."

I pursed my lips. "If it worked twice before…"

"I know you're eager to find out who might be after you, but there's no use jumping to conclusions," she said patiently. "If you publicly accuse Vernice and she's *not* the one then you'll be branded a liar. Or worse."

I ground my teeth instead of answering. It wasn't fair. Horace was innocent, but Felix was just taking his forced confession and waiting for the murderer to strike again. Worse, everyone else was doing the same. Garwood and Vernice had stopped by to congratulate me on finding the poisoner (and for, I suppose, not dying the night before). I glowered at Vernice, not even bothering to hide my disgust at her. I hated this feeling of being handcuffed and having no recourse—or even an idea of how to get out of this.

Ilara had asked me to dine with her, as an apology for missing the dinner the night before, so instead of stewing, I dressed in a dinner gown and met her in my private dining room. I'd intended to discuss the tariff situation with her, perhaps strategizing the best way we might approach the council, but I ended up just venting about the investigation, leaving out, of course, my vigilante part in things.

"And you think this man is innocent?" she asked.

"Yes," I said. "It's a gut feeling. He's got a wife and children. There's no way he'd risk all of that just for...anarchy. But I can't prove that he's being paid off, not until he changes his confession. Not without jeopardizing his family."

She tapped her hand against her chin thoughtfully. "If you don't believe it was him, then who are your suspects?"

For that, at least, I had no good answers. Obviously Vernice. Perhaps even Beswick—especially as I still didn't know if he knew I was The Veil. But would he go to so much trouble to kill me? Surely it would be worse for business if I was dead, even if I was also trying to take him down? It was suspicious that he'd declined my invitation.

"Didn't you say you were conducting your own investigation?" she asked when I didn't respond. "I take it the trail has come up similarly cold?"

"Yes, but that's my fault," I said. "I've been too preoccupied with other matters and I let this one fall to the wayside."

"Running a kingdom is a lot of work," Ilara said with something of a sympathetic look. "I've left my advisors in charge, and I'm still bombarded by letters every day. Your advisor is...the Lady Katarine?"

I nodded. "She was married to my brother."

"She seems quite strict with your time. I hear she keeps you locked in your room all morning." Ilara cast me a worried look, as if she was afraid she'd overstepped.

"There's a lot to cover," I said, trying to pull my attention back to the dinner. "And I don't mind spending time with her, really. She's nice, once you get to know her."

"I suppose I'm just surprised that you trust her," Ilara said, running her spoon along the plate. "I mean, her husband died. Wouldn't she be the prime suspect in his murder?"

"Believe me, that was my thought at first, too," I said. "But I guess it doesn't make sense. Why would she kill her husband—especially without any heirs? It would've been better if he'd lived."

"Forgive me, but...she doesn't appear to be a woman in mourning," Ilara said then shook her head quickly. "I'm sorry, that was out of place. I shouldn't be lecturing you on who to trust. You're smarter than I am, anyway."

I smiled. "No, your instincts are good. But I thoroughly vetted her, and I'm not convinced she had a motive."

"Some might point to you as the culprit," Ilara said thoughtfully, tapping her finger against her chin. "Perhaps even poisoning your own glass to throw off suspicion."

At that, I laughed. "Anyone who's been around me for more than five minutes would know that's not the case. I was perfectly happy in my life until Felix came barging in. August would've made a better sovereign than me, Kat a better queen. I'm just... trying not to screw up."

"Let me let you in on a little secret about us royals," Ilara said, leaning across the table. "None of us know what we're doing."

"Yeah, but most of you have been bred for this kind of thing," I replied, sitting back. "You've been doing this for a while. I got thrust into this a month ago."

"True." She picked at her food. "If I were you, and I'm merely offering this as a suggestion, I'm sure you thought of it already—"

"It's fine," I said with a wave of my hand. "What is it?"

"Perhaps it's time to take control of the investigation," Ilara said, casting me a nervous look. "Ask your captain if you can interrogate him yourself. You have a very kind face, Brynna. Perhaps he might change his tune. Especially if you promise immunity to his family."

"Then Ver...whoever put him up to it would say that he was lying," I said, shaking my head. "Just trying to save his skin and his family."

"Then perhaps he can give you something to work with," she said. "After all, sometimes the smallest clue can lead to the biggest discoveries."

⇒————→

I had my doubts that Princess Brynna could get the man to talk, but perhaps The Veil could. In any case, it was worth a shot, as Riya reported they'd gotten nothing out of the man after a night of questioning. She escorted me down to the training greens early, where Felix was conducting a drill with his youngest soldiers. If I had to guess, I would've pegged them at ten or eleven. Each wore the same look of focused discipline as they jogged around the courtyard, remaining stoic even as Felix barked orders to them.

"Quit nagging them," I said, coming to stand next to him. "They look fine to me."

"A good unit remains in sync," Felix said, his focus on the children. "If they think, eat, breathe, and move the same, they'll have each other's backs. And a good unit remains thick, no matter the circumstances."

"As thick as you, Riya, and Joella?" I asked. "They think the world of you, you know?"

"I know," he said. "What can I do for you? I'm obviously a little busy. We're not scheduled to meet until after dark."

"I want to interrogate the prisoner," I said. "As The Veil."

"I...don't think that's a good idea," Felix said, before raising his voice to yell, "*Halt!*"

The twenty kids came to a stop in unison then turned to face him.

"Marten, your turn was a half-second too slow. Paulson, you're now a breath too fast, pull it back some. The rest of you are fine. Now, get to the weapons arena and pair off. I want to see some bruises on your arms later."

The soldiers saluted with a loud grunt then dispersed in an orderly fashion.

"Why do you want to talk to the prisoner?" Felix said, turning to me.

"Because I think I could do better than you can," I said, watching the children dissipate. Yet again, I was strongly reminded of Celia's camp.

"Can you? I think we proved last night that we're more than capable."

I scowled. "You got lucky."

"*We* don't get lucky. We do our job. And you should let me handle it. You have enough on your plate."

Another set of soldiers—this time looking thirteen years old—came marching in. "Felix, just let me question him. It's not a matter of who's better at their job. You're the Captain of the Royal Guard and I'm a vigilante. If anything, he's probably more willing to trust that I won't murder him after he speaks. And I'm better able to use the information he gives me. I was talking with Ilara—"

He turned to me, eyes wide. "You spoke to the Severians about this?"

"Just in basic terms," I said. "It's fine, we have a queen-to-queen agreement going on."

"Does that agreement include when she and the rest of her group are leaving?" he asked. "Because it's getting a little ridiculous that she's still in the castle."

"I like her company," I said. "And she still may be our ticket to Beswick's contracts."

"Did you ask her if she knew about them?"

"Well, no..." I cleared my throat. "We haven't broached the subject of Beswick yet. I don't want to tip him off. But for right now, I want to focus on the poisoner. This may be our last chance to find out who's behind all this."

Felix chewed his lip. "Fine. I'll rearrange the schedule so our guards are the ones watching him. Don't go down there until I give you the signal."

"Sure thing."

"And don't..." He sighed. "Don't get physical with him. Remember, he's—"

"I know he's innocent," I replied. "That's why I want to talk to him."

For all my bluster, I wasn't sure how I would get through to Horace. He was motivated by love for his family, which meant he was pretty much immovable. Unless, of course, I could promise protection for them. It wasn't impossible, especially if I knew who was putting him up to all of this.

When the clock struck eleven, I pulled the mask over my face and descended the desolate staircase. Joella was at the door, nodding at me as I breezed past her into the basement of the castle. Felix waited for me at the end of the hall, saying nothing as he unlocked the cell door and left it open for me. The stench of refuse and death came at me, but it wasn't the worst thing I'd ever smelled before.

Horace lay on a pile of hay, his pale face reflecting the torchlight. There was no light in his eyes.

"Do you know who I am, Horace?" I asked, lowering my voice.

He nodded, barely.

"Who hired you to kill the princess?"

He opened his mouth to speak, but nothing came out except a wheeze. He blinked a few times then tried again—and still, nothing but air.

I knelt beside him and close to his mouth. I smelled something sweet—death.

"*Shit.*" I jumped to my feet and ran out the cell, leaving it open —he couldn't escape even if he wanted to. Felix was waiting at the end of the hall, and he looked up in concern when I ran to him.

"Something's happened to our informant," I said. "He's been poisoned."

While Felix tended to him, checking his pulse and asking questions Horace had no chance of answering, I picked up the wooden glass he'd been drinking out of and sniffed. There it was— that same sweet poison someone had intended for me.

"I don't know if I can do anything for him," Felix said.

"I might be able to," I said, looking out of the cell. "I know of a Nestori woman outside the city who may be able to identify the poison and whip up an antidote before he dies. But I have to leave now. And you can't—"

He met my gaze. "Where is it?"

"She lives about a few hours' ride from here," I whispered, not wanting to tell him the truth. "If I leave now, I can be back before dawn."

He clenched his jaw, as if on the verge of telling me no, but instead said, "Who are you meeting?"

"An old friend," I replied. "She won't talk to me if you go with me, though. So I have to go alone."

"Brynn—"

"Felix, look, if you want answers, I can get them for you, but we're going to have to bend the rules a little bit, okay?" I rested my hand on his arm. "I don't want this guy to die, so I have to go now. I promise, I'll ride out and ride back as quickly as I can."

He nodded. "Be careful no one sees you leave. And be back soon."

# Chapter Twenty-Seven

Riya helped me tack up a horse quickly, and then I was off, galloping through the dark city with my mind racing. I had no idea if it was a Kulkan poison or not, but the Nestori were experts in the earth sciences, as they called them. I just hoped I was quick enough to save Horace's life.

I traveled under the bright moon, the wind whipping at my face. If I'd half a mind to, I could've continued running to the Kulkan border and beyond. But a man needed my help—an innocent man, I was convinced.

The city of Forcadel may have been the most populated, but the country was vast. Looking at it on a map was nothing compared to galloping across the low, grassy hills that spanned as far as the eye could see. Every so often, I'd make out a small village or trading post along the way, or maybe even a one-house farm.

After a few hours, a forest appeared in the distance, and my hands began to shake. I hadn't been back here in a long time, and there was no guarantee I'd even be let in the front gates. But it was my only option, and if it required me to eat crow, so be it.

And the large bag of coins in my saddlebag didn't hurt, either.

Almost as soon as my horse hit the tree line, the whistles began. Codes from sentries in the trees, telling other sentries about my location, my physical appearance, my direction. The message would get carried back to Celia before I reached her, and she'd decide whether I was welcome or not.

The fortress appeared out of nowhere, large tree-trunk walls with sharpened point tips, two large torches out front. The thick gates remained closed, and my heart sank.

But as I drew closer, there was movement—the gates were opening. I exhaled in relief; Celia wouldn't let me inside to kill me. She had plenty of people to do that out here.

The horse came to a stop in the center of the small village. Houses for sleeping, eating, laundry, and more lined the perimeter, and in the center, the weapons house, the small training arenas. It hadn't changed from when I'd run away from here in a panicked state, but I hadn't expected it to.

I dismounted and held onto the reins as a shadowy figure walked toward me. She stepped into the light and my heart began to pound in my chest.

Celia looked as young and fierce as the day I'd first laid eyes on her at thirteen. She had Nestori ancestry, but I was sure it was greed that kept her looking so young. She wore a pair of leather breeches and a long white tunic, her black hair cut short around her ears.

But the smile on her face, that was the most foreboding.

"Hello, Celia," I said as evenly as I could.

"Well, good evening." Her voice was smooth, touched with amusement and something else. It didn't escape my notice that she hadn't addressed me yet—by the name I went by in camp, Larissa, or my real one. "To what do I owe the pleasure of your visit?"

"I need Nicolasa's help," I said, turning to face her fully.

"So you need *my* help," she corrected with a knowing look.

"Surprised you're asking. You've amassed quite a debt, you know."

I tossed a bag of gold on the ground. "There. Happy?"

"Gold is meaningless," Celia said.

I tried not to roll my eyes. "It's kind of important, and time-sensitive. A man is dying, and I need an antidote. So please, take the gold and let me talk to her."

Celia motioned to her left and I took off running. Nicolasa and Callum were the healers in the camp, as they could do things with plants that normal doctors couldn't. Nicolasa, in particular, was fluent in the magical sciences. If anyone would know what the poison was, it was her.

"Nicolasa?" I said, walking into the healing hut.

"L-Larissa?" The Nestori woman poked her head out of the back room, surprise evident on her face. She was Forcadelian, with long black hair that she'd tied at the base of her neck, and a kind face that remained so even after all the sadness she'd endured here. She was usually the first person new kids saw when they arrived.

"My sweet girl," she said, walking over to me and cupping my face. "Did they catch you finally? Are you back for good?"

I didn't know the story Celia had told anyone, if there even was one, so I shook my head. "I just need a little help from you. It's about a poison."

"Have you ingested it?" she asked.

"No." I pulled the goblet from my bag and handed it to her. "Can you identify it?"

She sniffed it. "Smells like aranecea, a quick acting poison. It's a wild leaf that grows in the northern part of the country. Far away from here, close to Kulka."

So it was a Kulkan brew. "Any ideas who might be trafficking in the stuff?"

She tipped the goblet over in her hands, thinking. "It's a fairly uncommon poison in Forcadel, but Nestoris use it often to burn off warts and whatnot."

"You don't have any here, do you?"

"Not that I know of," she said. "Where did you get this goblet? And who's trying to poison you?"

"It's not me," I replied. "It's the...princess of Forcadel. This was her goblet and she and I both think it's the same poison that killed her father and brother, too. Luckily for her, she sniffed it out before she drank it."

"Lucky indeed. This poison isn't an easy death," she said. "It starts with horrific pain, like your stomach is burning a hole in your insides. Then you sweat and thirst like you've never had a drop in your life. Finally, you lose feeling from your toes all the way up to your fingertips. You die because you can no longer breathe."

"The prime suspect is currently suffering from it," I said. "Which further proves that he's a mere puppet. But a puppet with children and a wife who'd like to see him live a few more decades."

"The prince's wife, did she mention similar symptoms when he died?" Nicolasa asked.

"She said she just woke up and he was dead," I said.

"Then it's not the same poison," she said. "Or the prince's wife is lying to you. It's always the spouse, you know."

"I don't think it is in this case," I said with a chuckle. "Do you think you can brew an antidote for it?"

"Can the man speak?" she asked.

I shook my head. "Just air through his lips."

"Then it is too late for him," she said. "The poison has taken root in his body. He'll be dead by dawn."

"Clearly whoever hired him didn't want him to talk," Celia said, making me jump. I glanced over my shoulder to where she stood, leaning against the doorpost with a curious look on her face. The hairs on my neck rose, but I kept my face passive.

"Excuse me, Larissa," Nicolasa said, ducking her head as she rose. "I have to tend to my crops out back."

I didn't want to be left alone with Celia, but I also didn't want to show her weakness.

"So..." she began softly, walking to the bowls bearing leaves and flowers. "You've been busy these past few weeks."

"I'm sorry I barged in unannounced," I said then paused. "And for Jax."

"Jax had it coming, I'm sure," she said with a small chuckle as she plucked a white flower from the bowl. "I told you that you'd be back in power one day."

"Oh?" I quirked a brow. "Premonition? Or premeditated?"

"I don't think you'd be here if you thought I was responsible," she said. "And besides, why would I want *you* dead, my lovely little princess?"

"Doesn't mean you didn't kill the other two," I replied, leaning back on the table. "So eager to get me on the throne that you cleared a path?"

"I think your time in the castle has made you paranoid," she said, tossing the flower back into the bowl. "It's certainly made you a little stupider."

"In what way?"

"Come on, Larissa," she said, crossing her arms over her chest. "Do you really think, if a Kulkan was responsible, they would use a Kulkan poison?"

"I don't see why they wouldn't."

She glanced at the ceiling. "If you were a peasant and the only people involved were the local authorities, perhaps. But we're talking about the deaths of kings and princes. Your Captain Llobrega is no slouch, and neither are you. It's not hard to believe you both would uncover the truth rather quickly."

"So you're saying they wanted me to think it was a Kulkan?" I said slowly then nodded. "Because they're trying to frame someone. Vernice, perhaps."

"Or, perhaps, distract you from something else entirely," Celia said. "If I were you, I would ask myself what's to be gained by murdering the princess? Or at the very least, what's to be gained by sending her on a two-day wild goose chase when the main suspect is as good as dead already?"

"Discord on the Council, anarchy. Exactly what the prisoner said he was after." I shook my head. "Perhaps that's the end of it, after all."

"I don't believe that, and I don't think you do, either," she said, pushing herself off the table. "You've got a long ride back to the kingdom. I suggest you spend some of that time thinking about it."

She was almost to the door when I spoke again. "If I'm back in power, as you say, why haven't you come to ask me for a favor yet?"

"Because I have nothing to ask," she said, with a light shrug. "Life is good in the camp, for now. Besides, you're young. I may need something in ten years."

I rolled my eyes. "So I'm just supposed to wait for that day?"

"I suppose you could ask your captain to bring his soldiers here and raze the place, if you were so inclined." She winked and closed the flap behind her.

It was, indeed, a long ride back to Forcadel. I mulled over Celia's advice, bouncing through ideas and scenarios as fast as I could think of them. The only real solution I came up with was that perhaps there was someone trying to sow discord on the Council. Vernice was out; she was too smart to use a poison that could be traced back to her.

I supposed Niemen could be behind it, and by extension, Katarine. And as little sense as that made to me, I still had a duty to pull that thread until it unraveled or ended.

When I arrived back in the stables, the sky was turning pink. I handed my horse off to Riya and kept walking until I reached the dungeons. But the soft sound of crying told me the man had already passed. Felix and his guards stood at attention, and the woman I'd seen the night before was crying over the dead body of her husband. Her two children were nearby, their tears quiet, but no less heartbreaking.

Felix caught my eye, and we walked to a private spot. "Did you find an antidote?"

"Yes, but it was too late for him anyway," I said, showing him the vial. "The poison starts with stomach pains then slowly paralyzes the body." I gave him a side-eye. "Was that...how August died?"

"No stomach pains," Felix said. "He just didn't wake up. It doesn't sound like it was the same potion."

"We should ask Katarine, to be sure," I said. "She was the last person to see him alive." I looked over my shoulder. "Did you get anything from his wife or children?"

"The first they'd heard of him being involved was when we arrested him," Felix said.

"How did someone get in to poison him?" I asked. "I thought your guards were keeping an eye on him?"

He swallowed hard, glaring at the wall. "I have a feeling...there might be a problem in my ranks. I'd hoped it wouldn't come to this, that it was just my failure to protect August and your father. But I had a tight guard around him. People I trusted. Either someone's not doing their job—"

"Or they're involved," I said. "I'll ask Katarine about August. If we know what we're looking for, we could isolate the poison." I looked behind me as the wife and children walked out of the cell, covering their faces as they wailed in misery. "I don't believe it's Vernice, though."

"Why not?"

"Too sloppy," I said. "If a Kulkan was trying not to get caught, they wouldn't use a poison from their homeland. But if they were trying to frame someone, they would." I ran my hand across my face. "At least, that's what Celia thought—"

He grabbed my arm. "Celia? You spoke to..." His face went slack. "The Nestori was Celia's."

"Nicolasa is her name," I said, staring into the dark prison cell. "She's the only one I know who would know about the poison, and she did. Celia just happened to wonder why I decided to show up for the first time in three years." I loosed a shaky laugh. "Surprised she didn't ask for that favor she's been talking about. I mean, I'm back on the throne, I'm sure she'll be knocking—"

"Brynn." Felix rested his hands on my shoulder. "Say the word and I'll take care of her for you."

I brushed his hand off. "She's not our biggest problem right now. There's a murderer on the loose and our best lead just died." I exhaled, shaking my head. "I just hope it was worth it to him."

# Chapter Twenty-Eight

I spent the morning pacing my room, thinking about what I'd missed and how I might pick up the trail. Everyone was a suspect, and no one was. It was hard not to get discouraged, especially as Beswick had taken a backseat and my timeline to deal with him was growing shorter by the day.

I was now convinced that, although Vernice wanted me off the throne, she wasn't trying to kill me. At least not actively. Beswick remained a suspect as well, but only because I wanted him involved in some way. And although Katarine and the Niemenians were also suspects, that wasn't a bridge I was willing to cross until I had more information, especially as Felix wouldn't take kindly to me investigating his only remaining best friend.

But if I was going to find a killer, I needed to go back to the previous murders and investigate. Perhaps I would uncover something that Felix and his team missed.

The next morning, I had Felix take me to my father's quarters on the top floor of the east wing of the castle. He unlocked the engraved double doors at the end of a long hallway, revealing a sitting room that was bigger than the entire butchery I'd been living in. Gold adorned everything, from the chairs to the columns —even the red velvet drapes had gold stitching. Ostentatious could take a lesson.

"You know how many people we could feed by selling one of these drapes?" I said, nodding to the floor-to-ceiling windows.

"It will ease your mind to know most of this was here before your father took possession, and that when August was to be king, he asked if he could redecorate."

"Can I?"

"Absolutely." He smiled. "You're free to move in whenever you like, as well."

"Oh?" I spun around. "You trust me that much now?"

"You've left the castle twice and come back unscathed," he said, brushing past me. "But when we get back to Beswick's investigation, I'm going with you."

"Fine," I replied. Did I actually miss him? "Just take me to his bedroom."

The room was a bit homier than the other rooms, with a large bed in the center and floor-to-ceiling curtains on the window. There was a musty scent to the room, but I only supposed that was because it hadn't been touched in several weeks.

"What did you want to see?" Felix asked.

"I don't know," I replied, walking to the small table in the corner of the room. It was similar to the one I took my meals on. "What did he have for dinner the night before he died?"

"Some braised fish, potatoes and carrots. He ate with Garwood." Felix spun around. "His man found him not breathing when he brought breakfast."

"Did you keep the dishes?"

"Obviously not, as we had no idea he'd been poisoned," Felix said, leaning against the wall. "But we questioned everyone with access to his food. Most have worked in the kitchen for decades."

"So had our place setter," I said with a pointed look. "I wish we could've questioned him more before his death. Did he tell you *anything*?"

"No," Felix said. "Other than confessing to the crime, of course."

"Falsely confessing." I ran a hand through my hair. "Are there any deals my father was negotiating? Anyone get the short end of the stick who would want him dead?"

"No more than usual," Felix said.

"And who did August meet the night he died?" I asked. "What was he eating? What did he drink?"

"He and Katarine met with Zuriel," Felix said, crossing his arms over his chest. "I don't understand why we're going through this exercise."

I wiggled my eyebrows at him. "Sometimes it takes an outside perspective to see something you missed."

"Is that what Ilara told you?"

"Down, boy," I said with a chuckle. "I'm merely walking through the list of suspects again, double and triple checking. There's got to be something we've missed. A suspect we haven't considered yet. Maybe one of the other Councilmembers, like Zuriel."

"Could've been Garwood."

"Felix, come on." I rolled my eyes. "Garwood and my father were best friends. His sister was my mother, for crying out loud."

"Both excellent covers. He could've killed them both, expecting to put himself on the throne, but when you showed up, he manipulated you into doing what he wanted."

I turned around to argue with him, but stopped at the teasing smile on his face. "Are you making fun of me right now?"

"Maybe a little," he said. "I understand you want to find the culprit, but perhaps you should let it go and let me handle it. I can't believe I'm saying this, but you should focus on Beswick instead of this. Because we have *this* covered."

"Yes, I can't believe you're saying that," I replied, tilting my head at him. "Maybe you're the poisoner."

"Brynna, if I wanted you dead, I would've shoved you off a rooftop many weeks ago," he said, pressing his hand against the small of my back as he led me out. "C'mon, let's get out of here. I think we can have the attendants get it ready for you to move into."

"But I'm so at home in my locked tower..."

My father's murder scene was a dead end, so I turned my attention to August's. In this case, there was a witness to the death, and one who was friendly to me. Still, I wasn't going to let our friendship cloud my judgment. She may not have had a clear motive, but that didn't mean she didn't have one.

When she arrived for my morning tutoring session the next day, I let her dive into the details of how we'd taken over a port city in the west from the Kulkans, and why that meant the mayor there needed to be from a certain family, but I didn't absorb what she was saying. I bided my time, waiting for a lull in the conversation then painted a pensive look onto my face.

"You were with my brother when he died, weren't you?" I asked.

"Yes," she said, looking up from the book she was showing me. "Why?"

I leaned forward on the table, making sure to keep my face curious and not accusatory. "Did you notice anything about August before he died? Remember what he ate or drank?"

"That whole week was a blur," she said, looking down at the book.

"Felix said you were entertaining Councilman Zuriel," I replied, hoping to prod her along. "In the main hall."

"Right." Katarine nodded, casting me something of a worried look. "Zuriel was trying to get a leg up, since August was to be coronated soon. Most boring dinner of my life."

"Most important dinner," I corrected her. "Do you think Zuriel could've been behind the poisoning?"

"No. At least, it would've been incredibly dumb to invite us to dinner then poison August."

"What else do you remember about the night he died?" I asked. "Did he complain of stomach pains, or chest pains?"

"No, we just had dinner and went to bed," she said, sitting back. Her cheeks had become pink, which set off warning flags in my mind.

"But that night, do you remember anything?" I pressed. "Like did he cry out in his sleep, snore, anything?"

Her face was now blotchy red. "I'm a heavy sleeper, Brynna. I just woke up and…"

I nodded, but my mind raced. Felix had said Beata had found him dead. There was a big difference between finding your husband dead and the maid finding him dead. And if they were sharing a bed, and if it were the same poison, August would've at least done *something* to alert Katarine before he died.

"Why are you asking me?" she asked quietly.

"Just curious," I said with a fake smile. "Can we continue with our lesson?"

"Of course."

I couldn't shake the feeling Katarine was lying to me. But if I went to Felix, he would shut me down. He was already pushing me out of the investigation, and I didn't like that either. So if I wanted the truth from her, I'd have to get it myself.

And perhaps burn a few bridges along the way.

That night, I donned my vigilante mask but didn't leave the

castle. I went down the usual path, free of guards and witnesses, but didn't continue into the garden where Felix normally met me. Instead, I took a left turn into the cupboards and waited. After half an hour, I heard his annoyed panting as he came into the kitchen.

"Have you seen her?" he asked.

"No, sir," Joella replied.

He let out a string of filthy curses, to which I had to stifle a giggle. I hadn't known his vocabulary was so large.

Once he'd stormed off like a petulant child, presumably to search the city for me, I left the closet and crept down the hall. Felix's downfall was his regimented schedule; the guards passed the same spot every fifteen minutes. So when one set passed, I moved to the next hiding spot. And so on and so forth, until I was in front of Katarine's door.

Instead of going in, I opted to break into a room one door down. It was yet another empty guest room, the same four-poster bed, the same musty linens. I went to the window and opened it, looking out onto the courtyard. I was at least a hundred feet from the ground, and with my dark clothes and the clouds overhead, I could move out onto the ledge without being seen by the patrolling guards below. I wriggled closer, reaching the lighted window and squinting as I searched the room for Katarine. She was sitting at her chair in her dressing gown, her long blond hair flowing down the front of her body. She looked almost like an exquisite doll, right down to her rosy cheeks.

Perhaps I should've thought this through a little more. I doubted she'd just up and spill the beans about what she was doing the night of my brother's murder. And she didn't seem like the kind of woman who'd leave once she had undone all her trappings, so going through her things would be out of the question. She did mention she was a heavy sleeper, but that could very well have been a lie.

I shifted when the door opened then relaxed when Beata

appeared, grinning and unpinning her hair as she crossed the room.

And then, to my utter surprise, Beata leaned down and kissed Katarine, who tangled a free hand in her hair, and kept her there. Their chaste kiss soon turned into something much more, and I pried myself away from the window to give them some privacy.

Katarine and...a servant? That seemed ridiculous. She was to be queen, supposedly in love with my brother. She'd *slapped* me when I'd insinuated that she hadn't loved him. Perhaps the lady doth protest too much, but...this was a little more than I'd been expecting.

Disappointment settled on my chest. Would Katarine have killed my brother so she could be with Beata? Was she capable of such a thing? And was she, perchance, also responsible for my father's death? Was it some conspiracy from the Niemenians?

I chanced another look inside. Beata was curled up next to Katarine on the chair, and Katarine was toying with the other woman's dark curls; Katarine's face had a youthful glow I'd never seen before. And even Beata, who always seemed so kind, was beaming from ear to ear.

I turned away once more, torn between betrayal and amazement. Now, of course, it was clear why she hadn't seen my brother die. Had he known his wife was in love with someone else? Had they even slept in the same bed?

I left the ledge and made my way down to the kitchen, finding a guard who seemed most relieved to see me and having him point me in the direction of Felix. He spotted me immediately and came jogging over, fury etched on his face.

"Where the *hell* have you been?"

I kept walking, not sure I could look at him without revealing all my hurt. "In my room, asleep."

"Bullshit, I checked there."

"I was sleeping on the roof, then. Whatever."

"I checked there, too."

I rolled my eyes. "I didn't leave the castle, just had some questions to get answered. Are you ready to go?"

"Not until I find out where you were and what you were doing," he said, grabbing my shoulders so I would face him.

I stared into his eyes for a few moments, debating if I should tell the truth. Finally, I decided it would be better to have it in the open, and gauge his reaction to the news. "I asked Katarine about the night August died. I...didn't like her answers. So I decided to investigate her on my own."

His reaction was swift. "*You searched her room without her permission?*"

"No, I spied on her," I said.

"And that's better?"

"No, because..." I shook my head. "It doesn't matter. I found out she's a liar. And now my main suspect in the deaths."

Felix's face shifted into something unreadable. "Why?"

"I saw her sharing a passionate kiss with someone who isn't my brother. She said she loved him." My shoulders drooped. "She lied to me."

"Brynn." Gently, he lifted my chin to face him as he spoke. "Before you fly off the handle, I suggest you talk to Kat yourself."

"Why?" I said, unable to tear my gaze from his. "So she can tell me another lie?"

"Because I think Kat would appreciate being able to tell her side of the story in full context," he said, dropping his hand from my chin. "She's a good person, and a good woman. She would never do anything to intentionally mislead you. Perhaps she might've not wanted to share her personal life with you."

"But—"

"If you still don't like her answers, then I'll arrest her or do whatever you want me to do. But you owe it to your brother, and to Kat, to get the full story."

# Chapter Twenty-Nine

In the back of my mind, I knew Felix was right. But it still didn't erase the hurt I felt. I had allowed Katarine to join my inner circle. She knew my secrets, why would she think to keep one from me?

As I waited for her to arrive for our morning session, my mind ran wild with theories about conspiracies and Katarine and what she might be up to. I had no illusions that she would be honest with me, but perhaps in her lies, I could suss out the truth.

The lock turned over and she breezed inside, looking for all the world to see like her usual, buttoned-up self. Was she really capable of the passion I'd seen the night before? Or was she too constrained after a life of royalty to let anyone but a select few into her inner circle?

"How long have you and Beata been together?" I asked before my anxiety got the better of me.

She froze, her eyes widening in fear. "W-what?"

"I asked how long you and Beata have been together."

"W-we haven't... I don't know what you're talking about," she said, but the fidgeting and rapid eye movement gave her away. As did the blood-red color of her cheeks.

"Katarine," I smiled humorlessly, "I saw you together last night."

Her hand flew to her mouth, and her eyes filled with fury. "You...you were *spying* on me?"

"You lied to me, so don't even begin with that look." I got to my feet. "I knew you weren't telling the truth about my brother's death, so I wanted to find out for myself what you were hiding. I didn't mean to intrude on a private moment."

"You saw nothing," she said, her face now a glorious shade of purple. "Whatever you saw wasn't what you think it was. Beata is a servant—"

"Unless she's also a prostitute paid to cuddle and make eyes at you at night, I doubt that's the truth," I said, folding my arms over my chest.

Katarine exhaled a shaky breath. When she spoke, her voice was tiny. "Please don't send me away."

"I won't, as long as I get the truth out of you," I said, sitting back down and kicking out the chair across from me. "Now have a seat and start talking."

"I don't exactly know what you want me to say," she said, perching on the edge of the chair and averting her gaze.

"Let's start with the basics: Did you love my brother, as you claim?"

"Of course I loved him," she said hotly then retracted. "But it's not... I loved him like a dear friend. The same way I love Felix. They were the only ones I had as a lonely girl in this castle. They protected me, stood up for me. Helped me find my place."

"But you didn't love him as your husband."

"Our marriage was arranged, out of either of our hands," she said. "It didn't matter if I loved him or not. But I did, as I keep telling you. His death was...completely unexpected. I miss him

235

every single day."

"Did he know about you and Beata, or did that start after he died?"

"Of course he knew. He was the one who..." She stared at her hands. "He...We'd come to an agreement. I would bear him two children to cement our treaty and that would be the end of that... part of our relationship. He and I would be free to seek other companions as necessary."

"So he approved of your relationship?"

"There's nothing..." She swallowed, gathering her thoughts. "It's a flirtation at best and a few stolen kisses here and there. Beata was always around as my attendant, and she just had the most beautiful eyes." For a moment, her eyes went soft before she buried her face in her hands. "But I knew if anyone found out I was with someone who wasn't my husband, it would be the height of scandal. I wasn't pregnant yet with his children, so..."

I blanched, not wanting to get *that* personal with her. "So what changed? You two looked cozy last night."

She wiped a tear off her cheek. "It's been...hard since August died. He was my very best friend, and with Felix so distracted, I've been feeling rather lonely. And Bea is just..." She sniffed and dabbed a handkerchief against her nose. "I've been weak."

"But do you want to be with her?" I asked. "For real?"

She barked a sardonic laugh. "I'm the youngest child of the kingdom of Niemen. My only purpose in life was to marry your brother and bear heirs. Now that my husband is dead and I'm childless..." She sighed. "I'm not much use to my sister anymore. So now I suppose I'm at your mercy."

"You didn't answer my question," I pressed, leaning in closer. "Do you love her or—"

She loosed a heavy sigh. "I don't have that luxury. For you and me, marriage is about alliances. Treaties. Love will never factor into it."

"It's a yes or no question. Do you love her, yes or no?"

A smile curled onto her face, similar to the contented grin she'd worn the night before. "I am fond of her, yes."

"Why?"

She glanced up at me, confused for a moment then gathered her thoughts. "She's got a beautiful spirit, and she's so smart. Brynna, she's a better strategist than me sometimes." She laughed and that smile on her lips grew. "You know she had a scholarship to study navigation, but she declined it just to stay in the castle. To stay with me." She sighed. "It would have been better for us both if she'd gone."

"She appears to only have eyes for you, Kat," I said. "And you her."

Katarine inhaled deeply and looked away.

"So what happened the night August died?" I tilted my head in her direction. "The truth, please."

She swallowed, gathering her thoughts. When she spoke, it was even and clear. "August and I had been trying for a child for many months. But even though I'd been a willing partner, there was nothing, even after a year. There were a few months where I'd been late to my bleeding, but it had come anyway. Both Beata and August thought I might be barren. After all, my mother had six children. It shouldn't have taken that long for me."

"Then my father died," I said.

"Yes, then your father died, which made it all the more important that I become pregnant with the heir. Beata had heard about a Kulkan Nestori who specialized in fertility. So in the middle of the night, Felix snuck us out to meet with her. She made me urinate in a bowl then mixed it with some flowers, and told me to come back in three days' time to get the results." She sighed, blushing once more. "Beata thought, since we were already away from the castle, we could spend the evening together. So we did." Her flustered face turned sad. "When I returned at dawn, August was dead."

"And there were no witnesses to it," I said. That was something. "Who else knew you were leaving?"

"No one except those in Felix's inner circle," she said.

"I'm starting to think that Felix might have to work on that circle of his," I replied then paused. "I hate to ask this, but do you think Beata…?"

"No," Katarine said with a fierce shake of her head. "August actually…well, he liked Beata. For me. He's the one who promoted her to be my attendant so we could spend more time together. And his death put our relationship in jeopardy—"

"*Relationship*?" I said with a teasing smile. "I thought you said it was just a flirtation?"

She flushed again and looked at her hands. "I'm not used to having conversations about it. I'm sorry—I'm not trying to be deceptive."

"Is there anything else about yourself that you've been hiding from me?" I asked, sitting back in my chair and crossing my arms over my chest.

She cast me a curious look then gazed down at her lap. "I do enjoy a good game of cards. A bit of a gambler. I took Felix and August for their coin purses on several occasions."

"Then we'll have to play soon," I said, reaching across the table to take her hand. "And don't worry about your future here, either. I'd be stupid to let you go after all the knowledge you've imparted on me. Just please, don't lie to me anymore."

She smiled and squeezed my hand. "I promise."

"Now," I said, releasing her. "I think we were going to learn about my great-grandfather's naval victory against Kulka?"

"Well?" Felix asked when I met him downstairs that evening. "Do you want me to arrest your sister-in-law?"

"I think she can stay," I replied with a look. "But I have to know...did you know?"

He rolled his eyes. "Of course I knew. Kat, August, and I were best friends."

"And did August really encourage her and Beata?" I asked, thoughtfully.

Felix grinned, which surprised me. "August was the worst. Always trying to set others up. He noticed how Kat stared at Beata and went through a bunch of trouble to get her promoted to their main attendant. A lot of the uninformed thought that August and Beata were the ones sleeping together. But he was the prince, so it wasn't questioned."

"Would've been nice if you'd told me that," I said, as we walked out of the iron gate and into the city.

"It wasn't for me to tell you," he said. "I don't spill secrets, Brynna. Especially those belonging to my friends. But I knew once you spoke with her, you'd understand."

"I might've found something new," I said. "The night August died, Kat said you helped her and Beata meet with a Nestori woman, right?"

"Yes, I had Joella escort them out." He narrowed his eyes. "Why?"

"I'm thinking whoever killed August did so on a night when his wife was away," I said. "Even if they didn't share a bed, she still would've heard him struggling from the next room over. So my question to you is: which of your guard knew she was leaving that night?"

"I'm telling you, it wasn't anyone in my guard," Felix said. "I only informed four: Riya, Joella, Coyle, and Zathan. And I would trust them with my life."

"Maybe you shouldn't."

He stopped me with a hand to my arm. "Brynna, my team is not under investigation. And besides that, even if they were, *you* don't need to investigate them. I thought you were letting me handle this?"

"Fine," I snapped, sticking my hands on my hips. "What else have you found?"

"Riya spoke with one of Beswick's men, who gave us the contract Horace signed. He owed Beswick three thousand gold pieces, and to pay it off, he'd been working as a dockhand to help smuggle in Severian and Kulkan goods."

"Great, that doesn't tell us anything," I replied.

"It gives us an angle. Perhaps one of the Severians contacted him."

"To what end?"

"We're exploring every avenue. That's why there are five of us, and one of you." He stepped back. "If you really want to help, just stay out of our way."

*And it doesn't occur to you that one of the five people investigating could be a party to the crime?* But I didn't voice my concern. Somehow, I was sure he wouldn't hear it if I did.

# Chapter Thirty

I was convinced someone in Felix's so-called inner circle couldn't be trusted. Felix was obviously too close to the situation, and blinded by his own loyalty to his troops, to even question if they were capable of betrayal (which they obviously were). If I wanted the truth, I would have to investigate them myself.

The tricky part would be conducting such an investigation under their noses, keeping one step ahead of Felix *and* the murderer.

The next morning, to my extreme delight, Katarine arrived about the same time Beata brought my breakfast. I'd insisted they both sit and eat with me, even though neither of them did anything more than nibble.

"It is nice that you know," Beata said, her cheeks a rosy color as she held Katarine's hand. "Although I really must be getting to work."

"You can tell them I was being persnickety about my hair," I replied. "Or I wouldn't get out of bed, or whatever else people might say about me."

She cast me a look instead of responding, to which I laughed.

"The only thing people are upset with you for is letting Ilara stay," Katarine said. "It's really been quite long, you know. Time for her to pack up and go back home."

"She's ill," I replied, having heard from her handler as much when I inquired about dining with her. "And I still want to help. What are my options?"

"Few and far between," Katarine replied. "You don't control tariff amounts, especially in the farther cities on the rivers. You'll have to seek permission from your Council for that."

"And I doubt they'd be interested." I sighed. "What else do I have?"

"Kick her out?" Beata replied with a frown, surprising both Katarine and myself. "What? She's taken over a complete wing of the castle. It smells like weird herbs and cows over there. The entire castle staff is furious."

"Come on," I said with a gentle laugh. "Be nice, they're our guests."

"I have to agree with Beata," Katarine said, squeezing her hand. "The sooner she's on her way, the better I'll feel." Then she brightened. "But in good news, today we'll be meeting with a designer to redecorate your father's...I mean, your bedroom."

I grimaced. "Can't you do it?"

"No, Brynna," she said with a shake of her head. "This will be fun."

"I hear the designer coming is one of the best in the city," Beata said, standing to clear the table. Katarine and I both helped, much to her fussing. "Do you know what they would say if they found out I had the princess helping me clean her own table?"

"The only people in this room are the ones who matter," I said with a smile. "And you two had better bring your appetites tomorrow, because I hate dining alone."

For the second time that week, I walked into my father's royal chambers—or rather, my new chambers. Felix had said I could move in as soon as it was refurbished. And as much as I hated spending the city's money on myself, the decor was dreary and masculine. If I could control one thing, it would be my space.

"I'm glad Felix is letting you move in here," Katarine said, pulling open the curtains to let more light in. "You two seem to have a good relationship now."

"You could say that," I said, glancing out the open door to where Coyle was waiting. I was still looking for an opportunity to spy on them, but it was hard to do that when they were guarding me. "But they're still here all the time."

"Oh, well, that's to be expected," Katarine said with a laugh. "You are still the sovereign."

I sighed as I took in what was left of the decor. "This wallpaper is ugly."

"It's from your great-grandfather," she said with a disgusted look. "Dreadful, right?"

Just then, the designer walked in the door, arms laden with drawings and fabric swatches. He introduced himself as Charles, and spent ten minutes talking about how honored he was to be designing my room before barraging me with ideas for furniture and fabric.

"The latest trend is a four-posted bed, carved from Niemenian wood," he said, showing me a sketch of a very nice, very large bed that could've slept ten people.

"I suppose, but shouldn't I be buying Forcadel-made furniture?"

"If you want," he said, sticking his tongue out in disgust. "But the Forcadel designs are so bland."

"I'm a bland person," I replied, pushing aside the furniture designs. Something caught my eye—it looked like blueprints. I pushed aside the fabrics and sketches until I found it, noticing immediately that the drawing of the royal suites lacked any markings of secret exits. Those were probably a closely-guarded secret. But how closely-guarded was the question...

"Something the matter?" Charles asked.

"I was thinking, perhaps, of moving some walls," I replied, as my mind turned over an idea. I still needed a way to give Felix and his guards the slip if I was going to spy on them, but up until now, they'd only shown me the exits they knew about. But what if there were others that even Felix didn't know about?

"Maybe adding a second door over..." I glanced behind me, trying to keep the excitement out of my voice. "There. Wanted to see what was over there."

His eyes lit up. "Well, Your Majesty, if you're looking to make significant architectural changes then we'll need to consult the official plans of the castle."

*There it is.* "Fantastic. Where can we find them?"

"They're down in the archives," Katarine replied. "Under lock and key, for security reasons, of course."

"Of course." I shifted. "But perhaps I could get to them? Since I am, you know...going to be queen?"

She glanced at Charles, who seemed to be salivating at the prospect of major renovations. "I believe you and I will be granted access. But we'll have to leave you behind, I'm afraid. The archive is accessible to royalty only, and the plans just to Princess Brynna."

"Don't worry," I said as he pouted. "I'm an excellent sketch artist."

⇒————

The royal archives were not, as I'd assumed, in the catacombs of my castle, but rather on the other side of the market square, in an old building next to the church. Luckily, Felix was busy drilling his young charges, so he wasn't around to decline my request to leave the castle in the royal carriage. Joella and Coyle sat on the back as Katarine and I climbed in for the short jaunt.

"Do you really want to move a wall?" Katarine asked as we set off.

I shrugged. "That room is stuffy. At the very least, I'd love some more natural light. And if I'm going to be stuck there, I might as well make it my own."

"Mm."

The archives were much larger than they looked outside, with stacks and stacks of scrolls and old books, with one window in the front offering spotty light. Katarine rang the bell in the front and an older woman came hurrying forward.

"Can I— Oh!" She wiped her hands on her shirt and bowed low. "Your Majesties."

"I'm no longer a majesty," Katarine correctly quietly. "Princess, this is Alfie Torrelas, she's your royal archivist."

"At your service," she said with a bow. "What can I help you with?"

"We'd like to see the castle blueprints," Katarine said. "So that the princess can better understand the architecture for possible improvements."

Alfie paused, but only for a moment, then disappeared into the mounds of paperwork.

"You and Alfie are friends?" I asked.

"I wouldn't say friends, but friendly," she replied, running her finger along a dusty table nearby. "I spent a lot of time here learning the ins and outs of Forcadel's history over the years. Most of the books we've been using are on loan from her."

The archivist returned with an old scroll in her arms and hesitantly looked at Katarine. "I apologize, but the laws say only the royal family may have access to these."

"She's family," I said, waving her off.

"No, no," Katarine said with a warm smile. "I think I might go look through the history books. Perhaps find something more on that naval battle we talked about this morning."

I watched her go for a moment before turning back to Alfie. "Let's see what you've got."

Alfie unrolled the scroll, revealing a detailed front view of the castle. "The last survey of the castle was completed about a hundred years ago." She pointed to the seal on the bottom of the map. "And, as an aside, only the sovereign can request to see it, as obviously, it contains every entry and exit to the premises."

"Every one?" I asked with a grin. "Show me the royal suite."

She flipped through the pages until she found the bottom one, displaying the fourth level of the castle, where the royal wing lay. I ran my finger along the center hallway, mapping the castle in my mind until I hit the king's office—and the exit into the stables. As I'd suspected, there were other exits in almost every room of the royal wing, including two in the royal bedroom.

"I do hope you aren't really considering knocking down walls," Alfie said, after a moment. "It's such an old castle—"

"Do you mind if I take a sketch of this?" I asked. "Have a pen and paper? And...be sure not to tell Lady Kat about it."

Realization dawned on her old face and she nodded, rushing to procure me the drawing materials. I drew two sketches, one I could give to the royal designer to play with and one that marked the exits. I hid the latter inside my tunic for safekeeping.

"Let me ask you a question," I said. "Did my brother ever look at this map?"

She thought for a moment then shook her head. "I don't believe so. The last person to look at it was...your father, I believe." She nodded, as if her memory was coming back to her. "There was an issue in the kitchen with a wall when he first ascended the throne. Why do you ask?"

"No reason." I smiled. "No reason at all."

⇨————→

We returned to the castle, where the designer had somehow procured more designs and fabrics in our absence. I gave him the first drawing and he used it to offer options for walls we could destroy and what that might do to the space.

"And here, if you wished to create a larger sitting room." He gestured to a wall near the window with fading wallpaper. "We could take some of the library."

"Oh, Brynna," Katarine said with a frown. "Don't take your library. It's so nice."

"Can we take a look at it?" I asked, walking to the door. Coyle stood in the main room at the front door, his gaze on me as I passed into the bedroom. Was it a good sign he wasn't following me closely? Did that mean Felix didn't know about the exits? I'd have to test that theory.

The library was actually much smaller than I'd thought—more a second office, if I had to call it anything. Only one wall held a shelf of books, and otherwise it was mostly treasures and trinkets. Out of the one window, the bay was visible on the right side, which meant that was the southern wall, where I would find my exit.

"Oh yes, very small indeed," Charles said, walking into the room and frowning.

"I just can't see why you'd want to make the bedroom bigger," Katarine said. "It's big enough."

"Why don't we go back into the bedroom and take another look?" I suggested. "I'm not sure I see your vision, Charles."

He and Katarine left, bickering and not noticing that I hadn't followed them. I would only have a few precious moments, so I hurried to the southern wall where my secret map said the exit would be.

The secret exit Felix and I used was hidden in front of a statue, but this one had nothing in front of it. I surmised that perhaps there was a lever that unlocked the door. I pushed, kicked, tapped, but nothing budged. The two sconces on the wall...they looked just a little different than the other ones. So I pulled one, and it came forward, but the door didn't. The other sconce was the same.

"Oh, *come on*," I muttered. My arms weren't long enough to grab onto both, so I hooked my heel onto one, and then grabbed onto the other. With a breath, I jumped into the air and yanked them both forward. The door softly clicked behind me, and I scrambled inside, shutting it before Kat and Coyle heard me.

"What the..." Coyle's voice came from the other side. "Oh, great."

"Where is she?" Katarine's soft footfalls echoed in the room. "She can't disappear, can she?"

"Princess?" Charles called. "Princess, where did you go?"

"Felix is going to be furious," Coyle said. "Come on, let's alert the forces so they can try to head her off before she gets too far."

I waited for him to come through the door, but he didn't, so before they panicked too much, I hurried out into the hallway, calling for them.

"Charles? Kat?" I said, turning right and left. "Where'd you guys go?"

"Oh." He sighed in relief. "Where did you go?"

"Privy," I said, walking toward them. "Sorry, I thought you heard me tell you. Why'd you guys leave?"

Coyle gave me a curious look, but then shook his head. "Just wanted to make sure you stayed put."

"Please, Coyle," I said with a laugh. "Where would I go? Climb out the window?"

He stared at me for a long time, and I was sure he could see right through me. But, finally, he nodded and walked out into the main room again.

# Chapter
# Thirty–One

It was sorely tempting to walk out of the castle by myself through my newfound exit, but like a good vigilante, I met Felix by the garden door. I was curious; would he mention my jaunt to the archives? Had Coyle told him I'd momentarily vanished?

But if he knew, he didn't mention it, and we set off into the night.

For weeks now, we'd had the same routine. Stop by Ruby's, pay her a few gold coins, then stake out Beswick's location. Sometimes, we would get lucky and be able to eavesdrop on his conversations. More often than not, he would take dinner at one of his restaurants until midnight then retire to his manor in Mariner's Row.

But tonight, I didn't mind the downtime, because it would give me a chance to lay the first pieces of my master plan. In order for my ruse to work, I needed to slip out of the castle undetected. And for that to happen, Felix and his guards needed to believe I was indisposed.

"You've been coughing a lot tonight," Felix said after I cleared my throat again. "Feeling all right?"

"Yep," I said. "Fine."

We grew silent for a moment and I hid a grin from him as I thought about Phase Two, flushing out the leaker. It would be a gamble that I'd set the trap correctly, but I was running short on time.

Slowly, I looked over at Felix, clearing my throat. "I think I might have another lead on our poisoner."

"Really?" He turned to me. "And you're just telling me this now?"

I chose my words carefully. "It's something my contact at Stank's mentioned. A merchant who supposedly deals in Kulkan poisons. They'll be coming back to town tomorrow night. We may want to keep an eye on my food—and who touches it."

"I doubt they'll try again, now that we've got someone to pin it on," Felix said. "Or if they do, they probably won't use the poison."

"True," I said, thinking quickly. "But the merchant might be able to lead us closer to our real culprit. It's worth looking into."

I felt his gaze on me and turned slightly to catch his scrutiny. There was something unreadable in his eyes behind the mask.

"What?" I asked.

"Just thinking," he said. "Have you... have you ever thought about training someone else? Like a successor or protégé."

"I don't know who else would want this job," I said with a shrug. "You don't get paid, you don't sleep, and you don't have much of a life. Nobody loves Forcadel like I do."

"I do."

"Do you want to be The Veil?" I asked, turning to him. "Ready for a change of career? You feeling comfortable in that mask yet?"

"Hardly." He tugged at the cloth on his eyes. "My point was there are others who would wear the mantle in your place. In a way, it's good that nobody knows your name. When you disappear, someone else can pick up where you left off, and the city won't be the wiser."

I chafed at the idea of someone else wearing my mask. "They won't do it as well as I do."

"Of course they won't. But you'll be overseeing things as queen."

"After my coronation, maybe I could go out once a month—"

"No, Brynna."

I scowled at him, then remembered my plan. I made a show of coughing loudly and wiping my eyes.

"You okay?" Felix asked.

"Sure," I said. "Allergies must be bad."

"Do you have allergies?"

I cast my gaze at the sky. "No."

The next morning, when Beata delivered my breakfast, I only picked at it. By lunch, I was starving, but still didn't eat. I grimaced and pretended not to remember anything Katarine told me during the day, making sure to avidly protest any mention of illness. More importantly, during the course of the day, when I was alone with the four different guards in Felix's inner circle, I spoke to them about the poison investigation, telling them I was closing in on the merchant, but changing one small detail about where Felix was to meet me that evening.

I asked Riya, who escorted me and Katarine to the school room, to keep Felix away from the stables so I could leave without him.

To Coyle, who took me from the classroom to my tower for lunch, Felix was to meet me in the town square at eight.

Joella, who took me from my room to my office where I signed papers, I asked to have Felix meet me in my room for dinner.

And to Zathan, who came to get me for dinner, Felix was to

join me at the garden gate, as usual.

Then, all there was to do was wait.

As soon as I'd finished picking at dinner, Felix walked into my room looking honestly surprised to see me there. "I've had a very interesting day, Brynn. Would you like to know why?"

"I'm sure I could guess," I said, grimacing and holding my head. "But please, enlighten me."

"I've been told by three different people that you're closing in on the poisoner and three different places where I'm supposed to meet you to investigate them."

I nodded, keeping a smile off my face. *Gotcha.* "And what did three different people tell you?"

"That you'd asked them to keep me away from the stables, to meet you at garden gate, and to meet you at the town square."

I flinched and shook my head. *Oh, Joella.* Why did it have to be you?

"So which is it?" he asked. "And what the hell is going on?"

"I'm experimenting," I replied. "I wanted to see which of your people weren't loyal to you."

"And?"

I flashed him a fake smile. "All good. They all did exactly as I thought they would."

Felix frowned, narrowing his eyes at me. "What are you planning? And why are you screwing with my guys? Leave them alone."

"I'm not doing anything because they passed the test," I said, coming to stand slowly and making sure to exaggerate my grimace.

"Then you haven't gotten anything on the poisoner, have you?" he asked, sounding a little upset.

"No. I thought, perhaps, if one of your men was responsible, they might run back to their handler," I said. "But it turns out they're all clean."

"Of course they are," he said hotly. "They can be trusted. Your trustworthiness, on the other hand, is currently in doubt. What the hell is going on?"

"Nothing," I said, standing and holding my head, hiding a warm compress that I'd fashioned from the cup of evening tea Beata had sent up. "Felix, I'm not in the mood to argue."

"What's wrong? Are you ill?" He crossed the room and pressed his hand to my forehead, still warm and wet from the compress. "You're burning up."

"'m fine," I said, weakly pushing his hand away, but he grabbed it, his eyes filled with concern.

"Brynn, are you sure you didn't ingest any poison?"

"Calm yourself, Captain," I said with an eyeroll. "I can catch a little cold every now and again."

The furrow hadn't left his brow. "You're running yourself too hard. Beata says you haven't eaten all day and Kat said you weren't paying attention during lessons."

"I never pay attention."

He pursed his lips in a very convincing impersonation of a mother hen. "Brynn."

"Fine," I said, putting as much disgust into my words as I could. "My head is killing me anyway. Might as well take a night in."

He pressed his hand to my lower back as he guided me toward my bed. "I'll have Beata send up some more tea. And tomorrow, we're going to have a conversation about all these decisions you've been making, including confusing the hell out of my guards."

"Fine, fine. Just go." I curled up under the blanket and covered my eyes with it.

The door closed, leaving me alone. It was actually quite nice to lie there in the darkness, and exhaustion tugged at the back of my eyes. But I didn't succumb, waking when Beata tiptoed in with some tea.

After an hour, I flung the sheets off. I fashioned a body-shaped person out of pillows and covered it up. In the darkness, even I couldn't tell the difference. I padded to the door; the first test of Felix's trust would be if it were locked. But it opened with a soft click, and I grinned.

"Princess?" Riya rose from her post. "Can I get something for you?"

I opened the door wider, squinting in the low light and pressing a hand over my head. "I'm dying for a glass of water. Would you mind? And maybe find Beata and see about getting another cup of tea or something?"

"Of course." She jumped to her feet and dashed down the stairs. I waited a breath before following behind. Riya took a left at the bottom of the stairs, and I took a right. The hall was empty, and I grinned—I'd obviously convinced the entire castle. I had to duck into a room two or three times to avoid a passing guard, but finally—finally, I came to the dark library.

And with one pull of the lights, the door opened, and I was free.

I inhaled the warm night air and trotted out into the night, listening for the sounds of footsteps. When none were following, I made my way toward the stables, where Joella was standing guard with Coyle. I crept silently to the darkness, crouching low and waiting.

"Shame the princess has come down with something," Coyle said. "Though I'm sure it makes our life easier."

"Infinitely," Joella said with a severe laugh. "She's such a pain in the ass. And she makes Felix run all over the place after her. If you ask me, she should stay in the castle where she belongs."

"Think she'll stay after she's crowned like Llobrega says?"

"Fat chance." Joella stopped and turned behind her, as if she'd forgotten something. "Hey, I forgot to check on something for Riya. Can you handle this by yourself? I'll send over Monty after a bit."

"Sure, sure," he said. "Without Princess Pain in the Ass wandering around, things are pretty silent."

"You, too, Coyle?" I shook my head. Nobody liked me, it seemed.

I kept my distance from Joella as she most assuredly didn't seek out Riya but went out of the castle grounds. She grabbed a stashed black cloak from underneath a bale of hay right outside the castle, covering her royal guard uniform. When she got to the city center, I ascended to the rooftops to follow, keeping her shiny shoe buckles in view as I followed her to the eastern side of the city.

She finally stopped in a dark alley where another figure was waiting. I sat hidden behind the ledge, listening.

"...found the poisoner. Or a merchant ship, I think."

"Oh? Who is it?"

I released a low growl. I knew that voice—Ignacio.

"Not sure. She could also be bluffing," Joella said. "She's not nearly as smart as she thinks she is."

"I've heard that from multiple people."

"Oh, come on," I whispered.

Joella and Ignacio spoke in hushed tones, and I could only catch wisps of their conversations. When they parted, Joella kept to the shadows, her cloak billowing behind her.

I waited until she was far enough away that Ignacio wouldn't hear her scream then came up behind her with a knife. She jumped, but stopped moving as soon as the blade pressed into her neck.

"You little snitch," I growled. "I should slit your throat and cut out your tongue."

"P-princess?" she gasped, her body trembling. "What are you doing here?"

"I could ask you the same question," I said. "I saw you meeting with Beswick's man about the poisoner. You're lucky I don't kill you right here. Are you responsible for my brother's death?"

"You don't understand," she whispered desperately. "It's not what it looks like."

"Oh? Because I told you I was close to finding the poisoner, and here you are, telling the man who did it—"

"Beswick isn't responsible, I promise you," Joella said. "I swear to you, he's not."

I tightened the blade against her skin. "What's the word of a liar worth?"

"Brynna, please." She disarmed me with a quick break but didn't run. "Just listen to me for one moment."

I folded my arms across my chest. "Speak."

"Beswick has my sister in his little web. She was in a lot of debt, and he was going to kill her if she didn't pay or...get me to feed him information from the castle." She slumped. "I swear, I haven't told him that you're The Veil or anything else about that."

"Then what are you telling him?"

She licked her lips. "Information about what you're doing as princess, things to do with his business, that kind of thing."

"And that I was close to finding the poisoner," I finished with narrowing eyes.

She sighed. "I hadn't been able to bring him any news of value, so I thought he'd be interested in it. He wasn't." She shook her head. "I have to figure something out this month or else he's going to double my debt. I'm sorry, I'm...I'm desperate."

I clicked my tongue against the roof of my mouth, struck with a brilliant idea. "Maybe we can help each other, Joella."

"What are you talking about?" she asked with a nervous look.

"I'm going to give you something to give to Beswick, and in return, you're going to get me close to him."

Her eyes narrowed. "Why?"

"That's my business." I glowered at her. "As you've proven you can't be trusted."

"I'm working for Beswick, but I have no idea who poisoned

you," she said. "Or Prince August or your father. I swear."

"You lied to me about working for Beswick," I said. "So you've got to earn back my trust. Can you get a message to him?"

She nodded stoically. "When I have information to give Beswick, I go to the bakery in the town square. Buy three yeast rolls. Then I meet with him at his club on the eastern side."

"Then I suggest you hit up the bakery tomorrow."

"What am I going to tell him?"

"Tell him..." I smiled. "That the Severians are going to be making a deal with the princess and cutting him out. And if he'd like to see the new treaty, you'll bring it to him personally."

# Chapter Thirty-Two

"How are you feeling?"

I jumped at the sound of Felix's voice, nearly taking his head off. "Wha?"

"I asked how you were feeling," Felix said, sitting down on the edge of my bed.

"Like shit," I said. It was mostly the truth. I did feel like shit, but only because I'd gotten in just before dawn. Without Felix on my tail, I'd made the most of my free evening and taken out more than a few low-life criminals. But that, of course, meant I was struggling this morning.

"You're killing yourself," Felix said, laying his hand on my leg. "This can't continue, Brynn."

"Just a little head cold," I said. "I'll be right as rain in a few days."

"As long as you take it easy."

I rolled my eyes. "Fine, I'll take it easy today."

But once I was awake, I did anything but. Alone in my room, I paced and pondered. How I was going to get alone with Ilara today? And how I could put together a non-binding agreement that would cut Beswick out completely?

My opportune moment came when Joella switched out with Riya as my room guard around noon. I changed into one of my nicer tunics, pinning my gold circlet to my hair, which I'd braided about as well as Beata. Then, I went to fetch my new best friend.

"We're going for a walk," I said, appearing in the doorway and catching Joella's eye. "If anyone asks, I went to stretch my legs."

She nodded grimly and followed without saying a word.

Ilara had been put up in the southern wing of the castle; I'd thought it would be nice for her to have a view of the water when she woke up. As we entered the hall, I counted the Severian guards, marked by their brown and red uniforms, instead of the blue and white of Forcadel. They nodded to me, although I felt their eyes on me as I passed.

The attendant at the door jumped to his feet and bowed. "Your Highness, I wasn't aware that you'd be paying us a visit today. I thought you were ill?"

"I needed some fresh air," I said with a forced smile. "I thought, perhaps, Ilara would have a moment to speak?"

"Let me fetch her," he said, ducking into the room. A moment later, Ilara appeared in a shapeless white dress that ended just above her ankles. Her black hair was stick straight and falling to her hips at least, pinned back with a beautiful jeweled barrette.

She flashed me a wide, happy smile. "I'm so glad to see you're feeling better. I'd asked your captain if I could send you a healing tincture, but he declined."

"He's a little overprotective," I said, squeezing her hand when she offered it. "Would you like to take a walk with me?"

"Oh, please," she said, glancing behind her. "I'd love some fresh air."

With Joella trailing us, I took Ilara down to the gardens where we wouldn't be overheard. In order for this to work, I needed this conversation to remain between the three of us.

"It is so nice to get outside," she said, turning her face up to the sun. "I could spend every day out here."

"How are you liking your time here in Forcadel?" I asked, stopping to admire a particularly pungent white flower.

"Oh, very much." She beamed. "Yesterday, I spent some time in your fantastic square, before a kind merchant took me out for an afternoon sail around the bay. It's quite impressive, this city you have here. Even this garden is so luscious."

"I used to play here as a girl," I said with a soft smile. "My brother August would chase me, and I'd hide under that bridge or behind the well. Once, I thought it would be a good idea to hide in the well."

"Was it?" she asked with an amused smile.

"I know Felix heard me crying, but he ignored me until the morning," I said with a glower.

"Your captain has been in your life a long time, then?"

"Longer than I'd like," I replied. "I sometimes think he still sees me as that little girl stuck in a well."

"Perhaps," she said before turning to me. "I know you didn't just take me out for a walk to these beautiful gardens to stretch your legs."

"You're right," I said, looking at Joella and dismissing her with one look. "I wanted to talk about your agreement with Johann Beswick."

"Oh." She looked away. "I'm not sure I should discuss those with you. My minister of economics said—"

"Beswick is a crook, and he's also the one who's hitting the transports you're paying him to protect," I said, placing my hands on my hips. "So you're paying him a lot of money to get half your shipments."

Her mouth dropped open, and she covered it with her hand.

"It's not your fault," I said, by way of an apology. "Beswick likes to entrap people and make them believe he's the only one who can save them from their problems, when he's the one who put them there in the first place."

"We give him a thousand gold pieces per month to protect Severian glass from the border to the ocean, and another thousand to transport it into Forcadel." She furrowed her brow in anger. "But I'd long suspected it wasn't as official as we'd been led to believe. Beswick takes more than he should, and his methods of dealing with disagreements aren't ones I like." She sighed. "But as it stands, he's the only one who'll do business with us."

"Surely there are other merchants out there," I replied. "You can't just have Beswick."

She made a helpless gesture. "Of course not. But he's the only one who'll meet with me. I was devastated that I couldn't attend your dinner. Such an opportunity lost because I couldn't sit up."

"It's fine," I said, patting her hand. "There will be other dinners, I'm sure."

"Perhaps, but none that I will attend," she said sadly. "Your captain stopped by this morning and strongly urged us to pack up and leave before your coronation."

"He did, did he?" I'd have to talk to Felix about that. "Don't worry about him. There are others in the city you can meet with. I'll hold another dinner. Maybe tonight."

"It's no use, Brynna," she said sadly. "There aren't many who are willing to deal directly with us. It's a treacherous journey from Severia to the coast. Half our glass is damaged or stolen en route. We already sell it at the lowest price we can, so the profit margins aren't..." She sighed. "Unfortunately, my beautiful homeland lacks natural resources. And so we are where we are."

"I'm sure," I said. "What if I promised you a free royal guard escort for all your shipments to the coast?"

Her eyes widened. "Are you serious?"

"We'll have to finalize this with the Council," I said, hoping they would give me an out. Two thousand gold pieces per shipment was quite a lot of money for Beswick to lose; that would have to get his attention. "And it might not be forever. Just temporarily, until I can find a way to get rid of Beswick. Then, I promise you, I'll try to find you a better solution."

"Even one protected shipment would mean so much to my glassmakers," she said, tears in her eyes that she wiped away quickly. "And I suppose we'll begin the process of packing up our things. I'd hoped I could stay for the coronation festival, but I understand the situation I've put you in. I just hope we can return before the sandstorms become too terrible to travel in."

"Look why don't you just...stay," I said, after a moment. "It's ridiculous that you should travel during the middle of stormy season. Is your kingdom running fine without you?"

"One hopes."

"Then just stay until the coronation. Felix can deal with it. Let me handle this Beswick thing and then we can get down to the business of real negotiations, all right?"

She grinned brightly. "Thank you, my dear friend."

That night, I played like I wanted to go out, but Felix refused. I fought with him for an hour, finally breaking down into tears about how frustrated I was that things weren't going faster, how bad I felt, and so on and so forth. The poor bastard ate it up, tucking me into bed and drying my eyes. It made me feel a little guilty that I was tricking him, but if everything went as it should, he wouldn't be the wiser.

Once I'd been left alone long enough, I went to my door and opened it, finding Joella waiting down the staircase.

"I have a meeting tonight with Beswick," she said.

"Excellent," I said, joining her on the bottom step. "If it's a trap, I will kill you. And your sister, her daughters, and that new infant baby boy."

She stumbled. "What?"

"Do you think me an idiot, Joella?" I said evenly. "I wanted to make sure I had insurance. If you try anything stupid, I will end every single one of them. And don't think I won't, either."

It was a lie; but Joella didn't need to know that. She just needed a reminder of what was at stake.

She swallowed. "You went to my sister's house?"

"Of course I did." I continued walking, lowering my voice. "But if you don't screw me, there won't be any problems. Your nephew is a handsome little guy, isn't he?"

"Y-yes, he is," Joella said quietly.

We left the castle without another word.

As promised, she walked into Beswick's club, the guard at the front allowing her entry without a glance. Beswick was waiting in a room on the third floor. I had a good vantage point across the street, but I wasn't able to hear what he was saying. I pulled out the small crossbow I'd retrieved from the clocktower and loaded it with one of my listening devices with a fifty-foot string. Then I aimed toward the window and waited. Joella appeared exactly when I wanted her to, and right when she slammed the door behind her, I released the arrow. I pulled the cup to my ear and listened.

"...don't slam the door so hard."

"Sorry," Joella said. "I'm a little nervous."

"Don't be. Come sit at my table and tell me about this new treaty."

"She's offered Ilara a full royal guard from the border to Forcadel," Joella said. "Apparently, she's trying to undercut you. That's what she said."

"Ah, that poor girl. Does she really think it will be that easy?" He chuckled and my blood boiled. "I have ways of making sure that never happens. Perhaps I'll have my friends on the Kulkan border come with their hats out. It'll be interesting to see if the princess is so swayed by their sad remarks, too."

"I'll let you know what I hear," Joella said, standing. "But I can't... She can't know I was the one who told you."

"I have many spies, Lieutenant," he said evenly. "Although you've done well. This is the first I've heard of this latest development. Continue to get close to the princess and find out all you can, especially if she somehow surprises me again."

"I will." Joella stood. "And...my sister?"

"Oh, dear. Your sister's debts are long since paid." I could picture that evil smile growing on his face; I'd heard this a thousand times before. "But if you'd like to continue your employment in the captain's guard, you'll do well to keep feeding me information."

Joella said nothing but turned and walked out of the room. Poor girl; I could've told her that was going to happen. But also, if I was successful tonight, she wouldn't have to worry about him again.

"Asher, get the carriage, I'd like to visit our friends at the Hound's Tooth tonight." He rose and left the room. Once the room was empty, I yanked my listening device out of the window and wound it back up. Down below, Beswick stepped out of the building and into a waiting carriage. I counted four bodyguards with him—one inside, two on the front, and one on the back.

I loaded my crossbow with a sack of knockout powder and aimed at the carriage. It hit next to the man on the back, exploding in a puff of smoke. Not three seconds later, the back guard slumped forward and off the carriage.

I cursed as the vehicle came to a stop and the remaining three guards came to see what the noise was. They kicked their compatriot, calling to Beswick, who poked his head out. He glanced around at the sky, frowned, then called them back in. They took off at a much faster pace, and I followed on the rooftops.

I loaded up another knockout powder, but with the carriage

moving so quickly, I couldn't get a good shot in. Every time I got ahead of them, they'd take a left, and I'd have to scramble to catch up. I'd just have to go for it, I decided, and rushed forward, grabbing a well-placed clothesline as I wafted to the ground.

I landed in the middle of the road, and the horse screamed to a stop. Without missing a beat, I aimed and fired my crossbow, and the two men in front slumped over after a breath. The carriage door opened and both Beswick and his fourth guard came out.

"What the hell is this?" Beswick said, looking at the men on the ground. "Who the hell are you?"

I lifted my crossbow. "Your contracts, please."

"I'm sorry...what?" He cocked his head in my direction.

"The contracts you have with Severia and Kulka," I said, taking a step forward as the guards shared a confused look. "I want them. You will give them to me, or I will take them off your body."

"Oh, right, I think I've heard about you," Beswick said with a slow nod. "You're the little creature who keeps interfering with my business, or trying to, hm? Getting some poor souls out of deals, that kind of thing."

I didn't rise to the bait. "My patience is growing thin, Beswick. Give me the contracts, or this arrow goes into your chest. I promise you I'm a very good shot."

"And I am a very well-prepared man."

Footsteps echoed in the street behind me, above me, on the rooftop.

I was surrounded.

# Chapter Thirty-Three

"You see, my dear, I run a very tight ship," Beswick said. "When I don't arrive at the right time, my men come looking for me." He picked a dust bunny off his jacket. "Now I'm going to continue on my way. My associates will be more than happy to deal with your...complaints."

And with that, he stepped back into his carriage and it took off down the street.

With a quick glance around, I assessed my situation. Two behind me, including the back guard who'd woken from his slumber. One to my right and left, and two in front of me. I had no more knockout powder, just a knife that wouldn't do more than nick someone. My best option would be to find an exit and run like hell...

"Not so quick now, are ya?" one of the men grunted.

I smirked. "Well? I'm waiting."

But nobody moved—at least not toward me. Shadows appeared behind each of the men, and with one choreographed movement, the guards were disarmed. My heart dropped into my stomach as, too late, I realized who'd come for me.

Disembodied hands yanked me backward then tossed me over a shoulder and hurried away. I didn't need to guess who they belonged to.

"This is ridiculous," I said, struggling against the grip. "Put me down."

My captor said nothing but ducked into an alley and roughly threw me to the ground.

"Are you *insane?*" Felix barked, ripping off my mask with such ferocity that he probably took a clump of hair with it. "Going after Beswick like that? Alone?"

"I had an opening and I took it," I said, rubbing my stinging scalp. "I had it handled."

"You obviously didn't because half my squad is out there beating off Beswick's men," Felix said, pacing the room. "Do you know how stupid this was?"

"I'm getting the measure of it," I said, coming to stand. "I didn't realize he had men tracking his movements. I won't make that mistake again."

"You damn well won't, because you aren't leaving the castle again," he snarled.

"Oh, yeah?" I crossed my arms over my chest. "We had an agreement—"

"And you voided that the moment you got yourself surrounded by six men who could literally—*literally*—murder you with their bare hands."

"I didn't void *shit*," I shot back. "I said I had it *handled*. You didn't even give me a chance to—"

"Brynna, listen to yourself!"

"I am listening to myself. You, on the other hand, are not listening to me," I cried, throwing my hand in the air. "I made a damned mistake. I make those from time to time. I'm human. But that doesn't mean you can overreact like this!"

"This isn't a simple mistake," he said with a fierce shake of his head. "This could've potentially throw your entire kingdom into disarray. What am I supposed to tell the Council when you're taken prisoner by a known criminal? How am I supposed to tell them that you've been moonlighting as a vigilante and you're unable to make the next meeting because you're sitting in Beswick's basement, bloodied up?"

I rolled my eyes. "You're talking in hypotheticals now. I wasn't going to get captured."

"Yeah? Well your judgment is still impaired," he snapped. "Otherwise, why would you *lie* to me about being sick? Why go through all this trouble to entrap Joella—"

I exhaled loudly. "Because she's working with Beswick."

"You think I don't know that?"

My jaw fell open. "You *knew*? And you didn't tell me?" I shook my head, barely processing what I was hearing. "And more importantly, you let it go on?"

"I made sure to keep her off any important missions related to Beswick's interests," Felix said, wearing a look of moral superiority he definitely shouldn't have been wearing. "Gave her enough to keep her and her sister out of hot water."

"And that makes it better?" I blinked a few times. "Felix, that's treason."

"It's not treason. It's making the best of a bad situation," he replied. "That's something you have to do, from time to time, when you're in a leadership position. Not everything is black and white."

"It is, in this case," I said. "Joella is compromised. Maybe she didn't poison August, but *someone did*. And it's clear you don't have an objective view of this situation."

"That's bullshit," Felix said hotly. "I'd pin my entire career on their loyalty."

"Well, you shouldn't!" I shot back. "There were eight people who knew Kat wouldn't be in that room. August is dead, and Kat and Beata were meeting a Nestori woman, which leaves five people: Yourself and your so-called inner circle. Now if you don't see how that could possibly be an issue, maybe it's time you re-think your position here."

He licked his lips, and the bit of indecision felt like a victory parade. "Brynna, these people...the four I mentioned, I'd trust them with my life. I trust them with *your* life—"

"You trusted them with August's life and look what it got you."

He recoiled as if I'd slapped him.

"Felix," I said, not liking the way he was looking at me. "I'm not doing this because I hate you. I'm trying to find out who's responsible and, more importantly, who's trying to kill me. If I find out who in your circle is the leak, it'll lead me to the mastermind." I sighed. "Please let me do this, because you are obviously incapable of being objective here."

"So what part of August's death were you investigating when you took on Beswick?" Felix asked evenly.

It was my turn to be wordless. "Beswick is one of my suspects, so—"

"You're a piece of work, Brynna," Felix said, as a carriage rolled up behind him. "It's time you go back to the castle. And *stay* there."

A large procession of bloodied guards escorted me back to the castle, and none of them would look at me. But I didn't care. In my mind, they were all derelict in their duty, most of all Felix. I was still seething that he knew about Joella, and couldn't shake that he was hiding more from me. Perhaps he did know who the poisoner was, and he was protecting his staff. Perhaps he, himself, was the poisoner. It was a thought I hadn't completely dismissed, especially considering how much he hovered over me.

S. Usher Evans

Unsurprisingly, when I returned to my room, I was locked inside, but I didn't intend to stay there. In the few nights I'd been out on my own, I'd brought back more provisions for just such an occasion, including extra special gripping gloves I could use to climb down the tower. If I worked quickly, I could get back out there.

But when I ripped open the floorboard, my heart sank into my stomach. All my stuff was gone.

I frantically searched through the closets, the floorboards—anywhere I might've stashed a secret pouch of powder or an extra crossbow. But Felix had had this entire room picked clean. For not the first time that night, I released a long string of curses toward my captain, running to the door and banging with all my might. I didn't care if I broke the door down; in fact, I was hoping for it.

"Step away from the door."

Oh, how could he sound so calm. *"Screw you, you son of a bitch!"*

The lock turned over and the door swung outward. Felix walked past me, an unreadable look on his face. No less than ten guards waited outside the hallway as he closed the door behind him.

"We need to have a discussion about what happened tonight."

"Do we?" I asked dryly. "I'm so tired, Felix. I don't want to."

"Tough." He sat in the chair, wearing a stoic look and remaining quiet for a few moments. "I want to apologize for keeping Joella's involvement with Beswick a secret from you."

I snorted. "You? Apologize? That's new."

"Brynn, I'm trying," he said, and I made a gesture for him to continue. "She'd offered her resignation to me when Beswick first approached her, but we both thought it would be best if she continued on in a limited capacity. She's told me everything she told Beswick, on her honor, which—" He shook his head as I tried to interrupt. "Yes, I still believe to be worth taking."

"Beswick doesn't have her sister anymore," I replied. "Now he's just blackmailing Joella, or so he said last night."

"Which means that she remains stuck," he said. "Beswick has friends on the Council who could pressure me to fire her, and I would have no recourse."

"I wouldn't allow it."

"Godfryd would," he said. "And as it stands, I report to her. Technically."

"Godfryd is in bed with Beswick?" I shook my head. "Is everybody?"

"Yes, in one way or another," Felix said. "Which is why, even if you had proof of his treason, they might not do anything about it."

"Well, now we'll never know. I wasn't able to get the contracts because you interrupted me before—"

"Beswick was long gone before we showed up," Felix said. "I made sure of it."

My face warmed. He was right, but that didn't mean I wanted to admit it.

"I won't lie, you made a monumental mistake tonight," Felix said. "But I can also understand why you wouldn't include me in your planning. I understand why you suspect my men."

I sat up. He was being awfully mature about this—which raised some red flags. Was he concerned I might fire him? Concerned I might spill the beans on Joella and get her fired? Or, as I suspected, was he trying to win me over to prevent me from investigating him further?

"And you were right," he said with a sad shake of his head. "I haven't been objectively assessing suspects. Tonight showed me that I can't just blindly trust people to do what they say. Or to be as sick as they appear."

"If you want me to apologize for tricking you, I won't," I replied.

"I'm going to look at every one of the people you mentioned,"

Felix said. "Including Beata and Katarine. I don't think they're responsible, but they could have inadvertently said something to someone. Maybe even locate that Nestori witch."

"Good," I said, sitting up. "I'll help."

"Ah, no," Felix said with a smile. "You're not leaving the castle anymore. I thought we went over this."

I blinked at him. "But what was this apology if not telling me you were completely wrong?"

"I was wrong not to tell you everything, but I was absolutely right to save your ass, and absolutely right that you completely screwed up in going after Beswick by yourself," he said. "The two ideas are not mutually exclusive. Beswick had *nothing* to do with the poison, either, so don't even start with that."

At that, I was back on my feet. "You didn't even give me a chance to try to get out of it—"

"Because you shouldn't have gotten into it in the first place!"

I gnashed my teeth together, furious. "You can't just keep me in here. I'll tell people. I'll have you fired."

"Who? The Council?" He smirked. "Do you know the complete shitstorm you started by even mentioning that deal to Ilara?"

"I knew they weren't going to go for it," I said, though I wasn't confident in that assessment. "I was just giving him something to bite at."

"The only one who's going to get bitten is you, I'm afraid," he replied. "The Council has requested an emergency meeting in the morning for you to tell them all about your little chat. Based on the color of Garwood's face when he told Kat, I would clear your morning because you're going to get it. Unless, of course, you'd like to tell them that you put every other treaty we have in jeopardy so you could catch a low-level criminal?"

I swallowed. "I'll think of something."

"I'm sure you will. You're quite good at lying." He rose and walked to the door. "Have a good night."

I winced as it slammed shut.

# Chapter Thirty-Four

My door remained locked until midmorning when Beata brought my food. But she was accompanied by Riya, whose hatred of me was palpable. With eagle eyes on me, she kept a tight grip on her sword, waiting for me to rush her.

Just to screw with her, I jumped toward the door. Predictably, she unsheathed her sword with one movement, pointing it at me. Beata cried out in surprise, nearly knocking over the carafe. I sauntered over to the table and inhaled.

"Smells delicious. Thanks, Beata," I replied with my gaze on Riya.

"You need to mend fences around here," Beata said with a frown. "Or you'll find yourself without any friends."

"Don't tell me you'll stop being my friend, Beata," I said with a mock pout.

She scowled at me, the first negative reaction I'd gotten from Kat's chipper girlfriend in the weeks I'd known her. She wiped her hands on her apron and walked to the door, shaking her head at Riya, whose sword remained out and pointed at me.

"Down, girl," I said, sitting at the table and helping myself to some bread.

"Careful your food isn't poisoned, *Princess*," Riya replied. "None of us are too keen to test it for you anymore."

Proving a point, I slathered some butter on the roll and stuffed the whole thing in my mouth.

"Brynna, what are you doing?" Katarine asked, walking into the room with a stack of papers. She looked at Riya, who was basically snarling, and smiled encouragingly at her. "Riya, I think Felix needs you downstairs."

"It's not smart to leave her by herself," she said, but, nonetheless, put her sword away. "I'll be right outside."

"I'm sure you will," Katarine said, closing the door behind her. She looked at me and pursed her lips. "You have made quite a mess, my love."

"Have I now?" I said, taking a much smaller bite of the roll. "Please, do enlighten me."

"I have Garwood, Vernice, Godfryd, and even Zuriel banging down my door to speak with you this morning," she said. "They all want to know what could've possessed you to broker a deal with the Severian queen without their input. And a deal so clearly designed to favor the Severians."

"I was using it to get the attention of a hardened criminal," I replied with a smile.

"I'm sure that'll go over well," Katarine replied, shaking her head. "When the Kulkans and Niemenians find out, they'll want their own sweetheart deals. And it's not just that, the merchants will want to know why the Forcadel royal family is intervening. We have suppliers of glass other than the Severians. There are many on the border who swear allegiance to you. What will we tell them about how they'll suddenly have to cut their prices to stay competitive?" She exhaled. "This is a very big mess, Brynna."

"Well, then just have the Council veto it," I replied, grabbing an orange and peeling it, more to stay busy than because I was hungry. "That's what I thought they'd do anyway. Just veto whatever I said."

"They…Brynn, technically, they can't." She handed me one of the books she'd brought with her and opened it to a marked page. "International treaties are the sole responsibility of the royal. So if you signed—"

"It was a verbal agreement," I said. "I'll just tell her it's not going to work."

"First, you've got to talk to the Council," she said. "They've requested a meeting at noon today to talk with you. I suggest you and I come up with some ways to make them happy before then."

I might've felt more righteous in my shame had I actually procured something of value from it. But Beswick was out of my grasp, his contracts safely in his pocket, and I was nothing more than a princess in trouble with her Council. Still, I held my head high as I walked into the room, taking my seat and folding my hands on the table.

"Well, out with it," I replied. "I know you want to."

"You have potentially ruined several lucrative treaties with our neighbors," Garwood began. "I cannot fathom why you would enter into an agreement with the queen of such a poor country."

Katarine had advised me to keep my opinions and responses to myself, and just let them get their tongue lashing out of their system. To keep myself focused, I pressed my thumbnail into my palm, the pain reminding me that this was temporary, and that speaking would make it worse.

"The Kulkans will be furious," Vernice said. "They're already annoyed that you've allowed that desert-dweller to stay in the castle as long as she has. But they allowed it because they thought it was merely a place to land, not that you were devising ill-advised treaties."

I pressed my nail harder into my wrist.

Now Godfryd spoke up. "I have to send my already stretched forces to help move glass? *Glass*? You couldn't have bargained for something worth more value? The cost to move your soldiers won't even come close to the amount of money Forcadel could make off the shipments."

"It won't be our glass, it'll remain theirs," Garwood replied with a sharp look at me. "We're just the glorified escorts."

I glanced at the remaining two; Zuriel was waiting his turn, and even Octavius was actually awake. I would be curious if he'd have anything of value to add, or if he'd just echo what the others had said. Instead, surprisingly, Zuriel gave me a wink. Perhaps they weren't all angry at me after all.

"Well?" Garwood said. "What do you have to say for yourself?"

Slowly, I rose from the table. Katarine and I had practiced what I'd say, and the words came from my lips as if I were being controlled by some puppet master.

"It's clear I miscalculated," I began. "The Severians have a hard life, and I was swayed by their requests for help. I did not sign any official documents, therefore, any agreements I made are bound by my word alone. With your approval, I will undo what I've done, and seek non-royal means to help the Severians." I ran my tongue over my teeth with disgust. "I apologize for causing such discord on the Council."

"Well, now," Octavius said with a grin. "That sounds just fine, Your Highness."

Garwood shot him a furious look. "Verbal or not, it still constitutes an agreement. You can't go around agreeing to things without letting us know."

"It won't happen again."

"And I just cannot understand why you would think you could make such an agreement in the first place," Vernice said. "Perhaps it's time we consider that she is not the right person for the throne."

I quirked a brow, my thumbnail now close to drawing blood from my palm.

"Ana, don't be ridiculous," Garwood said. "She's the heir—"

"Heir, and nearly upending our entire economy," Vernice said. "It's just something we should consider. It won't take much to declare her unfit for the throne, and then the crown will pass to—"

"A drunk," I replied, deciding my thumb-in-hand tactic wasn't going to work anymore. "Is he fit for the throne? Or would you just consider him more malleable than I am? I'll remind you that our murderer remains at large."

"I thought Captain Llobrega captured him," she replied with a narrow eye. "And he died of—"

"He was poisoned to keep his silence," I replied. "Which means he was an innocent man."

"Now's not the time to talk about this," Garwood said. "We need to stay focused on how we'll resolve this Severian crisis."

"I think it's absolutely the right time to talk about it," I replied. "Since a Councilor just asked that I renounce my throne. Seems fishy, hm? Bitch can't kill me, so she'll have me declared unfit instead."

Vernice gasped and Garwood shook his head. "Brynna, no need to be rude."

I sat back and pressed my thumb into my palm once again, remembering that I was trying to get out of this Council meeting without too many bruises.

"We are not discussing Princess Brynna's fitness for the throne," Garwood said, casting a warning look at Vernice. "Maurice made his share of governing mistakes, and we gave him the space to recover from them. If you'll recall, Ana."

She sniffed, clearly still salty that I'd called her a bitch. But she deserved it.

"As long as this agreement doesn't become any more than a verbal discussion, I don't think we have to worry," Garwood said, glancing between me and Vernice. "The envoys from Kulka and Niemen are on their way, and we'll be able to smooth things over when they arrive, inform them that the princess merely made a mistake. It should satisfy them—as long as the Severians are gone from the castle, and that agreement is voided."

I nodded. So much for helping Ilara. "Agreed."

"Excellent," Garwood said, taking his seat. "Now, if no one else has any business to discuss, I'm sure that's enough excitement for one day."

# Chapter Thirty—Five

Unsurprisingly, there were two guards waiting for me outside the Council room, and I was practically frog-marched into my room and locked in. Katarine came shortly thereafter and spent the afternoon with me, drafting how I would approach Ilara and ways we could still help her. She wasn't pleased I'd called Vernice a bitch, but overall, thought that the meeting had gone as well as could be expected.

When night fell, the door turned over and Felix walked in, carrying a book under his arm and a blanket in the other.

"What are you doing here?" I asked, having not spoken to him since the night before. "Are you going to let me out?"

"No." He sat down in front of the fire, pulling off his boots and sitting back on the chair. "Since it's clear you can't be trusted, I'm staying here for the night."

I stared at him, dumbfounded. "Are you serious?"

"Clearly one of us has to be. Since you're too blinded by your own ego to set it aside for five minutes."

"That's rich, coming from you," I scoffed. "At least I'm trying to make a difference."

"By getting yourself killed."

I exhaled. "I'm making good with the Severians. I have breakfast with Ilara in the morning to kick them out of the castle. The Council's pissed but taken care of."

"Excellent," he said, cracking open the book. "But you still almost got yourself killed last night."

I scowled. "I didn't, actually."

"Go to sleep," he said, turning the page.

"You've *got* to be kidding me," I said, marching over to him. "Are you really doing this? Really, Felix? I'm a grown adult."

"Prove to me I can trust you in here and I will leave you alone."

I released a frustrated growl. "I don't have to prove *anything* to you."

"Then I'll stay here, reading this fascinating book on a Forcadel naval battle, and you can just stew."

That was it. I dove for him, knocking him out of the chair and onto the floor. We were a tangle of limbs and grunts as I struggled to get the upper hand. But he was quicker, slapping a metal handcuff around my left wrist then my right. I shot my leg out and kicked over the chair, screaming in fury as I struggled against the manacles.

The door flew open and three of his guards came running in, swords drawn.

"Stand down," Felix said, pressing his hand onto my back. "I have her handled."

I released another filthy string of curses, the worst I could think of, but all it made him do was laugh as he pulled me upright and marched me to the bed.

"Are you going to be nice?" he asked, unlocking my left arm.

In response, I reared back and tried to choke him. He grabbed my wrist and twisted it behind me, sending a shot of pain up my arm. I gritted my teeth and exhaled slowly, but didn't cry out.

"Since it's clear you aren't going to behave," he replied, replacing the cuff on my left wrist.

Then the bastard procured a second set of handcuffs and attached me to the bed.

"You cannot be serious?" I said, lifting my conjoined hands and tugging against the wooden bed frame. "Are you serious right now?"

"Yup."

He righted his chair, which had been kicked over in the scuffle, and sat down, picking up his book and kicking his feet up, exactly as he'd been before I'd attacked him.

I exhaled loudly through my nose. "As queen, I order you release me from captivity."

"Your royal orders only have weight if your captain gives them weight," he replied casually. "Also, you aren't queen yet."

"Queen enough."

"You keep missing the larger point," he replied, turning the page. "You don't get power merely because you have a crown on your head. You have power because the people have given it to you. They trust that you're the right one to lead them into prosperity. And if they think, for even a moment, that you aren't that one, you will lose your power and be nothing more than a scowling teenager."

"Thank you, Felix, for a lesson I've already received. But I'm telling you to unlock me and leave."

He just laughed and shook his head. "Why don't you think about what I just told you and we can talk in the morning? Katarine will be returning early to continue your lessons. It's clear you still need them."

"It's clear I'm going to murder you."

"Oh?" He looked up from the book and smiled, damn it. "Please, I'd love to see you try without your weapons."

"I broke a man's arm."

"You had the element of surprise and darkness. And right now, you're chained to a bed."

"I hate you so much right now."

"I know you do." He lifted the book and settled into the chair. "So perhaps you should just close your eyes and go to sleep so you don't have to look at me anymore."

I stood next to the headboard, glaring at his stupid face as he purposefully read. Oh, if he thought he could outlast me, he was sorely mistaken. I could spend hours on a rooftop, watching for signs of trouble. My righteous anger would keep me up all night. Because I would be damned if Felix Llobrega won this round, or any round, ever again.

I awoke with my handcuffs missing, but Felix still in my room. He was awake, reading his book with a half-eaten breakfast tray sitting in front of him.

"Good morning," he replied, closing the book with a loud sound. "Can I trust you not to stab me with the butter knife?"

I rolled out of bed and rubbed my wrists, too tired to argue with him. I was still wearing the same clothes from the night before, and my hair was coming out of the plait. But I made no move to fix it. It wasn't as if I was trying to woo Felix to my bed, unless I was going to murder him afterward.

I marched over to the table where my breakfast was waiting and plopped down, helping myself to coffee and a scone. There was an assortment of iced pastries and muffins, instead of my usual fruit, and the coffee was extra strong. It was clear Beata was trying to put me in a good mood.

Unfortunately, my breakfast companion ruined any chance of that.

"Are you always this beautiful in the morning?" Felix asked, a ghost of a smile dancing on his lips. "Your hair is...exquisite."

"I'm not used to sleeping a full night," I said, running a hand over my frizzing hair. "Why are you still here? It's day. I'm not going to disappear."

"I don't quite trust you," he said, grabbing another icing-covered pastry from my set. "And we have to talk about your meeting with Ilara today."

Yawning, I poured myself another cup and downed it in one gulp. "I'm going to tell her that the Council overruled me. Kat and I already talked about other ways we can help them." I paused, giving him a glance. "You know what would be the best option? If Beswick was just...out of the picture entirely. Then he wouldn't be able to stiff them."

"I'm sure that would be the best option. It's not the most realistic, but it's the best."

"If you'd let me out of my room, I could—"

"Brynna," he said with a sigh. "No."

Beata arrived shortly after that, and I was allowed to bathe and get changed into one of my nicer dresses. Felix was gone when I returned, but Katarine had taken his place, helping herself to the pastries.

"I heard you and Felix had a good night," she said with a wink at Beata.

"Don't even start," I replied, stepping into my dress. "I can't believe you condoned him handcuffing me to the bed."

"I mean, it's not my kink, but..."

I gasped and looked over my shoulder. Katarine wore a mischievous smirk on her face and Beata giggled as she tied the sash around my waist.

"This is grossly unfair," I said. "Two against one."

Coyle was my guard of the day, escorting me down to where the Severians were staying. It was clear nobody had told them they needed to vacate, as the earthy scents of perfumes and teas met my nose the closer I came to Ilara's quarters. I was let inside a room I no longer recognized. The curtains were of a thicker fabric, blocking the warm sunlight and leaving it rather chilly and smelling of sheep. Shaggy rugs sat on the floor made of torn fabric that I almost tripped over as I walked into the room.

Ilara had a beautiful spread before me, eggs and fruit arranged in an intricate pattern. I ate none of it, but smiled politely as she came out of her bedroom and joined me in the room.

"It is a glorious morning, is it not?" she asked. "I wish my handlers would let me open the windows more. But they're so concerned about my well-being."

"Yeah, I know all about that," I replied, rubbing my wrists. "I come with bad news. I'm...not going to be able to follow through with that treaty we discussed."

She smiled, clasping her hands on her knees. "I know. I had a feeling."

"I'm sorry, I didn't mean to get your hopes up." I chewed on my lip. "I was trying to do something and I was using our treaty to accomplish it."

"Did you do it?"

"Um..." I tilted my head to the side. "Yes and no. But it doesn't matter. The Council was furious with me for even considering it. And I'm afraid it's just made things worse."

"I understand completely. I've made a few mistakes myself in the course of trying to do the right thing." She stared at her hands. "I also assume you're here to ask me to pack up and go back to my country, hm?"

"They would like you to do that," I said with a wince. "Apparently, your presence is offensive to our richer allies who are on their way for my coronation."

She barked out a laugh then dissolved into giggles. "You certainly have a way with words, Brynna."

"It's ridiculous," I said with a laugh of my own. "But...I feel like I have to play by the rules for a little bit. Right now, it feels like the entire country hates me. Or at least everyone in the castle."

She tilted her head to the side. "Your captain, it seems, is quite fond of you."

"My captain is about to lose his job, his head, or his manhood, I'm not sure which," I snapped, glowering at the dark liquid as if it were Felix himself.

"Ah, well, I'd assumed something might have been going on between you." She shrugged. "It's not uncommon for the protector to become attached to the protected."

"Uh...no," I said as my cheeks warmed. "Felix just wants me to live long enough to sit on the throne. And we have differing opinions on the best way to do that. And right now..." I released a breath, thinking about him and his smug smile as he watched me all night. "Right now, he's not on my good side. He's decided I can't be trusted to wipe my own ass anymore."

"Mm, perhaps," Ilara said. "But I have to say, the way he watches you, it's clear that he has feelings for you. And perhaps whatever happened to make him react this way...his reaction isn't really the most rational because, well...love isn't rational."

My warm cheeks enflamed more. I thought he was concerned for my health out of duty. But what if he was in love with me, as Ilara was saying? Could I use it to sway him to let me out?

Ilara laughed as she patted my hand. "Brynna, be careful. A man's heart is every bit as breakable as yours. Felix seems like a good man."

I had my doubts about his goodness at the moment. "I'm not going to do anything to hurt him. Emotionally. But if I can manipulate him to loosen his grip, even a little...then it's worth it." I chewed my lip. I had plenty of practice in basic seduction, but Felix would require more than a flash of my ample bosom.

She laughed. "Perhaps you could try a little vulnerability. Have a conversation about your childhood. Commiserate. That kind of thing. You're such a closed-off person. It might be enough to mend whatever was broken between you."

"I don't want to *mend* it. I want him to get off my back."

"Oh, sweet Brynna, that's what I'm trying to help you with," Ilara said with a giggle. "If you can open yourself up, perhaps he'll trust you again. And when he trusts you again, he'll get off your back." She winked. "Or, you know, maybe get on it, if you want."

I rubbed my chin thoughtfully. "I guess."

"And in the meantime, I'll help matters by getting back on the sea as quickly as possible," she said with a smile. "I will miss you, Brynna."

"Me, too," I said, clasping her hand. "I hope this won't be the last I see of you."

She squeezed my hand. "The Mother wouldn't allow it."

# Chapter Thirty-Six

My breakfast with Ilara was the only excitement I was allowed, it seemed, because I was marched back to my room and locked inside. Even Katarine didn't bother to visit. My only company was Beata with lunch, who could stay for a moment. Since I'd slept the entire night before, I spent the afternoon standing at my window and seething out at the dark gray sky and rough waters. About mid-afternoon, a squall blew by, which gave me about an hours' worth of entertainment.

But I did spend some time thinking about what Ilara had said about Felix. I hadn't noticed a change in our relationship, but perhaps I'd just missed the obvious signs. I wasn't ever one for romantic entanglements. Tasha the butcher's son had been a convenient bedmate. There had been a boy in Celia's camp who I'd thought had pretty eyes, but I couldn't even remember his name now.

Still, this wasn't about romance, it was about manipulation. And for that, I had the perfect topic of conversation.

Like the night before, Felix arrived at nightfall with a book and a blanket, setting himself up on the chair. He set a pair of handcuffs down on the table before sitting and pulling off his boots.

"I hope you aren't going to try to fight me again," Felix said, resting his bare feet on the table near the fire. "I'm not in the mood, so I won't be gentle."

"Are you ever?" I asked, rubbing the small bruise he'd left on the back of my arm the night before. Then I glanced up at him. "Gentler than Celia, anyway."

His eyes met mine for a moment then he went back to his book.

"This kind of reminds me of her," I said, sitting back on the bed. "Some of the kids who tried running away would get handcuffed to their beds until they learned better. Usually only took one time, you know?" I shivered, keeping the memory at bay.

Felix still hadn't shown any sign he was listening, so I continued.

"The night I ran away...the first time," I said, sitting back on the bed and curling my legs under myself, "I almost thought Celia was waiting for me. I barely got past the gates of the castle before I was stuffed into a carriage and led out of town."

He turned the page, but I knew he was listening.

"I wasn't scared, really. Probably should've been, but I was pretty sheltered. All I knew was that if I allowed my father to marry me off to a Kulkan prince, I'd never see my home again. Never breathe in the salty air or get splashed by a wave. And whatever Celia had in store for me was a better option than that."

"Celia lives on the Kulkan border," Felix said. "That, at least, I know."

"But still within the country," I said. "She knew who I was immediately, but for the first few months, I was like any other runaway. I had to become useful or get the hell out. So I became useful."

He turned another page.

"I already knew how to use a sword, which gave me an advantage over everyone else there. Celia taught me how to defend myself without it, and with every other weapon in her arsenal. If I didn't win, I didn't eat. So I learned how to win."

"That certainly explains a lot."

I resisted the urge to roll my eyes. "At first, all she did was send me out as a scout. It annoyed me, because I could defend myself —"

"But perhaps she wanted to protect you," Felix said, looking up at me. "Sounds familiar."

"No," I said softly. "She wanted to use me. It's the reason I don't have a brand on my arm. She wanted to keep me scared enough to stay, but happy enough not to realize I could run back here and ruin her operation."

The smirk faded from his face. "So why'd you leave?"

A pair of lifeless eyes flashed across my mind and my heart skipped a beat. I'd wanted to open up a little, but there were some things that were too sacred to be used for this purpose. My cheeks warmed as the silence stretched out between us, and I struggled to come up with something that wasn't the truth.

"I told you, I decided I was over it," I said after a long pause. "I wanted to use my skills to help people. That's why I went out at night. And why...why I think you should let me out again. Because I can help people."

"Mm," he replied, flipping the page. "I don't think you want to help people. I think your ego wants to do what it wants, and doesn't care about who you are or what you represent. If you wanted to, you could use your position as queen to make Forcadel better."

"I tried that."

"No, you used your position to get to Beswick. You didn't use your position to help anyone but yourself, and it was selfish."

That word again. I hated it, especially coming from Felix's mouth. "How is taking out one of the most notorious crime bosses in the city *selfish*?"

"Because *you* won't let *anyone else* do it for you," he said. "I think you couldn't care less about your people, because if you did, you wouldn't want to be out there, risking your life, when you could do more as queen. If you wanted to, you could send any one of my guards out in your stead to investigate, but instead *you* drag both of us out in the middle of the night. All you care about is getting the glory as some masked vigilante." He shifted in the seat. "And since it's my job to keep you alive, here we are."

My face was burning as I struggled to find the words to refute him. But there was a sick feeling in my stomach now, one that very clearly wanted me to admit Felix had a point. When I'd begun my life as The Veil, there had been a purpose, a greater goal. But now, maybe I'd forgotten why I donned the mask. And that sat like a weight on my chest.

"Now, if you're done trying to manipulate me," he said, rising to his feet, "I think Riya might be a better watchman for you. At least she's wise to your bullshit."

I winced as the door slammed behind him.

Riya was now my nightly companion, arriving at dusk and leaving before I woke up. I barely saw Felix except in passing in the hallway, where he did his best to avoid my gaze. Confessions and apologies threatened to bubble from my lips in those brief moments, but I kept them to myself.

The Severians moved out of the castle within three days, but per Katarine, they were still unable to make the trek back home. Ilara had come down with a horrible illness, and had to remain ensconced in an inn near the water until she was well enough to travel. But she was out of the castle, which seemed to appease my

Council. They were still furious with me over the treaty incident, but with time and silence, they soon grew to a tepid dislike. Garwood had even resumed our weekly lunches, although I still let him do most of the talking. Mostly because I had nothing to offer.

The only people in the castle who still enjoyed my company were Katarine and Beata, who joined me for breakfast every morning before we continued our lessons. Beata had even started adding more sweets to my meals, but they didn't help.

"Not even a smile?" Beata asked, as she placed the plate of iced pastries in front of me.

"Not much to smile about," I replied, looking out the window. "Felix hates me, I'm stuck in my room all day only to be let out to be ignored by my Council. And worst of all...Beswick is still out there ruining lives and there's nothing I can do about it."

"But I had the cook make you chocolate," Beata said, holding one up hopefully. When I shrugged half-heartedly, she pouted and put it back down. "See, Kat? I told you it wouldn't help. She needs to get out of the castle."

"Like that'll happen," I replied dryly.

"Maybe I can work on Felix," Katarine said. "We could take another day trip out into the city, buy you some more dresses. He could even come with us, if he's so concerned about you."

"I wouldn't give you the slip," I said with a half-smile. "But I don't think going on a girls' trip would make me feel any better. I don't think anything would make me feel better."

Beata shared a look with Katarine, who rolled her eyes and shushed her as she took Beata's hand. "I'm sure that's not true. Let me talk to Felix about it. You've been very good as of late. He's got to loosen his grip a little."

"Good?" I muttered, casting them a look. They seemed very cozy, holding hands and giving me the same concerned, motherly look. Oddly, it made me miss Felix even more. Despite the pain in my heart, I forced a smile onto my face. "Thank you for taking such good care of me. I do appreciate you both."

Beata chuckled and rose, wiping her hands on her apron then kissed Katarine on the forehead. "I suppose I'd better get to it."

"Have a good day," Katarine replied, watching her as she walked out the door.

"I can see what August was talking about, if that's how you two were around him," I said, shoving the rest of the pastry into my mouth. "So what's on our agenda this morning?"

"I have a special treat for you today," she said. "You have a full day of citizen grievances."

I quirked a brow. "I haven't had one of those in a while."

"No, you haven't. The Council wasn't sure, after the last one..." She cleared her throat. "But they feel you can be trusted now. And besides, there's quite a queue."

I shook my head. I was getting tired of being treated like an impetuous child. "So they want me docile and stupid? Color me surprised."

"It's all temporary," Katarine said, taking my hand. "But for today, it's probably best to continue that trend. Don't agree to anything and don't—"

"I know, I know," I said. "Are you sure they want me and not a sack of potatoes?"

She smiled. "You've got a nicer shape than a sack of potatoes."

In the receiving room, I assumed the position and rested my chin on my hand. Galton was back, walking with purpose into the room with a thick stack of papers. He bowed low at the hip and straightened.

"Good morning, Your Highness. We have fifty citizens to meet with today, so please take caution not to spend too much time with each person."

"I won't," I mumbled. Now even the attendant was telling me

what to do? Had I really sunk so low?

The parade of citizenry was more or less the same as the first time. Merchants asking for help, disagreements between neighbors that needed my input. Requests to increase my budget.

"I'm sorry," I replied softly. "I'm unable to help."

The last woman nodded and walked away, taking a piece of my heart with her. I exhaled and sat back in my chair, holding my chin in my hand. Felix had said that I could help more people as queen, but I hadn't done any of that. Instead, I'd unilaterally denied even valid requests, all so I could regain the trust of my Council. It seemed to me that everyone should be working toward the prosperity of Forcadel and its citizens. So why did it feel like I was the only one who cared about that?

I glanced at the other end of the room where Felix was standing at attention, and the urge to reach out to him was strong. But just as I caught his gaze, he turned to leave, and Joella took his place.

"Oh, don't look so glum, Your Highness!" Zuriel strode in with a bright white smile. "I come bearing good news on the progress of your summer festival."

The summer festival, that was something to look forward to. Maybe if I strained my ears, I'd be able to hear the music from my locked tower. "Please, give me some good news."

"We have three hundred merchants in town or on their way," he said, showing me a sheet of paper. "Our inns are filling up and our coffers are, too, from all the import taxes. So much so that it appears we have a surplus for the year." He paused. "I came to ask for your guidance on what you'd like to do with it."

I hesitated. "What are my options?"

"We could commission a new art piece for the castle, perhaps. Or purchase some new flowers for your coronation ceremony. I may have a line on some blue flowers that grow along the banks of the Vanhoja River."

"Do I have to spend it on myself?" I asked, a pleading note in my voice.

Zuriel thought for a moment. "I guess we could give it to Godfryd. Perhaps the captain's guard would like a bonus. They have been working extra hard lately."

That wasn't exactly what I meant, but it would have to do. I cast a look at Joella and wished she was Felix. "That sounds fine. I know they'll appreciate it."

"I must say," he said with a grin, "this will be a festival to remember. I've never seen the people so excited to welcome you as our queen."

I wished I could smile, but I just didn't feel like it.

# Chapter Thirty-Seven

When I returned to my room, faces and sounds of disappointment echoed in my mind. I opened the window, leaning out and letting the wind cool my face. I wasn't sure how long I stood there, but Beata came and left with my dinner and I didn't have the energy to acknowledge her.

I needed out. I needed to walk somewhere without Felix or guards or anyone looking over my shoulder, without anyone judging my behavior or deciding if I'd been "good enough" to allow me to help others. I released my grip on the sill and craned my neck upward. Well, they may not let me out of the building, but I could still get a bit of freedom.

I climbed up onto the sill, holding onto the outside of the window. I leaned forward and grabbed the ledge above, hanging by my fingertips. I swung myself forward and backward then propelled myself up onto the roof, landing on my feet.

Rising, I stood on the edge of my roof and inhaled, taking in the sight of the kingdom before me. And for the first time in a few days, I exhaled a loud, freeing breath. The weight on my chest lessened. And with a smile on my face, I leaned backward to lie on the still-warm tile roof of the castle.

The stars were just starting to twinkle above me as the sky changed color. Another rare wind blew the humidity away from my face, leaving goosebumps on my skin. I rested my hands under my head and closed my eyes, imagining I was back at the butchery, catnapping until another night saving the kingdom.

"Son of a..."

Riya's dulcet tones echoed up from the open window, followed by a lot of banging and clanging. A few minutes later, Felix's angry voice came wafting out, too.

"I can't imagine she's gone far," he said. "Zathan and Coyle are at the bottom of the stairs, and—"

"I'm up here," I called, loud enough for him to hear.

"Y—Brynna? Where are you?"

"Are you on the *roof*?" Riya cried.

"Yep." I adjusted myself and sighed. "Come up if you want."

"Come back in here *this instant*," Felix barked. "What if you slip and fall?"

"I'm in no danger," I replied. "Why don't you come out and see?"

His fingertips appeared on the edge of the roof, followed by the rest of him. He wore a scowl as he crawled on his hands and knees toward me. "Brynna, this is exceptionally dangerous."

I sighed. "It's too hot in my room. The air doesn't move. The bed is warm and sticky, too."

"I'm absolutely sure that this has nothing to do with driving me crazy, hm?" He hadn't turned back around to admire the view, and his knuckles were white.

"Are you afraid?" I asked.

He glared at me. "I'm afraid of sitting on a sloped roof where the slightest wrong move could send me sliding to my death, yes."

I laughed and propped myself up on my elbows. "So don't

make any wrong moves and you'll be fine."

"Brynna, I have had a very long day, and I'm not in the mood for your games."

"This isn't a game, Felix. I just wanted some fresh air," I replied softly.

"So go out to the gardens. Or anywhere else that's not a thousand feet up in the air."

"You won't let me. You've trapped me in my room." I smiled, gazing up at the stars. "Lie down and you'll understand what I'm talking about."

Grumbling, he carefully turned onto his back. "What am I supposed to be seeing?"

"The stars, Felix. They're up in the sky."

"I can see the stars from the ground." He craned his neck toward the black sky then quickly returned to me. "There, I looked at them, can we please get back into your room?"

"I like being up here."

"No, you don't, you—"

"Felix, I'm being serious." I closed my eyes. "This isn't another ploy to try to convince you to let me out tonight. I've had a hard day, too."

"Pardon me if I don't believe you after all the stunts you've pulled."

His words stung, but they weren't untrue. "I'm sorry for lying to you."

"Are you drunk?" Felix asked, eyeing me. "Or is this another —"

"I'm just trying to apologize, you ass," I snapped. "Isn't that what you wanted from me? I'm acknowledging what I did wrong and promising to do better."

"It's just so rare. I didn't think it was possible."

I turned to him, ready to argue further, but stopped at the smirk on his lips. It drew a smile onto mine and a lessening of the

298

knot in my chest.

"Joella told me about the bonus to the soldiers," he said. "Thank you for that."

"Well, my options were to buy a painting, get some blue flowers, or give my soldiers a bonus." I turned back to the stars. "And after telling everyone else no today, I wanted to do something for somebody else."

"It'll get easier," he said.

I sighed heavily. "I don't want it to get easier. I want to help people. I didn't help anyone today except the guards and, no offense, they're doing just fine." I shook my head. "I want to help the poor people in Haymaker's District, like I used to do as The Veil. Now, I'm just one of the rich people who's part of the problem."

"See, there it is again," Felix said.

"What?"

"That ego," He sat up. "I don't believe for a second that helping the people in Haymaker's is about anything other than giving you glory. Being altruistic for selfish reasons isn't very altruistic at all."

I blew air out between my lips. "You just have no idea."

"Then illuminate me," he said.

"Being the Veil used to be a sacred thing to me. It was...it was penance for what I did. Even if that thing was unforgivable, it made me feel like I was doing my best to atone for it."

"Did you...kill someone?"

I couldn't help the sharp intake of breath that gave me away, so I continued staring at the stars, my heartbeat throbbing in my chest.

"You said The Veil didn't kill."

"The Veil didn't." I squeezed my eyes shut. "Brynna did. Or Larissa. Me. I killed a man before I became The Veil. Killing him made me The Veil. I decided to become The Veil after I..." I forced my lips shut to keep from rambling.

He was quiet for a moment. "Brynna, I'm sure that however it happened was an accident—"

"It wasn't," I said, replaying the scene in my mind. "We were robbing a carriage, and one of the guards was aiming for one of ours. So I..." I swallowed hard. "I shot him."

"To save your own," Felix said. "I can't imagine—"

"It was Holden Oleander."

I wasn't sure why the name of Felix's guard tumbled from my lips, but once it had, I regretted it. Felix sucked in a breath and released my hand, staring at me as if he'd never seen me before.

"You...*you* killed Holden Oleander?"

I averted my gaze so I wouldn't see his disgust. "It was the very first mission Celia gave me to lead. She wanted the diamonds they were transporting—I think they were for Kat, actually. It seemed like something that wouldn't hurt anyone, but...there were more guards than I'd thought. I tried to use knockout powder, but..."

Oleander's lifeless eyes flashed through my mind and I shuddered. But more terrifying was the deafening silence coming from Felix, so I kept talking to fill it.

"When I came back to camp, Celia wanted me to act like it was nothing. Like taking a man's life was...just a part of doing business. But I couldn't live with myself. I had to do something... so I decided to leave the camp and turn myself in." I was finally brave enough to open my eyes, but not brave enough to look at him. "To you, actually. I saw you and Fishen telling Oleander's family and I was ready to...just hope you didn't recognize me so you'd throw me in jail where I belonged." I swallowed. "But before I could get that far, I saved a woman from two street thugs. Fishen saw me do it and told me that if I really wanted to repent...maybe I could do it by helping people instead." A tear fell down my cheek and I didn't wipe it away. "So I did. Every time I put on that mask, I would remind myself why I was there. And maybe I strayed a

little from that in my pursuit of Beswick. But I'm not doing this...
I just wanted to find some forgiveness for what I did. To be able to
look at myself in the mirror and not be disgusted with what I saw."
I closed my eyes again. "Now I'm part of the problem. Sitting on a
throne and telling people I can't help them because I have to keep
all my gold for myself."

Felix was silent for a long time, and more tears fell as I
ruminated over what I'd said. The gentle touch of his thumbs
wiping the tears from my cheeks prodded my eyes open into his
sad, brown ones.

"Oleander's death was..." He paused. "Well, it was. But you
don't have to be part of the problem. You *can* help people—even
more than you have as The Veil. And when you're queen, I have no
doubts that you'll do everything in your power to destroy Beswick
and anyone else who's harming people in this city. But you have to
be careful that in the pursuit of one evil, you aren't unleashing
more." His thumb brushed against my cheek again, although there
were no tears to be found. "That's why you have to listen to us. We
all want what's best for Forcadel."

I stared into his eyes, words tumbling from my lips before I
could stop them. "I'm sorry. About...about Oleander. I wish that
I..."

His eyes shifted, but his hand didn't leave my cheek. Instead,
he pressed a sweet kiss to my forehead. "C'mon, let's get off this
roof already."

I barked a laugh, bolstered by the feather-light feel of his lips
lingering on my forehead. "Felix, we've been running on rooftops
for weeks now. Surely you're no longer afraid of heights."

"Heights, no. Sitting on top of a tall tower? Yes."

I sat up, wiping my face with my free hand. "Fine. I'll walk you
through getting back into the room, O fearless Captain of my
Guard."

# Chapter Thirty-Eight

Talking with Felix had lifted a weight off my chest, and not just because I was allowed out of my room again. Our relationship was damaged, but it wasn't broken. And I was surprised at how much I wanted it mended. Even though I wanted to visit Ilara in the city and tell her how I'd fared with her advice, I didn't broach the subject. Even the Council was starting to tolerate me again, and I wanted to keep things moving forward.

Two weeks before my coronation, I awoke to new ships in the harbor again—this time bearing the colors of Kulka and Niemen. Unlike when the Severians had surprised us, the castle had been preparing for their arrival for the past few days, or so Beata told me.

"This is a good thing," Beata said, as she worked on my hair. "It means the waiting is over. You're going to be queen soon." She leaned down to whisper in my ear. "And I know Kat's excited to see the Niemen delegation. Look at her."

Indeed, Katarine stood against the window, practically climbing out of it with anticipation.

"Leave her alone," I said with a small nudge. "It's not easy to leave home."

"I wonder who it could be," Katarine said, walking away from the window and wringing her hands. "Perhaps Silvia? Maybe even one of my cousins." She made a face. "I hope Ariadna didn't send a cousin. That would mean she doesn't find you very powerful. Better hope it's a sibling."

"Thanks," I drawled as Beata giggled.

As soon as I finished dressing, Felix arrived with news from the convoys he'd sent to greet the boats.

"We are to receive Lord Melwin of Kulka," he said, reading off the paper. "He's a ranking member of their Council."

"And from Niemen?" Katarine asked, a little breathlessly.

"Prince Luard von—"

He didn't finish as Katarine gasped so loudly it cut him off. "Are you serious? *Luard* is here?"

"Yes," Felix said with a smile. "And he's very excited to see you."

Tears actually gathered in her eyes. "I haven't seen him since I was a girl. I can't believe he came. Oh, what a wonderful day!" She twirled a few times, giggling, then stopped. "Oh, I've got to change. I can't let him see me wearing this. And my hair is so out of style—"

"Bea," I said, looking up at her. "Why don't you get Kat ready to see her brother, hm? Felix and I can finish up here."

"Come along, silly girl," Beata said, wrapping her arms around Katarine and walking her out of the room.

"That was weird," I said, after the door shut behind them. "I've never seen her so excited before."

"She hasn't had a lot to be excited about in a while," Felix said. "But it's a good sign that the Niemenians sent Luard, and an even better sign about Melwin. Both of them will be authorized to speak on behalf of their kingdoms." He paused. "It would be like you sending me to represent you in a foreign nation."

I turned, pensive. "Can I do that? Get you out of my hair for a bit? You'd probably like Kulka…"

"Funny," he said dryly, offering his arm. "Shall we?"

The receiving hall had been completely transformed. Now, giant blue flags hung from the rafters, and behind my throne, another banner bearing the Lonsdale crest. Like Felix, the royal guard wore their dress uniforms, navy-colored with glinting silver buttons down the front. But it wasn't just the usual squad of soldiers; even the younger kids stood at attention at the end of the room, their swords scraping the floor behind them.

"Your guards look very presentable," I said under my breath. "All of them."

He nodded. "It's the first day I've let the younger kids in the main throne room. If they embarrass me, I'll flog them within an inch of their lives."

"I'm sure," I said, as I released him and ascended the throne. But I stopped before I got there. There was a new cushion on the throne—in fact, even the dais on which it sat had new velvet coverings. Instead of the royal red, it was the same dark blue that matched the guards.

"What's wrong?" Felix asked.

"Throne's new," I said, pointing to it.

"It's about time, isn't it?" he said. "It's yours. Might as well be updated for you."

For me. For the queen. Why that realization hit me at that moment, I didn't know, but it was hard to breathe again. Perhaps in the back of my mind, I'd always thought I'd wriggle out of becoming queen. Perhaps find a more suitable ruler or maybe even be forced out through the Council. Vernice had certainly been trying.

And yet, there I was, looking down on the final few days of freedom before I would be chained to this newly refinished throne.

"Ah, I see you've seen the updates," Garwood said, coming to stand next to Felix and me. "I wanted to keep it a surprise, a little coronation gift for you. The chair was looking ragged and it just didn't do to have our queen sit on an old throne."

I nodded, unable to tear my gaze away from it.

"Brynn," Felix whispered. "Take a breath and go sit down."

I inhaled deeply, the air releasing whatever paralysis had taken root, and I climbed the dais and sat on the throne. It wasn't the most cushiony seat, but it was manageable, especially with extra padding between my rear and the hard gold.

"Do you like it?" Garwood asked.

"Yes," I said thinly as Felix left to join his guard on the side of the room. "I guess send in the envoys."

The doors opened and I had to force myself not to grip the throne. Unlike with Ilara, the first envoy came only flanked by two or three soldiers and Lady Vernice. His guards wore tunics made of dark brown fabric. Melwin himself was a middle-aged man, a head shorter than his flanking guards with a sharp, long nose and prominent cheekbones. His dark hair had been cut a little longer and combed over to one side. His tunic was a verdant green color, the color of the farmlands of Kulka. But based on the soft skin on his hands and the lack of tan lines on his face, he'd probably never seen a farm in his life except from a carriage.

He swept right up to the throne and bowed, some of his hair falling out of place. "Your Highness, I am Lord Melwin Bounderby from the kingdom of Kulka. I bring you good tidings of peace and luck on behalf of King Neshua."

"Thank you," I said with a nod. "I'm honored that you're here to witness my coronation." I looked at Vernice. "Always a pleasure, Lady Vernice."

She bowed, though not as low as Melwin then nodded to

Garwoood. "Leandro, glad to see you as well."

"Ana," Garwood said. "Melwin, what news from Kulka? The king is in good health?"

"Exceptionally, the whole royal family remains fit and happy. Prince Ammon and his wife have just welcomed their second child."

"Second?" I blinked. Ammon was the man I was supposed to marry. Could I really have been a mother twice over already had I stayed?

"Ah yes, he was your betrothed," Melwin said, his smile fading slightly. "He's quite the attentive husband. Princess Demetria was a Kulkan lord's daughter who was happy to take your place, once you decided against fulfilling the treaty."

I forced a smile onto my face as Vernice jumped on his conversation topic. "Yes, Princess. Melwin and I were discussing the open treaty. Have you given any thought as to how you would resolve it?" Her eyes glittered. "Melwin, you said that you have a son who would be eligible."

"Strapping young man," he said. "I've brought him if—"

"I don't think I'll be marrying anyone any time soon, as we've discussed, Lady Vernice," I replied with a glare at Vernice. "But perhaps we can talk about who else could fulfill my obligation. There are plenty of eligible young people in my court who would be more than happy to take up the mantle in my place."

Melwin frowned. "Unfortunately, the treaty was very specific. It should be a sibling to the crown or, of course, the crown itself."

"Ah." I looked around, opening my arms. "We're fresh out of siblings. I'm sure we can come to alternate arrangements."

He grumbled instead of responding, so Vernice inserted herself again. "I do hope you're planning on giving *my cousin* the same amount of hospitality you've given others."

Of course they were cousins. I could see the resemblance in their stink faces. "Lord Melwin, have you already settled in, or would you like me to find somewhere else in the castle?"

"I'd prefer to stay there. I don't want to be too close to the Niemenians." He bristled. "Loud, boisterous bunch there."

"I'm sure," I said. "Well, I hope that you'll enjoy your stay here. I know your cousin will see to it."

Blessedly, they took the cue and turned to leave. Once they were past the large double doors, I exhaled a loud breath and slouched.

"Vernice will keep asking about that marriage contract until it's filled," Garwood said.

I squinted at him. "Do you feel like being married off?"

He barked a laugh. "My husband might have a problem with that."

"True."

The door behind me opened and shut and I spun around to see who'd arrived. Katarine, dressed in a light yellow dress, hurried into the room with inflamed cheeks. She came to stand next to me.

"I'm sorry I was late," she said, her pale cheeks flushed.

"You just missed Vernice and her cousin," I replied then glanced at her. "Or were you counting on that?"

She shrugged and smoothed her shirt. "Lady Vernice is a wonderful Councilor."

"Spoken like a true diplomat," Garwood said, waving to the front of the room. "Send in the next one."

The doors opened again, but this time only a single man came strolling through. He looked as lively and fun as Melwin had been old and mean. His blond hair was almost white, styled and gelled so that it retained a messy look, and his rosy, pale cheeks told of a man who was used to smiling. His blue eyes were visible from clear across the room. Despite it all, I could clearly see the resemblance between him and Katarine, especially as she practically flew off the dais and into her brother's arms.

"Kat!" he cried, catching her and spinning her around the

room. "My word, look at you! You haven't changed a bit."

She grinned and swatted his shoulder. "Silly, I'm a decade older."

"Nonsense, still the same Kitty-Kat I used to chase around the castle."

"I think you've got a handle on the situation," Garwood said, turning to me as the siblings got into it. "You see, my dear, this is why you marry wisely. Your envoy loves his sister, and his sister loves you." He winked. "Now, if we could only have the same relationship with Kulka, we'd be in business."

"I'll get right on that," I said, pushing myself to stand. As Garwood left us, I approached the center of the room, where I'd yet to be noticed or acknowledged.

"It's so good to see you," Katarine said, drinking in her brother like she was dying of thirst. "How's the palace? How's Mum?"

"She's cantankerous and miserable, so the usual," he said, holding her warmly. "You look so beautiful. I'm sorry I couldn't make your wedding. And—"

Finally, I cleared my throat loudly. Luard looked beyond his sister to me, and his face reddened.

"Oh, Your Majesty." He stepped beside Katarine and bowed. "My apologies. I am—"

"We're past that. It's been far too formal in here for a while." I stuck out my hand. "Brynna. Princess."

"Luard," he said, taking my hand. "Envoy."

"Brynna," Katarine scolded, shaking her head. "I swear I've taught her manners, Luard."

"Don't even start with me," I said with a glance in her direction. "You've been hopping like a rabbit since this morning."

"I can't *believe* you didn't tell me you were coming," she said to her brother. "That was horrible of you to not mention it in your letters."

"I wanted it to be a surprise," he said grinning. "And also, I had to really work on Ariadna. She wanted to send Cousin Broward, can you imagine?" He glanced in my direction. "But I told her it would be rude to send such a bore to my sister's sister's coronation. After all, we're just so thankful that you've kept our Kitty-Kat around. I don't think we have room for you back in Niemen."

"I wouldn't let you have her if you wanted her," I replied with a wink to Katarine. "So, Luard. What news do you have for me from the queen?"

"Oh, the usual. She wants you to stop charging them so much to transport the ore to the ocean. Or just give us back the land you took from us six hundred years ago."

"Your sister tells me that would be a bad move, strategically."

"Traitor," he said with a shake of his head. "Well, I'm absolutely famished. Would it be rude to invite myself to dine with you two gorgeous women?"

"No ruder than asking me who I'm going to marry," I said with a shake of my head. "Let's go."

# Chapter
# Thirty—Nine

"And then, my tutor comes into the room, and I could have died," Luard said. "The girls, they were hiding behind a curtain and one of them *sneezed*. I thought for sure we'd been made. But my tutor had always been hard of hearing, so he sat his old ass down on the chair and proceeded to lecture for the next hour. None the wiser that two naked girls were hiding behind a curtain."

The Niemenian prince was like a breath of fresh air. We'd enjoyed a light lunch in the royal dining room and were now sitting in the brand new furnished royal bedroom. It was much more subdued than the previous furniture, continuing the theme of dark blues and whites. Luckily, Luard had been regaling us with tales of his adventures, so I hadn't really had a chance to think about how it was my room now.

"Ah, those were the days," he said, sitting back and sipping his wine. "My dear Kitty-Kat, I'm just so sad I never got to meet your lovely husband."

"I think you two would've gotten along great," Katarine said with a look to me. "Just like you and Brynn will get along while you're here."

"Yes, Brynn," Luard said, giving me a look. "You know, I hear that you're still without a marriage contract. I could offer myself to fulfill your husbandly needs."

I snorted and rolled my eyes. "I'm good, thanks."

"Don't tell me you're going to marry one of those dreadful Kulkans." He made a face. "They're so stuffy and boring. I'd, at least, give you a thrill."

"I've had thrills before."

"Not in the bedroom."

"So little you know," I replied, earning me a look of surprise from the rest of the room. "What?"

Luard hooted and grinned. "Oh, I like your little queen. She's got some fire in her."

"A little too much, if you ask me," Felix grumbled from the corner.

"You can't blame her," Luard replied. "Poor thing thought she was free from all this royal mess, and then you dragged her back into it. Surprised you haven't tried to escape yet."

I laughed. "That's an understatement."

"Speaking of escaping, what are the chances that we can get out tonight? I saw a raucous festival on the way up from the water, and where there's a festival, there's probably booze and fun."

"I would love to," I said. "But my babysitter won't let me out of his sight."

Luard snickered. "My love, you're going to have to learn the better points of giving your guards the slip."

"She's well-versed in that," Felix said.

"Not recently." I turned to him, expecting the answer but deciding to ask anyway. "Well? May I attend my own festival tonight?"

"Why not?" he said with a shrug.

I nearly fell out of my chair "Wait...really?"

"You'll be accompanied by us, of course. As the princess." He gave me a look. "And you have to stay with me at all times."

"Well, of course she'll be coming as the princess. What else would she be coming as?" Luard asked with a laugh.

But I jumped to my feet, grabbing Felix by the arm and pulling him into the corner. "Are you screwing with me? This isn't funny if you're screwing with me."

"The festival is well-guarded and staffed," he replied softly. "You'll be with a large group, including myself. And if we dress incognito, we should avoid a lot of unnecessary attention." He glanced at Luard, who was back to entertaining Katarine with his history, and then back at me, lowering his head to eye-level. "But you will *not* leave my sight."

"I promise," I said. I was getting a chance to escape of the castle, I'd do whatever he said.

"And you will drink and enjoy yourself and not think about anything else," he finished. "You've been entirely too moody lately. It's time you had a little fun."

I peered out of the carriage windows at the city, which had been transformed. Streamers in blue and white hung from every sign, men and women wore blue and white ribbons on their lapels. Even more than that, there seemed to be a lightness in the city. Perhaps the combination of having the festival and coronation wasn't the worst idea for a city that had seen so much tragedy of late.

"Your room looks nice," he said, by way of conversation. "I think it's time you moved into it."

"Kat did a good job," I said with a nod as I sank back into my carriage cushions. "Thank you, again. For letting me out of the castle."

"Promise me you won't try to slip away," Felix said, his gaze still outside.

"I promise," I said softly, and I actually meant it. As much as I liked to push Felix's buttons, I didn't like him to be truly angry with me. And besides that, I'd been off the streets for so long, I wouldn't even know where to begin.

"I love the summer festival," he said. "It's always been my favorite time of year."

"You said you hated it!" I turned to him in disbelief. "You gave me so much crap about wanting to have my coronation the same weekend as the festival, and said—"

"We hate the festival because we normally can't participate," Felix said with a laugh. "Which is part of the reason I said yes to you coming. Now, we can enjoy while working."

I turned to him, tilting my chin upward in a playful look. "Ah, so you didn't do it for purely altruistic reasons, hm?"

"They're still pretty mad at you for what you did to Joella. Anything I can do to mend that break, I will." His gaze was serious. "You don't want the people protecting you to hate you."

I nodded. "Understood."

We took the long way around to give the others time to make their way to the city center. When the carriage finally rolled to a stop, Luard, Katarine, and Felix's five guards stood at the ready. Felix and the guards were similarly dressed, and he and I took an unmarked carriage down to the festival grounds while the rest would join on foot. If I hadn't known any better, I would've considered us a collection of young people, out to enjoy the festival. And perhaps that's all we were. For tonight, I supposed I could set aside all my fear and just enjoy the evening.

The closer we drew to the event square, the more festive the decorations. My likeness had been printed on fliers and posters that hung in windows, although it didn't look quite right. But I appreciated the effort.

We strolled into the festival grounds, entering a crowded space full of laughter and conversation. Felix and Riya pressed in on either side of me as we moved through the populated entrance toward a spot that had less people. The event had taken up a full city block down by the water, with vendors selling their wares out of pop-up tents and face painting and exhibits. And food—all kinds of delicious-smelling food. Fried, steamed, grilled, blackened, there seemed almost too much for any nation to eat, but based on the number of people with bowls of seafood, there was enough. My food at the castle was exquisite, of course, but there was nothing like biting into a steamed crustacean that had been caught and seasoned not an hour before.

Luard was in his element, even without his royal sash and flashy attire. He asked every vendor about their wares before moving onto the next, delighting in everything he saw. Finally, we reached a vendor selling drinks, and his eyes lit up.

"First round is on me!" he said with a grin, handing cups of dark red liquid around to everyone.

"Here," Felix said, taking a sip of a drink before handing it to me.

I inhaled deeply—it was a turtoil, a fragrant summer drink of wine, brandy, berries, and cinnamon. The taste brought back memories of my childhood and this festival when my father was king. I sipped the drink slowly.

"You absolutely must try one of these pastries," Luard said, thrusting a buttery bread into my face. Felix plucked it out of his hand and took a bite first, before handing it back to me.

"Are you really going to take my food before I eat it the entire night?" I asked. "What if it's a slow-acting poison?"

"Oh, I'm not testing for poison," he said with a mischievous grin. "I just want some."

I rolled my eyes and broke the bread in half, revealing a purple berry center. I handed half to Felix and nibbled on mine as we continued through the space. Although Luard thrust another turtoil into my hands once my glass was empty, Felix only took a small sip.

"It's not that strong," I said, the buzz barely noticeable in the back of my mind. "You could have one."

"I'll have a beer at the end of the night when you're back in the castle," he said. "Some of us still have to remain vigilant."

"A beer, hm?" I said, sipping. "Learn something new about you every day, Felix."

Luard made a noise of surprise and dragged us into a tent filled with paintings. Landscapes of Forcadel, ships in the bay, and more paintings of my face. The artist proudly stood in front of his work, beckoning Luard and Katarine closer.

"They say hanging a painting of the queen will bring you luck," he said.

Felix caught my eye and I had to turn away to keep from laughing. The man had painted my face fifty times but didn't notice me standing in his shop. My laughter quickly fell away when I saw the back room. A painting of a hooded figure standing in the moonlight hung in the center. But when I reached the back of the room, there wasn't just one—there were hundreds. Big paintings, small paintings. Plates, vases, canvases, even a small stone. All with The Veil.

"Ah, you like these?" he said, appearing at my side.

"It's incredible," I said, choking back tears.

"She was incredible. She saved my life six months ago from a band of thieves. I was returning home late from my gallery and I was jumped. She appeared like an angel from the heavens, but she fought like a devil. Right hook, left hook!" The man mimicked a punch. "Upper cut! And before my eyes, all seven men were down."

I was now very sure this was an exaggeration, because the most I'd ever been able to take at once was four. And they were teenagers.

"That day, I dedicated my life to painting her. To let everyone know what a hero we had walking amongst us." He looked to me. "Why are you crying, Highness?"

It was probably the turtoil, but seeing these paintings brought a lump to my throat and a tear down my cheek. I wiped it away hastily and forced a smile onto my face.

"It's just so beautiful. Have you seen The Veil recently?"

"Oh, no. She comes and goes as she pleases. But I know, when I'm in trouble again, she will come help me. Because that's what she is."

The tears were now threatening to become all-out sobs. "I'm sure she will."

"B—oh, here you are," Felix said, throwing back the flap. "I've been looking all over for you..." He trailed off when he saw my face, and then what I was looking at. "Come on, the group is ready to move on."

I nodded and thanked the man, slipping a gold coin into his hand and promising him I would buy one of his paintings after the festival.

"That was...something," Felix said. "Did he say something to you? Are you all right?"

"Fine," I said, dejectedly. "Come on, let's get moving."

I wasn't in a mood to continue with the festival, the joyous air fell flat on my sadness. But I couldn't deprive my guard of their fun, so I followed along behind them as they continued to explore the festival.

# Chapter
## Forty

"What really happened in that tent?" Felix asked, falling into step beside me.

"I saved him, apparently, from some muggers. And he's been painting my likeness ever since." I wiped my eye before another tear fell. "It just...it reminded me of the good I used to do. Of how I used to make a real difference for people." I laughed. "Plus, I'm sure the turtoil has something to do with it."

"You said they weren't that strong," Felix said.

I lifted a shoulder.

"What you missed, Brynn, was the entire front of the gallery. Where your face—your real face—was front and center. You may have been a hero to him as The Veil, but you will be a hero to everyone as queen. I promise." He nudged me. "There's no way you couldn't be, not with your stubborn nature."

I laughed and glanced around at the festival once more. I'd done my best to ignore my face plastered inside every tent, but there it was. Perhaps he was right.

"I just wish I could've taken down Lord Beswick," I said. "I feel like I failed."

"You haven't failed, Brynn. You have all the time in the world, and more resources as queen."

"But without those contracts, I can't prove a thing," I said. "And you know that Kulka and Severia aren't going to give them up."

"Here," Joella said, appearing with three cups of turtoil. "Buck up."

I took the cup gingerly and stared into the red liquid. Those were the first words Joella had spoken to me since the Beswick incident.

"Thank you," I said, taking a hesitant sip. "Will you sit with us?"

She nodded and plopped down on the other side of me. "It's a good day to be here. The full festival won't begin until tomorrow, so it's not as crowded as usual."

"This isn't crowded?" I asked.

"I take it you never went?" Felix asked.

"It's well-lit and well-guarded." I took a drink. "It didn't really need my help so I never came as The Veil. And when I was a girl, my father wouldn't let us go."

"Oh, we went," Felix said with a devilish grin. "August and I would sneak out and get completely wasted."

I turned fully to him. "Are you serious? *You* snuck out?"

"Of course, your brother was a terrible influence." He laughed. "It's part of the reason I'm so good at catching you. I know all the exits and entrances to the castle. By heart."

"Not *all* the exits," I said coyly, but the smile evaporated from my face. Beswick and Zuriel had turned a corner, deep in conversation and trailed by five armed guards. Felix rested his hand on my thigh, squeezing once before standing and helping me up.

"Ah, Princess!" Zuriel said, his face blossoming into a grin. "And Captain. So wonderful to see you two out and about, enjoying the festivities. Especially considering all the attempts on your life recently."

"It's more important to be seen amongst my people," I said through gritted teeth.

"And also," Felix interjected, "it would've been criminal to miss such a wonderful festival."

"Too right you are," Zuriel said with a firm nod. "I was just conferring with Lord Beswick. This festival is merely the beginning. We will have shows and carnivals and, of course, all the coronation festivities to attend."

"It will be masterful," Beswick said to me. "I spared no expense in putting this on for you."

My cup nearly fell out of my hand. "You paid for this?"

"But of course!" He tilted his head. "It's my honor to be a sponsor, especially this year, when it's so important that our kingdom celebrate our new queen."

My vigilante mind spun rapidly, wondering what he might be covering up, or how this might be connected to something nefarious, but Felix placed a calming hand over mine and I forced myself to smile.

"I know the people appreciate your generosity," I said, almost automatically. But I would not thank the man. Not in this lifetime anyway.

"I hope, Princess, that you might consider extending an invitation to Lord Beswick for your coronation dinner," Zuriel said, glancing at the man and back to me. "As he has been so generous with the festivities."

"The princess will consider it," Felix said with a tight smile. "But we should really be getting back."

Beswick and Zuriel bowed, the former's gaze landing on Joella for a second longer than necessary, and walked away.

Once he was out of earshot, I exhaled so loud, it caught the attention of several passersby.

"I hate that son of a bitch," I said, downing the entire turtoil in one gulp and wishing it had more brandy in it. "I hate him so much I could scream."

"Likewise," Joella said, glaring at his retreating back.

"Third," Felix said.

"And yet, you won't let me do anything about him," I replied. "Not even now, when there's a thousand people packed into a small square. When I could oh-so-easily pickpocket him and get those contracts out of his jacket pocket."

"You wouldn't get close," Joella said. "Besides that, he knows your face."

"Yeah, but maybe there's a way after all," I said, my heartbeat thumping as Beswick entered a large tent in the back of the festival with half-dressed girls beckoning men to come inside.

"Brynna..." Felix said with a heavy sigh.

"Felix, listen to me," I said, grabbing his arm and resting my other hand on his chest. "I have an idea, and I promise you Beswick won't even know I was there."

He didn't say no, but he didn't look convinced.

"Please, just...trust me," I whispered. "I know—*I know*—I can do this. And this is my last shot to get to him. *Please*."

I locked gazes with him, pouring every bit of my desperation into my eyes and praying he would be swayed. Somewhere in the depths of those brown pools was the man who'd let me roam free for a few blessed weeks, the same one who'd seen me dispatch villains and common criminals.

Slowly, he lifted his hand to cover mine on his chest. "Tell me your plan."

I could barely contain my excitement as Felix and I waited behind Titta's tent for Joella to retrieve her. Soft music echoed from inside the space, with the occasional giggle or moan. Felix wore a tempered look of disapproval with crossed arms—a warning that he was ready to put a stop to my plan if he felt it was too risky.

Titta rounded the corner then stopped short. "Oh! Princess, this is a surprise. Or are you here on Veil business?"

"Afternoon, Titta. I'm here on business," I said with a vigilante-like grin. "I saw Lord Beswick come into your establishment a few moments ago."

"Ugh, yes. I have to pay my girls extra to entertain that ogre." She made a face, but it faded quickly to one of curiosity. "And I suppose you'd like to join them?"

"Not exactly," I said. "He knows my face, and unlike you, hasn't connected the dots. But if one of your girls could see fit to get him to take his jacket off, even for a moment, I would be very appreciative."

Titta nodded slowly. "And what else will you give me for this favor?"

I glanced at Felix and he nodded. "I have nothing to give right now but a promise of a future favor. After all, next week, I'll be in a better position."

Her eyes lit up. "Now that is interesting. I've been looking to start another club, but your city keeps declining my request."

"Ah, well." I waited for Felix to say something. When he didn't, I grinned. "I will make sure it's approved."

"Excellent," Titta said. "Tired of Beswick getting all the good buildings in this town, anyway. He's in the back, paid for an hour session. Follow me."

I shared an excited look with Felix, who shook his head in disgust. "What? No snarky comment about how I shouldn't promise things to people?"

"I'm merely letting you enjoy the moment," he replied. "We'll save the lectures for later. I'm sure Vernice will love that you're giving special treatment to a skin bar."

"Please, she's a frequent patron," I said with an eye roll.

"Which I'll be glad to remind her of if she says anything."

Based on the muscle twitching in his jaw, he had another comment ready, but he kept quiet as Titta opened the back flap to her tent and let us inside. Unlike the large room in her dance hall, the tent was segmented into private rooms. She put her finger to her lips and pointed at one of them, letting us into the empty space next to it.

"Thank you," I whispered as she left us.

Beswick's low voice filtered through the white fabric. I lay down at the hem of the fabric and lifted it up just enough to see through. Beswick sat on a chair in the center of the room as two scantily dressed girls swayed their hips around him.

"Gabriela, why don't you come work for me?" Beswick asked as the girl slid herself over him. "I would pay you extra. I'd even get you out of that little legal trouble you've run into."

"Oh, Mr. Beswick, you drive a hard bargain," she said, her voice low and breathy. She caught my eye for a split second then returned to her charge. Perhaps Titta had informed her of what was going on because she didn't even give me a second glance.

"What about you, Amaris?" Beswick asked.

"Mm, maybe," she said with a grin. "But you'll have to pay me triple to get me to leave Titta's."

He laughed loudly. "I like a girl who knows her worth."

I lowered the hem and sat up, chewing on my lip as I thought about what to do next. I lay back down and lifted the fabric then crawled through before Felix could stop me.

My heart thumped wildly in my chest and I stood upright, and to their credit, neither Gabriela or Amaris even looked in my direction. But Gabriela spun around behind Beswick, running her hands down the front of his body and pressing her chest to the back of his head.

"Aren't you a little hot?" she purred into his ear. "Perhaps you'd like to take this jacket off?"

"I thought I had to pay Titta extra for that service?" he said.

The girls smiled as Amaris sat on his lap, undulating and distracting him while Gabriela came to me. She shook her head and shrugged. I nodded to her and gestured for her to stay put. It was time for me to put my pickpocket skills to the test.

I pulled off my tunic, leaving just my breast bindings, which were about in the same place as the girls' fabric. Then, making my footfalls soft, I walked up behind Beswick and began swaying, sliding my hands through his greasy hair.

"Mm," he moaned, and it took everything not to vomit on him. Amaris caught my eye and slid off his lap, to stand between his legs, bending over and giving him a full view of her chest. Keeping my breathing steady, I slid my hands down his chest until they reached his belt buckle then back up.

My heart stopped when he grabbed my hand, but he merely pressed it against his cheek then, to my horror, kissed my palm. I kept rubbing my other hand over his body, until he finally released me. I had been standing behind him for entirely too long, so it was now or never.

Barely breathing, I reached into the left pocket and struck gold, yanking out the contracts.

"Wh—"

Amaris took the initiative and pressed her lips to his, climbing on top of his lap. I took two steps back, lightheaded from lack of air, and let Gabriela resume her position. I fell to my knees and crawled out, grasping my chest in relief.

"Um."

I looked up at Felix, whose face had gone red.

Then I remembered my tunic was still in the other room and all I wore was a binding and pants. I slapped the contracts into his hand and lifted the hem of the tent again, grabbing my tunic from the ground and crawling back out.

⇒————————→

We dashed out of Titta's tent, not stopping until we were outside the festival grounds, hidden away in a desolate alley. I gulped in the precious air I'd deprived myself of, from exertion and nerves and, now, excitement as I pulled my tunic back over my head. Then I bent over, grabbing my knees and trying not to vomit.

"What happened in there?" Felix asked.

"You don't want to know," I replied, taking a deep breath as I straightened. "But we need to move quickly. Once Beswick finds out those are gone, he'll come for Titta. You should put a few extra guards around her girls until we can get him taken care of."

Felix hesitated, looking at the envelope in my hand. "Are you sure that's what you need?"

"I'm...honestly afraid to look," I whispered. "Because I don't want to go back in there and try again."

He took the paper from me gently, unfolding the pages and reading with a furrowed brow. The longer he read, the more my stomach filled with dread. If I hadn't gotten them, we couldn't arrest him. And then Gabriela, Amaris, even Titta, would be in danger.

"Brynn," he said, his breath tickling my ear. "You did it."

A wave of relief washed over me as I yanked the pages from him, reading them five times before the words made sense. It was a contract between Beswick and Ilara to provide security services— and also to import goods without paying tariffs. Illegal and definitely treasonous.

"See?" Felix said softly. "You're not a failure."

I actually cried out in relief and dove into Felix's arms, tears welling as he wrapped his arms tightly around me then plucked me off the ground, spinning me around a few times.

He put me down, and I stared into those dark brown eyes, now with nothing but pride in them. With a soft smile, he wiped my wet cheek with his thumb, his warm breath on my face. My heart pounded as the seconds drew out between us, and I struggled to find the words to express my gratitude to him and to fate, for allowing me this sweet victory.

I lifted my head, intending to thank him or say something more profound, but the words died in my throat. There was something new in his eyes, something that sent twin shocks of fear and exhilaration into my stomach. My tongue swept across my lips, tasting salt and anticipation as he tucked a lock of hair behind my ear and sent an electric charge down my back.

Slowly, he lowered his head and captured my lips in a sweet kiss. My mind went blank, and I tilted my chin upward, inviting him to continue. When he didn't, I opened my eyes into his, surprised to find a rolling storm of emotions there. He seemed to be waiting for me to react, to push him away.

But we both knew I could fight him off, and he hadn't crossed any lines I hadn't left open for him. As angry as he made me, as frustrating as his rules and protectiveness was, what I felt for him had gone beyond friendship, or even that of a queen to her captain. And now that he'd stepped over that line, I wanted more.

I took a step toward him, sliding my hands over his strong chest, the soft fabric of his tunic sending chills up my spine. The taste of him remained on my tongue, and, craving more, I pressed a soft kiss to his jaw. He tensed, swallowing hard. I swiped my fingertips across his stubbly cheek, in need of a shave, to brush the short hair on the back of his neck.

He released a soft sigh, and then his lips were on mine again.

This time, there was nothing soft or chaste about it. My back hit the wall, his hand resting on the base of my skull as he assaulted my mouth. It was all I could do to keep up, too distracted by the way his body fit against mine, the thoughts of what might happen if we continued. The sensation of his tongue moving with mine, the way he moaned when I gripped the front of his shirt and pulled him closer. If I let him, he would have me right there against the wall. And I was definitely considering it.

But just like that, it was over.

"We need to go," he whispered, his face flushed and lips swollen. "Beswick and contracts."

I nodded, the papers dangling in my hand. "Can we...continue this later?"

He kissed me, but this time only for a moment. "Let's go."

# Chapter
## Forty-One

Felix and I rushed back to the castle, my lips still tingling from his kiss. It was hard to stay focused. All I wanted was to ask Felix to meet me in my room. But Titta and her girls were counting on me; making out could wait.

Riya sent a messenger to Garwood's home with an urgent message to meet me in my office and there, I paced by myself. Felix had left to get Riya, and I wasn't sure why I expected him to return, but I wanted him to. Perhaps he was preparing celebrations. Or the arrest warrant.

Finally, after an eternity, Garwood arrived, and I didn't even give him a chance to take off his traveling clothes. "You need to give me permission to arrest Beswick."

He blinked a few times. "I'm sorry, what?"

"Arrest Beswick. I need you to help me convince the Council to do it tonight."

"Just take a deep breath," Garwood said, pulling his hat off. "And explain to me why you want to arrest one of the most prominent businessmen in the city."

"Because he's a crook, and I can prove he's been engaging in treason," I replied.

"Why don't you start at the beginning?" Garwood said, sitting on the chair.

I told him a modified version of the truth, that my investigator had been looking into him for several weeks now, spurred by rumors of his treasonous activities.

"I know, Brynna," he said. "I hear all the time from constituents who are too far in debt to him, and want something done about him. But unfortunately, there's nothing *to* be done."

"Ah, well, there used to be," I said. "I'd heard whispers that perhaps he was dealing under the table with Kulka and Severia."

Garwood nodded. "Hence why you entered into that ill-advised agreement with the queen."

"Yes," I said. "It was designed to flush out Beswick, and, I'm glad to say, it worked." I pulled the contracts from inside my tunic. "Read these."

Garwood pulled out his glasses and read through the papers. His brow furrowed, but I couldn't decide if he was surprised, angry, or perhaps just confused. The longer the silence stretched out, the more anxious I became.

"Brynna, I'm afraid this isn't as much as you think," he said, pulling off his glasses. "Certainly not enough to make an arrest."

"W-what are you talking about?" I said, coming to my feet. "It's...it's illegal for a Forcadel business to agree to anything without the sovereign's permission."

"And who do you think brokered this agreement between Severia and Beswick in the first place?" Garwood asked.

I blinked. "Who?"

"Your father, of course."

I lowered myself to the chair, sounds of confusion and disbelief bubbling from my lips. "He...did what? Why would he do that?"

"Well, our merchants wanted to get Severian glass for a fraction of the price, but the Severians wouldn't budge. So Johann stepped in and promised them he'd protect our interests."

"And he's also the one they need protection from!" I leaned back in the chair. "He's the one taking half their glass. How could anyone think this was a fair deal?"

"It's very fair to our merchants in Forcadel," Garwood said. "They get good quality glass at a cheap price and they pass those savings onto the rest of the citizens."

"But the Severians—"

"Are not your people, and therefore, not your concern. If Queen Ilara wanted something different, she could assign a few of her royal guard to helping guard their shipments."

"She can't afford that," I said. "It's a vicious cycle. They can't get ahead. Just like all the citizens in Forcadel who owe money to Beswick. He gives them just enough rope to hang themselves."

"I know that some of his dealings are unsavory," he said evasively. "But it's a necessary evil we have to live with. He does a lot of good—"

"If you say his paying for the festival was a *good* thing..."

Garwood pursed his lips. "He did pay for it. He pays for it every year and he's responsible for bringing in all the vendors and artisans. It brings an incredible amount of revenue to the city, and boosts morale." Garwood cleared his throat. "He's also made a sizable donation to support your coronation."

"Give it back," I said, standing. "I don't want his money anywhere near my coronation. I want him *hanged*."

"I understand—"

"You understand *nothing*," I cried, slamming my hands down on his desk. "You say we have to live with him because he's rich. But he's only rich because he's bleeding our citizens dry. Severia might not be my concern, but the people of this city are. And I can't idly stand by while a common criminal continues to keep them from prosperity. Now, *find* me something I can arrest him with, or I will replace you on my Council."

Garwood threaded his fingers together. "I'm not sure there is anything, Brynna. Beside your father's approval of this treaty, the rest of the Council has agreements or deals with him. Vernice negotiated a similar deal with the Kulkans, and from what I understand, gets a lovely cut of the profits. Godfryd lives in a Beswick-owned manor on the south side of town, and Beswick often gives scholarships to young children so they can join the king's guard. And Octavius—"

"Is a drunk and frequents his taverns."

"Well, he is a drunk, but he's also a gambler. But all his debts are brushed aside, of course."

"Of course." I swallowed my frustrations. "So I have to replace my entire Council just so I can take this guy down, huh?"

"Inadvisable. You need some semblance of consistency, especially considering the turmoil at the throne these past few weeks."

I could've just screamed. It just wasn't fair—after all I'd done, all the sacrifices. Crawling around on my hands and knees, running across the rooftops of this city. And even as queen, Beswick remained firmly out of my reach.

"I'm sorry, Brynna. If there was something I could do, I would. But my hands are tied."

I nodded and stood, grabbing the contracts off his desk and leaving without another word.

I returned to my newly furnished room and punched a few holes in the air to keep myself from crying. I couldn't keep a single thought in my head for more than a moment. I was scattered, I was exhausted. I needed my captain.

But my captain didn't show.

When the clock struck midnight, I finally walked out into the hallway, finding Joella waiting with a stoic look on her face.

"Where is Felix?" I asked. "I sent for him hours ago. We need to talk about what to do about Beswick."

"He told me to tell you he's taking care of Titta," she replied. "And that you should get some rest."

I narrowed my eyes. "So he knows about Garwood? He knows that the Council is doing nothing?"

"Yes," she said with a sigh. "He said not to worry about it."

Dumbfounded, I returned to my room. While I was grateful he'd thought to take care of Titta and her girls, it didn't solve the *larger* problem. Despite his advice, I didn't sleep, sitting on my windowsill and staring out into the night, my mind buzzing with anger, betrayal, and I wasn't sure what.

But when I didn't see Felix at breakfast, lunch, *or* a very annoying dinner with Lord Melwin and Vernice, I was fit to be tied. No one was giving me any news, other than continued assurance that everything was fine. But I didn't want to hear that.

I marched outside, grabbing Joella by the tunic and slamming her against the wall. "Take me to Felix. *Now.*"

Too shocked to argue, she nodded.

We walked silently down to the barracks, perhaps the murderous look on my face enough to keep the younger guards away from me. Joella stopped in front of Felix's door and knocked.

"Captain? Are you in there?"

"Come in," came his gruff voice as the door unlocked.

I pushed past Joella, marching into the room.

"Brynna!" Felix said, nearly falling off the bed. I'd never seen him in such a state of undress. He was shirtless, with only a pair of black pants untied at the waist giving me a view of defined muscles on his stomach and hairless chest. His feet were bare, the stubble on his skin even darker than the day before.

"Where have you been?" I snapped, folding my arms over my chest.

"I'm sorry," he said, grabbing his tunic from the floor and sliding it over his head. I tried not to stare at the spot below his navel.

"Is that all you have to say?" I cried. "Felix, Garwood shut me down. My *father* sanctioned the contract with Beswick and it has the full support of the Council. And—"

"Brynna, that kiss was...a mistake."

I froze, all thoughts of Garwood out the door. "What?"

"It was a mistake. I got caught up in the moment and I forgot my place. I'm sorry."

"Sorry?" I put my hands on my hips, shocked that something could still shock me. "You're sorry for kissing me?"

"I'm your captain, Brynna," he said. "And besides that, even if we were to act on it, it wouldn't go anywhere. You've got to marry for an alliance—"

"I'm not even thinking about that right now," I barked, keeping my anger burning so I wouldn't break down into tears. "I just...I just want to be with you."

He cast me a look somewhere between terrified and nauseated. "I think, perhaps..." He licked his lips. "I should take another position in the guard."

I fell backward against the window ledge. "W...what?"

"It's for the best. Until you and I lose whatever...emotions caused us to make a rash decision last night. We can't be together. Not even for a little while."

My anger was losing to my tears. It was bad enough that Felix didn't want to be with me, but now he wanted to be out of my life completely?

"So that's how you feel?" My voice sounded far away.

"It doesn't matter what I want. It matters what's best for the kingdom. If I stay, if this becomes something more, then I won't be able to do my job effectively. I already haven't been able to do it effectively. Letting you get that close to Beswick, letting you out of the castle at all." He shook his head. "All it takes is a little pout and I lose track of what's right and wrong."

My frustrations from the day spilled from my eyes, and I let them. "Felix, Garwood said my father was responsible for the Beswick contracts. He sanctioned them. I'm no closer to taking him out than I was a week ago and now you're...talking about leaving. You need to stay and help me *fix* this."

"I'm...sorry," Felix said. "I know how much it meant to you."

"It's not about *me*! It's about this kingdom. He's a criminal and we're just letting him get away with it."

"You can readdress it when you're queen," he said. "But for now, just let it go."

My tears ceased as quickly as they'd come. I turned to the window and exhaled loudly through my nose. "So that's it, then? We failed, and you're just giving up like that?"

"I don't want to give up, Brynna, but I can't be around you anymore. It's what's best for both of us. You have others you can lean on. Kat, Garwood—

"Garwood is dead to me."

"Don't be a child."

I smiled. There was the old Felix. "I want you around, Felix."

"And that's precisely why I should leave," he said.

"Fine," I whispered, looking at the sill as my chest hurt. "Then pack your bags. I'm sending you to Kulka to marry one of King Neshua's sisters. You said I needed to make a strong ally, and they want me to fulfill their contract. So you can go, if you're so eager to leave."

I waited for his sharp intake of breath, for him to tell me that I was crazy for sending him away from the only home he'd ever known, but instead, I got silence.

"You've been telling me all this time that it's time to start thinking like a queen and not do whatever the hell I want," I said. "Well, now I'm thinking like a queen. I need their alliance, and you're the only person who's actually on my side in this castle. So you'll go there, marry one of them, have some Kulkan babies, and maintain the alliance."

He continued to say nothing.

"But if you disagree for any reason, please tell me," I finished, turning to him, finally.

"I don't think it's a bad match," he said after a moment. "In fact, it's a very smart move."

"So there are no objections?" I whispered.

He grasped the hilt of his sword tightly. "No."

"Good," I said after a moment. "Then make arrangements to find your replacement as captain."

"I will."

"And start packing. You're going back with the envoy."

"Agreed."

"And you have no objections at all?" I held my breath. For someone who fought me at every turn, to have him nod and bow as I dictated his life to him was strange.

"None."

And with that, I turned and walked out of his room, keeping my tears at bay until I was alone, and then I collapsed onto my bed.

# Chapter
# Forty–Two

"I suppose that will work," Melwin said with a slow nod. "He's noble-born, yes?"

"Oh yes," I said, my simmering rage keeping my voice calm. Felix had formally resigned his post this morning, naming Riya as his temporary successor until the Council approved her. All of this he'd done via a letter delivered with my breakfast.

Coward. I was glad I was sending him away.

I'd asked for the Kulkan envoy to come to my office first thing so we could discuss it in private. I doubted there would be any outcry from the Council; half of them thought Felix ineffective anyway.

"He'll make an excellent match to any of your eligible princesses," I continued. "He's well-educated in politics and can help mentor your soldiers."

"The fourth daughter of the king is just now twenty," Melwin said. "I'm sure King Neshua will be most happy to have her marry into such a strong alliance."

"It works for me," I replied. "And we will call my marriage

contract settled then?"

"I suppose, for now." He winked at me. "But you will have to marry eventually. Must keep that strong Lonsdale blood on the throne. You know, your great-great uncle married into the Kingdom of Kulka."

"I'm sure I'll get around to it eventually," I said with a smile. "Thank you for being so understanding."

"But of course! We value our alliance with your country." He beamed. "I'm sure you're excited about your coronation this week, hm?"

"Ecstatic," I replied, lacking the energy to even pretend I was anything other than miserable.

He left shortly after that, and I was alone to sign and stamp papers. Normally, I dreaded this work, but today, I was grateful for the monotony. It was better than jumping back and forth between disgust at my government and fury at my captain.

Around lunch, there was a knock at the door, and Joella, Coyle, Riya, and about ten other guards filled my office.

"Are you here to arrest me again?" I said, sitting back.

"No," Joella said. "We're here to formally protest the removal of Captain Felix and his impending departure to Kulka."

I rolled my eyes. "Take it up with him. It was his idea."

Joella made a noise and looked at Riya, who stepped forward. "I don't believe that. He wouldn't willingly leave us for another kingdom. Not unless you forced him to."

"I didn't force him to *do* anything. It's usually the other way around, in case you forgot," I replied, picking up a paper on the order of linens for the castle. Why was I even responsible for ordering linens?

"Brynna...this isn't some ploy so you can continue as The Veil, is it?" Joella asked. "Because the rest of us will make sure you stay at the castle."

To be honest, the thought hadn't even crossed my mind. There was nothing but disgust and hurt for all the men I'd trusted in my life so far. This was why I hadn't gotten close to Tasha. No chance of heartbreak with him. Just mediocre sex and no questions.

The worst betrayal, though, was my father's. To find out he'd been in cahoots with Beswick, even as I'd worked to take the slumlord down, was a hurt that I wouldn't soon forget. And Garwood, acting like he had no recourse. Both of them disgusted me.

"The Veil is dead," I replied softly. After all, what purpose did I have if the leadership around me wouldn't even take action on the evidence I'd presented them? There was no winning there. Not unless I took a dark turn.

"Brynna—" Joella began, but stopped when I threw down my pen.

"Look, if you're that attached, you can go with him. He'll need attendants and...friends in the castle." I sat back. "I'm sure you would all enjoy the vacation."

"Our home is here, Princess," Riya said. "As is Felix's."

"Then, again, you should ask Felix why he was so eager to leave." I offered them all a freezing look. "If there aren't any other issues, I have a lot of work to do before my coronation."

The next day, I wrote an order to Godfryd to reorganize the entire guard, replacing Riya, Joella, Zathan, and Coyle with another set of guards whose names I didn't bother to learn. That same day, I officially moved into the royal bedrooms. Through it all, I waited for Felix to barge into my room, declare he saw through my ruses and was putting a stop to it all.

Instead, I found Katarine waiting for me in my bedroom one evening.

"Care to share what's going on with you?" she asked softly. "Felix's guards are up in arms, and now I hear you're marrying him off to someone else. You've moved into these bedrooms and you've declined to meet with me for the past week."

"I assumed you would've been spending time with your brother," I replied. "I apologize for not seeing him more. I haven't been in the mood for parties."

"Don't avoid the question."

I bit my tongue to keep the hurt from showing on my face. "Felix wanted to go. And it's time I moved into here since my coronation is in two days."

"Brynn." She rose to her feet. "You don't have to hide from me. Tell me what happened."

"I told you, Felix wanted to leave," I said, pulling the tunic over my head. Then, because I just couldn't hold it in any longer, I added, "because he didn't want to stay. With me."

"Ah," she said with a nod. "I thought it might be something like that."

"I don't even know why I care so much," I said, wiping my cheeks and turning away from the closet.

"Because you do. And so does he." She sighed. "I only suppose he told you that he couldn't do his job well if he had feelings for you?"

"Yeah. How'd you know?"

"Because he told me the same a month ago," she said with a smile. "I counseled him to think long and hard about what he wants. In my view, his love for you is an asset. It makes him more protective of you."

Felix had been in love with me for at least a month? I wished Katarine hadn't told me that; it just made my chest ache more.

"He was exceptionally hurt when you lied about being sick to sneak out, and devastated when you threatened Joella," she continued. "And I pointed out that it seemed to go beyond the hurt of a protector to the one he's protecting, or even friends. So he confessed to me. I only suppose, perhaps, you confessed to him?"

"He kissed me," I said, trying not to relive that moment in my mind. "He looked at me like...like I was the only thing that mattered. Then he tells me he wants to be reassigned far away from me."

"You're thinking with your heart. You need to look at it from his perspective."

I squinted at the ceiling and made a face. "The perspective that he's a complete asshole and should be kicked in the groin?"

"That he's a man who loves very deeply, and often in conflict with his love of country. He knows, as you must, that a relationship between the two of you would be fleeting. Your marriage must further the interests of Forcadel."

"*Why* is everyone always so interested in who I marry?" I knew the answer, but it was frustrating all the same. "I miss my old life. I could just sleep with who I wanted, and nobody cared."

She laughed. "I know you're hurting, but it's for the best. And in fact, sending Felix away is a smart move for you both. He'll be out of sight, and useful to the kingdom. You'll be able to focus on the business of governing."

It was all just so adult. And I hated it. Hated that, on some level, I agreed with Katarine. I really couldn't be with who I wanted; that much had been clear since I was thirteen. In two days' time, I would have to bury all remnants of the rebellious girl I'd once been in favor of a stoic queen. Because it wasn't about me, it was about my kingdom. And they needed someone steady.

"I'm sorry that it has to be this way." She took my cheeks in her soft hands and kissed my forehead. "But you will heal eventually. And one day, you two can become friends again."

She left me to my empty bedroom with the gas lamps burning and a dark bed I hadn't yet slept in. When I did, it would be admitting defeat, and admitting that my life was no longer mine to control.

I walked to the floor-to-ceiling window and stared out onto the city. The festival lights were visible in the distance, lights paid for by Beswick. It made me sick to know just how much he'd ingratiated himself into my city. How much he took advantage of its weakness and the people. And how those in this castle just let him get away with it.

I walked back to my closet, locating another tunic in the back —a dark purple one. With my chest throbbing, I dressed myself and walked out of the bedroom, expecting to see a guard standing in the center room. But there were none; perhaps Felix hadn't told the new guys about the escape routes.

But there wasn't even a guard at the garden exit when I walked out.

I had no agenda for the evening, other than to stretch my legs and get some fresh air. I stopped by the bell tower to gather whatever was left of my supplies—some knives, my weighted ropes, and one small bag of knockout powder. My crossbow only held three arrows, but I didn't really see a reason I'd need them. I just wanted my things, in case Felix decided to clean me out. I was actually a little hurt he hadn't even taken my spare cloak and mask.

But sliding the fabric over my skin was like coming home. For the first time in weeks, I had a firm grip on the world through the black slits in my mask.

I took to the rooftops, ambling without purpose or agenda. The warm, sticky air clung to my skin and made me sweat. But it was glorious to be by myself, to actually *be* myself. I'd learned early on in Celia's camp that I was the only one I could count on. No one would take care of me, no one would rescue me. And thinking someone would was a good way to get myself killed. I wouldn't forget that lesson again.

Down on the street, a shadow crept behind an old woman. I leaped over the edge of the building, running up behind the thief and dispatching him before the woman even knew he was there.

She hurried home, the thief limped away with an injured shoulder, and I resumed my patrol on the rooftops.

Perhaps this was how I maintained my sanity. Keep my attention on these lowlifes, and leave the big fish to...

I came to a stop, realizing I'd traveled to Sailor's Corner and Titta's bar. But the lights and music weren't on. In fact...the place was empty. Ransacked.

My heart fell into my stomach and I turned away, furious. Beswick had ruined another set of lives, thanks to my meddling. I'd been too cocky, thinking I could do anything under Felix's rule of law. I just prayed Titta and the girls had gotten out—but I wasn't confident. Beswick would've found them, and he would have destroyed them for daring to cross him.

As much as I wanted to blame someone else, this was purely my fault. I'd allowed myself to be hamstrung by the rules, by niceties and politics. When actual people were being hurt because Beswick assumed he was the only one who could break the law. He went low because he thought no one else would sink to his level.

But as I stared at that dark building, I decided I was finished playing by Princess Brynna's rules. It was time to put a stop to him once and for all.

# Chapter
# Forty–Three

"I would like to take you up on that offer to invite Lord Beswick to my coronation dinner, Lord Zuriel."

Garwood gave me a look of surprise, but the rest of the Council nodded approvingly. It was the final meeting before my coronation ceremony, and we were finalizing details for the dinner that would occur that night. I waited until the middle of discussions in order to make my request, hoping it would come across as innocuous.

"I think that's an excellent idea," Zuriel said, clapping. "He's given so much money toward your coronation and the festival, after all. It's only right to thank him for his contributions."

"But it's short notice," Vernice said, sounding as if she'd rather he not be there at all. "Would he even be available?"

"An invitation from the princess? Of course he would be," Zuriel said. "I know he regretted not being able to attend the last one."

I nodded and let the planning continue, keeping my responses metered and leaving the invitation to Beswick where it was.

Especially with Garwood's gaze on me.

When the meeting was finished, I acted quickly to devise an escape route before he could question me. But Zuriel was faster than either of us.

"Your Highness, may I have a word? It's about your coronation parade tomorrow," he said, flashing a grin.

"Absolutely," I said, hurrying around the table and taking his arm. "We can walk and talk, as I have work to do in my office."

Once we were out of the room, he cleared his throat. "I'm very excited about the procession. Though I'm concerned about the royal guard."

"Hm?"

"Apparently, there's a leadership vacuum down there," he said. "Or they're protesting the resignation of Captain Llobrega. I'm not sure which it is."

I cleared my throat, forcing myself not to look annoyed. "The good captain felt he wasn't doing his duty effectively and tendered his resignation. I couldn't change his mind."

"He was so young to take that position from Captain Mark," Zuriel said, shaking his head. "It's a lot of responsibility. But now I hear he's returning to Kulka with their envoy?" He flashed me a smile. "The two of you were so close, I'm surprised you'd let him go."

"As I said," I replied softly. "It was his decision. But you were saying something about an issue with the royal guard?"

"Yes, well, we'd hoped to have the guards march in front and behind the carriage, a real show of force. But since they're in a bit of disarray, I can't find anyone to speak to who knows what's going on. Perhaps you might be able to go down there and ask?"

"Get Godfryd to order them." I didn't ever want to return to the barracks, if possible. "I'm sure they'll be ready to march. They do enough of it."

"That they do," he said, patting my hand. "Well, I won't keep you, I know you have lots of work before your ceremony tomorrow." He beamed. "I wish you the best of luck."

"Thank you, Lord Zuriel," I said, glancing around to make sure no one was around. "And please, inform Lord Beswick that it would break my heart if he didn't come to my dinner tonight. It's important that I thank him personally."

Zuriel bowed. "If I have to march him here myself, I will do it."

I returned to my office, but didn't stop at the desk. Instead, I walked through the secret door and hurried into the dark passage. Without anyone watching me inside the royal suite, I was able to find all the secret exits, mapping how they connected and forked and, more importantly, where they let out. Of the seven exits in the royal suite, three connected at the bottom floor and led out the garden door. The library deposited me in the barracks, connecting with another door that had been locked but was somewhere on the second floor, I guessed. The final two passages, a second bedroom exit and one in the dining room, let me out into the stables, exactly where I wanted to be.

Starting at the stable door, I walked the length of the passage, counting the steps and the time it would take me to drag a body. I waited at the door to the dining room, listening for sounds of activity. But the room was empty, although the tablecloth had already been set. I ran my fingers along the edge of the round table, counting the chairs and taking in all that was there, from the vases sitting on short columns to the hanging glass chandelier that would be lit before the dinner began.

I practiced a few moves, including the timing it would take to get from the secret door to the other, before I heard voices coming from the hallway. I dashed back into the passage and closed the door just as they came in.

"Can't believe we have to drag all this stuff up here. Can't the princess dine on the first floor?"

"Get used to it."

I left the two attendants and walked the length of the passage, exiting into the bedroom. There, I dug in my closet, finding my cloak and mask, along with the rest of my gear. I would've given anything for a trip to Kieran's ship, but I had what I had.

I ventured back into the passage and left the gear and change of clothes by the door. I stared at it for a moment, uncertain. Perhaps one final trip to the bell tower was in order, just in case there was something there I'd missed. Besides that, I had a few hours to kill, and my anxiety might eat me alive if I stayed stagnant.

I slipped through the second exit, walking down the passage chewing my lip nervously. I would've missed the form standing in my way, except there was no getting around him. Felix wore a white shirt and dark pants instead of his uniform. But at least he'd shaved. I supposed he needed to look presentable.

"So I hear Beswick is coming to dinner," he said, lifting his gaze to mine.

"I don't believe you're captain anymore, so I don't have to talk to you about what I choose to do." I tried to walk past him, but he shot out an arm, blocking my path. "And I also don't think you get to tell me where I can and can't go."

"If you go after him, I will have no choice but to fight you," he said. "And I'll win."

"Then you'll just have to arrest me," I replied, pushing his arm away. "*If* you win. Because now, I'm not playing nicely."

"And what will you do?" Felix asked. "You've already gone to the Council and they did nothing."

I tilted my head up, staring at his lips as I thought about what it had been like to kiss them. His gaze shifted for a moment then hardened.

"Brynna, answer me."

"You gave up the right to order me around when you resigned," I said, ducking under his arm.

He grabbed my shoulder and pushed me against the wall. "I still have the right to tell you when I think you're being unbelievably stupid."

I stared up, sighing. Then in one move, I slid down the wall, swinging my leg around and knocking him on his ass.

"No, unbelievably stupid was ever believing that I could get rid of Beswick under your so-called rule of law," I snapped.

"So what?" he asked, wincing. "You're going to kill him?"

"Yes," I said. "I'm going to string him up in the town square so everyone can see it. He deserves death for what he's done."

"What happened to the girl who spent three years repenting for the death she'd caused accidentally?" he asked, coming to stand.

"I think she decided she'd had enough playing nice," I replied, continuing toward the door.

"Don't make me hurt you, Brynn," he said, a note of pleading in his voice.

"Too late," I whispered, closing the door behind me.

If Katarine or Beata had any wind of my plan, they didn't mention it. Katarine had brought me the latest dress from the tailor, a gold-accented light blue dress with a lace top. Beata took extra time working on my hair, pinning in my diamond tiara to my hair and painting my lips red.

"You look beautiful," Katarine said, taking my hands. "Don't let Luard take up too much of your time tonight."

I patted her on the hand then rose. "Why don't you fetch him for me? Take your time, too."

"Why?"

I made a face. "I'm sure Melwin will want to talk more about this treaty."

"Mm." She narrowed her eyes at me. "And it has nothing to do with Lord Beswick joining you tonight?"

I paused by the door. "If it does, you two are better off staying away."

"Would it do any good to tell you that what you're planning is stupid?"

"Nope." I turned around to face her. "But if you want to help, then feel free to inform my guests that I'm already waiting for them."

She sighed and looked at Beata. "I guess you should remove that tiara and re-do her hair." She walked to the door, pausing momentarily. "Felix is going to try to stop you."

"Let him," I said, as Beata unpinned the bun. "He has no idea who he's messing with."

She made a noise and closed the door behind her.

"I suppose it's the tunic and mask tonight, hm?" Beata said softly, wiping off the red she'd painted on my lips. "Such a shame. That blue really brought out the color in your eyes."

Despite my nerves, I laughed.

Once I was dressed, I slipped through the bedroom exit and down the passage to the dining room. I pressed my ear to the door and listened.

"...thought Lady Katarine said the princess was already in here?"

"Perhaps she's on her way," Garwood said. "There's been a lot of miscommunication since the princess reorganized her royal guard."

"Well, why on earth would she do that?" Vernice replied.

"I believe," Zuriel said, "she and the captain had a falling out. I believe she's lost confidence in his ability to manage the staff."

"And she's sending him back with me," Melwin said. "It's probably for the best. He seems like he'd make an excellent husband to one of King Neshua's cousins. Though it's not as good as getting a royal sibling, especially if, as you say, they've had a falling out."

Garwood sniffed. "Who knows what the princess is thinking? I sure don't half the time."

"I suppose we'll have to get used to her, after all." She sighed. "I'd hoped perhaps she'd abdicate."

"She's a lot hardier than she appears, Ana," Garwood said.

More voices, this time Octavius. I'd never known him to be late to a party. "Ah, am I early?"

"Just in time," Garwood said. "And I see you've brought Johann."

I exhaled and smiled at the ceiling. He'd come. How perfectly delicious.

"Beswick, good man," Zuriel said. "Glad you could join us."

"Who could refuse an invite from our illustrious princess?" Beswick replied. "Though I'm surprised she isn't here to greet me. She was so insistent on my presence."

"We've sent a scout to search for her," Garwood said. "Please, have some wine."

"Yes, have some wine, you murdering traitor," I said.

I took a long breath and blew it out through my mouth. I would get one shot at this, and if I failed, it would be more trouble than just losing my shot at Beswick. There was an annoyingly Felix-like voice in the back of my mind, asking me if this was truly worth risking my crown and my kingdom.

To which I answered: Absolutely.

# Chapter
# Forty—Four

I opened the door slowly, walking out into the light. Vernice saw me first, releasing a blood-curdling scream and throwing her hand over her mouth. Knowing I had precious seconds before the guards came running in from outside, I cartwheeled over the table and slammed the door shut, turning the lock just as bodies hit the other side of it.

"W-who are you!" Vernice cried.

As much as I wanted to punch her lights out, I grabbed the bag of knockout powder from my belt and flung it at her face. She coughed for a moment, the powder pluming around her head. Then she fell to her knees, and to the ground. Zuriel and Melwin rushed to her side and inhaled the powder, falling on top of her in an ungraceful heap.

"Enough!" Garwood bellowed, walking forward with a vase in his hand.

I replied with my crossbow aimed at his face. Garwood dropped the vase and stepped back, joining the others against the wall.

"Back again, are we?" Beswick asked. He was the only one in the room who didn't look scared out of his mind. "I'm sorry to say I don't have your contracts on my person. I seem to have, ah, misplaced them."

Garwood gave me a look.

"I know," I replied, lowering my voice. "What did you do to them?"

"Oh, Titta?" He shrugged. "Not your concern."

I took two steps toward him, snarling. "You son of a bitch. I was the one who took your contracts, not them. They had *nothing* to do with it."

"But they allowed you access," he said. "I can't have that."

I opened my mouth, but the door splintered then flew open. Felix walked into the room, back in his soldier's uniform, although without the captain's pin. Joella, Riya, and Zathan filtered in after him, grabbing the cowering and unconscious Councilors and pulling them from the room. Then, it was just Felix, Beswick, and me.

"Please help me," Beswick cried, wearing a look of fear. "This crazy woman is trying to kill me."

"Put the crossbow on the ground," Felix said, pointing his sword at me. "And we can resolve this amicably."

"There's only one way we resolve this," I replied, tilting my crossbow toward the ceiling.

"Good—"

I pulled the trigger, sending an arrow flying to the ceiling and the rope holding the crystal chandelier. I easily stepped back as it came crashing down on top of the table, the lit candles sparking the wine-soaked tablecloth into flames.

Felix jumped over the table, landing two feet away from me. I stepped back, unsheathing my sword and rushing toward him. He was slow with his weapon, but it was still heavy, and my arms shook with the weight. But this wasn't the time to play nicely.

With a cry, I pulled his sword to the other side then shot out my foot to connect with his midsection. He bent forward, and I clasped my hands together to come down hard on the base of his skull. He fell forward with a thump, and stayed there.

A lump of emotion swelled in my throat, but I stuffed it down, turning back to Beswick.

I picked up my crossbow from the floor and grabbed Beswick by the shirt, tossing him toward the open door and pressing the tip of my arrow to his back.

"Start walking."

We didn't have much time. Surely, Riya and the rest had seen the open door to the secret passage. But the dining room table was now burning, and soon the fire would spread. If I was lucky, the guards would focus on it instead of me. After all, what did they care about a common criminal?

We walked through the passage, his hands in the air as he stumbled forward in the darkness. We walked out into the stable, and instead of continuing, I shoved him inside an empty stable I had ready for him. There, I'd stashed a chair and some rope.

"Sure you want to stop?" he asked as I tied his arms and legs together. "The captain won't be out for long, and soon—"

"He's no longer captain," I replied. "Keep up with the latest political intrigue, Beswick. He's nothing more than a common soldier."

He shrugged, noticing that his hands were cuffed together. "So now, little girl, you have me. What shall you do with me?"

"Oh, I have big plans for you," I said with a low chuckle.

"You do? Well, I daresay you'll have some trouble. If it's not already been made clear to you I own this city. I own that Council and everyone in that castle."

"You don't own the princess," I said.

"Oh, I will. Eventually, she'll come to me with a favor. And I, of course, will grant it. I've already gotten her approval, you see, by her inviting me to her table for her coronation dinner. Only the *most* important to her are allowed at such an event."

I began to laugh. "So sure of yourself, are you? Did it ever occur to you that she might have planned to invite you to separate you from your guards so I might be able to take you?"

"You got lucky, little one. The princess wouldn't be caught dead cavorting with a criminal such as yourself."

I spun and yanked my mask off. "Wanna bet?"

The pure shock on his face was quite possibly the most delicious thing I'd ever seen. "That's...not possible."

"Oh, isn't it?" I said, leaning against the box. "I've been here, Beswick, protecting my city against scum like you. And now I find out you've infiltrated the entire Council? I thought Garwood would see reason, but he's just as corrupt. So now I have to clean house. Starting with you." I pulled my crossbow and aimed it at his chest. "See, it's no longer about merely trying to dismantle your empire. For me, it'll be enough to drag your lifeless corpse into the town square for everyone to see it rotting in the summer sun. Maybe I'll stick it next to me tomorrow at my coronation, just to prove a point."

Beswick's eyes widened as I walked closer to him.

A loud explosion echoed somewhere in the distance, the force rattling the windowpanes.

"What did you do?" I said, running to the window. A plume of smoke was winding toward the sky from down by the docks. I stepped back. Perhaps it was an accident; I'd investigate later. But then there was another, and another—black orbs coming from the water. Cannon balls or...something worse.

"What's going on?" Beswick asked.

"Somebody's attacking the city," I said, grabbing my mask and putting it back on. "You stay here, I'm going to figure out what the hell is going on. Unless you want to save me a trip and enlighten me."

He shrugged, a nervous smile on his face. "For once, Your Highness, I had nothing to do with this."

⟜———•

I raced out of the stables, around the front of the castle, and out into the city. Smoke billowed from buildings down by the shore, and that was as much as I needed to see before I took the front steps two at a time. Explosions sounded every few moments, people screamed, children cried, and the world shook as if it were ending.

I kept my pace toward the docks; there, at least, I'd be able to see who was shooting at us. It had to be coming from the bay, though I wasn't sure what navy would have such firepower. Ours certainly didn't...unless there was something Godfryd wasn't telling me.

As I dodged people, animals, and other things in my way, I ran through a thousand scenarios for why this could be occurring—especially on the eve of my coronation. A coup, perhaps? Beswick?

No. I slowed as I came across the remnants of a building, completely destroyed. But it hadn't just imploded, something had blasted it from the inside, sending debris across an entire city block.

I recognized the two buildings beside it, and my stomach turned over in sickness. It was Tasha's butchery. I stood in front of it for a moment, glancing around for the small family who might not have been in there. But I knew they had been, and they were currently buried under the rubble.

Turning away, I swallowed the bile threatening to come up. There was no way anyone from Forcadel could've wreaked this kind of havoc. Which meant we were being invaded. I couldn't imagine that the Niemenians would've done this; not with the king's brother and sister in my castle. But perhaps Luard had been a ruse. Or Melwin had been.

A whistling sound got my attention, and at the last moment, I dove away from a building just as a black ball crashed through the top. I lifted my head, confused, and then the orange plume exploded outward, shattering the glass. I only barely managed to take cover under an abandoned shop cart.

"What the *hell* is going on?"

I left the destroyed building and continued running toward the docks. Finally, sweat dripping down my neck, I arrived at the docks, where I found a bay full of ships. That, of course, was nothing new, but these ships all bore...

A Severian flag.

"Are you serious?" I cried then ducked for cover as another volley of cannonballs exploded from the ships, flying into the city, leaving plumes of dust in their wake and more screaming.

I spun back around, searching the bay for any with a Forcadel flag, but...dread slipped down my back. Godfryd had been telling me for weeks that our naval posture left us open to attack. Maybe this was what she'd been warning me about.

The lead ship fired another missile, and then three more fired after it. Then five more behind it. There was an entire navy in my bay, firing on my city, and I had no idea how to stop them. I was one girl with one sword; they were an armada.

No. I was a queen. And I may not have had an army, but I had my captain and my general back at the castle. We would be able to negotiate the cessation of hostilities, at least. Perhaps figure out why the hell the Severians thought they should open fire on our citizens.

So with one last look at the bay, I turned and raced back toward my castle.

The front of the castle was void of any guards, but I told myself it was because Felix had ordered them to help the citizenry, not because they'd abandoned their posts. I took the steps two-by-two, pulling my mask off. There might be questions, but I didn't care. Our country was under attack and we had a lot more issues than whether I was a vigilante princess.

Finally, the throne room was dead ahead of me, and I just prayed that was where my Council was, and that they wouldn't be too angry with me about Beswick. But again, we were under attack. There were more important things to worry about. And Felix... well I hadn't hit him that hard.

I threw open the doors and ran into the throne room, glad to see a crowd assembled.

"I'm here, I..."

My feet skidded on the tile floor as the rest of me froze in shock. My entire court was on their knees, swords pressed to their necks. Felix, Kat—even the Council. Felix's guards were there, Joella and Riya wearing twin looks of fury. Standing over them were new guards in royal clothing, the ones I'd seen since Felix had resigned.

"Well, so glad of you to join us again, Brynn."

And sitting on my throne, looking for all the world as if she owned it, was Ilara.

# Chapter
# Forty-Five

I stared at her for a few moments, still trying to wrap my head around what I was seeing.

"Please, call off the bombs," Ilara said, picking up the goblet and sipping from it. "I have my prize, and as long as she cooperates, there's no need to continue killing my new subjects."

"Y-your new subjects?" I spat out.

"Yes, one must start a reign off on a good foot," Ilara said. One of her men brushed past me, and a few moments later, I heard the telltale sound of another explosion.

"Calm yourself," she said as I spun around. "It's merely a flare. A signal to my ships to cease their attacks. That the city is mine."

"The city isn't *yours*," I said, one hand on my sword.

"Brynna, love, let's not be hasty," she said, shaking her head as two guards at her side moved toward me. "I know you're quite a capable fighter, but you can't take down an entire army. That's why you came running back here, hm? Looking for guidance from your little captain?"

I glanced at Felix for a moment then straightened my

shoulders. "My navy will come back."

"And they'll encounter a hostile defense," she said with a smile. "The position in the bay is quite good to fend off any external forces, as you well know. You just have to get inside the bay itself, take over the two towers at the mouth."

The fact that I'd been officially out-maneuvered was starting to dawn on me, but I didn't give in to it. There had to be something I hadn't thought of. I just needed to stall.

"What is that weapon you're using?" I said. "The one blowing up my city?"

"*My* city, darling. They're exquisite, aren't they? We get the explosive ore from the sands of Severia. I think they make cannons just a little more potent." She shivered, as if the idea were delicious to her.

"I don't understand. What the hell are you doing?"

"I'm...taking over your country," she said, with a small laugh. "I know you've been a bit distracted lately, Brynn, what with screwing your captain and playing at being a ridiculous vigilante. But while you wasted your time focusing on a small fish like Beswick, you missed the bigger picture."

"Kind of hard to see the big picture when it came to my door begging for help," I said evenly.

"Oh, I thought you might've figured me out a few times," she said with a smile. "But you're just so easily distractible. A little nudge and you're off on some other wild goose chase. So simple." She put her hand to her mouth and coughed weakly. "And so easily fooled by a poor queen in ill health."

"Look fine to me now," I muttered. "So it was you who killed my father and brother?"

"Of course, dear, of course. I'd expected to arrive to find a city in chaos, but instead I found a princess on the throne. One who, according to my sources, has been saving the city from under a mask. I thought I might come as a woman needing help, as that

S. Usher Evans

seemed to be the best way to get under your skin." She beamed. "It appears to have worked."

My face was on fire, but I forced myself to look angry.

"And now, dear, it's time for you to make your exit," she said, and two bodies practically appeared out of nowhere behind me, grabbing my arms before I could wrestle out of them.

"We can talk about this," I said, realizing what was happening. "Beswick won't be picking off your glass shipments anymore."

"Do you think I care about silly old glass, Brynna? They said you were too focused on that criminal, and now I see it for myself." She lowered her head to my level. "I don't care about Beswick, shipments, or any of that. I wanted your kingdom, so I took it. You made it very easy, too."

I mouthed wordlessly, my heart thumping in my chest.

"And it was so easy to infiltrate your guard with your captain distracted by his nightly excursions." She tilted her head to Coyle. "And with the help of my good friend Lieutenant Coyle."

"Traitor," I muttered. If only I'd spent a few moments focusing on him instead of Joella. He wasn't on his knees with the rest, and neither was Lord Zuriel.

"I made sure to reward them handsomely. See, as your good friend Beswick says, everyone has their price, hm?"

"And what price did she give you to betray your country?" I asked.

"That's my business," Coyle said, lifting his chin higher.

"Oh, don't worry. You didn't get fooled alone. Beswick was easy to manipulate. We begged him for a compromise, and he said he'd bring us into the city to sell our wares and try to pay him back. Such a fool. Didn't even notice all the soldiers I smuggled in with the artisans. Didn't even ask why I had so many young, strapping individuals." She shook her head. "I believe he, like the rest of your city, thought us to be poor, stupid sand-dwelling vermin. Your underestimation was to my benefit, so I thank you very much for it."

"Please don't do this," I whispered then looked to my Council. To Felix. "At least...don't kill them. Just...take my life instead."

"My dear, not a single hair will be harmed as long as they swear fealty to me," she said. "And as for you...I have great plans for you."

The room went dark as a bag fell over my head, followed by a painful blow to the head.

⇨———————

I woke up in motion. Lights flashed in front of my eyes, and my head swam. Birds chirped somewhere in the distance. I certainly wasn't dead, but I wasn't sure how long that would remain the case.

"Are you awake?" Felix whispered beside me.

"Barely," I mumbled, my tongue not working quite yet. "What's happening?"

"We're being taken somewhere. I don't know where. Forest border, perhaps."

"Where's Kat?"

"I'm here." A foot nudged mine. "Brynna, what happened?"

I wished I could say I didn't know, but I did. I'd been played. I'd put my trust in a kind face and an easy out, and ignored what was right in front of me. I'd been so consumed by Beswick, I'd completely ignored the arrow coming toward my head.

People were dead because of me. No matter how much I tried to avoid that reality, it was the truth. Had I not sent away our navy, Tasha would still be alive. Countless others would be as well. My kingdom wouldn't be in the hands of some...

I closed my eyes to the darkness. I couldn't even disparage her in my mind. She'd outsmarted me in every way.

"It's all right, she hasn't killed you yet," Felix said.

"Why are you two here?" I asked.

"We refused to swear loyalty," Felix said.

"Did she..." I swallowed. "Did she kill anyone else?"

"No. Everyone except...Coyle is in the dungeons." There was no masking the disgust in his voice. "What she plans to do with them I have no idea."

"So he's the one who poisoned my family, huh?" I shook my head. "Did you even investigate him?"

"His hands were clean," he said. "But...he was the first one at Horace's house."

I snorted. "Of course he was."

"You didn't know he was dirty either," he snapped.

"Somebody was," I shot back. "And now we're all going to die out here because neither of us could see the forest for the trees."

"I wouldn't be so sure," Katarine replied calmly. "If she wanted you dead, she would've done it in front of the crowd. To send a message. We're out in the middle of nowhere now. Probably close to the Forcadel border."

The carriage rolled to a stop, and my body tensed. Despite everything, I was glad to have Felix and Katarine with me.

"I'm sorry," I whispered. "To both of you."

"I'm sorry, too," Felix replied as the door opened. Rough hands pulled me out of the carriage, walking me forward and keeping me upright, even as I stumbled over roots. I kept Katarine's voice in my mind, and the hope that if Ilara was going to kill me, she would've done it by now.

The mask was removed, and I squinted in the brightness. Katarine had been right—this forest was very familiar, and very close to the Forcadel-Kulka border. As much as I could, I canvassed the scene. Ilara was dismounting from a gorgeous cream-colored horse (probably a Severian variety), but the rest of her soldiers remained on their mounts or on foot. Katarine and Felix remained off to the side, flanked by guards.

"What are we doing out here?" I asked Ilara, who was taking

360

care to pull off white leather riding gloves. "You could've just killed me in the throne room."

She laughed as she handed her gloves to a nearby warrior. "My darling Brynna, don't be silly. We're friends. Why would I kill you?"

"Because you took over my kingdom."

"A kingdom you said you didn't want," she said. "All this time, Coyle told me how you argued with your captain, begging him to let you leave. Let you get out of this horrible burden that was unfairly placed upon you." She shrugged. "So, I'm giving you an out."

"An...out?"

She smiled, and damn if I didn't believe she thought she was my friend. "You're not a queen, Brynn. You're a free spirit. Responsible for only yourself. And all you have to do is just...keep walking."

I couldn't believe what I was hearing. "You want me to go?"

"I'll have your captain and lady certify your death," she said, pointing to them. "You'll be absolutely free to live as you want. Travel to Kulka, or even countries beyond. Become a nomad. Continue protecting innocent citizens from violent crime. Whatever you want, as long as you stay away from Forcadel." She smiled. "That's mine now."

The little voice inside me, the one that had kept me tethered to Forcadel, even after my father tried to sell me off, was crystal clear.

"No."

"Excuse me?"

"No way in the Mother's name am I leaving you alone in my city," I said, raising my chin higher. "It's not yours, it's *mine*. I know every inch of it, from the slums to the castle. I've bled for Forcadel. And I'm not going to walk away just because some desert-dwelling scum got the better of me this time."

"Are you absolutely sure that's the course of action you want to take?" she asked, walking toward me.

I glanced at Felix, who was beaming, and Katarine, with tears in her eyes, and then looked back at Ilara, my decision final.

"Yes."

"Very well."

Slicing pain shot from my stomach to my brain, and a guttural sound escaped from my lips. I looked down at the knife hilt sticking out of my stomach. My legs quivered and then gave out from under me as blood filled my stomach, bubbling up to my lips in tangy, metallic spit.

"*Brynna!*"

"Calm yourself, Captain," Ilara said, her voice somewhere in the distance as pain took over my consciousness. "I'll give both of you one chance to change your minds. If I have your loyalty, I will give my word that no harm will come to your guard. I assume they'll follow suit once they know their queen is dead and their captain has sworn fealty to me?"

"There's no—"

"Ah," Ilara said, raising her hand. "I doubt you'd want everyone under your charge to be strung up in the town square. Dead children make such a horrible sight." She leaned in closer, muttering something else I couldn't hear.

Felix said nothing, but his face had gone white.

"And as for you, Lady Katarine, I will need an education on the particular ins and outs of Forcadel. I hear you're the person to do it. If you comply, I will make you my attendant, bestowing upon you all the rights and privileges therein…including my blessing to marry whomever you choose." Her eyes glinted. "And if you refuse, I'll make sure to add that pretty little maid of yours to the long list of the dead."

She swallowed, saying something I didn't quite catch. My hearing was starting to fade. Slowly, I lifted my head to capture Felix's gaze, burning the memory of his pale, frightened face in my mind.

I opened my mouth to speak, to tell him to fight the bitch, but couldn't push air out. The disembodied arms holding me let me go, and I fell to my knees then my side. I lay there, something wet dripping out of my mouth as my pulse thudded in my ears.

Katarine dipped her head once, and then Felix followed.

I closed my eyes and fell into darkness.

# Chapter
## Forty-Six

The next few days passed in a blurry, feverish haze. I barely knew whether I was alive or dead, for I was sure that I had passed between worlds. I dreamed of my father and my brother, staring down at me from thrones high above me. I dreamed of Katarine crying rivers so deep that I drowned in them and Felix standing as still as the mountains in the distance.

There were moments of lucidity, where I could hear Felix's voice softly talking in my ear, but I couldn't force my tongue to work to answer him. Then I fell back into the blackness, plagued by dreams that made no sense, and yet I couldn't tear myself from them.

I awoke slowly, lethargically, as if I wasn't quite sure if I was waking at all. But the pain in my stomach had been missing from all my other dreams, so I assumed this vision was real. I licked my dry lips, wishing for all the world for a cup of water to fill my parched mouth. If this was living, I would've preferred to be back in my dream world.

I lifted my hand to check my wound, but found it tethered via a metal shackle to the bed.

"What the...?" I tugged harder, my brain finally catching up with the rest of me. I was shackled to a bed? Wounded, gravely. Thirsty, too. So my odds of escape were slim.

The rest of my memory came back to me and I sank back into the bed. I was supposed to be dead. I wished I couldn't remember the scream of horror that had erupted from Katarine's lips, the fury and shock written on Felix's face. I wasn't sure how long it had been, but they surely thought I was dead at this point. And perhaps I still would be.

There was the possibility that a kind passerby had seen me bleeding out and had seen fit to save me. There was, of course, the much larger chance that someone knew who I was and was holding me for ransom. Boy, would they be surprised when they found out just how much I was worth. Dethroned queen—not even queen. Dethroned princess.

I heard voices outside and steadied myself for whatever would walk through the door. The flap opened and I actually sighed in relief.

"Nicolasa?" I croaked. "You saved me?"

"I was called," she replied, walking over to me. She carried a pail of water, which she dipped a silver ladle into and poured liquid coolness into my mouth. "I'm glad you're still with us."

"Where am I?" I whispered.

"In a safe place," she replied, ladling more into my mouth. "Just drink. You've had a rough go of it, but I think you'll survive."

"Thank you," I said, leaning back now that my mouth wasn't as parched. "For saving my life."

"Like I said," She pulled out a small vial which she poured into my mouth. It tasted like metal and blood. "I was just called."

"Oh, Larissa, you are quite welcome."

My addled brain finally made the connection, and I sank back into my pillow.

"That will be all," Celia said to the healer. She said nothing as she jumped to her feet and ran from the room. When she was gone, Celia turned back to me, cocking her head to the side and scanning my body with her light green eyes.

"My, my," she said, taking a seat at my bedside. "You've looked better."

"I didn't ask you to save me," I said, wincing as the wound in my side protested movement. "And I refuse to remain in your debt, so you might as well kill me."

She chuckled, leaning back in her chair. "You have such a poor perception of me."

"Why the handcuffs then?"

"For your own protection, my dear," she said, running a single, long nail down my cheek. "I know how you like to run. I'd be happy to remove them, once you can be trusted."

"Trusted to what? I already knew where your camp was."

"Trusted not to run back to your kingdom half-dead," she said, removing her finger. "You've lost a lot of blood. Nicolasa has performed a miracle here."

"A miracle I'm sure you'll bill me for."

Celia sat back, resting her hands behind her head. "I'm glad to see you haven't changed. Still the wide-eyed little girl I found in Forcadel, trying to escape a marriage she didn't want any part of."

"Cut the crap, Celia. Why did you save me?"

"Because you're my queen," she said softly. "This bitch on the throne now needs to die. She's been there a week and already everything's in the shitter."

"A...week?" I'd been out for seven whole days. "And she's already taken over?"

"More and more of her henchmen arrive from across the great sea. Most of them had infiltrated the city through that summer festival."

"I knew there were too many Severian merchants," I said.

"Mm. Your captain, it seems, has sworn fealty to her as has your Council. Her little sea attack seems to have cowed your army. Or, perhaps it's because they struck when your army wasn't around to protect the city."

My face flushed, a feat considering I felt I had no blood left. "I miscalculated."

"I told you to think about who might benefit from your distraction," she said, sounding like a disappointed tutor to a misbehaving pupil.

I closed my eyes, rather than respond.

"You won't make that mistake again, will you?" It was more a statement than question.

The silence stretched between us, so I cracked open an eye.

"Will you?" Celia repeated.

"Don't see how I can, considering I don't have a kingdom anymore," I replied.

"Oh, that's not the Larissa I know," she said. "When you got knocked down, you picked yourself back up and went back in for another round."

I lifted my wrist weakly, letting the shackle speak for itself. "Seem to be stuck to the bed."

Celia leaned forward with a key in hand and unlocked the band. I rubbed my wrist and tried to sit up, but the wound in my stomach had different ideas.

"What's the point?" I said softly. "Maybe I should just let her have it."

"You'd let a foreign queen sit on your family's throne?" Celia asked.

I shrugged as much as my wound would let me. "Foreign or no, she'd be a better queen to the people of Forcadel than I would be."

"Are you so sure? Her soldiers fill the streets, kicking rich and poor from their houses as they take over. Half your King's Guard have been imprisoned, and your captain has been sucking up to the new queen to keep the other half safe." She shook her head. "Your people need you."

"How would I even begin?" I asked helplessly.

"That, my love, is why you are queen and I am not," Celia said, rising and walking to the door. "But rest assured you have the breadth of my forces at your disposal when you do figure it out."

I laughed. "Of course. Because I'll owe you another favor and also be queen."

"Well, I'm not stupid." She lingered in the doorway and tapped her finger against the frame. "But perhaps it irks me to see someone foreign on the Forcadel throne. I'd rather it be the evil I know than the one I don't."

"Celia, I don't...I have nothing," I whispered.

"You're alive, aren't you?" she said. "You're still stubborn, aren't you? Once your wound heals, you've still got your fighting skills, don't you?" She shrugged. "If you're capable of being The Veil for three years, I wouldn't bet against you now."

I didn't have anything to say to that, so I remained quiet.

"Oh, and one more thing," Celia said, a smile curling onto her face. "Now that you're awake, Jax will be tending to you. I know he'll be *exceptionally* glad to see you."

Of course he was. "Arm all healed then?" I asked dryly.

She just chuckled and closed the flap behind her. But Jax was the least of my worries.

Celia was right. I had my brain, my body would be healthy soon, and I had my loyalty to my kingdom. Though I didn't know how I'd even begin, I knew one thing:

I was going to get my kingdom back.

# Acknowlegments

Thanks to my parents, who continue to show faith and support for my work and my crazy schemes, and for letting me crash at their house between home purchases.

Thank you to my bevy of beta readers: Kristin, Alice, and Chelsea.

Thank you to Dani, my magnificent line editor.

Thank you to my typo checkers, Lisa, MC, Mom, and Bettina.

And finally, thanks to the Sush Street Team for getting the book off the ground:

Tom, Kristin, Lindsay, Grace, Becca, Sammy, Emily, Sierra, Jessica, Anna, Ray, Jean, Elizabeth, Allen, Theresa, Lisa and Cyra.

# Also By the Author

## Lexie Carrigan Chronicles

Lexie Carrigan thought she was weird enough until her family drops a bomb on her—she's magical. Now the girl who's never made waves is blowing up her nightstand and no one seems to want to help her. That is, until a kind gentleman shows up with all the answers. But Lexie finds out being magical is the least weird thing about her.

Spells and Sorcery is the first book in the Lexie Carrigan Chronicles, and is available now in eBook, paperback, audiobook, and hardcover.

## The Razia Series

Lyssa Peate is living a double life as a planet discovering scientist and a space pirate bounty hunter. Unfortunately, neither life is going very well. She's the least wanted pirate in the universe and her brand new scientist intern is spying on her. Things get worse when her intern is mistaken for her hostage by the Universal Police.

The Razia Series is a four-book space opera series and is available now for eBook, Audiobook. Paperback, and Hardcover.

# Also By the Author

## THE MADION WAR TRILOGY

He's a prince, she's a pilot, they're at war. But when they are marooned on a deserted island hundreds of miles from either nation, they must set aside their differences and work together if they want to survive.

The Madion War Trilogy is a fantasy romance available now in eBook, Paperback, and Hardcover.

## empath

Lauren Dailey is in break-up hell, but if you ask her she's doing just great. She hears a mysterious voice promising an easy escape from her problems and finds herself in a brand new world where she has the power to feel what others are feeling. Just one problem —there's a dragon in the mountains that happens to eat Empaths. And it might be the source of the mysterious voice tempting her deeper into her own darkness.

Empath is a stand-alone fantasy that is available now in eBook, Paperback, and Hardcover.

# About the Author

S. Usher Evans was born and raised in Pensacola, Florida. After a decade of fighting bureaucratic battles as an IT consultant in Washington, DC, she suffered a massive quarter-life-crisis. She decided fighting dragons was more fun than writing policy, so she moved back to Pensacola to write books full-time. She currently resides with her two dogs, Zoe and Mr. Biscuit, and frequently can be found plotting on the beach.

Visit S. Usher Evans online at:
http://www.susherevans.com/

Twitter: www.twitter.com/susherevans
Facebook: www.facebook.com/susherevans
Instagram: www.instagram.com/susherevans